Dreaming of Rome

T.A. WILLIAMS

Dreaming of Rome

CANELO

First published in the United Kingdom in 2019 by Canelo

This edition published in the United Kingdom in 2020 by

Canelo Digital Publishing Limited
Third Floor, 20 Mortimer Street
London W1T 3JW
United Kingdom

A CIP catalogue record for this book is available from the British Library.

Print ISBN 978 1 78863 831 9
Ebook ISBN 978 1 78863 097 9

Look for more great books at www.canelo.co

Printed and bound in Great Britain by Clays Ltd, Elcograf S.p.A.

To Mariangela and Christina, as always, with love.

Chapter 1

It was a magical setting, and everywhere she looked there was romance in the warm evening air.

But not at their table.

And that was just fine with her.

They were sitting under a parasol on the west side of Piazza Navona in the heart of Rome. She was sipping Prosecco while he had opted for a cold beer. The sun had dropped low on the horizon by now and the ground was already in the shade, although the residual heat from the scorching July sun still radiated up from the cobbles. The top of the obelisk rising from the centre of Bernini's spectacular Fountain of the Four Rivers in the middle of the square was tipped ruby red by the last rays of the setting sun, and the shadow it cast against the buildings on the opposite side lengthened by the minute. All around them in this pedestrians-only area were crowds of happy people, mostly tourists, laughing and chatting. Along with the tourists were also lots of Romans, like the man sitting alongside her.

Conversation between the two of them wasn't exactly flowing, even now. In the car on the way back into the city centre, he had barely uttered a word and Jo hadn't wanted to disturb his concentration as he weaved the battered little Fiat in and out of the traffic chaos that Romans accept as an everyday fact of life. She had lost count of the times she had found her right foot stamping the floor in search of a non-existent brake pedal, her hands gripping the seat belt apprehensively as he slipped confidently between lines of cars, often four or five abreast, narrowly avoiding being crushed by buses that sliced imperiously through the traffic. Gradually she had started to relax as she realised he knew what he was doing, but her palms were sticky by the time they reached their destination; a tiny, narrow road where he had a flat with a garage – a rarity in the centre of the city.

Jo had been encouraged by the presence of his dog. Throughout the journey, Daisy the Labrador had stood braced on the floor behind her, tail wagging, swaying with every movement of the car. The back seat was folded down so she was right behind Jo and she leant forward from time to time to stick her big black nose out of the window as she spotted something of note – normally another dog. On several occasions she felt compelled to bark a greeting or a challenge, and Jo's right ear was still ringing now as a result. However, the confident attitude of the big dog had reassured Jo, although the idea of what sixty or seventy pounds of canine bone and muscle flying forwards might do to both of them if Corrado misjudged a manoeuvre and crashed the car was something she preferred not to contemplate.

Now safely in the heart of the Eternal City, Daisy was stretched out on the cobbles at their feet, resting and recuperating in her turn after the events of the day, while the two humans at the table searched for something to talk about. It had been kind of Corrado to offer Jo a lift back into Rome, but it was pretty obvious he was just being polite. Still, he was the brother of the man her sister was going to marry – practically a brother-in-law – so she knew she had to make an effort.

'I'm glad everything went so perfectly today, Corrado. Lunch was amazing.'

'My mother didn't do it all on her own. One of the chefs from the restaurant came along and they did it together.'

Her sister's decision to marry into a family who owned a hotel and restaurant clearly had its advantages. 'Well, the result was wonderful. I've never had zucchini flowers stuffed with mozzarella and anchovies before. They were exquisite. And the chicken with peppers…'

'You liked the *Pollo alla Romana*? It's one of my mother's specialities.'

'It was terrific.'

The conversation lapsed once more, but Jo really didn't mind. She sat back and stretched her legs, careful to avoid the sleeping dog, as she soaked up the atmosphere here in the ancient heart of this wonderful city. The temperature, after the intense heat of the day, was now perfect and she felt pleasantly relaxed. It had been hard work making conversation in Italian with her sister's future in-laws and it was good to be able to speak English again now with Corrado. And he spoke it perfectly.

'Do you work in London, Joanne?'

'Yes, and it's just Jo. Only my parents call me Joanne these days.'

'And what do you do… Jo?'

'I work for a conservation charity.' She gave him the name and saw recognition in his eyes. He had removed his sunglasses and she noticed for the first time that his deep blue eyes were strangely hypnotic, when he bothered to look at her.

'Do you enjoy your job?'

'I love the work, but my boss can be a bit of a pain.'

'And what do you do there?'

'I report to the CEO and the board. I'm responsible for coming up with proposals as to how we spend our money. Like all charities, we have finite resources and there's an awful lot of work to be done around the world.'

'Sounds like a big job for a young woman.'

'Not so young. I'll be thirty in a few weeks' time.'

He smiled and it lit up his face. 'Still younger than me.'

As his interest strayed out across the piazza once more, Jo studied him surreptitiously over the rim of her glass. She already knew he was the elder of the two brothers. His younger brother, Mario, was twenty-eight, just like her sister. This had emerged today at the lunch to celebrate Mario's engagement to Angie, and Jo was here from England to represent their family after their father's hip operation had prevented their parents from coming over. From the look of Corrado, she reckoned he was maybe two or three years older than she was, probably in his early or even mid thirties.

The unsettling thing about him, however, was that he was gorgeous.

He was tall and, unusually for a Roman, he had light brown hair. His shoulders were broad and she felt sure he must work out, although maybe not obsessively. His forearms were strong and his expensive polo shirt fitted immaculately across his well-developed chest. His face was lightly tanned and there was no doubt about it, he was a really handsome man who wouldn't have looked out of place on the catwalk or in a blockbuster movie. As she sat there, it didn't take long before she realised that quite a few of the women walking past shared her opinion, some of them even smiling in his direction even though he made no attempt to respond. She settled back and enjoyed the show, smiling in her turn. The fact that her relationship with Corrado was purely that of a future family member suited her fine. One thing was for sure, she wasn't in the market for a man who looked like a Hollywood idol. She had had her fill of handsome men, and she knew to her cost that they couldn't be trusted.

She reflected that this was just about the first time she had sat down for a drink with a man alone since Christian, the love of her life with whom she had genuinely expected to spend the rest of her years, had decided *she* wasn't, after all, the love of *his* life. He had demonstrated this by walking out on her on a frosty morning five months earlier in order to fly off to even colder Iceland to be with a fellow model called Helga. The rest of the winter and the spring had been tough for Jo. She had sought to bury herself in her work and forget about him, but without a great deal of success. Things at work had been mixed; she had been promoted to this new higher position, but this had brought her into direct daily contact with the irascible CEO, Ronald, and she was finding working with him seriously challenging. And, as if that wasn't enough, thoughts of Christian and his six-foot-tall Icelander girl-friend continued to plague her quieter moments.

Now, for the first time in months, she found herself in the company of a very good-looking man, but without the pressure. He was courteous and attentive, but there was nothing in his behaviour that indicated any kind of romantic interest towards her, which was definitely for the best. Apart from his good looks, getting involved with her sister's future brother-in-law would have been complicated, to say the least. He wasn't wearing a ring and today he had come alone to the family gathering out at the estate in the country, and she wondered idly if there was a woman in his life. If there was, Jo wished her well. Hanging onto a hunk like this would be fraught with danger and almost inevitable heartache.

'And your parents have a farm, Jo?'

'Not a very big farm. It's more of a smallholding really, near Woodstock, just outside Oxford.' As usual, she added the qualification. 'Not the Summer of Love Woodstock in the USA. This is a little place just to the north of Oxford.'

'I know it well. I often used to drop into the Wood-stock Arms for a drink.' Seeing her surprise, he went on to explain in more detail. 'I went to university in Oxford and I used to go riding most weekends at stables just outside Woodstock.'

'So that's why your English is so good. What did you study?'

'Chemistry at Trinity. I'm a chemist.' For the first time he looked a bit insecure. 'Sorry, that's stating the obvious.'

The conversation then lapsed once again as she saw his eyes follow a pair of very pretty girls who walked past their table, arm in arm. He followed their bottoms with his eyes until the girls were lost in the crowd. Jo did her best to stifle an upsurge of annoyance. Christian, too, had had a habit of losing interest in her any time an attractive woman appeared on the scene. Corrado the chemist was clearly cut from the same cloth. Resignedly, she took a large mouthful of Prosecco and swallowed hard. Alas, half of it went down the wrong way and she dissolved into a coughing fit so severe, the dog even got up and laid a big heavy paw on her knees, subjecting her to a puzzled look.

'Are you all right?'

Corrado had returned his attention to her now, but as she had tears in her eyes and her face was flushed, she would have preferred it if he had still been looking elsewhere, even if it was at other girls' bottoms. She retrieved a tissue from her bag, wiped her eyes and blew her nose. Finally, she caught hold of the Labrador's paw and gave it a squeeze before answering.

'Fine, thanks. Sorry about that.' She glanced down at the dog. 'Thank you for the support, Daisy. Now you can go back to sleep.'

As the dog settled back down on the cobbles again with a heavy sigh, Jo also sat back and growled at herself. It was so frustrating that even now Christian could still mess with her head and it annoyed her immensely. She blew her nose again and did her best to dismiss the thought of her ex. Unaware of what was going on in her head, Corrado made another stab at conversation.

'So, apart from your work, how do you spend your time? Angie tells me you do a lot of riding, just like her.'

Jo shook her head. 'I used to, but these days I don't get out to the country as often as I'd like. I'm too busy and, besides, I've never been in Angie's league.' There was still a drop of Prosecco in her glass, so she took a cautious sip. 'To be honest, when I get a bit of free time, my hobby is butterflies.'

'Lepidoptera? Well, well. So, have you got a big collection?'

She shook her head. 'I don't collect them. I wouldn't dream of killing one. I love butterflies and I take loads of photos, but I hate butterfly collectors.' Jo could hear her tone harden, but this particular bee had been buzzing about in her bonnet for years. 'It's all so Victorian. Collectors go round with nets and "kill jars". See it, catch it, kill it, mount it. Like those old photos you see of men with handlebar moustaches and ladies in long skirts standing with one foot on some poor dead tiger or giraffe. And they wonder why there are so many endangered species these days.'

She caught Corrado's eye and summoned a smile.

'Sorry, Corrado. I don't mean to sound so bitter. It's just that I wouldn't ever want to kill anything, whether it's walking on land, flying about or swimming in the sea, and I don't understand why anybody would, unless it's for food.'

'I can see why you chose to work in conservation. We're making a right mess of the planet, aren't we? But for butterflies, you should spend more time out at the Country Club with Mario and Angie. They don't use weedkiller and it's all organic. There are all manners of butterflies there. What time is your flight back to London tomorrow? Maybe I could take you out there again.'

Corrado and Mario's family owned a large estate about twenty kilometres outside Rome with a restaurant, hotel and riding stables. It was a big undertaking and Mario had just taken over running it as his father gradually stepped back. Angie had been working there in charge of the stables for the past year and had fallen in love with Mario in the process. However, as far as Jo knew, Corrado the chemist was not involved with the business.

'That's very kind, Corrado, but I've got a very early flight, so I won't be able to make it.'

'Well, next time then.'

'Indeed.'

Conversation lapsed once more and Jo glanced at her watch. It was just after nine and she knew she would have to be up really early next morning so as to get out to Rome's Leonardo da Vinci airport – known to all Romans simply as *Fiumicino*, the nearby town – in good time for her flight. She resolved to head back to her hotel pretty soon, knowing she needed to get as much sleep as possible in readiness for what would be a busy week at work. After the enormous banquet they had been served for lunch, she couldn't face the idea of any more food, so dinner was out of the question. Then just as that thought occurred to her, it appeared that Corrado was reading her mind.

'How about dinner, Jo? It's a bit touristy here, but the food's very good.'

She shook her head and was about to explain that she couldn't possibly eat another thing when they were interrupted by a voice.

'*Ciao, Corrado. Come stai, amore?*'

Jo looked up. The voice emanated from a very pretty girl in her twenties who proceeded to drape herself around Corrado's shoulders and do her best to nibble his ear off. For a second, he caught Jo's eye and had the decency to look just a little bit embarrassed, before fending the girl off and replying.

'*Ciao, bellissima.*'

Jo sat back and listened to their conversation. It was conducted at pace and although she had studied Italian at school and had been doing an evening class for some years now, she still found it hard to follow. What was clear, however, was that the girl was thanking Corrado for something that had happened a few weekends earlier and was asking when it could be repeated. Although unfamiliar with all the vocabulary being used, you didn't need to be a qualified interpreter to understand the nature of what had taken place and what was being proposed. To her surprise, however, Corrado sounded evasive and when the girl eventually left, it was without any kind of commitment from him to meet up again. From the expression on the girl's face, she was more than a little miffed, and the parting glance she shot at Jo was brimming with venom, presumably identifying her as Corrado's latest conquest.

'Sorry about that, Jo. An old friend.'

Jo nodded but didn't comment. Once again, unhappy memories had been stirred by the scene. After a brief pause, she made one final attempt at conversation.

'And what sort of chemist are you, Corrado? Where do you work?'

'Just on the outskirts of Rome. We started off doing clinical testing: everything from pregnancy, to allergies, to bowel cancer. Not the most glamorous stuff, I know, but very important all the same. Now we're moving into all kinds of other stuff. You might be interested in what we've been working on recently: non-plastics. We're working on alternatives to plastic for packaging, cups, straws and all manner of other uses.'

'That's interesting.'

He smiled. 'I'm sure in your conservation work you must come across all sorts of problems caused by plastics. Hopefully we'll have cost-effective, natural, biodegradable alternatives before too long. Some already exist, but the trick is to drive the price right down so industry automatically chooses these over traditional plastic.'

'That sounds amazing.' And it did. In many ways, he and she were working in the same field. 'Although our main thrust is conservation, we're generally all about saving the planet, and plastics are one of the worst scourges of the modern era. I'd be very interested to hear more about your work some time. So, are you glued to a microscope all day?'

'I wish. I seem to spend all my time at conferences or seminars or, even worse, talking to accountants and bankers. The chemistry's the bit I've always liked. The business bit can be a pain.'

Jo reflected that he would appear to be a whole lot more than a simple chemist and she resolved to ask Angie for more information. After another glance at her watch, she finished the last of her Prosecco and turned towards him.

'Well, it's been very nice to meet you, Corrado, and thank you so much for giving me a lift back into town, but I think I'll go back to my hotel now and have an early night. I need to be up at five tomorrow morning for my flight.'

'Sure you're not staying for dinner? Not even a salad or something?'

'No, thanks. I'm still full.'

'Well, let me give you a lift back to the hotel, at least.'

She shook her head. 'There's absolutely no need to get the car back out of the garage again, thanks. I saw a taxi rank as we came into the square. I'll hop into one and I'll be home in no time. My hotel's just off Piazza Barberini, so it's not far.' He looked as if he was going to protest, but she stood up and waved to him to remain seated. 'Really. You stay and finish your beer. Besides, Daisy looks as if she's worn out. By the way, I've been meaning to ask; how come you've got a dog with an English name?'

He smiled. 'In honour of my old landlady in Oxford. She was a faithful friend as well.'

He stood up. As he did so, the Labrador sprang up, tail wagging. 'Don't be fooled by Daisy. She has boundless energy. No, I'm afraid I have to insist upon walking you to your taxi, if not your hotel. Mario told me to look after you and a promise is a promise. Your sister would murder me if I let anything happen to you.'

He motioned to the waitress who came across remarkably quickly. He pressed a bank note into her hand, smiled, and told her to keep the change. The girl blushed and smiled back, and Jo felt pretty sure it was less for the unexpected tip than for the contact with his hand. Together, they walked back up the square, the dog trotting happily alongside them, and Jo enjoyed the exercise after a day spent mainly sitting down. As they reached the big fountain, he glanced across at her and made a suggestion.

'Your hotel's in Piazza Barberini. That's only twenty minutes or so on foot. My four-legged friend here needs some exercise, so if you feel like walking, I'd be happy to accompany you. It's a lovely night.'

He was right; it was a delightful evening. Dusk was falling now and lights were coming on all round the square. Street traders were peddling strange fluorescent disks like little flying saucers that went spinning into the sky around them, and the fountain illuminations behind them suddenly flickered to life, bathing the sparkling waters with light. A band of Peruvian musicians in traditional dress were just setting up and Jo had no doubt the piazza would become an enchanting place as the evening progressed. For a moment she hesitated, tempted to tell him she would, after all, like to stay on and take him up on his invitation to dinner, but then good sense kicked in. If she only got a few hours' sleep tonight she would be shattered all week. Still, she thought to herself, a short walk through the streets of Rome was not to be missed, even though heels and cobbles didn't go too well together. She rarely wore heels, but had decided to dress up for the engagement party and she wasn't that steady on her feet on the uneven stones.

'That's a great idea, Corrado. I'd like that. This is my first trip to Rome and all I've seen so far has been from the inside of a car.'

He stopped for a moment and Jo did the same. At their feet, the dog hesitated, waiting to see which way Corrado would choose. After a few seconds reflection, he came to a decision.

'It's a pity you haven't got longer or we could go past the Colosseum, but it's too far out of the way for this time. We'll go via the Pantheon, though, and then, if you can spare ten minutes more, I'll show you the Trevi Fountain. At least you'll see a couple of the important landmarks and they're both pretty much right on the way back to your hotel.'

'Wonderful, thank you.'

He led her across to the east side of the piazza and into a narrow lane. Austere *palazzi*, centuries old, rose up on either side of them, massive iron gratings covering their lower windows. The buildings were all shades of pink, orange and ochre, faded by exposure to the sun. The crowds showed no signs of abating and their progress was slow, but Jo didn't mind in the slightest. She savoured the atmosphere of the place and knew that she would have to come back to Rome some day soon and dedicate some serious time to seeing the sights.

Within a very few minutes they emerged from the narrow lane into another piazza and she found herself confronted by the massive façade of the Pantheon. In the midst of the square there was another big marble fountain with, alongside it, a bored-looking horse standing between the shafts of a carriage, while its driver sat and relaxed with a cigarette, nearing the end of a long, hot day. Street lights on the buildings around the piazza and floodlights on the Pantheon illuminated the scene. The square was full of tourists, most just wearing shorts and T-shirts, even though the sun had dropped below the horizon and the swallows in the clear night sky had been replaced by bats. A digital thermometer outside a shop indicated it was still almost thirty degrees and Jo was glad she had chosen her lightest summer dress for today, but even so, she was hot. As she stopped and looked around, she heard the dog panting at her feet. Underneath that sleek black fur coat, it must be pretty uncomfortable to be a Labrador in Rome.

She stood and gazed in awe at the building before her. It was sobering to realise that this imposing structure with its row of titanic columns had been erected centuries ago and it was still standing today. Corrado's brain must have been working along similar lines.

'If I remember right, what you see there was finished in the second century, but it was built on top of an even older

Roman temple. Just think, when this was built, Rome was in its heyday and ruler of most of the known world.' He turned towards her and smiled. 'I wonder what the ancient emperors would have made of today's government. Italy isn't exactly the ruler of anything any more.'

Jo was surprised, and pleased, to hear him speaking more freely and enthusiastically. Presumably history was one of his interests and it provided a ready subject for them to talk about and, as they continued their walk, she realised that he knew a lot about the illustrious history of his city.

Together, they made their way round the huge building and he pointed out the traditional small Roman bricks that had been used to build the bulk of the structure. Many of them were pockmarked with holes, but whether these were the work of the weather, animals, or the result of small-arms fire, was something neither of them could tell. As they reached the rear of the building and curled round to the left, the dog suddenly stopped in front of Jo, unsure of which direction to take. She almost tripped over the black shadow at her feet and might have fallen but for a strong hand on her arm, as Corrado caught her and steadied her. She bumped against his chest, straightened up, and found herself looking straight into his eyes sparkling in the reflection of the street lights.

'You okay, Jo? Sorry about Daisy. She has a habit of stopping a bit suddenly.'

His face was only a few inches above hers and the lights only served to emphasise the sculpted contours of it. As she collected herself and stepped back, she was reminded yet again that she was in the company of a very good-looking man. And she knew what that meant.

She immediately took a second step back and gave him a grateful smile.

'Sorry about that, Corrado. Heels aren't ideal for this sort of road surface. Thanks for catching me before I ended up head first on the cobbles.'

'You can hang onto my arm while we walk if you like.' From his tone, he was just being helpful, but she shook her head all the same.

'I'm fine, thanks. I just need to be a bit more careful.'

After making a tour all the way round the massive circular structure, Corrado led her off to the right, along yet another narrow lane. As they walked, Jo was unsurprised to see gift shops still open at that time of night, along with cafes and restaurants doing a roaring trade, many with tables out on the street, crowded with people. All around them was the background hubbub of people talking and laughing. There was no doubt that tourism was big business in Rome.

They weaved their way through the streets until they emerged into the surprisingly small piazza where the Trevi Fountain stood. This too was illuminated and the whole area was buzzing with tourists. Jo felt his hand catch hold of her arm as he steered her through the crowds until they managed to reach the low railings surrounding the fountain. She could feel people pushing from behind and she was glad of his supporting hand. As she stood and took in the scene, she heard his voice at her ear.

'Keep a tight hold of your handbag, Jo.'

She nodded and gripped her bag even tighter, although she was already holding it tight to her chest with both hands. Her main concern at this point, however, was that the momentary touch of his lips against her ear had been far more stimulating than it should have been. If she hadn't been surrounded by a mass of humanity, she would have moved out of his grip – just to be on the safe side.

'Daisy, no!'

Jo looked down as he shouted. The dog had behaved impeccably all evening, trotting along with them without a lead, but it was clear that her Labrador DNA was now propelling her inexorably towards the water. Jo felt Corrado jerk forward and saw him make a grab for Daisy's collar. He hauled her back and told her to sit. As she obeyed, his tone softened.

'Sorry, Daisy, but you're not allowed into the fountains. I know you're hot – I wouldn't mind jumping in myself – but it's forbidden. Okay? See the police car over there? You'd be arrested.'

Daisy looked up at her master and it looked for a moment as if she nodded. As for Jo, her subconscious suddenly presented her with an image of Corrado stripped to a pair of swimming trunks, plunging into the pool. Not for the first time this evening, she growled at herself and did her best to concentrate on the sight before her.

The fountain consisted of a natural rock base with what Corrado told her were Titans emerging from the rocks in all their rippling muscular grandeur. Along with them were horses and what might have been Pan with his pipes. Positioned above them all, Oceanus, the Titan god of the sea, looked on majestically, flanked by two beautiful goddesses. The floodlit water was a perfect translucent light blue and, beneath the surface, the bottom of the fountain was covered in coins. The significance of this was soon explained.

'Here, take this.' She felt Corrado pressing a coin into her hand. 'If you're serious about wanting to come back to Rome, you know what you have to do.'

Jo didn't hesitate. She reached out and threw the Euro into the water, watching it sink to the bottom. Beside her, she saw Daisy make a lunge to follow it, but Corrado had anticipated her move and was hanging on to her collar tightly. He looked up at Jo.

'So, did you make a wish?'

'I certainly did.'

'So, you think you'll be back again before too long?'

'Just try and stop me.'

Chapter 2

'Bloody hell, Jo, who's that?'

Jo smiled to herself at the disbelief, and more than just a touch of envy, in Victoria's voice as she looked at the photo.

'That's Corrado, my future brother-in-law. But don't get any ideas. I'm not planning to get involved with a future relative. Life's complicated enough without that.'

Victoria swiped the photo with her fingers to enlarge it. What she saw clearly reinforced her first impression.

'Blimey, Jo, what a hunk! He's even more stunning than Christian, and that's saying something.'

'Well, you're not the only one to think that. Half the women in Rome were giving him the eye as we were sitting in Piazza Navona.'

'Ah, Piazza Navona… I've seen the pictures. I really must get round to organising that trip to Rome we've been dreaming of for so long now.'

Victoria and Jo had known each other since school and had few secrets from each other. Both had started their Italian evening class three years ago and had taken a trip to Venice together the previous year. Next on their agenda were Florence or Rome, or both.

'Well, if all goes well and Angie marries Mario next spring, she's already said we're welcome to come and stay in their guest bedroom.'

'Fantastic, I can't wait. But, returning to Mr Fabulous for a moment, did you and he…?'

Jo shook her head vigorously and subjected her friend to a disapproving look.

'We most certainly did not.'

'But he's so amazingly handsome, Jo. And, besides, there's nothing to stop you and your brother-in-law from hooking up. It's not illegal or immoral or anything.'

'It may not be illegal, Vic, but that's never going to happen. Like I said, he's going to be my brother-in-law and if I did get involved with him and it didn't work out it could affect my sister.'

'But that's not the only reason, is it?' Victoria didn't give Jo a chance to respond. 'It's also because he's so good-looking.' Victoria's tone was heavy with irony now. She knew Jo so very well.

'You're probably right. I've had it up to here with handsome men. I should have listened to my grandma. She told me never to go out with good-looking men, to choose one barely a few shades better-looking than the devil incarnate. The uglier the better. Handsome men are too high risk.'

'Did she tell you that before or after you shacked up with Christian?'

Jo shook her head ruefully. 'Before. I thought she was talking rubbish. I should've listened to her. I know now that she was right.'

'So you're on the lookout for an ugly man?' Victoria's tone was now decidedly cynical.

'I'm not on the lookout for any man, Vic. I'm fine as I am.'

Victoria snorted. 'Don't be ridiculous. Surely you want to fall in love.'

'Been there, done that, didn't buy the T-shirt. I have no intention of falling in love with anybody, thank you. Love's an illusion.' Jo stopped and corrected herself. 'Love's a delusion. You think what you're feeling is love, when in fact it's just hormones or lust or God knows what. I've been fooled once. I won't be fooled again.'

Victoria caught her eye and subjected her to her schoolmarm stare. 'Just because it didn't work out between you and Christian doesn't mean it won't work with somebody else.'

Jo shook her head. 'You're wrong, you know, Vic. I thought… no, I was certain, that Christian and I were in love and that it would last forever. I managed to convince myself of that and look where it got me. I was wrong, and I'm not going to make that mistake again. Love's just an invention of novelists and playwrights, a temporary clouding of the senses that makes you believe the most ridiculous things.'

'So you got burned, Jo, that doesn't mean it won't work out better next time.'

'There isn't going to be a next time, Vic. Trust me, I know what I'm doing.'

Victoria swallowed the last of the Prosecco in her glass and stood up. 'I trust you, Jo, but I reckon you're wrong. Same again?' Before Jo had a chance to answer, Victoria had disappeared into the crowd.

What Jo hadn't told her best friend was that, since returning to London, the good news was that she had been thinking less of Christian. However, the annoying bad news was that she now found herself thinking far too much about her handsome future brother-in-law. This was so patently contrary to everything she had worked out for her own sake since Christian's departure that it made no sense. The man was gorgeous. Her granny would have been appalled.

'Here, Jo. And I got a bag of crisps to soak up the alcohol.'

Jo took her glass and sipped it, pretty sure that Victoria was going to resume the attack. She wasn't mistaken.

'So, any ugly men on the horizon?'

Jo gave her a grin. 'No men at all, Vic.' She glanced at her watch; the lecture at the Natural History Museum was starting in less than half an hour. 'What're you doing this weekend? Feel like coming out to Woodstock with me? I'm going to see mum and dad. We could go riding.'

Victoria grimaced and shuddered.

'That's very kind, but no thanks. Horses are big, they've got teeth, they stink and they crap all over the place. I can't imagine why you think they're so wonderful. It's all right for you: you've ridden since you were a toddler and you've got a sister who's an Olympic show jumper. Me, I'm more of a cat person – and you don't need to ride them.'

'Give me a horse, or a dog, any day.' Jo smiled. 'Or a butterfly.'

'You and your butterflies. You're just a glorified train-spotter. You go round with your notebook and pencil, ticking the different ones off on your list and loving it, don't you? And you don't even collect them either.'

Jo was about to launch into her familiar critique of butterfly collectors when she remembered her most recent rant on that subject. Annoyingly that reminded her, yet again, of Corrado. Doing her best to dismiss the image, she just shook her head.

'Anyway, I really must go. There's a lecture on the endangered butterflies of Europe tonight and I don't want to miss it. Do you want to come along as well? You might find it interesting.'

Victoria grinned.

'I'd need an awful lot more Prosecco before that could happen. No, you go and enjoy yourself. I've got a pile of ironing to do back at home and I know for a fact that'll be far more interesting that your helicoptera.'

'*Lepidoptera*, Vic.' Jo grinned and swallowed the last of her wine as she stood up. 'Enjoy the ironing. You don't know what you're missing.'

Her friend grinned back. 'Actually, Jo, I do, I really do.' She stood up as well, a more serious expression on her face. 'And I might just start looking at flights and hotels in readiness for a trip to Rome this summer. Might you be up for that?'

Jo nodded. The idea of returning to Rome appealed very much, but irritatingly it wasn't the image of the Pantheon that came to mind, but of Corrado.

–

A couple of days later, Jo got a call from her boss at nine o'clock at night. He had a habit of doing this and it was getting on her nerves. He was one of those people who got up late, came to work at ten and woke up some time around lunch. By mid to late afternoon he was firing on all cylinders and he appeared to have no consideration for the fact that his staff might have lives outside of work.

Since Christian's departure, of course, Jo didn't have a lot going on, but it was annoying all the same.

'Ronald, hi, what can I do for you?' She folded the corner of the page to mark the spot in the book she was reading, and sat back, expecting a lengthy conversation – or, as was more usual, a monologue.

'Jo, excellent. Listen, I've been thinking. Talk to me about sea horses, would you?'

Jo knew better by now than to express surprise. A few nights earlier his opening salvo had been to ask how to tell a sea lion from a walrus. Whereas most normal people would have turned to the internet for this sort of thing, he always picked up the phone and, increasingly these days, it was Jo at the other end. Suppressing a little sigh of frustration, she did her best to reply.

'Sea horses belong to the genus Hippocampus. Their main distinguishing characteristic is that the female deposits her eggs into a pouch on the male's body and he carries the young.' She decided to risk a bit of levity. 'Not sure how popular that would be if it applied to humans.'

'Humans…? Oh, yes, of course.' Humour had never been his strong suit. 'Anyway, are they under threat?'

'Ronald, *all* sea creatures are under threat these days.'

'Excellent.'

As head of a charity dedicated to conservation, particularly in the ocean, it was a surprising response, but Jo didn't comment. It all became clear very swiftly as he continued.

'Do they have sea horses in the Seychelles?'

'Definitely, all over the Indian ocean, mainly in shallow waters.'

'Excellent.'

Jo began to get an idea where this might be leading.

'Are you considering a visit, maybe? Some sort of research trip?' This would not be the first time he had managed to combine what he described as business with a sunny holiday.

'That's what I was wondering. I've got a book up here on my shelves all about the islands. Just let me get it.'

She heard movement at the other end of the line as he presumably reached for the book. There was a metallic creaking sound as if he was climbing a stepladder. However, seconds later there was a cry, a crash and a scream of agony. She pressed the phone closer to her ear.

'Ronald, Ronald, are you all right?'

There was a lengthy wait before she heard another voice that she recognised as belonging to Ronald's wife, Deirdre. 'Hello, is that you, Joanne? I'm afraid Ronald has had a fall. I'd better phone the emergency services.' And the line went dead.

Next morning when she got to work, she heard all about it from Melissa, his PA.

'Ronald is in hospital. Deirdre just phoned. It appears he's broken two bones in his leg. Nasty fractures, apparently. He's going to be in traction for a while and they say he'll be out of commission for at least four to six weeks.'

Jo's immediate reaction was that a four- to six-week period without Ronald would be almost as good as a holiday for her, but she kept her tone studiously sympathetic. 'Poor Ronald. What a pain… literally. Have you spoken to him?'

'Yes, I've just come off the phone with him now.' She grinned at Jo. 'As you can imagine, he's not a happy bunny.'

'Is there anything he wants me to do while he's off?' Jo's current position meant that she sometimes had to deputise for Ronald, although, so far, she had only ever got the jobs he didn't want. Visits to the UN in New York or formal dinners in Brussels never came her way. Over the past few months she had taken his place at a waste processing seminar in East London, a weekend in the coalfields of Belgium visiting decommissioned pits, and two days in Silesia learning about air pollution. For a moment she wondered if this might result in a trip to the Seychelles for her, but she doubted it. Still, she crossed her fingers that his accident might mean something a bit more exciting, although standing up in front of crowds had never really been her thing.

'Yes, a few bits and pieces. If you can, would you be able to drop into the drinks do at the French Embassy this evening? It's to raise awareness of the state of the oceans. You don't need to do anything except be seen.' Jo nodded. She had been planning a quiet night in, but a brief appearance at an embassy drinks party sounded rather appealing.

'No problem. What time?'

'From six to eight. He says the speeches will be around seven o'clock so all you have to do is to get there before that and leave again when they're all over.'

'Fine, I'll do that.'

'Great. I'll email them with the change. They're red hot on security these days for obvious reasons.'

Jo nodded absently. 'Anything else Ronald wants me to do?'

'Yes, there is, actually. He asks if you could fill in for him at the "Save the Planet" conference in Rome later this month.'

'Rome?' Jo felt a thrill of excitement. 'I'd love to, Mel.'

Melissa looked relieved. 'That's great. And you're sure you can go at such short notice? It starts a week on Monday and it lasts for five days.' She caught Jo's eye. 'Sure nobody's going to miss you?'

Jo shook her head. 'Nope. I'm a free agent these days.'

'Oh, I'm sorry. Didn't it work out with your oh-so-handsome boyfriend? You looked so good together at the Christmas party, I thought it was the real thing.'

'So did I, Mel.' Jo did her unsuccessful best to keep the note of bitterness out of her voice. 'But I'm afraid it all fell apart in February. No, I'm on my own now, but I'm fine with it. So, what do I have to do at the conference?'

'Just put in an appearance and be prepared to give his paper on some fairly radical proposals for eradicating plastic waste by the year 2030.' Seeing the expression of apprehension on Jo's face, Melissa was quick to reassure her. 'It's all right. That doesn't mean standing up in front of the whole conference. Yours isn't a plenary session, just a sideshow in a lecture theatre. It's a PowerPoint presentation and it's all prepared. All you've got to do is read from Ronald's notes and run the disk. He told me to tell you that these sessions often only attract a handful of people.'

Jo nodded. In fact, she knew almost all of it by heart because she was the one who had written it and prepared the slides for the PowerPoint presentation. One of Ronald's less endearing traits was that, time and time again, when Jo or one of her colleagues came up with a bright idea, they would subsequently find it appear in academic or industry journals a month or two later with Ronald's name on it. Although the idea of standing up in front of a bunch of academics, including a number of household names, was scary, it would feel pretty good to be able to present what was in effect her brainchild. And, anyway, she told herself, having to give a paper was a small price to pay for an all-expenses-paid return to the Eternal City.

She had a sudden thought. It would be good to include in the presentation an update on progress towards finding replacements for plastics, so as to eliminate the problem at source. And the person to ask about this was, of course, Corrado. And if she was going to Rome, she would see him there and get the latest news on that subject from him. This was a very appealing prospect. Annoyingly, her subconscious immediately queried whether her interest in seeing the handsome Roman chemist again was purely professional, but she did her best to banish any such questions. He was the expert and that was all. It made sense to consult an expert. Nevertheless, her subconscious wasn't convinced.

'I'm sure the plastics lecture will be fine, Mel. Let me have everything as soon as possible so I can check it all through before I go.'

How amazing to be going back to Rome! When she got to her office and turned on her computer screen, her eyes landed squarely on a close-up of a striking purple butterfly flecked with patches of white. The caption beneath it read '*Purple Emperor, apatura iris*'. The lecturer at the British Museum had been lamenting how rare these were becoming in Britain. He had, however, mentioned that they could be found in Italy. She found herself smiling. Now, if she could see one of those…

At the end of the afternoon she dashed home for a quick shower and a change of clothes before the drinks party. Melissa had told her French embassy events tended to be on the dressy side, so she chose the newer of her two smart dresses. It was a bit short, but fairly conservative all the same, and the light blue colour matched her eyes. She put on a pair of heels and checked herself in the mirror before deciding she would do. Before leaving, she called her sister in Italy to give her the news about her imminent return to Rome. Angie sounded pleased.

'That's great, Jo. Why don't you try to get a flight out a day or two before the conference so as to be able to spend the weekend with us first? You can stay out here at the Country Club if you like. Mario or I can easily pop in to pick you up.'

'Thanks, Angie, but accommodation's already booked in a central Rome hotel from Saturday.'

'Well, we'll pick you up when you arrive and bring you out here for dinner that night and then you and I can do the sights of Rome on Sunday. Sound good?'

'That sounds great. I did Piazza Navona and the Trevi fountain with Corrado last week.' As she mentioned his name, she found herself wondering if she would see him again or whether he would be tied up with the girl who had greeted him in Piazza Navona, or another of the same ilk. She repressed the usual upsurge of annoyance with herself that inevitably followed thoughts of him and decided not to mention him to Angie. To her surprise, her sister then did just that.

'He said you two got on well together. He's very much your type, too, isn't he?'

'My type?'

'You seem to have a habit of picking insanely handsome men after all. Like your male model, Christian, for example.'

Jo felt the colour rush to her cheeks and was quick to knock that notion on the head.

'Not any more, Angie. I've had it with handsome men. In fact, I've had it with any men, at least for now. They're more trouble than they're worth.'

Then Angie said something unexpected.

'That's probably for the good. I was going to give you a little heads-up about Corrado, just in case, but if you're not interested, that's fine.'

'What sort of heads-up?'

'Oh, just… it's a bit complicated. I'll tell you all about it when you come over.'

When Jo put the phone down she stood for a minute or two, turning over in her head what her sister had said, wondering what sort of revelation might await her in Rome. Finally, she gave a little snort and went out into the corridor, turning to lock the door. As she did so, Kevin from flat three opened his door and peeked out. As usual, there was a cheeky grin on his face.

'Evening, sweetie. You're looking ravishing. Is Prince Charming coming to pick you up in his glass coach.'

'Hi, Kevin. You want to get yourself a life, rather than obsessing about your neighbours.' She grinned back. He and his partner Justin had become very good friends of hers over the past couple of years. 'And there's no Prince Charming. You should know that by now.'

'So where are you going all dolled up like that? A visit to the Palace maybe? I hear Prince Philip makes a real mean curry.'

'The French Embassy for a drinks thing.'

'Interesting… you never know who you'll meet there. Some handsome Frenchman, I'm sure. Are you wearing your posh underwear, just in case you get lucky?'

'Probably not as posh as yours, Kevin, and I have no intention of "getting lucky", thank you. Now go back to your knitting and let me get on.'

'Don't do anything I wouldn't do.' He hesitated, looking a bit more serious. 'And you really do look a million dollars, you know.'

'You're so good for my self-confidence. Thanks, Kevin.'

'Good night, princess. And remember to hang onto your glass slippers.'

The drinks do at the French Embassy was surprisingly crowded. Jo got there well before seven as instructed and found the large function room already packed. She decided not to speculate whether this was entirely for the sake of the planet's polluted oceans or because the French embassy was renowned for its excellent champagne and foie gras nibbles. She spotted a few faces she recognised from other animal and conservation charities, but most people were unknown to her. Following her instructions, she accepted a glass of champagne from a passing waiter and started to 'be seen'.

She moved steadily around the room, sipping the very good champagne and smiling back at anybody who smiled at her. The name badge she had pinned to her chest would hopefully ensure that her presence would be noted. She stopped and spoke to a handful of people, among them a very tall American with a ponytail. He wasn't wearing a name badge and told her his name was Ricky. He didn't look a lot older than her and she was surprised to learn that he would be giving the keynote speech this evening. He was friendly and knowledgeable and she got on well with him. She wondered idly if he would be at the Rome conference, but didn't have time to ask before he was led away.

She had just reached the far side when she heard the unmistakable sound of a microphone being tapped and silence gradually spread over the room. A middle-aged man with what looked suspiciously like a jet-black hairpiece stepped onto a raised dais at one end of the room and welcomed the guests in French. Once he had finished there was a ripple of polite applause, after which he switched to excellent, if accented, English and did the whole thing again. Finally, he introduced the guest speaker as Professor Richard Paris from UCLA.

Jo listened to Ricky speaking informatively about efforts being made to collect and dispose of the Great Pacific Garbage Patch; a gruesome floating island of detritus the size of Texas out in the middle of the northern Pacific. This wasn't new to her, but it was interesting all the same, as was the speaker.

As the speech went on, she became aware of a man standing to one side of her. His arm kept brushing against her bare shoulder and she got the feeling it was on purpose. She was hemmed in on the other side by an elderly lady with a walking stick and was unable to follow her natural instincts and move away, so she had to grin and bear it. The man was tall, wearing a dark blue suit, but she couldn't see his face unless she were to lean forward and peer up at him. When the speech finished, he turned towards her and she saw him more clearly.

She instantly warmed to him. Victoria would have realised immediately why this was; he certainly couldn't be described as 'gorgeous' by any stretch of the imagination. It wasn't that he was ugly by any means, but he was unlikely to be featuring on the cover of *Vogue Hommes* any time soon. His dark hair was already receding and his nose was a bit squint, as if he had received a hefty punch at one point in his life. He was wearing an immaculate dark blue suit, striped tie, and a smile on his slightly crooked mouth. Jo found herself smiling back at him. Evidently taking heart from her reaction, he leant towards her.

'Good evening. Are you an academic, a financier or a freeloader?' He had the sort of accent you normally only get after spending your youth in a very expensive private school.

'If I can only pick one, I suppose it would have to be academic. I've got a degree in Zoology and a PhD in Conservation. But it's not as straightforward as that.' She indicated her name badge with the name of the charity on it and he leant forward and studied it, or her left breast, closely. Sensing that the old lady behind her had started to move away, she took a tentative step backwards. As she did so, he straightened up, presumably realising that his inspection had maybe been a bit too intrusive.

'I see. So, you're helping to save the planet, Joanne.'

'I'd like to think so.' He wasn't wearing a name badge so she threw the question back at him. 'And what about you? What do you do?'

'If I can only pick one, I'd have to describe myself as a financier, but there's a good bit of freeloader in there as well. Which reminds me, I see your glass is empty. Can I get us a couple of glasses of this lovely champagne?'

As he posed the question, a waitress appeared with a tray and he expertly slipped his empty glass onto it and helped himself to two replacements.

'If you don't want the champers, I'm very happy to drink both of these, but it would be nice if you joined me.'

Jo set down her empty glass and took a full one from him. She found she was still smiling. He sounded like a fun sort of guy and the wonderful thing was that this was a normal-looking man hitting on her for a change.

'And your name, Mr Freeloader?'

'Markus. Markus Finchley. I'm very pleased to meet you, Joanne.'

'Jo. Everybody calls me Jo.' She took his hand and shook it.

'Well, Jo, what are the chances of my being able to buy you dinner when this little shindig finishes?'

She took a sip of wine and thought it over. He looked and sounded on the level and he certainly didn't remind her of Christian, or Corrado for that matter.

'What did you have in mind, Markus?'

'I've got a car and a driver outside waiting for me. You decide. For such an outstandingly beautiful girl I should really whistle up a plane and pop us across to Deauville for oysters and lobster at *Les Vapeurs*.'

Jo assumed he was joking. Besides, she had only the vaguest idea where Deauville was and she had never heard of *Les Vapeurs*, but she knew she wasn't going to get into a car with him, let alone an aircraft, until she knew a lot more about him. Yes, he seemed okay, but, as she knew to her cost, looks can be deceptive. She kept her tone light as she replied.

'Shame on you, Markus. Think of your carbon footprint. But if you're serious about dinner, Knightsbridge is full of restaurants, and I'm sure there are a good number of French ones within walking distance.'

He reached into his jacket and produced a phone. He spoke quietly into it for a few seconds before replacing it again.

'Excellent idea. I've got one of my people onto booking us a table.'

Chapter 3

'*Buonasera, Joanna.*'

'*Buonasera, Vittoria.*'

Jo had been late getting to their Italian class and so they hadn't had time to catch up on events since Monday when they had last seen each other. Now that the lesson was over, they filed out of the classroom and Jo caught Victoria's eye. '*Vuoi un Prosecco?*'

'*Sì, grazie.*'

They headed out and across the road to the pub where they usually ended up on a Thursday night after two hours of Italian conversation. Victoria had always been keen on languages while Jo's grandfather had been Italian and her mother had insisted she and her sister should learn the language, forcing the reluctant girls to do Italian alongside all their other A levels. By mutual agreement this evening Jo and Victoria decided to revert to their native language as they found themselves a free table as far from the big screen football match as possible.

'Seriously, Prosecco or do you want something else, Vic?'

'Actually, I rather fancy a cup of tea.'

'Good idea. I'll join you.'

By the time Jo returned with the teas, Victoria had dug out her iPad and was flicking through the pages of Booking.com. She looked up as Jo set the tray down.

'Rome – I've been doing some research.'

'Hold everything. I've got some big news about Rome.' Jo sat down and told her friend about the week she was going to be spending over there. Victoria was predictably green with envy. However, Jo had a suggestion that soon put a smile on her friend's face.

'I've phoned the hotel and they tell me I've been allocated a big room with, wait for it, *two* queen-size beds! The hotel's right in the middle of town, near the Spanish Steps, so it couldn't be better. So, if you can find the time, why don't you come over for a few days, or for the whole week? I'd love the company and that way, you get a free holiday in Rome. You've broken up for the summer, haven't you?'

'Brilliant! We actually break up next week. I've got Marguerite's wedding on the Saturday – we work together – and I can't really wriggle out of it although I would dearly like to. I'm supposed to bring a plus one, but I haven't got one, so I'm going to be the odd one out as usual.'

Jo nodded understandingly. Victoria's failure to hook up with a good man was beginning to get to her and beneath the cheery exterior, Jo knew Vic was far from happy with her life. Since Jo's break up with Christian, the two girls had spent a lot of time together and Jo had been doing her best to provide, as well as receive, support. She gave her friend a broad smile.

'Maybe you'll find the love of your life at the wedding; they're supposed to be good places for romance.'

'Yeah, right. Last wedding I went to, most of the men were gay.' Victoria didn't look convinced, but she rallied. 'Anyway, I could get a cheap flight to Rome on the Sunday and stay on until the end. Thank you so much, Jo. That's fantastic!'

'I'm booked Saturday to Saturday. I'll email you the flights. I'm really looking forward to it.'

'Well, it sounds as if your boss – what's his name? – has finally done something good for a change.'

'It's an ill wind all right.'

Jo took a mouthful of tea and sat back, dreaming of Rome. As she did so, she had a thought.

'While you've got the computer out, take a look at the hotel. It's very close to the conference centre and it's quite something.'

It only took Victoria a few seconds to find it.

'Blimey, look how much rooms cost! Your charity likes the good life, doesn't it?'

'You're joking, Vic. If we were paying for it, I'd be in a cheap *pensione* – if cheap places exist in the centre of Rome – but it was all booked and paid for by the conference organisers for Ronald as one of the guest speakers. It's just my good luck I'm taking his place.'

Victoria read the blurb out loud and then they flicked through the photos together. It certainly looked swanky, but, as Victoria pointed out, it ought to be for the price.

'But it does look good. And, and like you say, it's bang in the city centre as well.'

After a bit, Jo changed the subject. 'Anyway, let me tell you about the man I met last night.'

She saw Victoria's eyes light up, although she couldn't miss the tiny flash of envy lurking there. Yes, the sooner Victoria got herself fixed up with somebody, the better.

'You met someone, Jo? And there you were, just a few days ago, telling me you weren't on the lookout for a man.'

'And I wasn't. I'm still not. But I was at a drinks thing at the French Embassy – a work thing – when I bumped into this guy.'

'The embassy, eh? What a glamorous life you lead! Did they serve those little golden chocolates like in the old adverts?' Victoria was grinning. 'And is this man a sexy Frenchman?'

Jo grinned back. 'Nope, no chocolates, and he's not French. He's English and his name's Markus.'

'Sounds a bit posh.'

'Yes, I suppose he is, but he's very nice.'

'And ugly?' Victoria was grinning now.

'Definitely not ugly, but certainly not in the Christian league.'

'Or your Roman hunk.'

'He's not *my* Roman hunk but, no, not like him either. And, remember, Corrado is going to be my brother-in-law. Nothing's going to happen there.'

'And what happened with Markus?'

'He took me to this amazing French restaurant where we had a really excellent meal, although it must have cost the earth.'

Victoria rolled her eyes. 'Where do you find these guys? The last time I went out for a meal with a man, it was pie and chips in the pub and we split the bill. So, this Markus isn't short of a bob or two, or did the two of you end up washing dishes in the kitchen to pay for it?'

Jo grinned and shook her head. 'I think we can take it he's loaded. He says he's in finance and he's got a chauffeur, no less. I have no idea what he does, but there isn't any doubt that he's got money. But that's unimportant. The thing is, he's a really nice guy.'

'Who also just happens to be rich…'

'No, really, Vic, I mean it. He looks normal. He sounds normal. He behaved normally. Whether he's loaded or not doesn't matter.'

Victoria eyed her sceptically. 'Whatever you say. And how did the evening finish? Did you and he…?'

'No, we didn't, Vic. And why do you always assume I'm ready to jump into bed with men on the first date?'

'All right, I believe you, although if a wealthy banker was buying me slap-up meals, I'd be all over him like a rash. So, are you seeing him again?'

'I don't know.'

'Do you want to see him again?'

Jo had been pondering that question herself over the last twenty-four hours. 'Yes, I think I do.'

'Did you give him your number?'

Jo nodded.

'Then you can be sure you'll be seeing him again.'

'*Buonasera, signore.* Mind if I join you?'

They both looked up and Jo saw what could have been a blush on Victoria's face. It was George from their Italian class. She knew that Victoria liked the look of him, but, as far as Jo was aware, they had never been out on a date. Maybe this would be the opportunity to get the two of them together. She was quick to offer him a place alongside Victoria and the red spots on her friend's cheeks deepened in intensity.

'Of course, George, take a seat. We've just been talking about Rome. We're going there in ten days' time.'

He sat down and, as he did so, Jo checked him out. He was a good-looking man, probably around their age, maybe a bit short on self-confidence, but very pleasant. He smiled shyly at the two of them.

'Rome sounds exciting. What's the event? Just a holiday or what?'

Victoria was looking a bit less overcome by now, but Jo waded in again to give her friend time to regain her composure.

'I've got to go over for a conference and Victoria's coming with me as a tourist.'

'Lucky you. I love Rome.'

'I've never been.' Jo was pleased to hear Victoria's voice sounding almost normal. 'And the hotel we're booked into looks phenomenal. Here, George, see what you think.'

Victoria pushed the iPad across the table and they both watched as he looked at the description of the hotel and checked some of the photos and the map. He must have seen how expensive the rooms were, but he was evidently too polite to comment.

'Looks amazing. And it's in a super position, too.'

'Do you know Rome?' Victoria reclaimed the tablet.

'I've been a few times, but mainly for work. But I always try to set aside a day, or at least half a day, to see some of the sights while I'm there.'

'That sounds like a great job, George. What is it you do?' Jo reckoned it might help Victoria's cause – if she really did fancy him – if they could discover a bit more about him.

He shook his head ruefully. 'All terribly boring, I'm afraid. I work for the government.' He smiled across at Jo. 'Just a civil servant. Nothing exciting.'

'James Bond was a civil servant, George. Don't do yourself down.'

He grinned modestly. 'Double-oh six and a quarter, at best.'

'So, what are the places we really need to see when we're in Rome?' Victoria readied herself to write down what he said.

As George reeled off a list of must-see sights, starting with the Vatican Museum and the Sistine Chapel, Jo studied him a bit more closely. He was wearing a spotless white linen shirt and she was impressed. Even just ironing that would take an age. For a moment she wondered who did the ironing. Maybe there was a woman involved. Victoria would need to find that out if she was thinking about embarking on a relationship with him. He looked fit and healthy, but maybe not in the James Bond league. She glanced at Victoria and what she saw reinforced her original impression: Victoria liked George and, by the look of it, George liked Victoria. She crossed her fingers under the table and made a little wish that George might turn out to be Victoria's Prince Charming.

'And, of course, your hotel's right by the Spanish Steps and only a short walk from the Villa Borghese gardens.'

'That all sounds great, George. Thank you so much.'

They chatted about Rome and collected lots of good ideas from him. By the sound of it, he had spent quite a few odd days sightseeing and he was a mine of information, from where to eat the best pizza to where the main pickpocket hunting grounds were. Jo was unsurprised to hear that the crowds around the Trevi Fountain were one of the crime hotspots, so Corrado had been right to tell her to be careful. Once again, thought of the tall Roman brought with it a little flash of annoyance. Who needed a Corrado when there was a Markus on the scene? In fact, why did she need a man at all?

—

Jo went out to Oxfordshire to see her parents at the weekend. Her mum came to pick her up from the station and drove her out through the traffic to the little village where they lived. When they got home, Jo was very impressed to find her father up and walking around without a stick, only a matter of days after his hip replacement operation. She was really pleased to see them both and soon found herself sitting out in the back garden with them, relaxing in the shade of the enormous mulberry tree. As her mother poured the tea, Felix the old black and white cat appeared and jumped straight up onto Jo's lap. She settled back to stroke him, enjoying being home again.

'So, tell us all about Rome, Joanne.'

Jo and Angie would always be 'Joanne' and 'Angela' to their parents. Both had tried to get them to use their abbreviated names, but without success. It was just one of the facts of life.

Jo had spent a long time on the phone with her mum on Sunday night, telling her all about the engagement party in Rome, but she happily repeated her tale, adding other details as they came to mind. Predictably, her mother was more interested in Jo's opinion of Angie's future husband than the delicacies served up for lunch that day. Her father, equally predictably, was more interested in the estate and the Country Club.

'So, it's a big sort of place, then?'

'Definitely. They've got a lovely hotel and restaurant, and the stables are a really big enterprise, with their own showjumping arena.'

Her father murmured in approval. From the expression on his face she could tell he was savouring the fact that one of his daughters appeared to have landed on her feet, even if their firstborn had not. Jo thought it best to steer them off the subject of weddings and went on to tell them both about her upcoming week in Rome for the conference.

'How exciting!' Her mother was beaming. 'So, you'll be addressing an international conference. You *are* doing well, Joanne, aren't you?'

'Well, technically, I'll just be giving a talk in a side room, but, yes, it's rather nice to be involved with something like that, especially as I wrote most of the paper anyway.'

'And will you have free time for some sightseeing?'

'I'll make sure I do. And Victoria's coming over for a few days as well.'

'How nice. How is she? Has she got herself a young man yet?'

Jo shook her head and braced herself for what she knew to be coming next. She wasn't mistaken.

'Well, I'm sure she'll find somebody. And what about you, Joanne? Have you found yourself somebody to replace that awful Christian?'

Jo shook her head. 'No, mum.' There then ensued a pregnant silence before Jo finally gave in. 'But I did go out for dinner with a very nice man the other night.'

As expected, she saw her mother's eyes light up. 'Really? Oh good. And what sort of man is this one? Not another model, I hope.' The note of disapproval in her voice was unmistakable. She had always mistrusted Christian and, of course, events had proved her right.

'No, he works in the city. Something to do with finance. And, before you ask, mum, he's just a normal guy.'

A look of considerable satisfaction spread across her mother's face. However, her next question had Jo on the ropes once again.

'Angela told me her future brother-in-law's awfully good-looking. She says you and he went out for dinner last Saturday. Is that so?'

Jo suppressed a snort. 'Yes, he's a handsome man, but then, so is Mario. And no, I didn't have dinner with him. He just gave me a lift back into the centre of Rome.' She saw no need to mention the drink in Piazza Navona or their little walking tour afterwards.

'That's good. Angela says he's a bit of a Don Juan.'

This came as no great surprise to Jo, but she had always resented her mother's interference in her affairs, so she chose to play it down.

'How he spends his time is of no interest to me, mum. He just gave me a lift into town and he behaved himself perfectly. He's a scientist like me and we talked about science. You don't need to worry about me and him getting together.'

'That's good to hear. I've always thought handsome men were more trouble than they're worth.'

Jo waited for her mother to make reference to how badly Christian had behaved and how she had been right all along about him. However, to Jo's relief, she must have thought better of it and said nothing. After a short pause, Jo decided to change the subject.

'I was thinking about going for a ride this afternoon. Mum, do you feel like coming with me?'

'I haven't been to the stables for months. But, yes, now I come to think of it, I'd rather like a short ride. It is a beautiful day, after all.'

Jo heaved a sigh of relief. This would give her a chance to do a bit of bonding and reassure her mother that her little girl was doing fine and still loved her. As she did so, she felt her phone vibrate in her pocket and pulled it out. It was a text message from Markus.

> Hi Jo. Feel like dinner on Tuesday? New floating restaurant on Thames. Interested? Really hope so. Markus.

She glanced across at her mother. 'It's a text from Markus, the man I told you about. He's asking me out for dinner on Monday.'

'That's nice. Are you going to say yes?'

Jo paused for thought, but only for a few seconds.

'Yes, I think I am.'

–

Dinner on Tuesday turned out to be a bit more than she had bargained for.

Markus picked her up from London Bridge station in his chauffeur-driven Mercedes, although it would have been little more than a ten-minute walk to the floating restaurant moored just the other side of Tower Bridge.

The restaurant had been created inside an old barge and Markus clearly knew the owner well. They were greeted with open arms and accompanied to their table by the man himself, who then returned with champagne cocktails while they decided what to eat. Jo looked around at the ostentatiously stylish surroundings then picked up her glass and clinked it against his.

'Thank you for this, Markus. What a super place!' A bit too much bling for her taste, but she didn't want to sound rude or ungrateful.

'I'm so glad you like it. I've only been here a few times – it's very new, you see – and I've always eaten well.' He took a sip of his cocktail and smiled across the table at her. 'You're looking stunning tonight, Jo, if you don't mind me saying so.'

She smiled back. 'Pay me as many compliments as you like, Markus. And you're looking very smart yourself.'

As she spoke, she realised 'smart' was the operative word. Christian would probably have turned up in faded jeans with strategic tears at the knees, and a soft cotton shirt deliberately unbuttoned to below the ribcage. And he would have looked as if he had just stepped out of a perfume commercial and knew it. Markus, on the other hand, was impeccably turned out in a light grey summer suit and a pink shirt with an expensive logo on the left breast. Somehow, Jo got the impression he would have been more comfortable wearing a tie but, in accordance with current fashion trends, he had decided to abandon it in favour of an open collar, but with just the top button undone. No, he wasn't classically handsome, but he had style, even if it was maybe a bit too old school and a bit too rich for Jo's taste. Still, he was charming and friendly and she was happy to be there with him.

They both ordered mussels as a starter and she opted for just a salad to follow, while Markus chose turbot. They drank Chablis Grand Cru and Jo had few illusions as to what that might cost in a place like this. They chatted about everything from the matches at Wimbledon the previous day to his recent trip to the Caribbean, and she gradually got to learn more about him. He worked, as she had imagined, in the heart of the City, and his job involved travelling all over the world. By the sound if it, this was usually done in a private aircraft and he inevitably stayed at only the very best hotels.

Feeling she should show off a bit in return, she told him about her upcoming trip to Rome and asked if he knew the conference centre by the Spanish Steps. He confirmed that he did and that it was a modern conversion of an old building and that it wasn't too enormous. This came as good news to Jo, who had been fretting about finding herself standing up in front of hundreds of people. He asked her what she would be doing there and expressed a surprising degree of interest in their proposals to deal with plastic waste although, somehow, she got the feeling this interest might be more for her benefit than for the state of the oceans. Nevertheless, it was a pleasant evening, although one thing gradually emerged more and more clearly as the night progressed.

She didn't see the relationship developing.

This, she told herself as she took her time over her 'summer pudding with green tea ice cream and black-currant jus', wasn't because of his physical appearance. It was the abyss that clearly existed between him, with his chauffeur, his private plane and his obvious propensity for spending money, and ordinary Joanne Green from Woodstock, with her little flat in south London and her sum total of only two 'smart' dresses. She didn't fit in his world and she knew she never would. And if she was honest with herself she knew she didn't even want to. Maybe it was because of her interest in the planet and the knowledge of just how much damage humans were doing to it with their cars, planes and extravagant waste, but it was also the realisation deep down that she'd never feel comfortable as a kept woman or a trophy wife. Christian, for all his faults, had never flashed his money around and that had kept things far simpler between them. With Markus it would be very different and she knew she didn't want that.

Nevertheless, by the time they left, she had had a very pleasant evening.

The unpleasant bit followed shortly after.

He insisted on taking her to a wine bar in Chelsea for a nightcap, although she knew she had already drunk quite enough, considering she had a very full day at work the next day. However, as the comfortable limousine made its near silent way through the streets of the capital, Jo felt his arm stretch out behind her back and encircle her shoulders, pulling her gently towards him. She didn't mind too much and she made no comment, not least as the chauffeur was only a few feet in front of her to act as a chaperone. She felt lips against her neck and she pretended he had tickled her, still trying to keep things low key. However, when she felt his hand land on her knee and begin to slide slowly but unequivocally upwards, she turned to face him.

'If you don't mind, Markus, I don't think I'm ready for anything like this. I'd rather you removed your hand from my leg.'

She looked him square in the eye and saw the reflections of the streetlights of Blackfriars' Bridge flick across his enlarged pupils as he stared unblinkingly down at her. Gone was the charming, friendly expression. This was now replaced by something much more visceral and primitive. His hand on her leg stopped moving, but he didn't remove it or his arm from her shoulder.

'Don't you like me, Jo?'

His voice was husky and she had a horrible feeling she knew what that signified. Getting into the car with him had been a mistake, chauffeur or no chauffeur. She decided to try diplomacy first and, if that didn't work, she would scream the place down.

'You know I do, Markus. I've had a lovely evening, but it's just that I want to get to know you better before we try to take things to the next level.' She kept her eyes trained on his. 'You do understand, don't you?'

There was a long pause, by which time they had crossed the Thames and the driver was turning west. Finally, to her considerable relief, she saw him relax and she felt him remove his grip on her. When he responded, his voice had returned to normal and his expression was once more affable.

'Of course I understand, Jo. You need time. That's quite all right with me.'

She heaved a surreptitious sigh of relief and slid a few inches further away from him. As she did so, she reflected that there was no doubt a certain kind of dinner companion who would have been only too pleased to thank her date in the way he was clearly expecting. But that wasn't going to be her tonight, or any night. She could feel her heart beating fast as she began to recover from what had been an unexpectedly scary moment. The feel of his eyes upon her, studying her like a piece of meat, had been every bit as unsettling as his touch.

She looked out of the window and concentrated her attention on the Thames alongside them until the car came to a halt in traffic. As it did so, her eyes landed on the London Underground sign announcing the entrance to Embankment underground station right beside them.

She didn't hesitate. She reached for the door handle and pulled it, relieved to find it wasn't locked. The door opened, and as she stepped out, she looked back over her shoulder at him. He was still sitting there, no doubt taken by surprise by her actions.

'Thank you for the lovely dinner, Markus. I'm afraid I need to go home. Goodnight.'

'Jo…?'

Ignoring his plaintive protest, she slammed the door behind her and disappeared into the crowds. Her overwhelming sensation was one of relief, closely followed by anger.

Chapter 4

The plane touched down in Rome in the early afternoon and the train whisked her into Roma Termini station in barely half an hour. It was almost exactly three o'clock when she walked out through the monumental glass-fronted lobby into the suffocating mid-July heat. She set off across to the car park on the right to look for Angie or Mario who had promised to pick her up. To her surprise, as she got there, she heard a man's voice and saw a tall figure coming towards her.

'Hi, Jo. Welcome back. I'm in the Kiss-and-Ride car park so I couldn't leave the car and come and look for you.' He stopped in front of her. 'Here, let me take your bag.'

'Hi, Corrado. This is very kind of you, but don't worry about the suitcase. It's got wheels. I'm sorry to trouble you; I was expecting to see Angie or Mario.'

As she spoke, she was unable to hide her pleasure at seeing him again. He must have heard it in her voice, but he made no comment.

'No problem. They've got a show jumping event out at the Country Club today and both of them are up to their eyes.' In spite of her protests he took the suitcase from her hands and picked it up easily. He weighed it in his hand, glanced across at her and smiled. 'You're travelling light, I see.'

Jo was delighted to hear him speaking more freely, without any of the reluctance she had sensed two weeks earlier.

'Not really. I normally just bring cabin baggage, but I had to put in some smart clothes for the conference, so it meant a suitcase.'

'Still, it doesn't feel as if there's a lot in here. That's impressive, seeing as you're here for a week.'

'I'm not one of those girls who's that bothered about clothes, to be honest.'

He caught her eye again. 'With a face like yours, you don't need to worry about what you wear.'

No sooner had he uttered the words than he turned away hurriedly, but not before Jo had spotted an expression of regret on his face. What on earth?

She had no time for further reflection as she was presented with another surprise. He led her across to his battered old Fiat, but the strange thing about it was that the vehicle was rocking from side to side. As she approached, she realised what was causing this. Daisy the dog was in the boot, jumping about excitedly as she recognised her master.

He reached down and opened the tailgate. As he did so, Daisy came leaping out, tail wagging furiously, and to Jo's further surprise, ignored Corrado and came charging up to her and almost knocked her over, such was her delight to see her friend again.

'Daisy, get off!' Corrado made a grab for her collar with his free hand as she went past, but Jo waved his hand away and crouched down to greet the Labrador.

'*Ciao*, Daisy. And it's good to see you, too.' She hugged the big dog to her before standing back up again. Corrado was looking apologetic.

'Sorry, Jo. She's obviously very pleased to see you.'

Jo grinned at him. 'And I'm pleased to see her too… and you, Corrado.'

And she was. Not, she told herself firmly, that she thought of him as anything other than a future relative and a good friend. What had happened the other night with Markus had brought home to her just how right she had been when she had told Victoria and her mum she wasn't interested in another man. Drop-dead gorgeous or not, stinking rich or not, none of them could be trusted. She reached down and ruffled the dog's ears. Maybe what she needed was a dog.

Unaware of Jo's reflections, Corrado lifted her case into the boot and then called the dog. As soon as Daisy had jumped back into the car, he closed the boot once more and waved Jo into the passenger seat. She got in and did her best to dissuade the excited dog from licking her neck as Corrado started the engine and headed for the exit.

'What did you call this car park, Corrado?'

'It's the Kiss-and-ride car park. You aren't allowed to leave your vehicle. It's just for setting down and picking up again.'

Then she surprised herself. Totally ignoring the warnings being screamed at her by her subconscious, she found herself leaning towards him.

'Lean over this way a bit, would you? We haven't said hello properly.'

As he slowed the car and did as instructed, she kissed him softly on the cheek, repeating to herself that this was simply a friendly kiss between one friend and another. Even so, the touch of his skin against her lips felt good, worryingly good, and she found herself wishing she had limited herself to a simple handshake. From the uncomfortable expression on his face, it looked very much as if he also wished it had been a simple handshake.

As they drove out through the barrier, he made a suggestion.

'The show jumping finishes at four and Mario says it'll all be done and dusted by six at the latest. If you like, I could take you to your hotel, wait while you check in and dump your stuff. You can freshen up and change or whatever, and then I could give you a whistle-stop tour of Rome in the car before we head out to the Country Club.'

'That sounds wonderful. Thank you so much.'

It took barely five minutes to get from the station to the hotel. Although the Saturday afternoon traffic was particularly heavy and the numbers of tourists on the streets had, if anything, increased since the last time she had been here, the little car managed to squeeze past the worst of it until they came to a halt not far from the top of the famous Spanish Steps.

'The daytime traffic exclusion zone starts here, so I'll have to leave the car and walk you to your hotel. It's only three or four minutes.' Corrado was double-parked but he didn't appear to notice as, ignoring her protests, he picked up her suitcase and, together with the Labrador, they walked the last few hundred metres. As they got there, a uniformed porter came out to collect her suitcase and Corrado and Daisy returned to the car in case a traffic warden came along. Jo walked into the blissfully cool marble-clad lobby and across to the reception desk. A friendly-looking girl in her twenties was waiting to greet her.

'*Buongiorno. Ben arrivata a Roma.*'

Jo mustered her best Italian and replied, although she felt pretty sure the girl must speak fluent English in a place like this, giving her name and saying she had a reservation. The check-in formalities were swiftly concluded and the porter took Jo up in the swish modern lift to the top floor. Her room was mightily impressive, about the same floor size as her whole flat in London, and it even had a charming little terrace looking out over the roofs of the city. It was absolutely delightful. Dragging her attention away from the view, Jo turned to reach for her bag to give the porter a tip, but he had already set her suitcase down on a wooden stand and was at the door. Before she could do more than murmur, '*Grazie*', he gave her a smile and a little bow and let himself out, closing the door silently behind him.

Jo wasted no time. She changed out of her jeans into a light summer dress and sandals and was back at the car in less than ten minutes. She found Corrado leaning against the front wing, deep in conversation with a remarkably pretty policewoman wearing the trademark Roman police white helmet, not dissimilar to a London bobby, apart from the pistol at her hip. It was immediately clear that she hadn't stopped to give Corrado a parking ticket. From the smile on her face as she gave him a little salute and walked off, their conversation had been anything but confrontational. Jo shook her head in disbelief and gave him a broad grin.

'You men… So, you just turn on the charm and they let you get away with murder?'

He grinned back. 'And you women don't do the same thing? Anyway, if you're nice to them, they're normally nice to you. Besides, she's very pretty and I told her so.'

'And she didn't clap the handcuffs on you for disrespect?'

His grin broadened. 'The handcuffs come later, if you're into that sort of thing.' Then, as if regretting his moment of levity, he opened the door and climbed back into the car. Jo followed suit.

'So, Corrado, where to?'

'I've been thinking about that. The best way to see the centre of Rome is on foot, like we did last time you were here. But seeing as we've got the car, I was wondering if you fancied taking a little trip along the Appian Way.'

Jo, like most people, had heard of this famous Roman road, but she wasn't too sure where it led. Corrado was happy to fill in the blanks.

'You know the old saying about all roads leading to Rome? In fact, it was the other way round – they were leading out. The majority were built several centuries before Christ, designed partly to facilitate trade but, above all, to make it fast and easy to move troops towards points of conflict.' While speaking, he started the engine and set off along the road. As he passed the policewoman, he waved to her out of the window and received a broad smile in return. Jo shook her head in mock despair.

'If you can tear yourself away from consorting with the Roman constabulary, you were going to tell me about the Appian Way.'

He glanced across at her and grinned. 'Yes, of course. Well, it's the most important road out of Rome because it led south towards the ports of Naples and, in particular, Brindisi on the east coast of Italy, and from there galleys went to all the Roman provinces around the Mediterranean. Anyway, the really interesting thing about the Appia Antica, as we call it now, is that it's been conserved in its original state for quite a bit of its length, right here in Rome.'

'You're not going to tell me we can drive along it?'

He nodded. 'I certainly am. It gets rougher and rougher and narrower and narrower until it becomes a cycle track and footpath, but we can certainly drive out of town on it for a bit if you like. And all the way along it you'll see ancient Roman ruins popping up all over the place.'

'That sounds terrific.'

What was even more terrific was the route he took to get there. They slowly made their way down the hill through the traffic past the imposing bulk of the Quirinale Palace and off to the left. Corrado was quick to explain where they were.

'Just over to the right of us are the Fori Imperiali, the very heart of the ancient city. I really recommend you come back here on foot one day and check the Forum area out. It's a mass of ancient Roman ruins as far as the eye can see. As for where we are' – he pointed straight ahead – 'I daresay you know what that is, don't you?'

Jo had been gazing in awe all round her, overwhelmed by the sheer magnitude and antiquity of the buildings they had passed, but now her eyes followed his pointing finger and she was confronted with one of the most recognisable buildings on the face of the earth. It was an enormous round structure, the size of a football stadium, formed of row upon row of perfect arches, reaching up to the height of a modern high-rise building. It was made of weathered cream-coloured stone and, even though bits had crumbled, it was still recognisably a massive, solid, imposing piece of architecture.

'The Colosseum! Wow, Corrado, that is quite something!' Jo was almost speechless.

'When this was built, Jesus Christ had only been dead for fifty years. Just think, Jo, what this whole area must have been like in its heyday.'

In spite of no doubt having seen it hundreds of times before, Corrado sounded as stunned by the massive building as Jo herself, and very knowledgeable. She glanced across at him.

'Thank you for bringing me here, Corrado. What a place!'

'You're welcome. But promise me you'll come back on foot. Or maybe I could come with you.'

Jo smiled at him. 'I'd like that.'

'Let's carry on. There's nowhere to stop here anyway and my canine friend back there needs a walk.'

'That sounds like a good idea.'

They carried on past the Colosseum and onto a wide avenue shaded by iconic Roman umbrella pines, some as high as three or four storey buildings. These lived up to their name, providing welcome shade beneath their branches. Corrado pointed out the Circus Maximus off to one side, and he told her about the chariot races that had taken place there. He was obviously very proud of his

Roman heritage. She was very impressed with the city, and with him.

It was a very hot day and the air conditioning either wasn't working or it wasn't turned on. Even with both windows wide open and wearing her lightest dress, Jo was sweltering, and the slightly cooler air under the trees was very welcome. As before, she had to share her open window with the Labrador but, fortunately, the dog was less vocal this time and Jo's hearing remained unimpaired. Soon the area became less built up and Jo was amazed to see how many trees and parks there were around them. The road narrowed further until they found themselves approaching a massive fortified gatehouse set in what looked like the old city walls. As they reached it, Corrado pointed straight ahead, through the arched gateway.

'This is where the Appia Antica starts. If you think the road surface back there was rough, just you wait.'

They squeezed through the narrow archway and across a more major avenue into another stone-paved little road. This ran dead straight between ancient walls and dusty buildings and the surface was indeed pretty bumpy. They passed underneath a concrete bridge carrying what looked like railway tracks and then, after a few minutes Jo saw a sign up ahead. Corrado had seen it too and he had a suggestion.

'These people make some of the best ice cream in Rome. Shall we stop?'

'You're the driver. You decide. But I must admit an ice cream sounds good.'

Corrado pulled off the road into a big courtyard and parked in the shade of another massive umbrella pine. As they got out of the car, he pointed to a terrace over to the side, with tables and parasols.

'The nice thing about this place is that Daisy can come with us.'

Together with the dog they walked across to the terrace. As they got there, they were greeted by the sight of a huge glass-fronted freezer positioned underneath an archway, with a host of different flavours of ice cream piled up into peaks in individual containers. Jo stopped and stared in awe. Apart from old favourites like vanilla, strawberry and chocolate, there were so many others on offer, ranging from fruit flavours like peach, hazelnut and melon, to ones with puzzling names like *Ricotta Stregata* and *Zuppa Inglese*, literally 'English Soup'. She pointed to them and Corrado was happy to supply a translation.

'*Zuppa Inglese* supposedly was inspired by the English trifle and it's certainly got a custardy flavour. *Ricotta Stregata* is actually made with ricotta cheese and there's a liqueur in it called "Strega". *Stregata* means bewitched and it's a bit of an acquired taste.'

As Jo's eyes ranged over the rainbow of colourful mounds from white coconut and red fruits of the forest, to lurid-green mint and jet-black liquorice, she glanced across at him.

'What are you going to have?'

He smiled. 'I'm a creature of habit. I always go for the same thing here: banana and *cioccolato fondente*, the really dark chocolate. What about you?'

Jo finally decided to have a bowl of meringue, strawberry and *amarena* – the latter a mixture of vanilla ice cream with swirls of sour cherry syrup.

'And what about a glass of Prosecco with it?'

'It's too hot for alcohol, Corrado, thanks. Just a glass of mineral water for me please, but don't let me stop you.'

'I'll have water, too. Apart from the fact that I'm driving, it's easy to get dehydrated on a day like today. Do you realise the temperature this afternoon's in the mid-thirties? That's almost blood heat.'

They placed their orders and then walked across to a table in the shade and sat down.

'Would Daisy like a bowl of ice cream as well?'

'Daisy would like all the ice cream on display plus a side order of a roast hog.' Corrado smiled as he reached down and stroked the dog's head. 'She's a Labrador and you probably know what they're like for food. No, if she's a good girl she'll get a wafer biscuit at the end, but that's that. Just like all of us, she has to watch out for her waistline, even if she doesn't want to hear it.'

'And you think my ordering a bowl of three sorts of ice cream qualifies as watching my waistline?'

'You're on holiday, Jo. Besides, I bet you didn't have lunch today.'

'A cup of tea and a biscuit on the plane, but no doubt I'll be having a mammoth meal tonight with Angie and your brother. Still, as you say, I'm on holiday until Monday.'

'And then? Angie said you're a speaker at the Save the Planet conference. I know a few of the people who'll be there. All big names in their fields. *Complimenti.*'

Jo grinned. 'I'm just the stand-in. It should have been my boss and he's very well known in the field of conservation and climate change. I hope I don't disappoint too many of the delegates who wanted to hear him.' She gave him a grin. 'Although to tell the truth, I wrote ninety percent of it.

'I can't imagine you disappointing anyone.'

At that moment a waitress appeared with two enormous bowls of ice cream and a bowl of water for the dog. As Corrado looked up at her, the girl gave him a big smile.

'*Ciao, Corrado.*'

He smiled back and jumped to his feet, accompanied by the Labrador. '*Ciao, Antonia. Come stai?*' He leant forward and kissed her on the cheeks while the dog stood up on her hind legs to be petted.

Jo looked on in disbelief. Was this yet another of his girlfriends? What was it her mother had said about him being a Don Juan?

'Jo, let me introduce you.' Corrado turned back round towards her. 'This is Antonia. She's the daughter of one of my very best friends. She's doing a doctorate in microbiology at the *Sapienza*, and she works here part time. Antonia, this is Jo, from England. She's Angie's sister.'

As Jo produced a big smile and said hello, she gave herself a serious telling-off for jumping to the wrong conclusion about her guide. After Antonia left, Jo watched the dog at their feet slurping the water and vowed to do her best to put aside her prejudices and try to appreciate Corrado for the knowledgeable, generous man he so obviously was.

'The *Sapienza*?'

'Rome University. It's where I did my first degree. It's one of the oldest universities in the world. Not quite as old as Oxford, but still… It was founded in 1300 or so.'

'Sounds like Antonia's a bright girl. And pretty, too. She should do well.'

'Well, you should know what that's like.'

Corrado then immediately transferred his attention to Daisy at his feet and, contradicting what he had just said about Daisy having to watch her figure, reached down and dropped a spoonful of banana ice cream into the now empty water bowl beside Daisy's nose. The dog jumped to her feet and the ice cream was vacuumed up in seconds. As Corrado engaged in this displacement activity and the dog licked the ground beside the bowl until it shone, Jo digested the fact that he had pretty obviously paid her a compliment but then had, equally obviously, immediately regretted it. Something strange was going on, but still, she thought to herself as she dug into the delicious ice cream, a compliment's a compliment.

The ice cream was superb and she forced herself to eat slowly, savouring the different tastes. As she did so, she broached the subject of his work.

'The paper I'm giving at the conference is on removal and disposal of existing plastics from the ocean, but I'd love to be able to include an update on new products being developed to replace plastic. Could you give me a few pointers?'

As a conversation starter, it worked amazingly well. He was obviously very keen to talk about his work and very knowledgeable about all the different facets of it. By the time she reached the end of her ice cream, she had filed away in her mind a number of key points to add to the presentation, which she felt sure would improve it. She thanked him most warmly.

Jo had just reached for her glass and was sitting back, slowly sipping the water and looking out over the dry gardens surrounding the terrace, when she spotted something and instantly leapt to her feet, grabbing her phone off the table as she did so.

'Sorry, Corrado. Butterfly.'

She hurried to the patch of yellow grass and straggly weeds that might once have been a lawn, leaving Corrado looking perplexed. She was vaguely aware of feet behind her and she turned to see the dog trotting along with her, tail wagging. She slowed and put her finger to her lips.

'Shh, Daisy. Don't frighten it off.'

Ahead of her, the butterfly she had spotted had also stopped, settling softly on the trunk of an ancient olive tree. Very slowly, Jo approached and zoomed the camera on her phone until the insect almost filled the screen. She took a couple of photos and then crept a bit closer. She took another photo and then stood in silent appreciation. It was a large cream-coloured butterfly with dark markings, but its uniqueness came from the twopointed tails that protruded from the bottom edges of its wings, giving it its popular name. A second or two later, she felt a tap on her shoulder and heard a whisper at her ear.

'Even I know what this one is. It's a swallowtail, isn't it?'

Jo glanced sideways and found herself barely a few inches from his face, so close she could even smell the banana ice cream on his breath and see a little spot of the dark chocolate that had strayed onto his chin. She nodded in agreement and whispered back.

'*Papilio machaon*, to give it its full title. Quite common over here, but a total rarity in England.' And then, to her own complete surprise, she reached up with a finger and wiped the ice cream off his face, adding superfluously, 'Chocolate.'

He jumped back as if he had been bitten, startling the dog and scaring the butterfly away from its tree trunk. Jo watched as it fluttered into the air and vanished over an ancient stone wall. As it disappeared from view, she was still trying to work out what on earth had made her reach out and touch Corrado like that and why it had produced such an extreme reaction from him. She risked looking at him and saw that he had now retreated several paces and was half-turned away, wiping his face with a tissue. Maybe, she thought to herself, seeing as he was a chemist, he had a thing about germs and infection and being touched. Whatever it was, she felt awful and very silly. His behaviour towards her had made it completely clear from the outset that he wasn't interested in any kind of intimacy with her and as he was about to become her brother-in-law she knew he was off the table anyway. So why had she suddenly felt it appropriate, or even desirable, to touch him like that or indeed to kiss him at the station? She took a deep breath and went towards him, ostensibly to stroke the dog who was sitting at her master's side looking a bit puzzled.

'Don't worry, Daisy, there'll be plenty more butterflies.' She risked a glance at Corrado who was looking more composed now. 'That's a first for me. I've never seen a swallowtail in the wild before.'

'That's good.' He stuffed his tissue in his pocket and summoned a smile. 'There are loads of them around here.' He glanced at his watch. 'Now, if you like, we could combine a bit of exercise – probably well-needed after all that ice cream – with a bit of butterfly hunting. Interested?'

'Absolutely, but only if you haven't got anything better to do.'

'No, I'm at your complete disposal today. I tell you what, the Appia Antica turns into a path for walkers and cyclists a bit further along. We could leave the car and have a walk. We've got bags of time before we need to head out to the Country Club.'

As they walked back to the car, Jo heaved a sigh of relief. He appeared to have returned to his normal welcoming self again, in spite of her faux pas. As she climbed back into the car, she was still turning over in her head just why on earth she had felt it necessary to touch him like that, but her subconscious stubbornly refused to provide her with any answer.

They headed off along the increasingly bumpy road, past high walls and a number of sturdy gates and security cameras. Evidently, this was a part of Rome where very well-heeled Romans chose to have their villas. She pointed to the ornate roof of one large house as they passed and looked across at Corrado.

'Are we in the stockbroker belt here?'

She saw him hesitate and she wondered whether she might have overrated his excellent English. But it soon became clear he had indeed understood.

'It's a highly desirable area with house prices to match. You're only fifteen minutes from downtown Rome and yet you're in the country.'

'I'm not sure I'd feel too comfortable surrounded by millionaires, though.'

'I'm sure they're not all Mafiosi.' He shot her a little grin. 'Probably at least one or two of them have made their money legally – even though we are in Italy.' From his tone, he was mocking her but also his fellow countrymen.

'Of course. It's just that I've gone off millionaires.'

He glanced at her again and raised his eyebrows. 'Bad experience?'

Jo hesitated but, seeing as she had been the one to bring up the subject, she decided to carry on. After all, although he and the rest of the family were evidently well off, his battered car and his job as a chemist seemed to indicate that he certainly wasn't in the millionaire bracket.

'The other night I was invited out for dinner by a guy with a chauffeur and a private plane.'

'In London?'

'Yes, we went to a floating restaurant and it was all very nice until we got back into his car.'

Corrado glanced across at her. 'He expected a contribution towards the bill?'

Jo nodded. 'Yes, but not in cash.'

'So, did you slap him?' He grinned. 'I bet you pack quite a punch.'

Jo found herself smiling in spite of herself. 'You'd better believe it. But, no, I jumped out of the car and left him to it.'

'Presumably not a moving car?' His tone was still light, but his expression had changed. 'The Italian name for somebody who behaves like that is *stronzo*. Unfortunately, there are a lot of them around.' He glanced across at her again. 'But you're okay? Not too shaken up?'

'No, I'm fine, although there was a moment when I was really quite scared. He had caught hold of me and he was just staring at me. Creepy...'

'Like I say, a *stronzo*. I understand now why millionaires aren't your favourites at the moment.'

'But you're right. It's not fair to accuse all of them of being like that. My mother always tells me I have a habit of thinking the worst of people.' As she spoke, she couldn't help reflecting that only a short while earlier she had done just that to him. 'Anyway, if you're a millionaire, I promise I won't hate you.' She did not, however, mention her vow to stay away from handsome men as she still believed them to be fundamentally untrustworthy. Maybe her mother had a point after all. Not for the first time she vowed to try to be more open-minded.

A few minutes later, as the road narrowed even more, Jo saw a 'NO ENTRY' sign up ahead. As they approached it, Corrado turned off to the right, through an imposing arched gateway. The car crunched up a gravel drive lined with trees for forty or fifty metres before pulling up in front of a charming old stone house sheltered among yet more massive umbrella pines. He parked beside a big, very swish-looking 4x4 and switched off the engine before turning towards her.

'We can leave the car here. I know the owner of this place and he won't mind.'

'Wow, some house! You certainly know the right people, Corrado.'

They climbed out of the car and went back along the drive, the dog bouncing happily alongside them. Clearly, Daisy knew she was going for a walk.

Corrado explained, 'The laboratories where I work aren't too far from here and Daisy and I often come for a walk along the Appian Way. She recognises the place. She loves it for her own reasons. As somebody with an interest in history, I love it too. I think it's quite amazing and I hope you'll agree.'

The countryside here was as flat as a pancake, but what it lacked in terms of topography, it more than made up for in antiquity. The road itself beyond the 'NO ENTRY' sign was barely the width of a small car, presumably designed for an ancient Roman-sized chariot or cart. As they walked along the stone-paved road surface, it was clear that a lot of money had been spent clearing and relaying the stone slabs. From time to time, Corrado pointed out grooves and ruts carved into stones by the passage of countless wheels over hundreds, if not thousands, of years. The fields on either side of them were full of little copses of trees inside which, Corrado assured her, were ruins dating back two thousand years or more. He then went on to more gruesome facts.

'If I said Spartacus to you, what would you say, Jo?'

'I'd say a big old Hollywood epic. I can't remember the actor. Was it Rock Hudson or maybe Kirk Douglas?'

'Very good. It was Kirk Douglas, along with a roll-call of some of the greatest actors of the sixties from Laurence Olivier to Tony Curtis. But did you know it was based on real events?'

'Erm, sort of.'

'Spartacus led the slaves' revolt against the Roman state in 73 BC. When he and his army were finally defeated, the emperor ordered that six thousand slaves be crucified all along this road from Rome to Capua. Just imagine.'

Jo shuddered at the image. It seemed impossible to imagine this lovely place the site of such barbarism. 'Although all we see today are the amazing buildings left behind, there's no disguising the fact that the Romans were pretty brutal people.'

As they approached a huge amorphous structure made of old Roman bricks so weathered and worn that it was impossible to tell whether it had been a house, a temple or some sort of fortification, Jo's mind was suddenly torn away from the sufferings of those poor slaves as she spotted a flash of orange ahead of her. She pointed, but Corrado had already seen it and he turned towards her, keeping his voice low.

'I've often seen these, but I've no idea what they're called.'

Together, they advanced towards the little shape as it flitted through the trees at the side of the road. Suddenly it stopped, settling on top of a low stone wall. Jo crept up to it and took a couple of photos. It was a delightful butterfly, a bit smaller than the swallowtail they had seen earlier. It had a distinct leopard-spotted pattern on its light orange wings and she felt sure she recognised it. She turned towards Corrado to tell him, but found that this time he was keeping a safe distance between the two of them, no doubt in case she chose to touch him again. With another twinge of regret, she whispered across to him.

'Unless I'm very much mistaken, this is a Queen of Spain fritillary. If my memory serves me right, its Latin name is *Issoria Lathonia*. We have fritillaries in England, but I was at a lecture recently where they said this one's incredibly rare.'

As she spoke, she spotted a light blue dot on the other side of the road and slipped carefully away towards it, trying not to frighten the Queen of Spain. All in all, she saw and photographed five species that were completely new to her as she strolled along the road with Corrado and Daisy. He was very good company, knowledgeable and considerate, and the dog was a delight. Although it was still immensely hot, she loved every moment of their walk and was genuinely sorry when the time came to return to the car.

Then, just as Corrado was bending down to open the tailgate, butterflies were suddenly blasted out of her mind as she had a startling flash of revelation. As her eyes alighted on her future brother-in-law's damp back and broad shoulders, she knew she had a problem. The scales fell from her eyes – particularly when they alighted on his backside – and comprehension dawned. Corrado might not be interested in her in a romantic way, but she had just understood that the same could no longer be said about her. Whatever reservations she had voiced about drop-dead gorgeous men, indeed men in general, there could be no doubt about it. She now knew she could well be in imminent danger of falling for this particular drop-dead gorgeous man and things would become very complicated.

Of course, she told herself firmly, this had to be just lust. After all, there was no getting away from the fact that he was a very good-looking guy and she hadn't had sex in months. As such, it was predictable. The very naughty thought occurred to her that she was only here for a few days and then she would return to the UK, safely out of his reach. A little fling with him might do her a lot of good. Then, no sooner had this thought crossed her mind than her subconscious hastened to point out the reasons why nothing could, or should, ever happen between them. First of all, his brother and her sister were getting married and this would only complicate things for everybody, particularly her sister. Second, he didn't appear in the least bit interested in her in that way. And third, but even more importantly, she just wasn't that sort of girl. Casual sex, however alluring, had never been her thing.

It was really, really annoying.

Chapter 5

When they got to Mario and Angie's house, tucked away in a corner of the Country Club estate and well hidden from the restaurant and hotel, they found they weren't the first guests to arrive. The smell of smoke from the back garden of the lovely old converted barn testified to the fact that there was going to be a barbecue. As they got out of the car, Angie and Mario appeared at the door and the dog made a beeline for Mario while Jo went over to give her little sister a hug.

'Hi, Angie. I hope you aren't too tired after all the activity today.'

Angie grinned back at her. 'You sound more and more like Mum every time I see you, Jo. And I'm fine. It's been busy, but it all went well and now we can relax.'

'And you're doing a barbecue? For how many?'

'Oh, I don't know. We've asked the people who've been helping with the show jumping today. With you two I expect there'll be twenty or thirty people.'

'Blimey, Angie, you'll be exhausted!'

'Calm down, 'Mum'. We aren't doing the food. Mario's got the boys from the restaurant to help out. All I've got to do is avoid drinking too much and falling into the swimming pool.' Angie glanced down at Jo's handbag. 'Bugger, I forgot to tell you to bring your swimming things. I tell you what, though, come in with me and I'll sort you out with one of my bikinis. I've got a few and I'm sure one of them'll fit you fine.'

Jo was torn. On the one hand, the idea of plunging into a cool swimming pool was very, very appealing, but on the other, the idea of appearing half-naked among a bunch of strangers was a bit daunting, particularly as, among them, would be Corrado. Still, she hugged Mario and then followed Angie up to her bedroom. Glancing back over her shoulder, she saw Corrado and his faithful hound heading round to the garden, the Labrador's nostrils flared as she smelt the meat on the barbecue. Upstairs, Angie sifted through her wardrobe and the sisters chatted. They had always been close, although Angie mocked her big sister endlessly for being too serious, and it was good to hear how happy Angie sounded. And not just because of her new fiancé and her upcoming wedding.

Angie was a regular member of the British Olympic equestrian team and it had been this that had got her the job at the Country Club stables in the first place. Today's event had been organised in conjunction with the Italian Equestrian Association and it was a chance for Italian Olympic hopefuls to showcase their skills. Clearly, the Country Club was establishing itself as one of the foremost centres for showjumping in Italy. Jo told Angie how happy she was for her and bullied her into phoning their mother there and then for a chat.

As Angie spoke on the phone, Jo tried a couple of bikinis on for size. One was a bit loose, but the other fitted her perfectly. There was just one problem: it was fairly minimal. Not obscene, but definitely on the scanty side. Jo felt pretty sure her mother wouldn't approve and it was this, as much as anything, that persuaded her to go with it. She felt she had to prove her sister wrong. Of course she wasn't just like their mum.

Angie checked Jo out as she finished the call to their mother and gave her a smile and a thumbs up. As she dropped the phone on the bed, she sounded impressed.

'Wow, Jo, you look great in that. Have you lost weight?'

'I don't think so. Maybe a pound or two.' In fact, over the past months since Christian's departure she felt pretty sure she had lost a bit of weight, but had stubbornly refused to weigh herself. 'Are you sure you don't mind if I borrow it? If it looks good on me, it must look even better on you.'

Angie shook her head. 'Not on your life. Besides, I'm wearing my new one.' She slipped out of her dress and Jo was impressed. She was wearing a lovely red and white striped bikini that looked like it was made for her. Even better, it was even tinier than the one she had given Jo, so hopefully all eyes would be on Angie rather than her.

Jo stuffed her underwear into her handbag and both girls put their dresses back on over the bikinis before heading back downstairs. As they walked through the house, Jo told Angie about her afternoon with Corrado and would have dearly liked to get more detail on the whole Don Juan thing, but they were constantly surrounded by people so that had to wait. Mario appeared with glasses of cold white wine and then he and Angie took Jo round, introducing her to the other guests. Jo liked Mario a lot and could see that he and Angie were really happy together. If it hadn't been her sister, she might even have felt a bit jealous of their happiness, but she did her best to dismiss Christian, and what might have been, from her mind.

Although the sun was dropping towards the horizon, it was still light and still very hot. One by one, the guests began to peel off their outer clothes and get in the pool to cool off. The pool itself was remarkably big for a private house, but Jo knew that Mario was a keen swimmer. She found herself wondering idly if his brother also liked the water and if he would make an appearance in a pair of swimming trunks. Whatever he thought of her, and however inadvisable it would be for her to give in to animal instincts, this was a sight she was dying to see. She couldn't spot him among the guests in the garden and she was just beginning to wonder whether he had gone off, when there was a shout, a splash, a squeal and another splash.

Out of the corner of her eye, Jo spotted a black flash shoot across the lawn and belly flop into the pool, closely followed by her master. It all happened so fast that Jo didn't even get the chance to see Corrado with his shirt off. It was only when he emerged from the pool, dragging a compliant but unrepentant Labrador behind him that Jo realised he was still wearing it. The soaked white cotton had turned transparent and she got a tantalising view of his body, registering the fact that she had been right about him working out. He looked amazing. He squelched up to Angie and Mario with the dog and proceeded to apologise.

'Sorry, guys. She waited until I was on one leg, getting into my swimming things, and then she made a dash for it.' He looked down at the bedraggled dog and waved his finger at her. 'We've been through this before, Daisy. Dog hair and filtration systems don't mix. Are we clear?'

The dog looked up at him and Jo felt sure she could see a broad canine smile on her face. The next thing Daisy did was to shake herself violently, soaking all four of them and producing hoots of laughter from the other guests. Jo looked down at herself and then at her sister. They both looked like contestants in a Miss Wet T-Shirt competition and she was very relieved to be wearing a bikini underneath. Angie caught her eye, shrugged and grinned.

'Is that dress cotton?'

Jo nodded.

'Then slip it off and I'll give it a short cycle in the washing machine, otherwise your eau de toilette will rapidly become eau de Labrador. In this heat, it'll dry in next to no time.' Seeing the doubt in Jo's eyes, she was quick to reassure her. 'It's all right. You'll have it back on within an hour or two, I promise. Mario, Corrado, let me have your shirts and I'll stick them all in together.'

As she spoke, Angie slipped out of her dress and started collecting garments from the others. Jo saw Mario pull off his shirt and then his brother followed suit. Jo restrained a sigh and turned away so as to remove her own dress as discreetly as possible. As she turned back and handed it to Angie, she felt sure she caught Corrado's eyes on her for a second before he turned back to his brother.

'Here, Mario. Keep an eye on Daisy for me, will you? I've got a leash in the car. I think I'd better tie her to something or she'll just go and jump in again.'

As he disappeared in the direction of the car, Jo couldn't help admiring the V-shape of his back muscles and his powerful thighs. She immediately looked away, but not quick enough, as her eyes met her sister's and she felt her cheeks redden. Angie collected the wet clothes and headed for the house. As she did so, she leaned towards Jo and whispered to her in English.

'I think you and I should have a little talk.'

'I'll come and give you a hand with the washing machine.'

Jo followed Angie into the kitchen and from there to the utility room, deliberately closing the door securely behind them. As Angie prepared the washing machine, she glanced back over her shoulder towards Jo.

'Corrado...'

'What about him?'

'I saw you looking at him and I recognise that look. It's the same one you had on your face the first time you introduced me to Christian.' Jo made to protest, but her sister knew her too well and held up a hand to stop her. 'I don't blame you, Jo, but you need to know about him.'

'To know what?'

'Don't get your hopes up. The streets of Rome are littered with his victims.'

'Victims? You make him sound like Jack the Ripper.'

'Not in a physical sense, but emotionally he's a killer.' Angie spun the dial on the washing machine and pressed the start button. 'You see, Jo, he's a use-and-discard sort of guy. You know what I mean? Mario tells me he's lost count of how many heartbroken girls he's had to take under his wing after they've been dumped by Corrado after one or, at the most, two dates.'

'So not interested in commitment?' Jo wasn't surprised, but this still didn't explain why he had been so jumpy with her.

'He just doesn't believe in all that stuff.'

'What stuff?'

'Are you girls coming for a swim?'

They both spun round to find the door now open and Corrado leaning against the frame looking as appealing as ever. He was only wearing a pair of swimming shorts and his well-toned body was a very appealing golden-brown colour, not olive-skinned like so many Italians. In spite of what she had just been told, Jo couldn't restrain an inward sigh of attraction. Meanwhile, Angie answered for them both.

'The stuff in the washer should be ready in half an hour. Another half hour in the sun and it'll all be dry. Yes, I'm ready for a swim. Coming, Jo? Here, take a towel.'

They filed out past Corrado into the sticky-hot Roman evening. The shadows were lengthening, but it was still sweltering and Jo was more than happy to follow her sister to the pool area. As she passed the table with a visibly miffed Labrador tied to it, she stopped to deposit her sandals, towel and bag. She bent down to give Daisy a stroke before leaving.

'I'm sorry you can't come with us, Daisy. Now, look after my bag, will you? It's got my passport in it.'

'Don't worry about Daisy. I'll take her down to the river for a proper swim later on.' Corrado patted the dog on the head before leading the way to the pool. As he got there, he smiled at her and then dived smoothly into the water, surfacing a few seconds later, and looked back at her, running his fingers through his hair. 'It's deep this end, shallow the other end.'

Reluctantly, Jo tore her attention away from him. 'I'll start in the shallow end. I'd like to keep my hair dry, if possible.'

She and Angie walked down the steps until they were in up to their waists, before ducking down and floating in the slightly salty water. It was wonderfully refreshing after the oppressive heat outside and Jo just let herself relax as she reflected upon what her sister had told her. In essence it was the same thing she had heard from her mother. Corrado was what her gran would have termed a womaniser and, although the girls he discarded along the way were no doubt all far from unwilling, it was disappointing to hear about this flaw in such a cultured and pleasant man. The other thing that was more than a little annoying was the fact that he clearly didn't see her in that light. While she had absolutely no desire to be taken advantage of and then discarded, it was a bit galling to feel that she didn't match up to his high standards. She knew she was bright and she looked pretty good, so why not her?

She did a slow, lazy breast stroke up the pool to the other end and back again, keeping her hair out of the water and relishing the cool, refreshing feeling across her body. Finally, she settled on the bottom step at the shallow end where the water reached just up to her waist, rested back on her elbows and relaxed. A minute or two later, she was joined by Angie.

'Cooled down?'

Jo nodded. 'It's wonderful.' She glanced around carefully, but saw that they were alone. 'So, tell me, Angie, what is it that Corrado does, exactly? I know he works in a company that's looking for ways of eradicating plastics,'

'He doesn't just work in it. He owns it. Straight after university – did he tell you he went to Oxford? – he set up his company, doing clinical testing. It's gone from strength to strength since then and they've just moved into brand-new custom-built laboratories.' She caught Jo's eye. 'It's really big business and he's working on government projects as well. His company employs hundreds of people. In fact, I wouldn't mind betting that half the women in Italy who find themselves peeing on a stick in the privacy of their bathrooms end up peeing on one of his.'

'Wow!' Jo was amazed. So her critique of millionaires earlier today must have seemed as if it was directed straight at him. Little wonder he had recoiled from her touch. 'And he lives in a flat in Piazza Navona?'

'He's got a flat near there, but he's also bought himself a lovely old house along the Appia Antica a couple of years ago.'

The penny dropped.

'Not one with a stone gateway and a long gravel drive by any chance? And has he got a big blue Range-Rovery thing?'

'So you've seen the place? It's fabulous, isn't it?'

Jo nodded. 'And the flat in the city centre? Is that where he... entertains his lady friends?'

Angie grinned and nodded in return. 'Mario calls it his *scopodromo*. The best translation I can come up with for that is "bonkodrome", if you know what I mean.'

Jo groaned. 'Oh, God... And yet, he's so... so nice.'

'He is! He's a sweetie. He's just wired differently from the rest of us.'

'Who's wired differently?'

They both looked up as Mario came floating towards them. Angie gave him a grin.

'Who do you think?'

Jo saw Mario roll his eyes.

'Big brothers, eh? Who'd want one?'

Angie's grin widened. 'Or big sisters.'

Jo splashed her sister with water before returning to the matter in hand. 'So, what's his problem, Mario?'

Mario and Angie exchanged looks, and Angie answered for him.

'Corrado doesn't believe in love.'

'He what?'

'Love… he doesn't believe it's a thing.' She smiled at Jo's expression. 'You see, he's a scientist. He reckons love's just an illusion, some sort of primitive urge to reproduce that's designed to confuse the brain.' She reached towards Mario and kissed him. 'But we know he's wrong.'

As she listened to her sister, Jo began to get an awkward feeling that she had heard this all before… from her own lips. How could it be that what had seemed so very sensible and logical when she had expounded it to Victoria sounded so wrong now? Or was he right? Had she also been right all along? Was it all just the brain playing tricks?

'Maybe he's got a point.'

Angie's expression turned to one of barely-concealed exasperation.

'Just because Christian turned out to be a bastard doesn't mean you didn't love him. Of course it's a thing, Jo.'

'I know...' Jo nodded to herself. She really had loved Christian. Or had she? Had she just fooled herself that what she was feeling was anything other than lust? Or was it simply that she had enjoyed the reflected glory of being at the side of such a handsome man? Had he just been a rather fine-looking accessory? She shook her head and snorted. 'In fact, I don't think I know anything any more, Angie. But I know I need a drink.'

She climbed out of the pool and went back to where she had left her glass along with her bag and towel. She petted the dog and then took a big mouthful of white wine and immediately regretted it. It had rapidly warmed up in the sunshine into tasteless tepid mouthwash. She set it down again and dabbed herself with the towel until she felt dry enough to go and look for another glass of wine. As it turned out, she didn't have to. As she put the towel down, a shadow fell across her. It was Corrado, with an ice bucket in his hands. Sticking out of it was the top of a bottle. Without a word, he picked up her glass, threw the remaining wine onto the grass and filled it with Prosecco.

'Life's too short for drinking warm wine.'

Jo looked across at him, remembering what her sister had just told her and a sensation of considerable regret spread across her. Apart from his physical appearance, she knew that she liked this caring, generous man a lot. How he could turn out to be such a pig as far as women were concerned was inconceivable and tragic. And disappointing. She summoned a smile and held up her glass.

'Thanks, Corrado, you read my mind. Cheers.'

She clinked her glass against his and savoured the ice-cold wine on her tongue. Feeling more than a bit exposed in her sister's teeny-weeny bikini, she decided to sit down and, as she did so, she felt a warm, heavy, hairy head land on her bare thigh. She looked down at Daisy and her smile broadened.

'The water was very nice, Daisy. I know you would've enjoyed it.'

'That's an idea. Jo, do you feel like coming down to the river with us? It's just over there in those trees. Daisy deserves a swim.'

'Of course.'

Jo glanced down at the remains of the wine in her glass and made a quick decision. It would be warm by the time they came back and it was too good to waste, so she swallowed the contents of the glass in a couple of big mouthfuls, feeling relieved that she had managed to do so without getting hiccups. She caught Corrado's eye and saw him do the same. Slipping into her sandals, she stood up again and prepared to follow him as he unclipped the dog from the lead and dissuaded her from heading back into the pool. There was just one thing worrying her – she was nearly naked.

She toyed with the idea of wrapping the towel around herself, but in the end decided not to bother. She wasn't her mother, after all, in spite of her sister's jibes. All around her most of the other guests were in a similar state of undress so, as it was still very warm, she told herself that if they could wander about in just their swimming things, so could she. The glass of Prosecco she had just gulped down may have contributed to this decision, but she soon found herself walking off across the field wearing next to nothing, with a near-naked man and a very happy dog alongside her.

The river was wider than she expected, but the water level was visibly low. Fortunately, there was more than enough for Daisy to be able to leap in and swim energetically after the sticks her master was throwing for her. There was a big tree trunk by the water's edge, and from the look of its smooth surface, it had been used by countless people before her as a convenient bench. Jo sat down and breathed deeply as she watched Corrado bend and flex as he sent a regular supply of missiles flying into the water for the dog to fetch. He really did have a lovely body, but she knew all too well that he was the carrot dangling in front of a donkey that would never get to taste it. She sighed to herself. It wasn't a lot of fun being a donkey.

Finally, he straightened up, turned and walked across to the log to sit down beside her. She couldn't help noticing that he kept a decorous distance between them and, in a way, it was a relief.

They sat in silence for a minute or two before she summoned up the courage to start talking. Without taking her eyes off the dog, who had settled in the shallows with just her nose sticking out of the water, looking for all the world like a hairy black crocodile, Jo did her best to sound casual.

'So, what did my sister tell you about me before you met me?'

'Why, has my brother been talking to you about me?'

'Yes, they both have, but I asked first. What has Angie told you?'

'Let's see. You're very organised, maybe a bit too organised, and a bit bossy. You're very bright and you're ambitious. You're stunningly beautiful, but you're always playing it down. You were with a guy for a few years, but it all went sour back in the winter. You're still getting over the break-up, and if I so much as lay a finger on you, she'll get the local Mafia to come and chop me up and feed me to the pigs.' She could hear the smile in his voice so she turned towards him and saw him nod. 'Yes, I think that was the gist of it. Sounds about right?'

'Probably dead right about the bossy thing, but then that's what big sisters do, isn't it? But I don't know if I'm terribly ambitious. Yes, I enjoy my job and I work hard, but having a fancy title after my name doesn't matter much to me.'

'And the stunningly beautiful thing?'

Jo felt her cheeks redden. 'That's not up to me to judge and, besides, it's what's inside that counts.'

'Well, for the record, I think your sister got that dead right.' Ignoring her blushes, he carried on. 'Now tell me what Angie and Mario have been saying about me.' This time he sounded more serious. 'Was it good or bad?'

'Well, it made me feel pretty silly. They told me about your beautiful house, the size of your company and about how well it's doing. I'm afraid I owe you an apology for going on about millionaires the way I did this afternoon.'

'You were fine. In fact, if you remember, you even said that if I turned out to be a millionaire you wouldn't hate me. That's good enough for me, but I owe *you* an apology for not telling you the truth about my house. I just thought it might be easier, in view of what you had told me about your bad experience with the rich *stronzo* in London, if I kept a low profile.'

'Well, I meant it when I said it was a beautiful house.'

'Thank you. I'll have to show it to you properly one of these days.'

'But why do you drive round in that little Fiat all the time if you've got that lovely new car?'

He smiled, a full, open smile that lit up his face. 'That's easy. Have you seen how battered the Fiat is? That's inevitable in a city like Rome. People bump into each other all the time – and often they don't stop. And then there's the smell of dog. All right, on a dry day like today and with the windows open it probably didn't bother you too much, but on a rainy day, I can tell you... Daisy's part of the family, but she's definitely not the most aromatic. But the main reason I don't use the Range Rover so much is because it won't fit in the garage below the flat.'

The *bonkodrome*, Jo thought to herself. So did the fact that today he had come to pick her up in the little car mean he had come from the flat and, if so, had he been there with some random girl? Shaking a sense of annoyance from her head, she nodded and replied.

'I can see the logic of that. Remind me in a few years' time that if I'm in the market for a low mileage 4x4, you're the man to ask.'

He smiled. 'I do use it sometimes, but you're right. It was a bit self-indulgent to buy it and not use it. Anyway, did Mario and Angie say anything else about me?'

Jo took a deep breath before she answered.

'They said you don't believe in love.'

She saw him blink as he considered what he had just heard. It took him a few moments before he replied.

'That sounds a bit melodramatic, but I suppose it's true.' He caught her eye for a moment. 'Don't get me wrong, I'm not saying people don't develop deep feelings for each other, but it's just the whole concept of love that I believe is an illusion.'

Jo found herself sitting bolt upright. Now he was even using her exact same words. Fortunately, before she was called upon to respond, he carried on.

'You're a scientist, Jo. You must have done chemistry and biology when you were studying zoology. If I say names like endorphin, oxytocin, vasopressin or dopamine, do you know what I mean?'

'Yes, they're neurochemicals,'

'Exactly, all in the brain. If you don't mind, let me take you as an example. When I sit here looking at you in that sexy little bikini, something happens in my brain. The amygdala, that's my core memory system, receives the image from my eyes as a series of electrical signals along the optic nerve. This results in a cocktail of these chemicals being sent to my limbic system, what's often referred to as the emotional centre of the brain. This produces a sensation that people have come to call love. But, in reality, it's just a bio-chemical reaction going on inside my head as banal as when my brain tells me it's time to have a sandwich or go to the toilet.' He gave her a little smile. 'But a lot more enjoyable.'

Jo let the reference to her sexy bikini pass and nodded slowly. She had studied many of the complexities of the brain and none of this was particularly new to her. Indeed, recently, she had been thinking along very similar lines. But, nevertheless, she decided to play devil's advocate.

'Surely that's just lust, though, isn't it?'

'Precisely my point. What we interpret as love is just physical attraction. You're a zoologist. Tell me, what's the principal, overriding motivation of all animals?'

'That's easy, continuation of the species. Reproduction is the imperative.'

'Exactly, so when I look at you and like what I see, what's actually going on in my head is the recognition of you as a suitable mate.'

'But surely there's much more to do with love than just sex?' Jo looked around for an example. Her eyes alighted on the wet dog lying in front of them. 'Take Daisy, for instance, you love her, don't you? And she loves you, surely?'

Corrado shook his head. 'If you took Daisy away with you tonight and fed her and exercised her, she'd soon forget about me.'

'But what about your feelings for her?'

'She's a good dog and, like I say, she's a fully paid-up member of the family, but I'd hardly call it love.' She saw him smile. 'I'm sure when Shakespeare was writing Romeo and Juliet he wasn't thinking of Labradors.'

Jo gave up. 'So, if you don't believe that love exists, apart from as physical attraction or some innate primordial instinct to reproduce, why have you got yourself a reputation for breaking so many girls' hearts?'

'That's not me, that's them, I promise.' His expression was serious now and she saw him drop his eyes. 'I'm still a relatively young, healthy man. As such, I have desires and urges and I like sex as much as the next man – or maybe even a bit more. But I have never, and I would never, invite any girl into my bed without spelling out quite clearly that my motives are purely physical.' He looked up from his feet and Jo saw an expression of sorrow on his face. 'I tell them, but they all think that I'll change my mind. But I never do. You women think you can change us, but it's easier said than done.'

'You realise you're coming across as a very selfish-sounding person? I'm sure you aren't. I don't know you that well, but you've been anything but selfish towards me.'

'I'm sorry if I sound selfish. I don't mean to be. I just want to be honest. What would be far worse would be if I were to do like so many men do and pretend to have all kinds of emotional feelings that I don't have just to get a girl into bed.'

'But surely you must realise the hurt you cause these girls? It's so selfish to go looking for them when you know you aren't interested in anything but sex?'

'But I don't go looking for them, Jo, I promise. They come to me and that's the truth.'

From what Jo had seen in Piazza Navona earlier that month, she had to concede that he probably was telling the truth. 'So, you've never been in love and you don't think you'll ever fall in love?'

He shook his head decisively. 'No. That would be an impossibility, seeing as I don't believe the phenomenon exists. And you?'

'Yes, of course I have…' Her voice tailed away into uncertainty. 'At least, I thought I had.'

'Don't let me put you off, Jo. I can only tell you what *I* think, but you're an intelligent woman and you know your own mind. If you think you've been in love, then good for you.' He looked up again. 'I'd be delighted if somebody were to prove to me that love exists. Just like I'd be fascinated to see a ghost or a flying saucer.'

Jo just sat there. She really didn't know how to respond to him. Luckily, she didn't have to. A minute later they heard a shout, and the dog came splashing out of the water, shaking herself as she did so, luckily sufficiently far away not to soak them this time. The shout came from Mario, calling to them to come and eat. Corrado also got up and held out his hand to Jo.

'Feel hungry?'

She took his hand and let him pull her to her feet. 'Now I come to think of it, yes, I'm starving. After that massive ice cream this afternoon I thought I'd never eat again, but I was wrong.'

He smiled as he released her hand. 'That's the limbic system for you.'

The barbecue was unlike any barbecue Jo had ever experienced before. Yes, there were sausages, but they were very different from the burnt hot dogs she remembered from her dad's efforts back home. These were probably as much as half a metre long, rolled like a snake into a flat coil the size of a side plate, and held together with a couple of wooden skewers. They tasted spicy, meaty and lovely. Along with them was the Roman speciality, *abbacchio allo scottadito*, and these little lamb chops were tender inside, crispy on the outside, and very, very tasty. To go with the meat were different salads, some of them with exotic ingredients like edible flowers or tropical fruits, sumptuous *peperonata* and a mountain of roast potatoes with rosemary. The Prosecco was replaced with a light red Chianti Classico wine from Tuscany to the north and a dry white Frascati from the south east just out of the city.

Jo was beginning to feel a bit weary as they reached the end of the meal. The sun had reached the horizon by this time and the shadows had lengthened considerably, although the air temperature was so warm, it came as almost a surprise to realise she was still only wearing a bikini. She was about to get up and return to the house to change, when she was galvanised into activity by a tantalising little flash of colour. For a second, it looked as if this butterfly might even have the purple markings of the endangered Purple Emperor, so she jumped to her feet, startling the others around the table as well as the dog who had been slumbering at her feet. She scrabbled desperately in her bag for her phone, forgetting that the last items she had put there had been her bra and pants. As she pulled the phone out, she managed to send her underwear flying across the table, her bra actually shooting off the edge.

Blushing to the roots of her hair, she grabbed her pants and leant over to see her white bra draped across a bemused-looking Daisy's head. She made a quick lunge and caught hold of it before the ever-hungry dog decided to try to eat it. As she straightened up again, stuffing the offending articles back in her bag, she received a round of applause from her little sister. By this time the butterfly had disappeared into the twilight so Jo dropped back onto her chair and took a big mouthful of cold mineral water in an attempt to calm herself down. As she did so, she heard her future brother-in-law's voice, barely repressing a fit of giggles.

'And what do you do for your next trick, Jo?'

Deliberately avoiding catching Corrado's eye, she did her best to behave like a grown-up and reply as calmly as possible under the circumstances.

'My next trick, Mario, will be to head back indoors and change.'

'Well, at least we all know you've brought your knickers, Jo. Mum would be proud of you.' Angie was shaking with laughter. 'So, what prompted that little flight of exhibitionism?'

Jo took a deep breath and explained about the butterfly. This, at least, succeeded in silencing the giggles. Mario sounded interested.

'What did you say that butterfly's called?'

'Purple Emperor, *apatura iris*. You can't mistake it. It's got wonderful purple wings flecked with white.'

'I think I know the one you mean. I'm sure we used to have them in the garden when I was a little kid. Corrado, do you remember?'

For the first time since the underwear incident, Jo glanced across at him and, for a second, their eyes met.

'I think I do. It's the purple colour I remember. Imperial purple just like the emperors wore back in ancient Roman times. But I haven't seen one for years, maybe decades.'

'Like so many butterflies, they're getting more and more rare nowadays. I went to a lecture at the Natural History Museum a week ago and the man said there were fewer and fewer sightings in Britain. It would be amazing if I could see one, maybe photograph it. That's what I was doing in my bag, looking for my phone.'

'I hope Daisy didn't try to eat your bra.'

'No, she behaved impeccably, thanks.'

Sensing his eyes flick down across her body, she repressed a little shiver of what had to be lust, stood up and glanced at her sister.

'Now, if you'd just tell me where my dress is, I think I'm going to go and change before I embarrass myself any further.'

The party showed no signs of breaking up, but Jo was definitely sleepy when she emerged, once again fully clothed, from her sister's room. As she walked down the stairs, she saw Angie in the kitchen, making coffee.

'Angie, I think I'd better call it a night. I was up pretty early for the flight and it's been a long day. A very enjoyable day. Thank you so much for everything, particularly the loan of the bikini. I've put it in your laundry basket if that's okay.'

'Of course. Do you want a coffee before you go?'

Jo shook her head. 'I'm fine, thanks. All I need is a taxi.'

'No need for a taxi. Daisy and I'll give you a lift.'

Jo turned towards the voice and saw Corrado, now fully clothed as well, at the open back door.

'Are you sure, Corrado? The party's still in full swing. I don't want to drag you away.'

'No problem. In fact, I need to get back to the flat anyway.'

Jo did her best to ignore whatever or whoever might be drawing him back to his flat and accepted the offer. After doing the rounds of the guests, she kissed Mario and Angie and agreed to call her sister when she surfaced in the morning to arrange where and when to meet up for their sightseeing tour of the city before Victoria's arrival in the afternoon.

As they set off in the car, Jo checked the time. It was barely ten o'clock, which was just nine o'clock English-time, but she was definitely tired. It had been a very full day and the heat had no doubt had a debilitating effect on her body. She glanced across at Corrado.

'Aren't you tired? I'm exhausted.'

He shot her a quick look as they passed beneath the lights at the entrance to the estate. 'I'm fine, and you don't look too tired. In fact, you look lovely.'

She gave him a weary smile in return. 'Thanks, Corrado, but you can save the compliments.'

She almost went on to tell him she wasn't the sort of girl who would respond to flattery as part of the seduction process, but decided against it. After their chat down by the river, she was ever more convinced that he and she should just remain friends, good friends. Handsome and charming as he undeniably was, she had no desire to become another notch on his bedpost, even if he turned out to be interested in her in that way – and, so far, he hadn't given any indication of that.

He made no further comment, which suited her fine. She did, however, make a mental note to buy herself a new bikini tomorrow when she was out and about with Angie. When packing for Rome, it hadn't occurred to her that she might find herself somewhere with a pool.

The journey back into the centre of Rome took less than half an hour and Corrado was able to draw up right outside her hotel to drop her off. She turned towards him and smiled.

'Thanks for everything, Corrado. I've had a wonderful day and a lot of it was thanks to you. Now I'm going to go in and sleep for twelve hours.'

She saw him smile back and she leant towards him to kiss him on the cheeks just as he leant towards her. In the half-light, there was a momentary muddle and her lips landed fair and square on his. Both of them jumped back like scalded cats and Jo found herself blushing again. Doing her best to compose herself, she hastily opened the door and climbed out.

'Thanks again, Corrado. I'm here for the week, so I expect we'll meet up again.'

'I'll make sure we do. Goodnight, Jo, and sleep well.'

She reached back in and patted the dog, getting a slobbery lick of her hand in reply, before slamming the door and walking up the steps and into the hotel. Behind her, she heard his car start and move off.

The same doorman greeted her, although the staff at the reception desk had changed. A dark-haired girl behind the counter smiled at her as she got into the lift and let it whisk her silently up to the top floor where she made her way along the carpeted corridor to her lovely cool room. After locking the door behind her, and without turning on the light, she dropped her bag on one of the beds and walked carefully over to the French window leading out onto the terrace. Letting herself into the clammy night air she stood resting against the balustrade, looking out over the roofs of Rome towards the unmistakable dome of St Peter's in the distance. Four floors below, she could hear car engines and people's voices echoing in the narrow street, while lights clearly illuminated the Spanish Steps and the Piazza di Spagna beyond. Even though it was almost eleven o'clock, the whole area was vibrant with life and she rested on her elbows, soaking up the atmosphere.

In spite of the stunning view, there was just one thought in her mind. The touch of his lips against hers, although involuntary, had sent a sudden lightning bolt through her whole body, rousing her from her somnolent state as effectively as if he had thrown a bucket of cold water over her. How on earth, after all she had heard about him and from him tonight, could a simple touch produce such a seismic reaction? She shook her head in blank incomprehension. Clearly what Corrado would have recognised as her limbic system was totally at odds with the logical part of her brain. Her sister had described him as a 'use and discard' sort of man. He had even warned her off himself, and he certainly was giving no signs he was attracted to her, so why should she feel such attraction towards him? As a scientist, it was unfathomable, and as a woman, it was frustrating. Where was this leading?

Her subconscious suddenly roused itself and supplied the likely answer: heartbreak.

Chapter 6

In spite of her best intentions she didn't sleep for twelve hours, mainly because, at first, her brain stubbornly refused to let her doze off, forcing her to turn over and over in her head the events of the day. However, when she finally got off, she slept like a log right through until her phone started ringing at just after nine o'clock the next morning. Peeling her eyes open, she reached for it and hit green. It was Victoria and she had news.

'Hi, Jo, it's me.'

'Hi, Vic, all packed and ready?'

'Yup, and I should be in Rome by six.'

Jo lay back against the wonderfully soft pillow and stretched, forcing her brain into gear. 'Take the train from the airport to Roma Termini station. Text me as you get on the train and I'll be waiting for you when you come out.' A thought occurred to her. 'And keep a firm hold of your bags at the station. Corrado says it can be a dodgy place.'

'So, you've already seen your hunky Corrado?'

'Like I've already told you, he's not *my* Corrado. And even less so after what I heard yesterday.'

'And that was?'

'It's a bit complicated. I'll tell you when I see you, all right?'

'It's nothing too drastic, though, is it? He's not gay, is he?'

'No, Vic, that's for sure.'

'You said that pretty quickly. So if he isn't gay, is he married?'

'Nope. Like I say, it's complicated.'

Victoria finally gave in. 'All right then. Anyway, Jo, I've got news of my own. Guess who came to Marguerite's wedding with me yesterday?'

In fact, it wasn't too hard to guess. Victoria had been out for dinner earlier that week with George from the Italian class and apparently it had been a good night.

'George?'

'George. And it went really well.'

'And you're going to see him again?'

'He says he's counting the days until I get back from Rome.'

After ringing off, Jo thought about calling her sister, but decided to wait until a bit later as she and Mario would no doubt have had a late night. She showered and dressed and went down for breakfast. This was absolutely amazing and she very nearly went back to bed as soon as she returned to her room, just to sleep it off. Instead, she decided to walk it off. She phoned Angie and they arranged to meet at noon by the Arch of Constantine on the edge of the Forum. This gave Jo two hours to herself and she wasted no time before heading out.

It was warm, but not yet suffocatingly hot at this time of day, although the cloudless blue sky promised a repeat of yesterday's heat. Jo made her way down the wide sweep of the Spanish Steps towards the Piazza di Spagna. As she walked down, she tried to count the steps, but lost count just after reaching a hundred as a wave of Chinese tourists almost swept her off her feet. She took refuge against the stone wall at the edge of the stairway until they had passed before continuing down to the square and across it into the narrow Via dei Condotti.

The name of the street was vaguely familiar to her and she soon discovered why. The first shop she came to on her left was Gucci with, right opposite, Prada. Then came Bulgari, Cartier, and a never-ending series of horrifically expensive luxury shops. Few of the shop windows deigned to show prices, but those that did very quickly convinced Jo to delay her purchase of a new bikini until she found somewhere a bit more within her price range. Even at this time on a Sunday morning, the street was crowded and an astonishing number of people were already carrying bags boasting big-name brands. Clearly, Corrado wasn't the only person in Rome to have money.

Thoughts of Corrado brought back memories of the previous day and the conversation they had had down by the river. He had been totally clear in his rejection of the concept of love, and she believed he meant it. Besides, she, too, harboured very serious doubts about whether the phenomenon really existed. How was it then that she had been so affected by that momentary touch of his lips against hers? She was an intelligent person and, as such, she knew full well that romantic involvement with him would be a disaster and, besides, he patently thought of her purely as his future sister-in-law. Given these undeniable facts, why had his kiss been so disorienting? This question continued to exercise her all the way down to the Forum, but without resulting in any conclusion.

A wide swathe of central Rome was a traffic-free zone, although she very quickly learned to be on the lookout for cycles, buses or, more dangerous still, electric taxis that swept up from behind almost without a sound. Before too long, she found herself walking past the Fori Imperiali and, as Corrado had said, she was immediately confronted by a dazzling array of monuments and ruined buildings dating back two thousand years, with the vast bulk of the Colosseum ever present beyond. By this time, it was almost noon and she hurried along to Constantine's Arch to meet Angie, who turned up ten minutes late and apologetic.

'Sorry I'm late, but Mario was giving me a lift and he had a last-minute panic at the restaurant – something to do with a delivery of fresh fish...'

'Don't worry. I've just been taking in the sights.'

'And how do you feel about more walking? Not too tired?'

'I've got a week of sitting down at the conference to look forward to, so I'm up for a bit of walking. And after last night's feast and this morning's breakfast – and I'm talking full English plus – I need the exercise, or I'll end up looking like the Michelin Man.'

'Don't be silly. You could do with a few more pounds. My bikini was almost hanging off you last night.'

'I don't know about that, but that reminds me, can you take me to a shop where I can buy myself one, but not for three hundred euros?' She caught her sister's eye. 'I've just walked down Via dei Condotti.'

Angie grinned again. 'Not for the faint-hearted. Don't worry, I know some nice shops with far more sensible prices. I tell you what, let's take a bus there now and then we can walk from there to the Vatican as our first port of call. I've got bus tickets.'

Angie led Jo along to a bus stop, conveniently situated under the shade of another of the massive umbrella pines. As they waited for the bus, they chatted, but Jo was careful to steer the conversation away from Corrado. That whole situation was too complicated for a hot Sunday lunchtime. When the bus arrived, however, Jo was in for a major shock. As it drew up, she found herself level with the side of the bus, just behind the front door. There was a colourful panel on there advertising a fashion show taking place at the *Palazzo delle Esposizioni* and, to her astonishment, the face of the handsome male model on the catwalk was one she knew only too well. She stopped dead and pointed, unsure if she was capable of speech, such was her surprise. Angie followed her pointing finger and did a double take.

'Bloody hell, Jo, it's Christian!'

Jo nodded blankly. The doors of the bus hissed open and a crowd of people poured out while the people ahead of them in the loose 'queue' – not a Roman concept – made a rush to get in. Jo felt Angie's hand on her arm and she let herself be dragged blindly up into the bus with her. She heard the door close behind her and just managed to collect her thoughts sufficiently to grab hold of a post and hang on as the bus set off. She saw Angie punch two tickets into the little time-stamping machine and beckon to her. As the bus came to a halt at traffic lights, Jo followed her sister down to the back of the bus where there were two free seats. She slumped down and blinked a few times, drawing breath.

'Fancy Christian being here at the same time as you, Jo!' Angie sounded as amazed as Jo felt.

'I know.' Jo shook her head and turned towards her sister. 'Still, I suppose it was bound to happen one day or another. He travels all over the world. If it wasn't here, it would've been London.'

'Do you want to see him?' Angie laid a supportive hand on Jo's arm. 'We could go to the exhibition place today if you like.'

'God, no. That's the last thing I want. That's all dead and buried.'

As she spoke, Jo realised that she really meant it at long last. It was almost five months since his sudden departure from her life and she had been struggling to rid herself of thoughts of him for most of that time. She glanced at Angie and hung on as the bus swung sharply round a double-parked car.

'I mean it, Angie. He's history. No, let him strut his stuff in blissful ignorance of the fact that I'm here. Besides, I doubt he's any keener to see me than I am to see him.'

At some point they must have crossed the Tiber, but Jo's mind was elsewhere. When Angie finally pulled herself to her feet and headed for the door, Jo had no idea where she was. They stepped down onto the pavement and as the bus pulled away Jo managed to rouse herself from her catatonic state and looked around. They were in a much more modern area of the city. The buildings were predominantly concrete and modern brick, and both sides of the street were lined with shops. She felt her sister's hand on her arm.

'What you need's a bit of retail therapy. That'll take your mind off Christian.'

She was right. By the time Jo had bought herself a new bikini her head had cleared. The bikini looked good on her, although it wasn't much less revealing than the one she had borrowed yesterday afternoon, and she felt sure her mother would disapprove, but she bought it as much to keep her sister quiet as anything else. While she was there, she also bought some badly-needed new underwear and a few other bits and pieces. By now, she had started thinking logically about Christian again. So what if he was here in Rome? It was a very big place. As they walked out of the shop into the sunshine and she stuffed her purchases into her bag, she gave Angie a grin.

'To paraphrase what they used to say in the old Westerns, Angie, this town *is* big enough for the both of us. There's no way Christian and I are going to meet up, so let's forget him.'

Angie looked relieved. 'And you really mean it about being over him? We've been very worried about you these past few months.'

Jo reached out and gave her a hug. 'Thanks, Angie. I really am over him. It's taken time, but I've finally got him out of my system.'

As she spoke, she found herself wondering what the catalyst for this sea change might have been, but was lost for an answer. It couldn't be Corrado, because nothing was going to happen there. And if it wasn't him? Maybe it was just the healing atmosphere of the Eternal City. Whatever it was, she told herself, it was working, and she mentally closed the compartment in her head marked 'Christian' and felt all the better for it. She released Angie and gave her a smile.

'So, where to now?'

'I thought we could start at the Vatican. That's barely a fifteen-minute walk from here. The only bad news is that the Vatican museum's normally closed on Sundays. Still, you can come back during the week if you've got time.'

They made their way through the baking hot streets, hugging any shade they could find, until they came out into a broad boulevard, at the end of which they could see the curved outline of St Peter's Square, with the Basilica and the Vatican behind. They walked up in the blazing heat until they reached the piazza. This was crowded with tourists and believers, and Jo stood in the shade, looking round in wonder and admiring the remarkable curved colonnade that ringed it. Above the colonnade, just to the right, Angie pointed out the surprisingly unassuming window from which the Pope appeared from time to time. After taking some photos, they went from there into the majesty of St Peter's Basilica along with hundreds, if not thousands, of other people and marvelled at the opulence of the decoration.

In spite of Jo's resolve to avoid food after her mammoth breakfast, she allowed herself to be persuaded to stop at an ice cream parlour on the way back towards the city centre. It was as they were sitting on the sidewalk under a parasol, drinking ice-cold water, eating frozen yoghurt and cooling down, that Angie got a phone call. It was Corrado inviting them for dinner that evening. Jo couldn't help feeling a little surge of excitement at the idea of seeing him again, although she put in a plea for a very light meal. Then, just before he rang off, she remembered Victoria's imminent arrival. Angie relayed the message to Corrado, who immediately extended the invitation to Jo's friend as well.

After a tiring afternoon, punctuated by very welcome cafe stops, Jo got a call from Victoria, telling her she had landed safely and was about to get on the train from the airport. Together, Angie and Jo walked up through the back streets to Termini station. It was getting even hotter by now and once they met up with Victoria, they decided to take a taxi back to Jo's hotel.

They went up to Jo's room and sat outside on the terrace and chatted in a precious patch of shade that grew gradually smaller and smaller as the sun came round. Finally, they were obliged to head back inside into the coolness of the air-conditioned interior. Victoria declared herself very impressed by Rome, the hotel and everything, and Jo was delighted for her. They had been best friends since school and had always looked out for each other. When Victoria heard that Christian was here in Rome, she declared herself fully prepared to go out and buy a baseball bat and set off after him. She had never forgiven him for the hurt he had inflicted on Jo and that spring she had been a tower of strength during Jo's darkest moments. Jo calmed her down and told her not to waste her time. As she had said to Angie, that was all over now.

After Christian had been dealt with, Victoria got her to recount her conversation with Corrado the previous evening. When Jo reeled off all the scientific jargon he had produced to support his theory of love being an illusion, she saw amazement on Victoria's face and a distinct lack of surprise on her sister's. After Jo repeated Corrado's protestations that he didn't go looking for women, Angie was the first to comment.

'He's right, Jo. He doesn't go looking for them. The women come to him.' She kicked off her shoes and stretched out on Jo's bed. 'And now his company's making an absolute mint, there are even more of them buzzing around. It's a heady combination: good looks and money.'

'He says he warns them off, but they don't believe him.'

Angie nodded slowly. 'Yes, I'm sure he does, but, let's face it, he could just say no and save them the inevitable heartache.'

This thought had also occurred to Jo. It might be without wanting to, but he was definitely taking advantage of these girls. It was such a pity, when she felt sure that deep down he was a good man.

By now, Victoria was dying to meet this strange-sounding man and Jo had to make her promise not to be too unkind to him when she did.

'Trust me, I really think he's a good guy. It's just… what was it you said, Angie? It's just that he's wired differently.'

'He certainly is.'

'Not that differently.' Victoria gave Jo a wink. 'This whole "love doesn't exist, it's a chemical reaction" crap sounds just like what you've been telling me for the past few months, Jo. Maybe you've got more in common with him than you think.'

'Seriously, Jo, you've got to stop thinking like that.' Angie reached across with her hand and caught hold of her wrist. 'It really does exist. Trust me.'

Jo nodded, more to make her sister happy than out of any conviction that love really was a thing but fortunately, just then, Angie's phone rang again. It was Mario to tell them that Corrado suggested meeting at his flat in Piazza Navona for a drink before dinner. When Jo heard that she was going to visit Corrado's *bonkodrome*, she wasn't sure she was that keen, but by then Angie had already accepted.

Victoria decided to have a shower and change before going out, and Jo opted to do the same. She told herself this was just to freshen up, not because she was going to see Corrado, but her subconscious gave her a hard time all the same. At just after six they went back out into the stuffy heat again and walked down to Piazza Navona, taking Victoria past the Trevi Fountain on the way. As they passed it, Jo was reminded that the Euro she had thrown in had worked remarkably well, bringing her back to Rome barely a couple of weeks after her first visit.

Corrado's flat came as a total surprise. Jo hadn't really known what to expect, but if she had found herself confronted by a heart-shaped bed and mirrors on the ceiling, she wouldn't have been that shocked. Instead, she found a charming rooftop apartment furnished with a very effective mix of modern steel and leather sofas and chairs, alongside exquisite antique cupboards and tables. The floor was strewn with sumptuous Persian rugs, and the walls punctuated with a number of delightful old oil paintings. It was a lovely welcoming place, and nothing like the bachelor pad she had been expecting.

The first face to greet them was black and hairy. Daisy was evidently delighted to have guests and clearly over-joyed to see Jo among them. In fact, Jo was almost floored by her friendly assault. Behind the dog, Corrado greeted them with a smile. He shook hands with Victoria, hugged Angie and kissed Jo chastely on the cheeks. Jo smiled back at him and told her subconscious that the invol-untary thrill that ran though her at the touch of his lips on her skin was nothing more than a natural reaction to the cool air-conditioned temperature. Mario was already there and the two men had obviously been discussing business matters, as the dining table was strewn with files and paper alongside an expensive laptop.

'Thanks for coming, ladies. Shall we go outside onto the terrace?'

They followed the direction of Corrado's outstretched arm and found themselves on the stunning roof terrace. It didn't overlook the piazza, but faced the other way, perched directly above the little side street where he had his garage. It was a good size and he had lined it with massive ancient-looking terracotta pots holding pink and white oleanders and lemon trees whose branches were heavy with bright yellow fruit. Jo wondered how on earth these had been brought up the narrow staircase to get here. They sat down around a table in the shade of a huge parasol and admired the view.

In front of them was a jumble of roofs, all clad in sun-bleached pink tiles. Over the centuries, bits had been added to existing buildings and new ones had been constructed. As a result, there was a delightful, if chaotic, combination of angles and shadows, with spires and cupolas popping up here and there through the sea of pink. In the far distance was another of the seven hills of Rome, studded with magnificent villas, shaded by equally magnificent umbrella pines. Jo sat back and took a deep breath. It was an amazing place.

'What can I get you all to drink? I've got cold champagne in the fridge if you like.'

They were all happy to accept, although Jo's subconscious went out of its way to remind her that a fridge full of ice-cold champagne was probably a prerequisite for any upmarket seducer. She did her best to stifle such thoughts and jumped up to help. She and the dog followed Corrado through to the ultramodern kitchen and she was impressed to see him open the fridge and remove a plate of thin-cut Parma ham rolled around chunks of freshly cut bright orange melon. This was followed by a bowl of succulent-looking prawns.

'Wow, Corrado, what a spread! I hope this is dinner.'

He hadn't heard her follow him and he wheeled round. There was no mistaking the smile that sprang to his face as he saw her and she felt herself smiling in return.

'Did you prepare all this? Impressive! Anything you want me to do?'

'Hi, Jo. It's kind of you to offer. Yes, I prepared this stuff, but it's all cold so there wasn't much to do. Actually, as I live alone, I do quite a lot of cooking. I enjoy it.' He closed the fridge door and surveyed her. 'You look amazing. You've got a bit of colour in your cheeks today and it suits you.'

'You're too kind, sir.' She did a mock curtsey and scrutinised him. He was as handsome as ever, but there was something else this time. 'You're looking a bit tired, if you don't mind my saying so.'

He nodded ruefully. 'I didn't get a lot of sleep last night.' He must have noticed something in her face as he was quick to explain. 'I've been helping Mario with his plans for the Country Club. As I told you, I'm a chemist, and I'm far less comfortable with the business side of things, but I promised him I'd take a look at the books for him.'

Jo nodded. So maybe he hadn't been here with his next victim last night after all.

'And what's the verdict?'

'The Country Club's doing pretty well. Dad set it up back when we were just kids and it's gradually grown since then. Now that Dad's taken a back seat, Mario wants to try a load of new ideas and asked for my opinion.'

'Sounds exciting. What sort of new ideas?'

'Starting with a spa, gym and health club. There's a natural hot spring in the grounds and my people have been analysing the water for him. It's remarkably pure and uncontaminated by nitrates or anything else, so it could form the basis for the spa. In fact, he's talking about maybe piping it across to his own pool so he could swim all year round.'

'Good idea. And what about the stables?'

'He'll keep them going, although there's no money in horses.' He caught Jo's eye and grinned. 'Unless you go to the races and bet on them. The horses cost a lot more than they bring in, but we're all agreed we want to keep that side of the business going, not least as it raises the profile of the place when they have big events like yesterday's.'

'Do you ride, Corrado?'

He nodded. 'I've ridden all my life. And you've done the same, haven't you?'

Jo nodded. 'Yes, although now that I'm working pretty hard in London I seem to get less and less opportunity.'

'We'll have to see if we can arrange a ride while you're here in Rome, or will your commitments at the conference keep you fully occupied?'

'That would be great, but I honestly won't know until I see the programme tomorrow morning. The organisers were supposed to leave a copy at the hotel for me, but I haven't seen anything yet.'

'Well, let me know if you have any free time.'

For a second his eyes caught and held hers and she noticed, yet again, the almost hypnotic hold in them. Yes, she thought to herself, he probably didn't need a fridge full of champagne to get the girls. Giving herself a mental shaking, she replied, 'I'd love that. Give me your phone number and I'll text you tomorrow.'

They exchanged numbers and then carried the food and drink out to the others. The dog followed the plates of food assiduously and plonked herself down on the floor as close to the table as possible, nostrils flared.

It turned out to be a most enjoyable evening. After an hour or so on Corrado's terrace, chatting about everything from the history of Rome to the outrageous price of the fabulous bikinis in Via dei Condotti, they went downstairs to a nearby restaurant for dinner. It was a little place a couple of streets away from Piazza Navona and Corrado and his canine companion were clearly well known there. They sat outside and in spite of her best intentions Jo had no trouble finding room for a starter of roasted artichoke hearts, followed by a *fritto misto* of calamari, prawns and whitebait, dusted with flour and quickly deep-fried. This was served on a dish with a sheet of thick brown paper underneath that did an excellent job of soaking up any residual oil, although the whole thing was remarkable light.

They drank a lovely crisp white wine called *Est! Est! Est!* from Montefiascone, near the Lake of Bolsena, to the north of Rome. Victoria asked about the unusual name and Corrado was happy to explain.

'Back in the Middle Ages, the servant of a bishop was sent out to look for a good wine and when he found one he was instructed to chalk the Latin word *Est*, "it is", on the door of the cantina. If the wine was really good, he was told to write *Est Est*. When he got to Montefiascone and tried the wine there, the result was *Est! Est! Est!'*

'And what did the bishop think of the wine?'

'He loved it. See what you think.'

They all agreed with the bishop, although Jo declined to drink too much as she wanted to keep a clear head for the conference in the morning.

When the party broke up, Angie and Mario went off to their car to drive back out to the Country Club, while Corrado and Daisy walked Jo and Victoria back to their hotel through the side streets of Rome. It was a delightful evening and by the time they had climbed back up to the top of the Spanish Steps, Jo was feeling pleasantly sleepy after a day on her feet, not to mention the food and wine. Even so, when they reached the hotel and Corrado kissed her softly on the cheeks, she was shaken wide awake as that same annoying bolt of lightning shot, unbidden, through her once more.

As they travelled up in the lift together, Jo caught Victoria's eye.

'So, what do you think?'

'Corrado? He's totally Drop… Dead… Gorgeous. If you hadn't called dibs on him already, I'd have jumped him and ravaged him right there over the dining table.' Jo started to protest, but Victoria waved away her protestations. 'Of course he's the one for you, Jo. So what if he's going to be your brother-in-law? By the way he was looking at you, I reckon he feels the same way about you.'

This time Jo had to set the record straight. 'You're joking, Vic. I touched his chin with my finger yesterday and he ran a mile.'

'Rubbish. But, anyway, the thing is there's more to him than just good looks and a body to die for... or under.' Victoria paused for effect. 'Seriously, the better I got to know him this evening, the more I got to like him. Christian had the looks but, I'll be honest, I never felt he was that sincere. Corrado comes across as a very different calibre of man.' She caught hold of Jo's hand. 'What are you going to do about him?'

At that moment the lift doors opened and they stepped out into the silent corridor. Jo waited until they were back in their room before giving her answer, grateful for the thinking time. As Victoria closed and locked the door behind them, she turned to Jo and put the light on.

'So, what happens next, Jo?'

'Nothing.'

'Nothing!? Why nothing?'

'Because there's nothing to be done. You and I know each other well enough by now. Apart from the family complications, I'm not the sort of girl who's happy to jump into bed with some random man just for a quickie.' She had the honesty to look up and give Victoria a wry smile. 'However appealing that might be with a man like Corrado. I've been doing a lot of thinking lately. In two weeks' time I'll be thirty. Maybe Mum's right. I've reached an age when I need to start thinking of the future, and one thing's for sure, there's no future for me with a man like him.'

Victoria nodded slowly. 'The same goes for me. But, in my case, I think I might just have found my man. I wish he was here.'

Jo found herself wondering whether, after all, her friend might end up with a life companion before she did. She was happy for Victoria and George, but deep down inside, she couldn't help experiencing envy — and regret. Even though she hadn't known him for long, she felt sure that in so many ways Corrado might have turned out to be The One. Why, oh why were things so complicated?

Chapter 7

Monday morning came as a shock to the system for Jo after two days as a tourist.

She left Victoria to her day of sightseeing and walked barely three hundred metres along the road to the conference centre shortly after half past eight, even though things weren't expected to start until nine thirty. Although it was early, the entrance hall was already buzzing and she had to queue to check in at the main desk. As soon as she was recognised as one of the speakers, she was handed over to a dedicated staff member in a smart blue blazer who supplied her with her name badge and a welcome pack. They spoke for a few minutes in Italian and Jo was relieved to hear it flowing reasonably fluently from her mouth. The girl then ushered her into a 'hospitality room', where she found herself among other speakers and distinguished figures. Most of these were household names in the sector and her apprehension grew.

She did her best to relax and accepted a little espresso from a waiter. As she was sipping it nervously, she spotted a familiar head crowned with a familiar ponytail standing out high above the crowd. As she was gathering up the courage to go over to him, he saw her and immediately smiled as he headed across the room over to her.

'Joanne, isn't it? I don't know if you remember me, but we met briefly at the French embassy in London.'

'Of course I do. You're Ricky from UCLA. I really enjoyed your talk.'

They shook hands and Jo was very pleased to see him.

'I see from the programme that you're standing in for Ronald. Do you work with him?'

'I work *for* him.'

'And how's that working out?' He caught her eye for a moment and she couldn't miss the twinkle in his.

'You know him?'

'I used to work with him when he was at UCLA. That's something you and I have in common. So, you two get on okay?'

There was a lot she could have said about Ronald, but she felt it better to bite her tongue at least until she got to know Ricky better. She opted for the diplomatic reply.

'It's a privilege to work for such an eminent scientist.'

Ricky laughed. 'Did he tell you to say that?'

In fact, that wasn't far from the truth, but again Jo steered clear of controversy.

'We get on fine.'

'Do you know what his nickname was at UCLA?' He lowered his voice a tad. 'The Pirate. His speciality was pirating other people's ideas.'

Jo couldn't restrain a smile this time and he smiled back and then changed the subject. As they stood and chatted, her apprehension subsided a bit. He was good company and she found she enjoyed talking to him. All too soon, however, he had to desert her and head off for an audience with some local dignitary. Jo was sorry to see him go.

As he disappeared, she went over to a table in a corner where she opened her welcome pack. Inside, among other things, was the programme of events for the conference and she almost fainted as she saw that she was scheduled to give the presentation on plastics in the ocean at three o'clock that same afternoon. She drained the coffee and was looking round for a waiter to order another one when she got an even greater shock.

'Excuse me, you're Doctor Green, aren't you?'

Jo looked up at the sound of the voice. She didn't need to read the name badge to recognise the elderly lady before her as none other than the chair of the conference herself, Professor Waltraud Dietrich of the United Nations, a legendary figure in the world of conservation. Jo jumped to her feet, upsetting the, fortunately empty, coffee cup and scattering papers and pamphlets across the table as she did so. She could feel her face burning as she shook the outstretched hand and replied.

'Professor Dietrich, what an honour! Yes, I'm Doctor Green, Jo Green.'

'Welcome to the conference, Doctor Green. First things first, please would you give my greetings and best wishes to Ronald. I know him well and I was so very sorry to hear about his accident.'

Jo assured her she would pass on her greetings and they chatted for a few minutes before the professor cut to the chase.

'I gather from Flavia that you speak Italian.'

Jo remembered seeing that name on the lapel of the girl who had accompanied her in here. She nodded hesitantly. 'Not terribly fluently, I'm afraid, but yes, I do speak it a bit.'

'Flavia told me she was very impressed with your Italian.' The professor lowered her voice a fraction. 'The thing is, we find ourselves in a bit of a predicament. In spite of this conference taking place here in Rome, none of the main speakers, myself included, can speak more than few words of Italian. Of course, that doesn't matter in here as the lingua franca of the conference is, of course, English, but it does matter to the media.'

'The media?'

'Yes, RAI television, Italian state TV. They're very keen to do an interview with somebody who can explain the ethos of this conference. For obvious reasons this has to be done in Italian. I could do it through an interpreter, but it would be so much better if it was in their own language.'

Jo's heart, which had been falling as she listened, now crashed to the floor. She stared stupidly at the professor and had to struggle to prevent her jaw from dropping.

'You want me to go on TV, in Italian?'

'Yes, if you don't mind.'

'But my Italian's really not that great, Professor Dietrich. Besides, I've never needed to explain the intricacies of conservation and climate change in anything but English.' She could hear she was gabbling, but she was unable to stop herself. 'I'm awfully afraid I'll make a complete hash of it. And as for explaining the ethos of the conference, I'd be hard pressed to do that in English.' She felt a rising sense of panic.

The great lady laid a calming hand on Jo's arm as she sought to reassure her.

'Please don't worry. I'm sure you'll be fine. What I would propose is that you and I get together later this morning once things have started. We can map out what you need to say, and then you and Flavia can sit down and make sure you've got the vocabulary to render it into Italian.' To reinforce her point, she gave Jo's arm a little squeeze before releasing it. 'Besides, I'm sure the Italian public will be as impressed as I am to see that scientists aren't all stuffy old men and women like me. Trust me, Doctor Green, they'll love you.'

'Oh, God...' Jo dropped her eyes to the floor, desperately hoping it would open and swallow her up, but to no avail. 'And you're sure there's nobody else?'

This time she spotted a distinct twinkle in the old lady's eye. 'To be totally honest, the only other candidate we have is a microbiologist from the University of Pisa, but Flavia tells me he mumbles so badly, she can't understand a word he says. No, much better to make the interview with a lovely young British scientist who speaks reasonable Italian. Nobody will mind a few mistakes.'

'Oh, God...' Jo didn't know what else to say. Although she had been bracing herself to stand up in front of twenty or thirty delegates to deliver Ronald's paper, the idea of appearing on television was truly terrifying. 'And when would this interview take place?'

'Straight after lunch today. I understand that it's accepted practice to invite the television people to lunch first so they can meet the interviewee informally.'

'So I would be expected to eat with them?'

'Yes, we have a private dining room reserved for VIPs like me' – Professor Dietrich smiled – 'and you. I can guarantee you a good meal.'

The lunch may well have been excellent, but Jo didn't taste a thing. When asked by Victoria later what it had consisted of, she was unable to recall anything except for the overwhelming sensation of fear gnawing at her innards. Around mid-morning she and the professor had met as planned and then, together with Flavia, Jo had rehearsed the main thrust of what she was supposed to say in Italian, but she was still terrified. By the time she was escorted into the VIP dining room, she had already been to the toilet three times that morning.

The presenter was unlike any TV presenter Jo had ever seen before. He was described as the TV channel's Science Correspondent and he bore more than a passing resemblance to the stereotypical image of the absent-minded Professor. In spite of the heatwave outside, he arrived wearing a tweed jacket with leather patches at the elbows and a bow tie, and he boasted the sort of handlebar moustache you could hang hats on. In fact, in a funny way, his bizarre appearance had a calming effect upon Jo's overstretched nerves. She gradually found that by concentrating on his eccentricities – and there were many of these – she was able to deflect at least some of the terror she felt.

She was relieved to find that the interview was not going to be broadcast live. Tweed Jacket informed her that it was being recorded now for transmission later on as part of the evening news. This further served to hearten Jo. She was able to take comfort from the thought that if she clammed up – or, the way she was feeling, passed out – there would be the chance for another take.

In fact, when the interview started, she lost count of the number of takes. The producer insisted upon making them repeat whole sections until she had almost lost track of what she had already said. At least this allowed her to practise her lines and by the end she felt reasonably happy that she hadn't disgraced herself. All in all, she was tied up with the TV crew for three quarters of an hour and she was flabbergasted at the end to hear from the producer that this would be edited down to probably no more than a two- or three-minute piece.

One positive effect of getting this interview out of the way was that when she rushed from there into the lecture theatre to deliver Ronald's paper, she was so relieved to have survived the TV interview that she was totally unphased to find the place completely packed, with some delegates even having to stand at the back, even when she spotted Professor Dietrich and Ricky in the front row. She was able to deliver what seemed to her a pretty seamless performance, including the update on alternative materials she had gleaned from Corrado, and it appeared to go down well.

Unexpectedly, at the end of the session, after some tricky Q&As, there was even a ripple of applause. As the delegates filed out, she received no fewer than three invitations to dinner that night, but she felt sure these had less to do with the oceans than with what Corrado would have identified as the delegates' overactive limbic systems. Jo refused them all cordially and was heading for the Ladies toilet to freshen up when she heard a familiar American accent behind her.

'That was a great paper, Joanne. And you're a natural. You knew the subject inside and out and you had the whole hall in the palm of your hand.'

She turned and smiled at him. 'Hello, Ricky. Thanks. I was scared stiff.'

'It didn't show. And I'm willing to bet quite a lot that you actually wrote that paper yourself. Am I wrong?'

'I suppose I did have a hand in it.' She grinned. 'Well, more like a hand, an arm and a shoulder.'

He smiled back at her. 'So, the Pirate's still up to his old tricks. Anyway, can I buy you a coffee? Or something stronger, maybe? You look like you could use it.'

'You know what I'd like? A cup of tea.'

He checked his watch. 'Of course, I forgot you're English. It *is* almost five o'clock after all.'

He led her to the coffee bar where she was delighted to find that the waiter produced a convincing-looking pot of tea, with some cold milk in a little jug alongside it. It turned out to be UHT milk with a funny taste, but it was still recognisably a cup of tea all the same. She and Ricky chatted and she learnt more about him. He lived in Santa Monica and was a keen surfer as well as a renowned environmental scientist. They got on really well together and she found she was looking forward to seeing him again the following day.

She got back to the hotel just before six feeling weary but content, and found Victoria with a broad smile on her face.

'Hi, Jo, hurry up and get changed. We've been invited out for dinner tonight.'

In spite of her fatigue, Jo felt a sudden spark of interest. She hadn't heard anything from Corrado today and in her quieter moments had found herself thinking of him far more than was normal for a future brother-in-law. There was no doubt about it: she could feel herself drawn to him like one of her beloved moths to a flame. She glanced across at Victoria.

'Dinner?'

'Yes.' Victoria was looking very smug. 'But I'm not telling you who with. Go and have a shower and get changed. Tonight, we've been invited to try the best pizza in Rome and you wouldn't want to miss that, would you?'

Food hadn't been high on Jo's agenda today, but now that she thought about it, she realised she was starving. Presumably she had eaten very little of whatever it was she had been served at lunchtime.

'Sounds good, Vic. So, who's invited us?' She felt pretty sure it had to be Corrado and she felt her spirits begin to rise.

'Not telling. It's a surprise. Now hurry up and get ready while I tell you about my day.'

As Victoria recounted what she had seen and done in the course of the day, Jo hurried into the bathroom, showered and changed from head to toe after the stress of the day. She emerged wearing a light summer dress and feeling much more buoyant. This didn't go unnoticed.

'You're looking more cheerful now. You looked knackered when you came in. Do I presume you've had a tough day?'

'I'll tell you about my day as we walk, Vic. I'll relive it in my nightmares for years to come.'

Jo was still recounting the trials of this eventful day to a sympathetic Victoria as they neared the pizzeria where they were to meet their mystery host. This was called *l'Aragosta*, the Lobster, and it was close to the river Tiber. It was little more than a few blocks from Corrado's flat and Piazza Navona so, as they walked up the narrow street towards the flashing pink and orange sign, Jo felt pretty sure she knew who would be waiting for them.

She was wrong.

To her surprise, as they passed through the gaudy plastic fly curtain at the door, the man who jumped to his feet to greet them was none other than George from Italian class. He pecked Jo on the cheeks and then kissed Victoria a lot more enthusiastically while Jo recovered from her surprise. Along with that was the unmistakable sense of disappointment that she wasn't going to see Corrado after all. She took a seat and waited until George and Victoria emerged from their grapple. In spite of an air-conditioning unit working overtime high up on the far wall, it was hot in there and she was glad she had opted for her lightest dress. The place was packed and she was pleased to see that many, if not most, of their fellow customers were Italians. This boded well.

'Jo, what can I get you to drink?'

There was a broad smile on George's face and an even broader smile on a slightly breathless Victoria's.

Jo knew what she needed. 'Fizzy water please. Lots of it. I've sweated more today than I have done for months.'

'It has been hot, hasn't it?'

Jo decided not to bother him with her saga for now. Instead, she changed the subject from her to him.

'So, how come you're here, George?'

'It's a work thing. All very last minute. I only found out myself that I was coming here at nine o'clock this morning. Shall I get some wine as well? We can't have pizza without wine.'

As Jo agreed, a cheerful but busy waitress appeared, placed plastic-covered menus in front of them, took the order for drinks, and disappeared again in the blink of an eye.

'And how long are you staying, George?'

'I'm not sure. A day or two, I imagine. It's all a bit uncertain.'

'And this is on behalf of Her Majesty's government? Are you sure you aren't James Bond?' From the blissful expression on Victoria's face it looked as though she thought he was.

'No, no "licence to kill". Just boring old stuff, but if it gives me a chance to come back to Rome and to see a certain person, that's fine with me.'

After ordering a *Quattro Stagioni* pizza, Jo let George and Victoria whisper sweet nothings to each other while she pulled out her phone and sent a text to Corrado. This, she told herself, was not so much because she was desperate to see him again but rather because the idea of going riding in the Roman countryside really appealed.

She almost believed it herself.

> Hi Corrado. Gave my paper today. Just one evening commitment on Thursday. Otherwise any evening after 5 for a ride would be great. x Jo.

She agonised for a full minute about that little 'x', but finally justified it to herself as common courtesy to a friend and future relative. Her subconscious might have been about to protest as she pressed Send, but her thoughts were interrupted by Victoria grabbing her arm.

'Jo, look up there. It's you.'

Jo's eyes followed her pointing finger to the television screen positioned high on the end wall of the room. Sure enough, it was her own face up there. She felt herself blush all over again as the stress of the moment came back to her. She watched in silence as Tweed Jacket asked her questions and she answered. It was impossible to hear more than a few snippets of the interview over the noisy hubbub of the crowded restaurant, but she took heart from the fact that the producer hadn't felt it necessary to put up subtitles. Presumably it must have been comprehensible. The interview only lasted a couple of minutes as he had anticipated, but to Jo it felt like an age. She found herself studying an untidy strand of hair hanging across her left eye, the undone button on her blouse that afforded a glimpse of a black bra beneath and an unmistakable drop of perspiration on her brow. When the screen returned to the studio, she felt as if she had just done ten rounds in the ring with the world heavyweight champion.

'Look at you, Jo! Fame at last, eh?' Victoria sounded impressed.

'I couldn't hear what you were saying, but you come across really well on TV.' George was clearly doing his bit as well.

'I've never seen myself on TV before. It's creepy.' Jo turned anxiously towards Victoria. 'Vic, you could see my bra. I wasn't obscene, was I?'

'For crying out loud, Jo, of course you weren't. I didn't even notice. No, you were great. I know you told me you were bricking it, but you looked cool, calm and collected. And a damn sight more attractive than old hairy whiskers opposite you.'

At that moment Jo's phone rang. It was Angie, saying pretty much the same as Victoria. After gushing about Jo's on-screen presence, Angie finished by talking horses.

'Mario was speaking to Corrado today. Are you up for an evening ride tomorrow? Corrado says he can pick you up from your hotel and bring you out here. It's pizza night at the restaurant here, so the four of us can go for a ride and then we can drop in there for a pizza afterwards. That way you won't need to worry that I'm spending all my time cooking.'

Jo didn't tell her she was having pizza this evening as well. Instead she agreed readily and then had a thought.

'Hang on a sec, Angie.' She looked across the table at Victoria and George. 'What about you guys? It's Angie and she's asking if I'd like to go riding tomorrow night. Do you want to come too?'

Victoria grimaced. 'You're joking. No, you go off and enjoy your smelly horsy evening. I'm sure George and I will be able to find something to do to occupy our time.' She and George exchanged meaningful glances. 'Say thanks but no thanks to Angie.'

A minute or two later, the pizzas arrived and Jo could see immediately why George reckoned this might be the best place for it in Rome. Her pizza was served on a massive plate, but even so, it was overflowing onto the chequered table cloth. It was heaped with ham, cheese, tomato, olives and artichoke hearts and had obviously come straight out of the oven. Best of all, it had a wonderful thin crust and so, in spite of its daunting initial appearance, Jo found she was able to eat almost all of it without feeling totally stuffed. She washed it down with cold white wine and sparkling mineral water and by the end she had got over the stress of the day and the shock of seeing herself on TV. She sat back and stretched, glad to have got the interview and the lecture out of the way and definitely looking forward to going for a ride tomorrow. This, she told herself, was irrespective of whether or not she was going to see Corrado again, but her subconscious treated that with the disdain it merited.

Just as she was finishing her single scoop of white chocolate ice cream, her phone vibrated on the table top. It was a reply from Corrado.

> Dear TV celebrity. If you're up for it, I'll pick you up from your hotel at 6.00 tomorrow. Corrado. PS You looked and sounded great.

She texted straight back.

> Terrific. See you then. J

She didn't put the little 'x' back in this time. He hadn't used one, after all.

Chapter 8

Tuesday at the conference was a lot less stressful than Monday, and Jo was relieved. She had slept well, but the strain of the previous day had taken its toll and she was delighted just to be able to blend into the crowd today and sit back. She spent a relaxing morning listening to experts talking about white rhinos, deforestation, melting ice caps and the appalling reduction in the numbers of hedgehogs in developed countries. She was delighted to meet up with Ricky again and they had coffee and a chat together during the mid-morning interval. He was a really nice man and Jo definitely warmed to him, although it was interesting that she felt no romantic attraction to him. Whether the reason for this was that her affections were elsewhere was a debate she and her subconscious were not prepared to undertake.

Professor Dietrich went out of her way to look for Jo among the crowds during the lunch break and congratulated her most warmly on her performance, both on television and in the lecture theatre. Apparently, the feedback on both had been very positive.

'I particularly enjoyed your paper on the plastic scourge. You were very knowledgeable. Some of the questions were pretty complicated and you had an answer for everything.' She gave Jo a little smile. 'You certainly did a lot more than read Ronald's notes. Very impressive.'

After lunch, Jo slipped back to her room for a short break before the afternoon sessions began. There was no sign of Victoria and Jo imagined she must be out sightseeing or with her boyfriend. She felt another little twinge of envy at their evident happiness together, but was very pleased for Victoria's sake that she had finally managed to find herself a good one.

Reluctantly, she pulled out her phone and called Ronald in his hospital bed in London with the news that his paper had been very well received. He sounded a bit sniffy at first, so she apologised for not calling him the previous evening, explaining how stressed she had been. He revealed to her that he had already received word from some of his colleagues at the conference of the success of her performances both on TV and in the lecture theatre and, to her surprise, he sounded remarkably complimentary. She felt almost sorry for him lying in hospital, but there was no doubt in her mind that the fact that he would be there for some time would make her daily life easier. She passed on Professor Dietrich's good wishes and promised she would drop in to see him upon her return from Rome.

Duty done, she phoned her mother, and by the time she put the phone down after relating the events of yesterday, her mum had been so excited to hear that her firstborn had been on TV, she had done no further probing about Corrado. This suited Jo just fine. She wouldn't have known what to tell her anyway.

The afternoon passed quickly and she managed to get away from the conference at half past four, looking forward to her evening on horseback. As she was walking into the hotel lobby out of the warm Roman sunshine, her phone buzzed twice. Once back in her room, she sat on her bed and saw that she had received two messages, but neither of them was particularly welcome. The first was from Christian and her heart fell.

> Hi Jo. It's me. I'm in Rome. I saw you on TV. Can we meet up? Love, Christian.

She snorted as she read it and almost exploded when she got to the penultimate word. 'Love'? How dare he, after what he had done to her?

She checked the other message and her spirits fell even lower.

> Hello Jo. I see you are in Rome for the Save the Planet conference. By chance, I, too, am here in Rome. Can we meet up? I think I maybe owe you an apology. Dinner one evening? Markus.

Jo's blood pressure was by now approaching boiling point. 'I think I *maybe* owe you an apology?' She repeated the words out loud and was now snorting so loudly she didn't hear the door open until Victoria walked in.

'Hi, Jo? Trouble at 't mill? You look like you're going to have a stroke.'

Jo passed her phone across without a word. Victoria took it from her and read the message from Markus that was still on the screen. Shaking her head in disbelief, she looked back at Jo.

'I knew I should have gone out and bought that baseball bat. Where is the bastard? "Might owe you an apology" for God's sake!'

'There's a second message from, guess who?' Jo could hear the anger in her own voice. The baseball bat idea definitely had distinct attraction. She watched her friend's expression darken as she read Christian's message. Finally, Victoria dropped the phone on her bed and sat down heavily alongside it, kicking off her shoes and snorting in her turn.

'Listen, Jo, we're in Italy, the land of the Mafia and the contract killer. Why don't you get some nice friendly mobster to rub the two of them out? I've got a few extra Euros; I'll even contribute to the cost.'

Jo couldn't restrain a little smile at the image. 'Don't think I'm not tempted.' She slumped down on the bed opposite Victoria who was looking pensive.

'So, if you don't get a hitman, Jo, what *are* you going to do?'

'For now, nothing. One thing's for sure, I don't want to see Markus again. He really frightened me, whether he meant to or not.'

'And Christian?'

'I can't see any point in meeting up with him either, although at least he doesn't scare me.'

'Well, you know you can count on me. I may not be a mobster, but I reckon I could give Christian a run for his money in a punch-up. He may be tall, but he's skinny.'

Jo grinned in spite of herself and reached across to squeeze Victoria's hand.

'Thanks, Vic, but it won't come to fisticuffs, or baseball bats, with either of them.' She glanced at her watch. 'I won't answer the texts now. I'll talk to Angie when I see her and then I'll sleep on it before doing anything.'

Victoria nodded. 'Sounds sensible. Now listen, there's something else we need to talk about.' Jo glanced up at the unusual note in her friend's voice and saw a distinct twinkle in her eye. 'You see, Jo, I didn't do a lot of sightseeing this afternoon.'

'You didn't?'

Victoria grinned. 'Unless you count the ceiling of George's bedroom.'

'So, things are moving on?' Jo grinned back. 'And, talking of moving, did the earth move for you?'

Victoria nodded vigorously. 'Oh, yes.'

'Well, good for you two. I was just thinking how happy you looked together.'

'The thing is, Jo, would you mind awfully if I didn't stay here tonight?'

'Of course not. *Viva l'amore* and all that.'

Victoria looked relieved. 'It was so nice of you to invite me along, I wouldn't want you to think I'm just dumping you.'

'Of course not. You young people go and have fun.' She was a full month older than Victoria. 'I'll be just fine on my own.'

'Well, at least this frees you up to invite the gorgeous Corrado back here and have your evil way with him, doesn't it?' Jo could see she was joking, but she protested all the same.

'We've been through this before, Vic. It isn't going to happen. Now, I'd better get changed into my jeans if I'm going for a ride.' She jumped to her feet and grinned at

Victoria again. 'And I daresay you could do with a shower yourself.'

Jo went downstairs at six o'clock precisely, so as not to keep Corrado waiting and saw that he was already there. This time, to her surprise, he had come by car right to the hotel and had brought the big flashy 4x4. He was leaning against the bonnet, chatting to a very pretty girl while Daisy looked on from the boot. As the dog spotted Jo walking towards the car, she sprang to her feet, gave a welcoming bark, and pawed at the window. As she did so, Corrado looked round and from the expression on his face he was equally pleased to see her, although he didn't bark. He said something to the pretty girl and came over to meet Jo. The girl gave him a little wave and walked off without protest. Jo found herself once more gritting her teeth at his knack for attracting women to his side like bees to a honey pot.

'Good evening, Jo.' As he approached, he held out his arms towards her while looking round in mock apprehension. 'No TV cameras trained on us? Now that you're a famous star of the silver screen.'

Jo gave him a big smile and kissed him on the cheeks. The touch of his skin against her lips felt good, too good, and she was quick to release him and go across to say hello to the dog. The tailgate opened automatically and Daisy launched herself bodily into Jo's arms. Both of them ended up on the cobbles where the dog straddled her and did her best to lick Jo's face until Corrado waded in to the rescue and returned the dog to the car. He stood over Jo and smiled down as she rested on her elbows and collected herself. He was wearing adherent grey riding breeches and polished leather ankle boots, and he looked even more appealing than usual.

'Sorry about that, Jo. Are you all right? No damage done? Nothing in your bag to break, I hope? Your phone?'

Jo had brought her new bikini and a towel in case there was the opportunity for another swim, as well as a skirt to change into after the ride. These had proved to be very effective padding and no harm had been done as she fell over. She accepted Corrado's proffered hand and let him haul her to her feet, but she was quick to relinquish it again.

'No, everything's fine, thanks.'

'I've never seen Daisy take to someone so quickly.' He caught her eye and winked. 'I think it must be love.'

'Yeah, right...'

Jo climbed into the wonderful luxury car. Inside it was very cool, in both senses of the word. She buckled up her seat belt and cast an admiring eye around. She knew next to nothing about cars and had little interest in them, but you couldn't fail to be impressed by the symphony of cream leather, rich polished walnut and deep pile carpet of the interior. She turned towards him and caught his eye.

'So how come you managed to drive right to the hotel this time? I thought it was prohibited.'

'Only up to six o'clock. After six, it's allowed.'

She nodded. 'I see. And you brought the big car. This one's a bit different from the Fiat, is it?'

He grinned. 'It's ridiculously big for driving round these crowded roads, but you shamed me into bringing it tonight. Why buy it if I don't use it? Besides, nothing but the best for a TV star.'

'Don't get too used to the experience. If I never have to appear on TV again, it'll be too soon. I was terrified.'

'It didn't show. And I was very impressed by your Italian.'

'Really? Did you think it was all right? I know I'm nowhere near your league when it comes to languages, but I hope I didn't let myself down.'

'Very much the opposite. *Complimenti*. And my friend, Annarosa, agrees. She saw the interview on the news and we were just talking about it as you came out of your hotel.'

'Annarosa?' Jo did her best to sound nonchalant.

'She works in our Research and Development section. She's a chemist like me. I gave her a lift into town to meet her boyfriend.'

Jo made no reply, although she couldn't help feeling pleased this hadn't been yet another of his girlfriends. Unhelpfully, her subconscious pointed out that she only had his word for this and, as she knew to her cost, not all men told the truth. She did her best to shrug this ignoble thought away – at least for now.

He started the engine and the car purred off down the road back into the thick of the traffic. At this time of day, it took a long time to creep out through the near-gridlocked chaos until they were finally beyond the ring roads and onto quieter roads in the country. They hardly spoke, Jo not wishing to disturb his concentration.

When they got to the Country Club, he turned right immediately after the entrance and they crunched down a wide gravel track to the stables. This was the first time Jo had been down here and she was impressed by the scale and style of the lovely old stone building, surrounded by more modern units. They drove into the yard and found Mario and Angie already there, saddling up four fine-looking horses.

Corrado parked in the shade and they climbed out. Jo was impressed to see that Daisy was very well-behaved around the horses. In fact, she seemed far more interested in her buddy, Jo, than in the horses. Jo scratched the dog's ears as she stood talking to the others.

'So, which one's mine?'

Angie pointed to a fine chestnut mare. 'This is Cleopatra. She answers to Cleo when she feels like it. I thought you'd like her, seeing as she's about the same size as your old favourite, Polly, back at home. And, like Polly, she's a fairly lazy character.'

'And this big black beast?' The next horse along was very handsome and considerably larger, several hands taller than Cleopatra.

Corrado answered. 'This is Bogart. He's my next best friend after Daisy.' He went over to the horse, stroked its head and addressed it in Italian. '*Amico mio*, it's good to see you. Feel like stretching your legs?'

The big animal rubbed his head against Corrado's hand and Jo's experienced eye could tell there was a close rapport between horse and man. Presumably it wasn't just women who found him irresistible.

They mounted up and Mario led them out and along the track until they reached open fields. The horses trotted comfortably and Daisy ran alongside with a happy smile on her face. It was only when they broke into a canter that the Labrador decided enough was enough and took up station in the shade of a tree and watched while the riders circled the field. Over to one side was a line of jumps and

Jo followed the others over them, first from one direction, and then back over them again from the other. They were out for almost an hour and Jo enjoyed herself hugely.

By the time they had unsaddled the horses and settled them back in the stables, the sun was setting and they all piled into the Range Rover to drive back to Mario's house for a swim. Jo went upstairs with Angie and changed into her new bikini. When she came back downstairs, she found the two men already in the water and the disgruntled Labrador tethered to a tree. Jo went over to make a fuss of her before joining Mario and Corrado in the pool. It felt wonderful. After swimming up and down a few times, she drifted to her familiar spot on the steps and rested back, letting the water gently rock her from side to side.

Shortly afterwards, Angie joined her and Jo told her about the two text messages she had received. Angie listened in silence before coming up with the same question Victoria had asked.

'So, what're you going to do?'

'I've been thinking about that. As far as creepy Markus is concerned, I'm just not going to answer, and I'll hope he gets the message that I'm not interested. As for Christian, there's a little part of me that's curious to see how he's getting on.' She looked across at her sister. 'After all, we were together for the best part of four years. I've watched his career take off in that time and I'd quite like to know how he's doing.'

'But that isn't the real reason, is it?' Angie really did know her so very well, so Jo grinned and ended up confessing.

'No, I suppose you're right. To be honest, Angie, another other part of me would like him to see me with a smile on my face and a spring in my step. I'd like him to realise that my life's good even without him. I'm over him now and I'm doing just fine.'

'And are you really?'

Jo nodded. 'Yup. If you'd asked me that only a week or two ago I would have probably still said yes, but I'd have been lying. It's only in these last few days that I've finally achieved some sort of closure.'

'And what might be the cause of this change?' Angie caught her eye. 'Somebody new?'

Jo felt her face flush, but hoped the red glow of the setting sun would provide sufficient camouflage. 'I don't know.'

'Really? Nobody come to mind? Nobody at all?' Angie was playing with her and Jo knew she couldn't stonewall forever.

'Well, I suppose it might be Corrado.' As she uttered his name, she looked round apprehensively, but both men were still heads down, ploughing methodically up and down the pool. She glanced back at her sister. 'Now don't worry, nothing's going to happen, but since getting to know him I've realised just what I've been missing all these years. Christian's a very good-looking man – and, boy, does he know it! – but he's nothing like as kind and generous or as knowledgeable and cultured as Corrado. If it wasn't for his attitude to women, Corrado would be the complete package.'

'It's a terrible shame. The two of you look good together.' But then Angie's tone hardened. 'Mind you, if he broke your heart I'd strangle him.'

Jo gave her sister a smile. 'He told me you'd get the Mafia to feed him to the pigs. I think he's a bit frightened of you. You can be quite scary sometimes. But what he's done is he's given me a target to aim for. I now know that the complete package does exist. I'll just have to keep on looking until I find it.'

Angie nodded understandingly and pushed herself back out into the deeper water for a swim. Jo relaxed in the shallows, her eyes half-closed until she felt ripples against her skin and saw that she had been joined by Corrado. In spite of what she had told her sister, she felt a frisson of excitement as his bare shoulder brushed momentarily against hers. The sun had disappeared below the horizon by now and all she could see of him was the outline of his face.

'Jo, do you like classical music by any chance?'

'I like all kinds of music, although I'm no expert on the classics.'

'Nor am I, but I was wondering; you said you'd got a thing on Thursday night, didn't you?'

'Yes, the conference finishes on Friday lunchtime so there's a drinks thing on Thursday night. As one of the speakers, I'm afraid I really need to be there.'

'Fine, but what about tomorrow night, Wednesday? I've got tickets to a charity concert in the grounds of a villa not far from your hotel and I was wondering if you might be interested. It's within easy walking distance and the star of the show's a famous Spanish classical guitar player who's so famous I've forgotten his name.' Jo giggled. 'There's no point asking Mario or Angie. We've tried in the past and it's not their thing. Last year I took them to an opera and they both fell asleep.'

Jo giggled again. 'Yes, Angie's always been more of a pop music girl. But, yes, I'd love to.' Her subconscious had by now pointed out to her that this would in effect be a date of sorts, just the two of them alone, but Jo stubbornly ignored any negative thoughts. 'Do I have to dress up?'

'No, not at all. It's in the open air. Just come as you are.'

'In my bikini?'

'Now, that would be interesting.'

They went over to the restaurant for dinner. This was the first time Jo had been inside the hotel and restaurant complex and she was very impressed. The restaurant itself was spotless and stylish, and the serving staff immaculately turned out in crisp white shirts or blouses. The manager herself led them across the large dining room and out onto the terrace shaded by a vine-covered trellis. This was dotted with lemon trees and gnarled olive trees all in wonderful old terracotta pots. Most of the tables were occupied, even though it was a Tuesday, but places had been reserved for them in the far corner, overlooking the flawless elegant garden with its illuminated fountain. It was quite dark now and Jo was fascinated to see a number of moths attracted by the lights. She kept a weather eye open in case something rare should come by, and checked that her bag – this time without underwear in it – was close to hand.

They sat down and a waiter brought wine and water without being asked, while Daisy trotted over to a water trough to one side and drank deeply. Clearly, she knew her way around this place. When she returned to the table, Jo saw her settle down between her and Corrado and a few seconds later, she felt a heavy hairy head land on her feet as the dog stretched out for a rest.

The meal was excellent. Lunch at the conference centre had been a buffet affair and Jo hadn't taken much. As a result, after a ride and a swim, she was quite hungry and she chose a salad with soft goats' cheese and honey as a starter, followed by a pizza topped with fresh rocket and slices of *bresaola*. She had always liked the salted, air-dried beef from the north of Italy. The pizza was excellent but she had to admit, but only to herself, that it wasn't quite as good as the one in George's best pizzeria in Rome. Thought of George made her wonder how he and Victoria were getting on. Once again, a little twinge of envy ran through her, but she brushed it away.

She accepted one glass of red wine, but refused a refill, preferring to stay on mineral water. When Angie queried this, Jo was quick to explain.

'I'm going to need a clear head tomorrow. There's the possibility I may get asked to be on a panel for a Q&A session.'

The other reason she wanted to stay sober was to avoid the very real risk of giving in to the temptation to leap on her future brother-in-law, who was looking ever more desirable whatever his drawbacks, and tear his clothes off. This, she told herself, had nothing to do with love. This was pure, unadulterated lust and, for once, both she and her subconscious were on the same page. This must never happen.

At the end of the evening, Corrado gave her a lift back into town. The journey was mainly spent in silence apart from loud snores from the weary dog in the rear. When they reached the hotel, Corrado pulled up right outside and extended his hand formally.

'Well, good night, *cognata*.'

Jo understood the word and what he was trying to say with it. *Cognata* was the Italian for sister-in-law. Clearly, he was reminding her of the true nature of the relationship between the two of them and the inadvisability of their straying towards anything more. Jo nodded to show she understood and shook his hand.

'*Buonanotte, cognato*. And thanks for everything.'

It was, however, with a sense of considerable regret that she headed back to her room. It was dark in there and, as expected, there was no sign of Victoria, and Jo found herself gazing out over the beauty of the Eternal City with an acute sense of loneliness. Maybe it was because of this that, without sleeping on it as she had promised, she picked up her phone and texted a reply to Christian.

> I'm here till Saturday but tied up tomorrow and Thursday. How about a coffee after I finish work on Friday? Meet by the fountain in Piazza Navona at 3.00? Jo

She did not, however, reply to Markus.

Chapter 9

Wednesday did involve a panel session, as Jo had expected, but she felt it went pretty well. The fact that she had Ricky sitting alongside her added extra reassurance. One of the questions was even on the research Corrado and his team were doing, and she vowed to herself to thank him for the valuable information he had passed on to her. She turned her phone back on again as she left the conference centre at the end of the afternoon and immediately saw she had two messages. One was from Christian, agreeing to their rendezvous on Friday, and the other was from Markus.

> Hello, Jo. I'm not sure if you got my message yesterday. I'm in Rome and I wondered if you felt like having dinner with me one night. Call me. Markus.

Jo toyed with the idea of replying in no uncertain terms, telling him to take a hike, but decided on balance that the best reaction was to ignore him and hope he went away. She hadn't given him her home address in London or the name of the hotel she was staying at here in Rome, so she felt pretty confident he would take the hint and this would be the last she heard of him.

She showered and changed, taking a bit more care than usual over her appearance. Even though it was to be outside in the open air, the fact that it was a classical concert made her choose a light summery dress rather than shorts, but she opted for sandals rather than heels as Corrado had said they would be walking. He had arranged to meet her in the hotel lobby at seven. She was dressed and ready by six-thirty, so she went out for a short walk first, looking for a present for her mum and some sweets or biscuits for her colleagues at work. As she was walking around in the oppressively humid heat, looking in the shop windows, she had a surprise.

As she emerged onto Piazza di Spagna, just at the bottom of the Spanish Steps, she spotted Corrado sitting at a table under an awning, drinking what looked like a little espresso. Alongside him, very close alongside him, was a woman. His arm was around her shoulders and his other hand was gripping hers on the tabletop. Jo stopped dead and retreated into the shadows, wondering what to do.

Given that nothing was ever going to happen between her and Corrado, he was free to drink coffee with whomsoever he chose. It had nothing to do with her, and she didn't need her subconscious to reinforce this. However, annoyingly, it patently did bother her to see him with another woman. The fact that this was totally illogical did not escape her, but she was powerless to help herself.

After lurking there indecisively for a couple of minutes, she saw from her watch that it was almost seven, so she took a deep breath and marched across the square and up the steps without a sideways glance. She had no idea whether he'd seen her or not and she didn't look back, even when she reached the hotel and popped in to deposit the packets of biscuits in her room. After a few mouthfuls of mineral water from the bottle in the fridge, she checked her appearance and headed back downstairs again just as the bells of the church of Trinità dei Monti struck seven.

Corrado was waiting by the lift, this time minus the Labrador. He was wearing grey trousers, an immaculate white shirt and a dark blue linen jacket. He looked very smart and she was glad she had decided to dress up a bit. As he saw her, his eyes lit up and she found herself wondering if they did this automatically every time they saw a woman. Dismissing the thought, she went over and kissed him on the cheeks. After seeing him with the other woman, she found his touch less stimulating than the previous evening, so maybe, she told herself, the message was finally getting through to her limbic system that he and she really were never going to be anything more than in-laws.

'Hi, Jo. Good day?' He looked weary.

She nodded. 'Yes, thanks. Far less stressful than yesterday, thank goodness. And you? How's your day been? You look a bit tired.'

They walked out into the street and the heat hit her again like a slap in the face. If anything, it was even hotter and more humid tonight than any of the previous days. She looked up and, for the first time, saw ominous grey clouds on the horizon. As he turned right and started walking up towards the church, he answered.

'It's been pretty hard going, to be honest.' She glanced up at him and for the first time registered the signs of strain as well as tiredness on his face. 'Do you have any experience of cancer?'

Jo did a double take and stopped dead. 'No, why? Has somebody got cancer?' A cold shaft cut through her body.

'Not you, Corrado?' She looked down and saw she was gripping his forearm with both of her hands.

He laid his free hand on top of hers and summoned a weak smile. 'No, thank God, not me, but a very close friend of mine. His doctors have been doing scans and other tests to discover how far advanced it is and I've been talking his wife through what all the medical jargon means. In fact, I was having a coffee with her just now.'

'And is it bad?'

Corrado nodded sadly and made no attempt to remove his hand from hers, or her hands from his arm. 'It's really bad. The doctors have given him three months and, from what I've seen of the results, I seriously doubt if he'll last that long.' He glanced up at her and the expression of anguish on his face made her squeeze his arm supportively. 'We were at school together. He's only thirty-six, less than a year older than me.' She saw him take a deep breath. 'I've just spent half an hour trying to encourage his wife, and all I managed to do was to start crying myself. Poor girl, she ended up trying to comfort me.'

Jo felt a total rat. Once again, she had misread the situation. Her mum was definitely right about her habit of judging people too harshly and jumping to the wrong conclusions. Taking a deep breath, she wrapped an arm around his and hugged herself tightly against him.

'Do you feel like going to a concert after something like that? Why don't we just go for a quiet meal together or even just do nothing? Maybe you'd be better off at home.'

He shook his head. 'No, definitely not. I'm looking forward to the concert. It'll take my mind off things. Besides, I enjoy your company and that'll cheer me up as well.'

'I thought that was Daisy's job. By the way, who's looking after her this evening?'

'She's looking after herself. I gave her a huge bone-shaped biscuit thing and left the TV on for her. She'll be fine.'

'Is she a documentary or a soap opera sort of girl?' Jo was doing her best to bring a smile to his face. It worked.

'You know they say dogs can't see things on TV? Well, I'm sure she does. If there's another dog, or a wolf, or even a bear – I'm not sure her eyesight's that great – she gets up, goes over to the screen and either barks or wags her tail depending on how she's feeling.'

Jo gave him a final squeeze and released her hold on his arm. As they walked past the church and onwards gently uphill, the panorama over the rooftops of Rome to the left of them would have been outstanding if the view from her terrace hadn't already spoiled her. Even so, it was a delight to look out over the sea of pink roof tiles interspersed with towers, spires and cupolas. The huge bulk of Castel Sant'Angelo down by the Tiber initially shielded the Vatican from their sight but, as they walked further along, the massive dome of St Peter's gradually emerged into view in the distance. It was a magical scene and a magical evening. Whatever their relationship, or lack of it, Jo was very happy to be here with Corrado and hoped her presence would help to cheer him up.

The concert was scheduled to take place in the private walled gardens of a stunning Renaissance villa. As they walked in past two security guards, they were offered cold champagne by immaculate waiters. Clearly, this was a very upmarket affair. The seats were set up in a semi-circle around a low stage and on their way there, Corrado stopped regularly to greet other guests and to introduce Jo as his future sister-in-law. He was obviously very well-known and she got the impression he was well respected, too. From the finery on display, Jo felt seriously under-dressed and she grabbed his arm and grumbled in his ear when she got a quiet moment.

'"Don't dress up," you said. "Come as you are," you said. "It won't be a dressy affair," you said. Just look around you, would you? I'd need a mortgage to buy some of the clothes these ladies are wearing. In comparison, Corrado, I feel like a tramp.'

He slowed and turned towards her, his mouth so close to her ear she felt sure she could feel the touch of his lips.

'You're the most beautiful woman here, Jo. Like I told you, you could have come in your bikini and you'd still be the most elegant.'

Whatever her good intentions, a shiver went through her. Yes, he knew the right things to say all right. Not for the first time she questioned what terrible act she had committed in a previous life to find herself saddled with such a desirable, but untouchable, future brother-in-law. Now, if Angie had gone for one of her buck-toothed, horsy friends in Woodstock instead of Mario, this problem surely wouldn't have arisen. She sighed once again and took a sip of the very good champagne.

They made their way to their seats and she saw that these were right in the middle at the front. She gave him a quizzical look.

'The best seats in the house. You certainly know the right people.'

He smiled back. 'To tell the truth, I'm one of the trustees of the charity and we do tend to get preferential treatment. Mind you, I've probably donated enough money over the past few years to buy this villa!'

Soon the lights were dimmed. As she waited for the concert to begin, she suddenly became aware of little pinpricks of yellowy-green light flashing in the darkness all around them. To somebody interested in flying insects, these were an added bonus to an already magical evening. Although they were technically beetles, rather than butterflies, the sight of fireflies in the Roman sky was a real treat and Jo felt genuinely sorry when the stage lights came on and the fireflies faded from view.

The concert was introduced by a very glamorous lady in a silver sheath dress with a gravity-defying décolleté, who talked about the work of the charity. Corrado whispered to Jo that this was a very well-known TV personality. The presenter repeated what Corrado had already said, that the charity's raison d'être was similar to that of Jo's own organisation. They were trying to raise money to help clean up the oceans and protect species in danger of extinction. As the lady finished speaking, Jo swallowed the last of her champagne and carefully set the glass down under her seat. Yes, she thought to herself, with free champagne and a big-name hostess, this was quite some event. No doubt tickets hadn't been cheap and the charity stood to do very well out of this evening.

The concert itself was delightful. The first part was an excellent string quartet who played a number of well-known works by famous composers. Although, as Jo had said, she wasn't a classical music aficionada, she recognised and enjoyed most of the pieces they played. This was followed by an interval during which more champagne was served, this time accompanied by a mouth-watering selection of canapés. Jo wondered if Corrado had intended to go out for dinner after the concert, but these were more than enough for her. She tapped him on the arm after eating her third deep-fried, Japanese-style king prawn in breadcrumbs.

'This food's amazing, but I'm full already. There's a limit to how much caviar and wild salmon a girl can eat, you know.'

He smiled down at her. 'I came to a similar event last month so I knew what to expect. I should have warned you. But you can't be completely full yet. You haven't had the profiteroles. Save a bit of space. I promise they're worth it.'

Jo wondered idly who had accompanied him the previous month, but immediately did her best to chase the thought away. She did, however, follow his advice and try the profiteroles when they came past. They were twice the size of any she had ever tasted before, smothered in rich sticky chocolate sauce and filled with cream. She could almost feel the pounds settling on her hips as she ate them – she had to have two, after all – and she rounded on him with mock irritation.

'I get it now. You're trying to fatten me up so I'll have to struggle to get into my bridesmaid's dress, aren't you?'

He gave her a grin as she licked the chocolate off her fingers. 'That's the first time I've ever been accused of trying to get a girl into a dress, rather than out of it.' Seeing the expression that leapt to her face, he hastened to apologise. 'Sorry, that's in bad taste. I don't see you in that light, I promise.'

Jo glanced at him. 'How you spend your life's none of my business.' Nevertheless, she knew she owed it to herself to query his choice of words, even though her subconscious was screaming at her to let it go. She took a mouthful of champagne for a bit of Dutch courage. 'But, seeing as we're on that subject, what is it about me that prevents you from seeing me in that light?'

He dropped his eyes and hesitated before answering. It was such a long pause she found herself seriously regretting embarking upon this topic. If only she had had the good sense to steer clear of anything so intimate. Finally, he replied, his voice low and his tone unexpectedly serious.

'This'll probably surprise you, but I've been doing a lot of thinking over the past few days about that exact same subject. I suppose there are three reasons really why I've been trying hard not to see you in that light. First of all, you and I are going to be part of the same family before long and we'll be seeing a lot of each other. If you and I had a crazy little affair and then, inevitably, split up, that could seriously screw things up for the two of us, and for Angie and Mario as well.' Jo nodded in agreement, but he didn't see, his eyes still firmly fixed on the shadows at his feet. What she hadn't been able to miss, however, was the fact that he had indicated he maybe did find her attractive and had been trying to avoid temptation. What the possible ramifications of this might be remained to be seen. After another, shorter pause, he continued.

'And the second reason is that I know you aren't that sort of girl. You're beautiful, you're intelligent, you're sexy, you have a body to die for, and you're very, very desirable, but I know you're looking for more than just sexual gratification, and we both know that's all I can offer. So it should never happen.'

Jo was repeating in her head the adjectives he had used to describe her. There could be no doubt he was indeed indicating very clearly that he did, after all, find her attractive and, in spite of everything, she felt almost relieved to know there wasn't anything awful about her that had been putting him off. He lapsed into silence again and she gently prompted him.

'You said there were three reasons, Corrado.'

This time he finally looked up, straight at her. His expression was gentle, but serious.

'I like you too much. You're bright, you're kind, you're fun. You're far too good a friend to risk losing. Of the three reasons, this one's the real deal-breaker. I want to keep you as a friend.' His expression softened and she saw a look of almost apprehension in his eyes. 'That's if you'll have me as a friend.'

Jo felt her eyes tingle with emotion. She reached out and caught hold of his hand and squeezed it.

'That's the sweetest non-declaration of love I've ever heard. Of course I want you to be my friend. For what it's worth, I've really enjoyed being with you these past few days and I know I like you a lot, an awful lot but, like you say, it's all just too complicated.' She looked up at him. 'Yes, Corrado, you can be the big brother I never had. Please can we be friends and remain friends forever?'

A smile spread over his face. 'It's a deal. Friends forever.'

She felt his fingers tighten against hers and for some reason she had to fight to stop the tears.

The second half of the programme was an exceptional Spanish guitar player. Jo had learnt guitar at school, but had never progressed much beyond a very hesitant rendering of Bob Dylan's 'Knock, Knock, Knockin' On Heaven's Door', even if she had now forgotten most of the chords. How on earth anybody could play an instrument so perfectly was beyond her. However, she only listened with part of her brain. The other part was fully occupied in analysing her reaction to what Corrado had said.

She had been close to tears, but why? Was it just that she was so pleased to be friends with such a nice man – apart from his hang-up when it came to relationships? Was it maybe sadness at the realisation that it was now firmly established between them that theirs would always only be a platonic relationship? And if that made her sad, did this mean that deep down she was physically attracted to him? The answer to that was, of course, a resounding yes. She couldn't fool herself even if she wanted to. The very first time she had clapped eyes on him she had registered, without a shadow of doubt, that he was very appealing. He was right about her, of course, but just for a moment she wished she *were* one of those girls happy to jump into a good-looking man's bed and devil take the hindmost. He looked good, he felt good, he sounded good and he even smelt good. Yes, she reflected to the notes of Rodrigo's 'Concierto de Aranjuez', there was definitely something about him. One thing was for sure though; although she had said she wanted him to be like a brother to her, she knew she'd never really be able to think of him in that way, but at least she now knew they could be friends – however unsatisfactory that might prove to be to her limbic system.

It was a delightful evening and it ended in an unexpected way. As they were making their way slowly back to the hotel after the concert had finished, she felt a drop of rain on her face, followed by another. These weren't little spots of rain, but substantial drops that splattered as they made contact with her skin. Seconds later the darkness was split by a blinding flash of lightning and the heavens opened. As the thunderclaps threatened to deafen them, the rain came pouring down so hard, it felt like walking into a bathroom shower. She felt his arm stretch around her shoulders and pull her protectively closer to him. Between the crashes of thunder, he shouted in her ear.

'I was afraid of this. The forecast was for heavy rain after midnight. I thought we'd get away with it. After all, it's barely ten now, but I'm afraid we're in for a soaking. There'll be no chance of finding a taxi now so all we can do is walk and get wet.'

Jo was finding it remarkably cosy pressed up against him, even though she could already feel the water running down the skin of her back as far as her pants. Her hair was plastered down across her head, but she really didn't mind. After the clammy heat of the evening, the rain was refreshing, cooling, but definitely not cold. She twisted her head so she could look up at him, and smiled in the streetlights.

'So we get wet. Who cares?' She wrapped an arm around his waist, pressed herself tighter against his chest and, to her surprise and his, started singing, quietly at first, but then louder as he joined in with her. The song that came spontaneously to her lips was Gene Kelly's famous 'Singin' in the Rain'.

She couldn't remember all the words, but it didn't matter. Corrado laughed out loud as the rain fell even harder and he relaxed his grip on her shoulders. He caught her by the hand, splashing through the puddles and spinning round a lamppost, mimicking the legendary scene in the old movie. They laughed all the way back to her hotel and they were still laughing – and streaming with water – as they came in to the lobby. Corrado reached out his arms and the two of them hugged warmly.

'Right, you're home. I think I'll just carry on, seeing as I couldn't get any wetter if I tried.'

'You could come up to my room and dry off if you like. I'm sure the concierge will be able to get you a taxi in a little while.'

She was still laughing, but the smile was wiped from her face as an image elbowed its way into her head and wedged itself stubbornly in place. It was the image of the two of them up in her lovely big room, next to her lovely big bed, stripping off each other's soaking wet clothes and drying themselves off with the lovely soft white bath towels before falling onto the bed and into each other's arms. It was one hell of a graphic image and, in spite of the cooling effect of the water on her skin, she felt herself blushing bright red. He must have noticed, but he made no comment. Maybe he thought it was just reaction to the rain. He pulled her towards him again and kissed her on the cheeks.

'I'm looking forward to the walk home. It's been a great evening.'

'It really has.' She stopped him and was unable to resist the urge to pull his face back towards her and deposit a tiny, soft kiss onto his lips. She caught a look of surprise in his eyes, but he didn't stop smiling. Then she stepped back, still blushing.

'Goodnight, friend, and thank you.'

'And a very good night to you too, friend.'

As he disappeared back out into the deluge, she glanced across at the dark-haired girl behind the reception desk and saw her smile.

'It looks like you've had an exciting evening, Signorina.'

Jo smiled back before heading for the lift.

'It's a night I'll always remember. Always.'

Chapter 10

Jo and Victoria met up for a quick lunch together the next day in a sandwich bar a block away from the conference centre. The storm had blown itself out during the night and the only remaining signs of the torrential rains were occasional puddles, fast evaporating away in the hot midday sunshine. Victoria was looking and sounding very happy and she told Jo that things between her and George were proving to be amazing. So amazing, in fact, that she even dropped the L-word into the conversation a couple of times. Jo was impressed – and a good bit envious, irrespective of whether she believed in love or not.

'Good for you, Vic. I'm really happy for you. And do you get the impression George feels the same way about you?'

Victoria nodded. 'Very much so. He's already talking about when and where we can meet up back in London.'

'That's really great. I like him a lot, too. I think this one's a keeper.'

'Dead right. And what about you and your hunky chemist?'

'That's my future brother-in-law you're talking about, you know.' Jo told her the story of the open-air concert and their drenching, and Victoria laughed at the image of the two of them dancing through the downpour. She must have picked up on something in Jo's tone or expression as she didn't waste any time.

'It sounds to me as if this has to be the man for you, Jo. He's handsome, he's great, he's loaded and he makes you laugh. Now all you've got to do is to see what he's like in bed and you're good to go.'

'It's the bed part that's the problem. All he feels for me, if he feels anything at all, is lust.' She caught Victoria's eye. 'Now, don't get me wrong, Vic. I've got nothing against good old-fashioned lust, but sex with him would just mess everything up. It's not just me, it's Angie and Mario as well I have to consider.'

'Yes, I can see how that could get complicated. But surely there's the possibility that he'll have sex with you and realise he loves you and you can ride away into the sunset together, happily ever after.'

Jo shook her head. 'He made it quite clear to me that his other girls all start out with that idea in their heads and it all comes to nothing. I may look daft, but I'm not that daft. No, I'm afraid the only solution is the one we've come to. We'll just be friends.'

Just at that moment, her phone rang. She picked it up, looked at the caller ID and glanced up at Victoria.

'Guess who? Hi, Corrado, how are you?'

'Fine, thanks, and dry again. No ill effects from your soaking?'

'No. I had to dry my passport and banknotes with the hair dryer, but they're fine and, remarkably, as you can hear, my phone still works.'

'Great. I was wondering about tonight. You've got a drinks thing, haven't you? How long's it going to last? Would you like to have dinner with me afterwards?'

Just friends or not, Jo's heart gave a little leap. She had been hoping to see him again. After all, she was off back to London in just two days' time.

'Supposedly six to eight. After that I'll be free and I'd love to see you, but I really mustn't have another big meal.'

'Well, how about this for an idea? I said I'd like to show you my house; you know, the one on the Appia Antica. Why don't I come and pick you up at eight and we can have a light snack back there?'

Jo's subconscious, which had been behaving itself so far today, suddenly presented her with an image of herself dressed in a stunning and very revealing long black evening dress, her hair piled up on her head like a Hollywood diva, standing by his dinner table, reaching out her arms towards him as he walked over to her with a smile on his face and love in his heart. As his fingers ran up her bare arms and flicked the thin straps of her dress off her shoulders, his lips pressed gently against...

'Oh, God...'

'Is something wrong, Jo?' His voice on the phone sounded worried and, from the expression on her face, so was Victoria.

'Um, no, I just dropped something.' Jo deliberately refused to meet Victoria's eye as she thanked her lucky stars that this wasn't a video call because her cheeks were burning redder than the tomatoes in her sandwich. 'Um, yes, that sounds great, Corrado, thanks, but I could take a taxi. There's no need for you to come and collect me.'

'It's not a problem. See you at your hotel at eight. Don't worry if you're delayed. I'll wait.'

As he rang off, Jo dropped the phone back on the table and braced herself to meet Victoria's eye.

'He's invited me to his house for dinner tonight.'

Comprehension dawned on her friend's face. 'I see. So just the two of you, alone in a house with lots of beds.' She grinned across the table. 'Well, if nothing else, it'll be a good test of your willpower.'

'No, not completely alone. The dog'll be there.'

'Oh well, that's all right then. No problem.' Victoria's grin had just broadened.

Jo gritted her teeth. Today was Thursday and she was going home on Saturday. That meant she had another day and a half to get through – a day and a half to prove to her limbic system that she was more than just a slave to her animal instincts. Victoria was right. It wasn't going to be easy.

However, before Jo's dinner date, she found she had another daunting, and very unwelcome, experience waiting for her. At five o'clock as she waded through the crowd of other delegates hurrying towards the exit of the conference centre to go back and change in readiness for the evening's events, she was suddenly confronted by none other than Markus standing outside on the pavement barely a dozen paces ahead of her. As she spotted him, so she saw his eyes alight upon her. As they did so, a broad smile appeared on his face and he raised his hand in greeting.

Jo's first reaction was to stop, and all her instincts were telling her to go back into the hall and hide, but no sooner had this thought occurred to her than she realised this would only delay the inevitable. As far as she knew, this door was the only way out and all he had to do was to wait. What on earth could she do? Then, as she stood there, racking her brains for a solution to her dilemma, she spotted a friendly face on top of a very tall body. It was Ricky coming up behind her and this gave her an idea. She reached out and caught hold of his arm as he reached her.

'Hi, Jo. Is something wrong? You look as if you've seen a ghost.'

'Something like that. Listen, Ricky, can you do me a big favour?'

'Sure. Anything.'

'Can you be my boyfriend for a couple of minutes?'

He looked puzzled, but amused. 'Well, you could never be accused of going for long relationships. A couple of minutes? Wow, you're some maneater.'

'It's a long story. I'll tell you later. For now, just play the part of my boyfriend.' She managed a weak smile. 'We're very much in love, by the way.'

'But of course.' Without batting an eyelid, he stepped forward, caught hold of her and hugged her tightly to him. 'Darling, how wonderful you look tonight.' He put on an exaggerated English accent and sounded like Noel Coward. Jo had a sudden urge to giggle in spite of her predicament.

'Thank you, darling. You say the sweetest things. Now, let's go outside, shall we?' Lowering her voice, she whispered surreptitiously. 'The guy by the door is an arsehole.'

'Of course, darling, what else?'

Ricky was definitely entering into the spirit of the charade now. He stretched an affectionate arm around her shoulders and together they headed for the door. As they stepped out into the warm Roman evening, Markus took a step towards them. He was still smiling, but he clearly hadn't been expecting to see Jo in the arms of another man, particularly not one who was about six foot six.

'Jo, how lovely to see you again.'

'Markus, fancy meeting you here.' Jo was well aware it sounded corny, but she had never been terribly good at improv. 'What brings you to Rome?' She gave Ricky's hand a little squeeze.

'Business. Maybe you didn't get my texts?'

'I'm afraid my phone got soaked and it's still drying out. I just hope it still works.' As if suddenly remembering, she pointed towards Ricky with her free hand while ostentatiously hugging him tightly with the other. 'Sorry, I should have introduced you. This is Richard. He's been in the US and he's just come back.'

'Ah, right, I see.' She saw Markus weigh up the evidence before him and come to the inevitable conclusion. 'Well, I thought I'd just drop by to say hello. Now, I'd better leave you to it. I hope you enjoy your stay in Rome.'

And with that, he turned away and left.

'So, darling, where are we going now? Back to our love nest or somewhere even more exciting?' Ricky sounded highly amused. Jo gave him a real hug and reached up on tiptoe to give him a peck on the cheek.

'Ricky, you were amazing.'

'That's what my wife tells me.' He was grinning. 'Well, sometimes.'

'And she's right. Look, I've got to shoot off now, but I'll explain it all to you at the cocktail party. But really and truly thank you. You got me out of a hole.'

'Pleased to have been of service, Jo. See you later.'

The drinks party took place in the main lobby of the conference centre and it was packed. Jo easily located Ricky looming above the crowd and gave him the background to their encounter with Markus. She saw him shake his head sadly.

'Just as well I didn't know that before or I wouldn't have been so nice to him. You were dead right about him being an asshole.' He gave her a little smile and a mock bow of the head. 'On behalf of the fifty point four percent of the population of this planet with male chromosomes, I would ask you to accept my apologies. We aren't all like that asshole.'

Jo grinned back at him. 'And on behalf of the forty nine point six percent of the population of this planet with female chromosomes, I accept your apology. Thank you.' She clinked her glass of Prosecco against his bottle of beer. 'So, what now? Straight back to California?'

'Pretty much, with a couple of stopovers. I've been away for almost a month now. The kids won't recognise me if I stay away any longer.'

Jo got him to produce some photos of his family. He had a very pretty and surprisingly petite wife, three boys and a baby girl and an attractive weatherboard house with palm trees in the garden. They made a great, happy family and she was pleased for him, and more than a little bit envious. As she had told Victoria, maybe the time was coming to settle down herself. The only problem was where to find a suitable partner. And now that Corrado had provided her with a tantalising glimpse of what the complete package might look like, she knew it wasn't going to be easy. And she wasn't going to settle for second best.

She did the rounds of the delegates, shaking hands, exchanging business cards and receiving a surprising number of kisses from male and female delegates alike. There was a relaxed, end-of-term atmosphere and she was delighted to find she appeared to have been accepted into this gathering of scientists far more illustrious than she was. Professor Dietrich came along to greet her and the old lady surprised Jo by adding her own kisses to her cheeks.

'Thank you so much for your help, Joanne. You did me a real favour and you did it beautifully. I look forward to seeing you at future conferences. I must make sure I tell Ronald how well you did.'

Jo blushed and thanked her warmly. At least, she told herself as the great lady walked off, even if her love life wasn't exactly prospering, her career definitely hadn't been harmed by this week in Rome.

She ducked out of the party at a quarter to eight, which just gave her enough time to rush back to the hotel and change out of her heels. Maybe she and Corrado could do a bit of moth-hunting later on. After all, they wouldn't be doing anything else…

When she came back out again, she found Corrado waiting with the Range Rover and the dog. This time Daisy was out of the car and sitting obediently at his side. When she spotted Jo, she jumped to her feet and wagged her tail so hard the whole rear half of her body wagged with it, but she obeyed the command to wait until Jo crossed the road towards her.

'*Ciao*, Daisy. And it's good to see you too.'

Jo bent down to make a fuss of the dog before straightening up and smiling at Corrado. He was wearing shorts and a Harley Davidson T-shirt and he looked, unsurprisingly, stunning. She reached up and kissed him on the cheeks, studiously avoiding the messages her amygdala was signalling to the rest of her brain.

'*Ciao, amico mio.*'

'*Ciao, amica mia.*' He gave her a welcoming smile that reached deep inside her. 'Wow, I haven't seen you with your hair up before. You look beautiful.'

'I'm afraid I'm a bit overdressed. I could pop back into the hotel and slip on my shorts if you like.'

'You've got to be kidding. That dress is perfect.'

Jo took a deep breath and assumed a nonchalance she didn't feel. 'Well, if you're sure. So, we're off to the Appian Way again?'

'If that suits you?' He registered her nod of the head. 'You said you didn't want a big meal and I've taken you at your word. I've just got some cheese and a few other bits and pieces.'

'That sounds perfect.'

When they got to his house, she quickly discovered that the 'few other bits and pieces' covered virtually the whole table top. Apart from seven types of cheese, there were artichoke hearts, sundried tomatoes and huge green olives in olive oil, a board loaded with ham, salami and sausage and a mixed salad with every conceivable ingredient in it. There was smoked salmon on squares of toast, little kebabs of grilled chicken in a spicy tomato-based sauce and even spicier meatballs. Altogether, there was enough food there to feed a very hungry family. Two or three times.

'Wow, Corrado, are you fattening me up for Christmas?'

'You don't need to eat it all. It's all stuff that'll keep.' He grinned at her. 'This way, I've got my next few days' meals already prepared, so that frees me up.'

He told her all about the beautiful old house which dated back three hundred years, and pointed out a number of larger sculpted stones set in the walls, that had clearly been scavenged from older, almost certainly Roman buildings. The floors were delightful old terracotta tiles, worn down by the passage of countless feet over the centuries. The ceilings downstairs were vaulted, made of handsome old bricks and supported by tree trunks. He didn't offer to take her upstairs and, on reflection, Jo felt relieved; Victoria's words to her about willpower came to mind and she knew full well there was only so much of it she could muster. It was an amazing place and Jo fell instantly in love with it. She even told him so.

'Now, don't take this the wrong way, Corrado, but I think I've fallen in love with your house. It's the only way to describe how I feel about it, but this clearly can't be lust.' She grinned at him. 'I mean, I like the house, but I don't want to bear its children.'

'It's all right. You're allowed to use the word. I do it myself. I *love* the banana ice cream from along the road, for example. I *love* cool, crisp autumn days, I *love* sailing out to Ponza and the Pontine islands. I love all those things. It's just the whole emotional relationship thing that leaves me cold.'

It was another very warm night and Jo could have questioned his choice of idiom, but she thought it better

to move the conversation away from such potentially troubled waters.

'Well, however I say it, I think it's a spectacularly
wonderful house.'

'I'm very glad you like it. I tell you what, let's leave the
food for ten minutes and go out and see the garden. The
sun hasn't disappeared quite yet. You never know, we may
even be able to find you a butterfly or two.'

She grabbed her phone out of her bag, but then paused,
pointing at the table covered with the food he had just
removed from the fridge.

'Is it all right to leave this? Daisy won't steal food, will
she?'

Corrado shook his head. 'Absolutely not. There aren't
many rules in this house, but that's one she has learnt and
which she obeys.' He glanced down at the dog and ruffled
her ears. 'You're not a bad old dog, really, are you?'

'But you don't love her?'

'Oh, all right, I suppose if I can tell you I love ice cream,
it won't hurt to say I love my dog.' He caught her eye and
smiled. 'Love me, love my dog, as the saying goes.'

'Well, I definitely love your dog.' Concerned at the
direction the conversation was taking once again, she
turned away from the table and headed for French
windows set into a wonderful stone arch in the far wall
of the huge open-plan living room. 'Is this the way out?'

Corrado and Daisy led her out into the garden and she
was immediately hit by a cocktail of scents emanating from
flowers, bushes and Mediterranean herbs. Strongest of all
was lavender, but as they walked, she caught rosemary,
roses and wisteria in the evening air. As he had said, the
top third of the sun's orb was still just visible above the red

horizon and it was light enough to see what a wonderful garden he had. There were palms, fruit trees and vines, as well as a delightful swimming pool that looked as if it has been hewn out of solid rock. It even had a little waterfall feeding it. This, even more than the Range Rover and his wonderful stone villa, brought home to Jo that she was in the presence of somebody who inhabited a very different world from hers; a world where money was no problem. For a moment, the thought of money gave her a vivid flashback of Markus's Mercedes, the floating restaurant on the Thames and the two-hundred-pound bottle of wine. Somehow, seeing the luxury of Corrado's home made it a bit easier to control the baser urges coming from her brain on this sultry Roman night. As she had already told herself a hundred times this week, nothing must ever happen between them.

Luckily, she wasn't given much time for further reflection as she spotted a black and white shape settled on a huge buddleia bush. It wasn't the elusive Purple Emperor, but nevertheless she was delighted to find it was yet another very unusual butterfly she had been hoping to see. She beckoned Corrado over and pointed out how unusual it was. It wasn't the fact that it was quite a big butterfly with fan-shaped wings, nor the fact that it had appealing zebra stripe markings that made it special. She glanced up at Corrado and whispered, 'Have you seen one of these before?'

He shook his head. 'No, it's a new one for me.'

'Well, watch this. Hang on, I'll video it.'

She took a couple of photos and then switched the camera to 'video'. Once she was ready, she whispered to him again.

'Very gently, brush your fingers close to it so it flies off. Go on.'

He did as instructed and, sure enough, the butterfly took flight. She captured it as it did so and then turned the lens on Corrado's face. He was looking perplexed and she laughed.

'It flew off backwards...' He looked straight at her and shook his head. 'I've never seen anything like that before.'

Jo stopped filming and explained.

'No, it just looked as if it was flying backwards. *Iphiclides podalirius* is its Latin name. In Britain it's called the Scarce Swallowtail, but I don't know if it's got a common name over here. This butterfly has markings like a head where its rear really is and vice versa, and the long tails at the ends of the wings look like proboscises. It's very clever, when you think about it. As a predator pounces, it gets a real surprise to see its prey fly off in the opposite direction to what it was expecting.' She gave him a big smile. 'Nature's amazing, isn't it?'

So was dinner. The food was excellent and his company equally so. They chatted about everything from conservation to chemistry, from shopping to sailing and she thanked him again for all the information he had given her on replacements for plastics. He told her about his yacht that he kept down on the coast and showed her a couple of photos. It looked fabulous. He told her a lot more about himself and his business, his interests and his life, and she did the same, finally finding herself recounting the circumstances leading to her break up with Christian.

'I feel so very stupid, looking back on it. I genuinely thought everything was going fine between us.' She caught his eye and shrugged. 'It had been four years and I was even starting to think about wedding dresses and that sort of thing. And all the time, he was planning on dumping me for another woman. Well, maybe not all the time, but certainly towards the end.'

'So, when you told me you'd been in love, it was with this guy?'

'That's right. And he kept telling me he loved me, too, almost to the very last day, which I now know it was all a pack of lies. That's why I'm coming round to thinking that you might have a point when you say this love thing's all an illusion, or a delusion.'

'I'm really sorry for you, Jo. I can see how badly it must have hurt you.' He paused for a moment. 'To be totally honest, that's the other reason I refuse to buy into the whole everlasting love thing. If films, plays or books teach us anything, it's that love almost always leads to tears. Why should I expose myself to the risk of getting kicked in the metaphorical teeth when I can be just as happy without getting involved?'

Jo took a big mouthful of ice-cold mineral water. 'So, you're not a fan of the whole "better to have loved and lost, than never to have loved at all" thing?'

'Not me. Tennyson was a great poet, but I disagree with him about that.'

Jo nodded sadly. Maybe Corrado was right. Maybe she was right. Maybe the happy smile on Victoria's face this week was nothing more than a reflex reaction to having sex. Statistically, it was more likely than not that she and George wouldn't end up together for life, so there was most probably heartbreak ahead for both of them. And after her experience with Christian, Jo wouldn't wish that on anyone.

Her thoughts were interrupted by a movement and a low-pitched whine from under the table. Corrado interpreted for her.

'That's Daisy telling me she wants to go out for a pee. Do you feel like a short walk and then I'll drop you back into town?'

'Absolutely. I'm just sorry to make you drive again. Why don't we call a taxi to take me back?'

Her subconscious helpfully pointed out to her that the other solution would be for her to spend the night here with him, but she resolutely stamped all over it. It wasn't going to happen. It mustn't happen.

'Nonsense, I'm happy to do it. In fact, I'll take the Fiat and spend the night in town. Just remind me to put the leftovers in the fridge first.'

They walked down the drive and along the Appian Way. Dusk had fallen by now and it was remarkably quiet, apart from an occasional aircraft heading for Rome's other airport, Ciampino, to the south of them. As her eyes adjusted to the dark, she saw stars twinkling up above and hardly a single light anywhere around, although the orange glow in the sky behind them reminded her of the proximity of the city. She reached across and caught hold of his arm for support on the rough cobbles and he made no objection.

They walked for about ten minutes before turning back. The black dog had a spooky habit of disappearing from sight, blending into the darkness, only to reappear from a totally different direction, her eyes glowing green in the starlight. A handful of fireflies also appeared and danced around them. It was a magical evening and she was happier than she had been at any time this year. As they returned to the house, she felt she should tell him.

'Corrado, I just wanted to say thank you for everything. I don't just mean your incredible generosity and for devoting so much time to looking after me. Being here this week has been the best thing that's happened to me for ages, years, and it's down to you. I'm so very glad to be your friend.' She was still holding onto his arm so she gave it a squeeze. 'Thank you. Very much.'

'You're very welcome, Jo. I just hope you come back and see me again before too long.'

'Of course I will. And there's always Mario and Angie's wedding coming up, isn't there?' She had a sudden idea. 'I know! What're you doing tomorrow night?'

'Nothing special, why?'

'Right, hang on a sec.'

She reached for her phone and called Angie.

'Hi, Angie. Are you and Mario free tomorrow night?'

'Yes, why?'

'As a little thank you to Mario and you, I'd like to take you both out to dinner along with Corrado. No, no objections, I know a little pizzeria not far from Corrado's flat. It's called *l'Aragosta* and the pizzas are really good. And it's not too expensive. Is that okay with you? But, my treat, all right?'

Jo had to argue with her sister for another couple of minutes but she finally got an agreement out of her. Putting the phone away, she returned her attention to Corrado.

'So, have we got a deal?'

'There's no need for you to do this, Jo. Yes, I know *l'Aragosta* and you're right about the pizza there. Really good.' As they walked in through the entry archway and up the gravel drive towards the house, he reluctantly agreed. 'You're on my turf here in Rome. I should be paying, but if you insist, then I accept with thanks.'

Jo helped him put the food away before they went out to the little car. By the time they got to her hotel, she was feeling pleasantly sleepy and even the feel of his lips on her cheeks as they said goodnight to each other didn't wake her up too much.

'Thanks for everything, Corrado.'

'I'm the one who should be doing the thanking. I enjoy being with you. A lot.'

'Me too. Goodnight. See you tomorrow.' She gave him a smile, patted the dog and then went up to her room.

It had been a lovely night. And the good news, she told herself, was that she had only one more day to go before her overtaxed willpower could be allowed a well-earned rest.

The bad news, of course, was that this would mean separation from Corrado.

Chapter 11

Friday morning at the conference passed quickly, ending up with a plenary session and the adoption of a number of proposals to be transmitted to governments at the highest level. Just how seriously these would be taken was, of course, anybody's guess. Governments hungry for re-election every five years were mostly far more interested in short-term political gain than the long-term survival of the planet. As a result, by the end, Jo, like most of the delegates who filed out of the hall with her, was feeling a bit depressed at the short-sightedness of their political leaders. Even a hug from Ricky and an invitation to California didn't cheer her up as much as it should have done. Added to this was the knowledge that she was going to meet her ex in less than two hours' time. As a result, Jo was feeling a bit low as she walked back to the hotel at half past one.

She went up to her room and changed into shorts, T-shirt and sandals and went for a long walk to clear her head. Angie had told her about the Rome craft festival down by the river Tiber, so she headed there first. From Ponte St-Angelo all the way along the river bank to Ponte Cavour were artisan stands selling everything from olive oil and vinegar to purses, bags, ceramics, leather goods and bracelets. She bought her mother a chopping board made of olive wood and, on an impulse, she bought a tea towel depicting statues of muscular Roman gods in various states of undress for Kevin and Justin, her lovely neighbours back in London.

As she walked around, she tasted little samples of pecorino cheese and buffalo mozzarella, spicy sausage and smoked ham, dried fruits, different breads, biscuits and sweets. As a result, she felt no need to stop and have lunch, not least as she knew the dimensions of the pizza that awaited her that night. The thought of the evening to come reminded her that this would be her last sight of Corrado for months, and her overriding sense was one of regret: regret for what might have been but could never be. Doing her best to stay positive, she reflected that this would also be her last chance to see her good friend, Daisy, but in order to do this she realised she needed to book a table outside the restaurant as she imagined the Labrador wouldn't be allowed inside, much as she would love to follow her nose in there.

With the help of the little map of Rome she had got from the hotel, Jo managed to navigate her way through the maze of little streets as far as the pizzeria and it was the work of a moment to book a table outside on the pavement for four people plus a dog for seven thirty that evening. Although her flight home the next day wasn't as early as last time, she knew she would have to be up and ready to leave the hotel by seven o'clock next morning, so a late night probably wasn't the best idea. She texted the time to Angie as well as to Corrado, adding in her message to him that he really had to bring the dog.

By this time, it was almost three o'clock and her reunion with Christian was fast approaching. She had spent most of yesterday and all this morning regretting having agreed to see him again. Although, as she had told Angie, part of her wanted to show him how happy she was without him, the fact of the matter was that she wasn't really that happy. Yes, she felt quite sure she was over him now, but only at the expense of being alone. The more she thought about it, the more she realised that this week in Rome with Corrado had been so magical that deep down she knew life back in London would feel very flat in comparison. Still, she told herself, Christian didn't need to know that.

She got to the fountain in Piazza Navona at five to three and it came as no surprise to her to have to wait almost twenty minutes before she spotted the tall, elegant figure of her ex. He strode across the crowded square towards her as if he was still on the catwalk. He never walked anywhere like a normal person, and she distinctly saw three or four women do a double take as they recognised him. One even took his photo as he strode past. Jo sighed to herself as a host of uncomfortable memories came crowding back. He came up to her and held out his arms to hug her. She took a step back.

'Hello, Christian.'

He stopped, registering the fact that she was not, after all, going to fall into his arms and dropped his hands to his sides.

'Hello, Jo. How are you?'

'I'm fine, thanks.'

'You're looking good.'

Inevitably, the first thing to cross his mind had to be her appearance. To him and his world, looks were everything. Either by accident or design he was standing facing the sun and she studied him for a few moments before replying. He was still the same wildly handsome man she had lived with for four years. His hair was a good deal longer than the last time she had seen him, his skin was delicately tanned a very light honey colour and she felt pretty sure this had not been achieved by exposure to the damaging rays of the sun. Whether it was spray tan or basting and roasting in a tanning salon was difficult to tell, but he looked good all the same. However, she deliberately didn't return the compliment.

'Any particular reason for your wanting to meet up?' She wanted to make it clear that this had been his idea, not hers.

'Not really. I was just so surprised to see you on TV, I had to get in touch. Shall we go and sit down?'

Jo led him across to the same cafe where she and Corrado had sat that very first day she had met him. As they took their seats, she found herself drawing comparisons between the two men. As far as classic good looks were concerned, Christian was probably ahead by a point or two, but as far as everything else was concerned, he wasn't even in the same league. Yet again, Jo gave a surreptitious sigh for what might have been with her soon-to-be brother-in-law.

'What can I get you?'

Christian was clearly on his best behaviour and Jo found herself wondering yet again if he had an ulterior motive for wanting to meet up.

'Just a sparkling mineral water, please. It's so hot.'

'I know. I'll have the same. The humidity the other night played havoc with my hair. Yours is looking good, though. It's longer than I remember.'

'That's because I haven't had time to go to the hair-dressers. I've got a new job and I'm working all hours.'

Reluctantly, she told him about her new position at the charity as the waiter brought them their drinks. In return, he told her about his career, which appeared to be going from strength to strength. He recited a list of cities, from New York to Prague, where he had been over the past five months and she was impressed. Things were looking good for him. But that wasn't all.

'And, of course, my big news is that I'm engaged.'

Jo blinked. She had been expecting pretty much anything, from an appeal for money to an attempt to win her back, but this?

'Really? To your Icelandic lady?' She was still trying to digest what he had just said.

She saw him flick his fingers through his fringe dismissively and, for a moment, she even managed to feel sorry for six-foot Helga. It was a gesture she recognised so well. It was his way of indicating that something no longer interested him; be it the remains of the food on his plate, a half-read magazine, or a person.

'That all ended almost immediately.' He shook his head. 'Iceland in winter is so dark and cold and boring. You wouldn't believe how boring. No, that didn't last. My fiancée's American. I met her in New York last month.'

'Last month?' Jo was genuinely gobsmacked now. She knew he had a habit of being impetuous, but engaged within a few weeks of meeting somebody? 'And you're already engaged?'

'Yes, amazing, isn't it? We just clicked on all levels.'

'But that's…' For a moment she felt like telling him he was crazy, but then it occurred to her that maybe he wasn't so silly after all. If he really felt so strongly about this girl, did it matter that they had only known each other for a short while? She had only known Corrado for a matter of days, but she knew that, deep down, she had developed powerful feelings towards him. In her case, she and Corrado knew it couldn't, it mustn't, develop, but Christian didn't have these same constraints. She found herself wondering whether, if things had been different, if the complicated family situation hadn't existed, she, too, might have thrown caution to the winds and declared herself to Corrado. Maybe Christian was doing the right thing after all. She sighed internally.

'And is she a model, too?'

'No, she works for a charity.' He grinned at her over the rim of his water glass. 'Quite a coincidence, isn't it?'

'It certainly is.'

Before she could say more, they were interrupted by an unexpected visitor. Jo spotted a black flash running across the piazza towards them and then the next thing she knew was a cold, wet nose nudging her, while two hairy paws scrabbled at her bare knees as the dog tried to climb onto her lap. She leant forward and caught hold of Daisy's collar, ruffled her ears with her other hand, and set her back down on the ground again.

'Daisy, you shouldn't be running about like this.' She looked back up again and searched for any sign of Corrado, wondering for a moment if Daisy had escaped from home and was running loose. Through the crowds of people, it was impossible to see far, so she stood up to get a better view. For a second, over by the fountain, she spotted a familiar tall figure with light brown hair, but he was almost immediately blocked from view by a trio of seriously overweight tourists walking down the middle of the square eating enormous ice creams. Then, as they strolled slowly by, she heard a piercing whistle. She wasn't the only one. Daisy, who had been standing up on her hind legs, pawing at Jo's belt, dropped back onto all fours and shot off. Jo stood there and watched her go. Within seconds, just as her master had done, the dog disappeared into the anonymity of the crowd.

'Friend of yours?'

Jo sat down again and looked back across the table towards Christian.

'Yes, a very special friend.' As she spoke, she wondered why Corrado hadn't come over to say hello. Of course, the sight of her with another man might have been a bit of a surprise, but as he and she had clearly established that there was nothing between them, he could hardly feel jealous, could he? Had he genuinely not seen her? She was still mulling it over as Christian turned the questioning to her.

'So, what about you, Jo? Have you found yourself somebody else?'

She hesitated, uncertain what to say. She had come here fully intending to tell him she was happy without him, even if she wasn't involved with anyone else. In the light of his news, she knew that was going to sound a bit pathetic, so she improvised.

'It's none of your business, Christian, but, yes, I've moved on.' This, she felt, was an acceptable white lie. After all, she had been promoted at work and had found some new friends – one in particular – over here in Rome.

He looked almost relieved. 'And who is he? An Italian, maybe?'

'Maybe.'

'Not the owner of the dog by any chance?' Something must have shown on her face as he nodded. 'Well, good for you. I had an Italian girlfriend once. They're fun, and so very good-looking.'

'Was that before you knew me, or while we were together?' This time she saw a guilty shadow cross his face, and her heart hardened. 'Anyway, Christian, I have to go. I wish you and your fiancée well for the future.'

'But we've only just sat down.'

Jo emptied her glass, stood up and opened her purse. She took out a five Euro note and put it on the table.

'This should be enough to pay for my water, even in a place like this. Goodbye, Christian, and good luck with the rest of your life.'

She shook his hand and left him there.

She walked off in the direction the dog had taken, hoping she would run into Daisy again along with Corrado, but to no avail. After a while she came out of the pedestrian zone into a chaotic world of double-parked cars and kamikaze scooter riders. With great care, she crossed the busy road running alongside the river and found herself on a narrow, ancient stone bridge, now off limits to traffic. She stopped and leant on the stone parapet, looking down into the murky brown waters of the Tiber, her head still spinning from Christian's revelation.

In spite of the beauty and antiquity of the Eternal City, she found herself feeling unusually dejected. Everybody was moving on – except her. Christian had already got engaged, her best friend appeared to have found happiness with George, her little sister was getting married, and the only person who had expressed interest in Jo herself was creepy Markus. Worse still, the only man whose touch had ever sent a lightning bolt through her whole body could never be more than a friend to her.

Humphrey Bogart's immortal words in her favourite film, *Casablanca*, came to mind. 'The problems of two little people weren't worth a hill of beans in the greater scheme of things.'

But that didn't help to take away the sense of loneliness that invaded her.

–

By the time evening came, she was feeling a bit better. This was mainly because her solitary walk around Rome had been interrupted at half past five by a text from Victoria.

> George flown back home. Can I stay with
> you again tonight? Fancy a cup of tea? Vic

Jo replied immediately and they agreed to meet in the cafe at the bottom of the Spanish Steps where Jo had seen – and misjudged – Corrado with his friend's heartbroken wife the other day. The expression on Victoria's face when she arrived was bittersweet; not dissimilar from the way Jo herself was feeling.

'Hi Vic, had a good week?'

'I've had a great week, a *really* great week.' Victoria sighed. 'It's just such a pity it had to end.' She slumped down in a seat alongside Jo, protected from the sun by a parasol, although the heat was still intense. 'What about you?'

'Good… no, a lot better than good. It's been wonderful, apart from a couple of incidents. And Rome is such an amazing place.'

'Isn't it just? I've been sightseeing for four full days and there's still heaps left to see. So, incidents? What incidents? Tell Auntie Vic all about it.'

Jo told her about her meeting with Christian this afternoon and his incredible news. Victoria sniffed and shook her head. Clearly this only served to further damn him in her eyes.

'What a moron! How can you get engaged to somebody after barely a week or two? Good luck and good riddance, is what I say.' She shook her head in stupefaction and Jo decided not to mention her reflections about the short space of time she had known Corrado. This was best left unsaid. 'And what else has happened? You said a couple of incidents.'

'I've met Markus.' Jo recounted the story of his sudden appearance outside the conference hall and the success of her stratagem with Ricky the American. This brought a smile to Victoria's face.

'Ricky sounds like a good guy. Pity he lives in America.'

'And the small matter of him being married and having four kids.' Jo returned her smile. 'Anyway, George has gone back to London?'

'Yes, he got a message saying he had to leave immediately, just as we were about to sit down to lunch. I went out to the airport with him and we had a sandwich together while he was waiting for his flight.' Victoria sounded despondent, so Jo did her best to cheer her up.

'But you'll see him again soon?' She and Victoria were on the same flight home at eleven the next morning.

'Yes, indeed. If all goes well, I said I'd cook him a meal tomorrow night.'

Jo felt glad for her and went on to recount what she had been doing this week and all about the time she had spent with Corrado. Her frustration must have shown through. Victoria raised an eyebrow.

'So, you're telling me you're just going to go home and forget about the delectable Corrado?'

'Well, not forget about him, but certainly try to concentrate on thinking of him as just a good friend.'

Victoria looked sceptical. 'People can change, Jo. He can change. How old did you say he is? Thirty-five?' Seeing Jo's nod, she continued. 'He'll mature, he'll change. You can take my word for it.'

'I'd love to think you're right, but nothing he's said or done has indicated that in any shape or form. I'm sure he likes me, maybe likes me a lot, but nothing's ever going to happen between us. No, it's quite clear that he's happy the way he is and that's that. As far as he and I are concerned, he's doing what he thinks is right, which is keeping things all above board, and I agree. We're going to be in-laws and that's the end of it.'

'And you haven't even kissed him?'

'Of course I've kissed him. We're good friends.'

'Jo, I'm talking *kissed*, not pecked on the cheek. Tell me you've at least tried.'

'Well, just once and only for a second. And that was by accident.' She conveniently forgot to mention the kiss she had bestowed upon him after their 'Singin' in the Rain' dash to the hotel. That definitely hadn't been an accident on her part.

'And how did it feel? They say you can tell after just the slightest touch, you know.'

Jo took a big sip of cold water before answering honestly. 'It felt amazing...' Her voice tailed off as she remembered the sensation.

'Oh, Jo.'

At that moment Jo's phone buzzed and she saw she had a message from Corrado himself. It was short and anything but sweet.

> Hi Jo. Very sorry but something's come up and I'm not going to be able to join you for dinner tonight. Thanks a lot for inviting me. Have a good flight home and I hope to see you again some time soon. Corrado.

She passed the phone across to Victoria and did her best to stifle the wave of disappointment that swept over her. It wasn't easy.

'That's a real bummer.' Victoria handed back the phone and squeezed Jo's hand. 'Was it going to be just the two of you? Somewhere romantic?'

Jo answered distantly. 'No, with Angie and Mario, and now you as well if you're free. I invited them to the pizzeria George took us to, as my way of saying thank you.'

'Well, maybe it's for the best if Corrado's not coming after all.' Jo could hear that Victoria was trying hard to sound encouraging. 'From what you've been saying, you've got yourself into an impossible position. I can imagine it's a bit like an open wound that stings every time you see him. This way at least you can enjoy your pizza without raking that all up again. And of course, I'll be there. I'll cheer you up, I promise.'

The pizza was as fabulous as the last time and their table for four was sheltered from the setting sun by tall buildings on both sides of the street, while a little breeze kept the temperature bearable. Mario and Angie didn't appear surprised by Corrado's absence and Jo read sympathy in her sister's eyes. They didn't, however, discuss the possible reasons for it. Victoria did her best to keep her promise to make it a cheerful evening and she succeeded – up to a point. Jo ordered a bottle of Prosecco as well as red wine for the table and probably drank a bit more than she should have done. While this definitely relaxed her, it also made her a bit pensive and a bit glum by the time she and Victoria walked back to the hotel together. It had been fun to be with her sister and Mario, the food had been great, the restaurant lovely, but the elephant in the room – or rather not in the room – had been unavoidable in spite of Victoria's best efforts.

Jo kept on wondering what sort of other commitment had prevented him from coming. Maybe it was a work thing. Her subconscious helpfully reminded her it could also be another woman and Jo made the mistake of suggesting this to Victoria as they walked through the dark streets towards home.

'Don't be so silly, Jo. He wouldn't agree to have dinner with you and then change his mind just for the sake of a bit of nookie.'

'I'm not so sure. From what he told me, his limbic system's all in favour of sex.'

'Limbic system? Jo, I'm an *English* teacher for Christ's sake.'

'Sorry, Vic. It's a brain thing. He told me himself he liked sex.'

'Jo, we all like sex. You too, if you can remember that far back. But he's not the sort of guy who would just blow you off for something like that. I don't know him as well as you, but I'm quite sure about that. I bet you find he's got a proper reason and it isn't just some random girl.'

'I wonder...'

Chapter 12

The flight home the next day was uneventful, apart from Jo nursing a hangover and a deep sense of regret for what might have been. She and Victoria parted company at Earl's Court and Jo travelled on down to her flat south of the river. As she came out of the station it was drizzling and grey, in spite of almost being August, and her sandaled feet were soon damp as she walked the last few hundred metres home. Somehow this matched her mood and she was in a sombre frame of mind as she climbed the stairs to the second floor and rummaged in her bag for her keys. As she did so, the door behind her opened and the smiling face of Kevin appeared, with his partner, Justin, grinning from behind his shoulder.

'Hi, Jo, or should that be *buonasera*?'

She felt a smile on her face for just about the first time today, so she put down her suitcase and went over to give them both a big hug.

'*Buonasera, Kevino e Justino*. How are you both?'

'We're fine. Just a bit bored. Why don't you come in for a cup of tea and tell us all about romantic Rome?'

'Just let me dump my case and I'll be there.'

Jo unlocked her door, collected the pile of junk mail interspersed with a handful of real letters from the doormat and pulled her case into the flat. It was hot and stuffy in here so she went round opening windows to let in some air before digging out the tea towel she had bought for the boys and going across the corridor to see them.

'Come in, come in.'

There was a wonderful smell of baking in their flat which was, as always, spotlessly clean. As usual, she felt a sense of shame that her place, in comparison, looked so permanently untidy.

Kevin appeared at the kitchen door. 'Justin's been making brownies. You arrived at just the right time. Now, come and sit down and tell us all about your adventures.'

Jo spent an hour with them, telling them all about Rome and the conference. She deliberately left out a lot as she knew Kevin was one of the biggest gossips in London. She did, however, tell them Christian's news and they were first predictably shocked, and then supportive.

'It just goes to show the man's off his head.' Kevin caught hold of her hand and gave it a squeeze. 'First he goes off and dumps the most wonderful girl in London.' Jo smiled; Kevin could never be accused of understating things. 'And then he shackles himself to some random woman he hardly knows.' He shook his head ruefully. 'And an American as well.'

'What's wrong with American women?'

'Three thousand miles of ocean for a start. What's he going to do? Move over there?'

'I don't know and I don't care. He's no business of mine any more.' She caught Kevin's eye. 'And I really mean that, Kevin.'

'I really think you do, this time. I'm so glad, sweetheart. Justin and I've been worried about you ever since that totally crazy man – even if he was totally gorgeous – went off and left. Haven't we, Justin?' As usual, he didn't wait for his taciturn partner to respond, although Jo caught a little wink from Justin as Kevin continued. 'But what about you and romance? Surely you must have met a few handsome Roman men, with their togas and their chariots and stuff?'

For a moment, Jo remembered the grooves in the stone slabs of the Appian Way, carved by the passage of countless chariot wheels. This memory was immediately followed by an image of tall, handsome Corrado and his loveable Labrador. The picture was so vivid it was almost as if they were in the room with her. But of course, her subconscious reminded her, they were a thousand miles away. Kevin, who never missed a thing, immediately picked up on her facial expression.

'Don't tell me you lost him.'

'Lost who?'

'I can see it now.' Kevin had always had a theatrical bent. 'There you are, standing by the Trevi Fountain, staring into the water, when a shadow falls across you and a Roman Adonis lightly touches your hand.'

'Adonis was Greek, Kevin.'

'Whatever… You turn towards him and it's love at first sight. One look into those deep brown eyes and you're hooked, forever hooked.' He took a sip of his tea. 'But then it all went tits up. How sad.'

Jo giggled into her mouthful of chocolate brownie and almost choked. It was a while before she could respond. 'Good try, Kevin. I did indeed go to the Trevi Fountain with a very handsome man, but he's my future brother-in-law. And he's got blue eyes.'

'How exotic! A blue-eyed Roman. Tell us all about your future brother-in-law. He sounds wonderful.'

Gradually Jo let Kevin wheedle more details out of her until she finally revealed Corrado's reservations as far as human emotions were concerned.

'How awful for you, sweetheart! There you are, totally smitten with him and he turns round and tells you he only wants to jump into bed with you.'

'That's definitely not what he said. He never so much as mentioned anything about wanting to jump into bed with me. And who says I'm smitten? Besides, who, apart from Jane Austen's heroines, gets smitten anyway?'

'We all do, darling, we all do.' To make his point, Kevin leant across and pecked Justin on the cheek. 'How on earth he can tell you he doesn't believe in love is beyond me. And with you, of all people…!'

'Well, he did. He's a scientist and he just doesn't believe in all that stuff.' She caught Kevin's eye. 'I'm a scientist, too, and I think he may have a point.'

To her surprise, Kevin burst out laughing. 'My dear girl, you really are a hoot, you know.'

'What's so funny?'

'Of course love exists. You of all people should know that, seeing as you're quite clearly in love with your Roman.'

'I'm what?' Jo was genuinely amazed. 'What on earth makes you think that?'

'It's not me who's doing the thinking, princess; it's you. It's as plain as the nose on your face. Just the way you talk about him, the look in those pale blue eyes of yours; I can tell. Anybody could tell. You're smitten all right.' Without giving Jo time to protest, he carried on. 'So, what are you going to do about it?'

'What can I do? Apart from anything else, he's there and I'm here. Besides, like I told you, whether I do or don't, he doesn't believe in all that stuff.'

'Says who?'

'Says him. He told me as much to my face.'

'Just you wait. When's the last time you saw him?'

'Thursday night at 10.42.' Catching his eye, she hastened to explain. 'There was a digital clock in the hotel lobby. I noticed it as I was waiting for the lift, that's all.'

'Yeah, right… And what's the last thing he said to you?'

'His exact words were, "I enjoy being with you. A lot."' This wasn't a particularly amazing feat of memory as she had been turning his words over in her head again and again ever since hearing them.

'What more do you want? He can hardly come right out and declare his undying love, seeing as the two of you have decided it doesn't exist. I reckon this is as good as it gets.'

'Name me one Shakespeare play with those words in it. Or a sonnet or a poem by one of the great romantic poets. Or even a fricking Valentine's card! It's no more than a statement of fact by one friend to another.' She got to her feet, suddenly conscious that the last time she had been to the toilet had been in Rome. 'That's all it is, just like me talking to you. Thanks, Kevin. Thanks, Justin. The tea was just what I needed and the brownies were delicious. *I enjoy being with you. A lot.* See? Friend to friend.'

As she picked up her bag, she remembered the tea towel.

'Here's a little souvenir for you. I thought of you while I was away. I'm sure you'll be very interested in Roman men.'

'Not half as interested as you are, princess.'

–

Jo spent Sunday doing her washing, writing a detailed report of the conference for Ronald – she knew full well he would be expecting one – and doing her best not to think of Corrado. She went out to the supermarket and then came back home and filled the fridge. After that, she phoned her parents and arranged to go and see them next weekend. If the weather was fine, she and her mum would go riding again, but, for now, the sky was still overcast and Jo's mood remained subdued.

She went into work on Monday morning with a sense of relief, knowing it would provide plenty to occupy her mind. She wasn't wrong. Not only had her own work accumulated in her absence, but she found that Melissa had passed a heap of Ronald's stuff on to her as well. As a result, she was still there at eight o'clock that evening, all alone in the office, ploughing slowly through it. Then, just as she was starting to think about calling it a day, she got a text message and her whole mood changed.

> Hi Jo. Apologies again for not coming on Friday night. It was complicated. I hope you had a good trip home and that you have happy memories of Rome. Daisy keeps getting up and sniffing about. I think she's looking for you. We both miss you. C

We both miss you. These four words sent a thrill throughout Jo's whole body. On an impulse, she pulled out her phone and swiped through her photos until she came to the ten seconds of video of the black and white butterfly in his garden. She played it as the butterfly flew off and then his face appeared on the screen, looking puzzled.

'It flew off backwards… I've never seen anything like that before.'

The clip ended and she was left with his face filling the screen but, annoyingly, with the *Play* arrow bang in the middle, obscuring all but his ears, hair and chin. She tried again, but ended up playing it over and over again more times that she would have been prepared to admit, before realising all she had to do was to pause the video. This image of his face helped a bit, but she would have preferred his normal expression, rather than the befuddled look brought about by the backwards-flying butterfly. Finally, she dropped the phone back into her bag, turned her computer off for the night and headed home.

Outside it had turned warmer and she was pleased to see that the pavements had all dried up. Maybe the weather was on the turn at last. She barely registered the trip on the underground, travelling on autopilot, lost in her thoughts. It was only as she walked out of the station at the other end that she realised she was starving. She hadn't stopped for lunch and her body was definitely telling her it was time for food. As soon as she got back home, she pulled a pizza out of the fridge and slipped it into the microwave. She knew it wouldn't be a patch on the ones she had eaten in Rome, but it would do the job. On an impulse, she opened a bottle of red wine and poured herself a glass.

So Corrado was missing her… Or at least, her subconscious hastened to point out, he *said* he was missing her. That wasn't necessarily the same thing. Maybe he was only being polite. Nevertheless, Jo thought to herself as she sipped the wine, he had taken the time to contact her, so that meant he had been thinking about her. Surely that was a good sign. As the pizza heated up, she wrote a reply.

> Hi Corrado. Great to hear from you. Do
> please give Daisy a big cuddle from me. Pity
> about Friday night. This means I still owe you
> a pizza. I had a wonderful time in Rome and
> a lot of it was thanks to you. I miss you too.
> Jo.

She debated for a moment whether to insert a little 'x' before her name, but decided against it. A little 'x' implied love and he had made his position on that subject totally clear. She gave a little sigh and pressed Send.

Chapter 13

By the time the weekend arrived, Jo was glad to get out of London. The sun had finally appeared now that August was upon them and the city had warmed up all too quickly. Her flat, the trains, the buses, the offices themselves were like saunas and she felt sure she had sweated off the few pounds she might have put on in Italy by the time Saturday came.

Corrado's message had cheered her greatly – even if it was cheer tempered by regret – and her workload ensured that, during the daytime at least, she had little time for introspection or melancholy. On Wednesday, she was summoned to the hospital to speak to Ronald. She found him grumpier than usual and she had to struggle hard to prevent herself from crowning him with the bag of grapes she had brought as he lay there complaining. She did her best to remember that he had been stuck here on his back for several weeks now and he must be getting very bored, as well as uncomfortable. He took her conference report without comment and read it in silence. Finally, just as she was seriously considering going out to get a cup of coffee, he raised his head.

'So, it sounds as though my paper went down well enough, even though I wasn't the one giving it.'

'It went down very well, Ronald. And a number of delegates referred to it at the final plenary session. I think Professor Dietrich and her team are going to incorporate most, if not all, of it in their proposals to the UN committee on Climate Change next month.'

'Good, good.' Jo relaxed a bit. 'What are you working on now?'

'I'm just working my way through the stuff that's accumulated while you've been off and I've been in Rome.' It had already occurred to her that even from a horizontal position he still could have dealt with a good deal of it, rather than leaving it to her, but it hadn't come as a surprise that he preferred to take it easy, knowing she would handle it when she came back.

'Any new ideas come to you in Rome? Did anything you heard from the other speakers excite you?'

By now, Jo knew him well enough to be cagey. In fact, a couple of things she had heard had really appealed to her, but she remembered Ricky's nickname for Ronald of the 'Pirate' and decided to keep her cards close to her chest for now. She gave him a vague reply and endured another half hour of interrogation before being dismissed.

One of the things that had genuinely excited her in Rome had been a dramatic new proposal for disposing of plastic waste, transforming the bulk of it into fuel. As more and more plastic detritus was beginning to be removed from the oceans, the next big problem would be how to get rid of it, and she had been formulating a couple of ideas of her own that she thought might be worth pursuing. When she got back to the office, she dug out Ricky's visiting card and sent him an email outlining a few suggestions. She felt sure that he, unlike her boss, wouldn't just steal her ideas.

It was good to go out to Oxford on Saturday. Her parents were delighted to see her and they spent most of the weekend talking. She told them about the conference and then listened to the latest developments for Angie's forthcoming wedding. In the course of the week, her mum and Angie had been having serious telephone discussions, and Jo found that the first decisions had now been taken. The vicar had been contacted and it had been decided that the wedding would take place here in the village in early April next year. As she heard the news, Jo felt a sudden shiver of disappointment. This meant she had another nine months to wait before seeing Corrado again.

Of course, she could always go over before then to spend a bit of time with Angie so as to see him again, but what was the point? Victoria had referred to her relationship – or lack of it – with Corrado as being like an open wound. Why risk enflaming it by deliberately going back and seeing him again? He would still be appealing, but he would still be an unattainable, forbidden fruit. He knew that and she knew that. No, the best thing to do was to hope that absence in this case would not make the heart grow fonder, but rather the opposite. Hopefully, as the weeks and months passed, she would gradually be able to get him out of her head.

She and her mum went riding on Sunday morning and then the three of them went to the pub for a roast lunch. Although high summer, it was still unusually hot for England, and sitting out in the beer garden under a parasol reminded her of her days in Rome. And being reminded of Rome also brought memories of its inhabitants – one in particular. It was almost a relief when her mother brought up the subject.

'Angela told me you spent a lot of time with her future brother-in-law while you were in Rome.'

'Yes, Corrado, he was very kind. He took me out and showed me the sights.' She went on to tell her parents about the glories of the Eternal City, finishing with the open air concert. Her father, surprisingly, was impressed. Normally he stayed well away from her romantic involvements, preferring to leave that area to her mother.

'Sounds like he's got a brain on him, Joanne. And a good bit of culture. I like that in a man.' He glanced across at her and nodded. 'You're an intelligent girl. You need an intelligent partner.'

'He's not my partner, dad, and he never will be.' Even Jo herself could hear that this denial had come out far too quickly. She did her best to explain before her mother joined in. 'He's a very nice man, but we're very different. Besides, he's going to be my brother-in-law.'

'Not that different. You're both very bright and cultured. Angela says he's very handsome and you're a very pretty girl. You could do far worse.' He grinned at her. 'Besides, Angela tells us he's worth a fortune.'

Jo was beginning to wish her little sister had confined her conversations with her parents to matters relating to her own relationship with Mario, but it was too late now. She did a bit more explaining, deliberately doing her best to leave out any mention of Corrado's views on love and sex. She had never discussed sex with her father and she had no intention of starting now.

'It could never work, dad. He's got his business there in Rome – and yes, I gather he's doing really well for himself – and I'm stuck in London.'

'But you're not irrevocably stuck in your present job, are you? By the sound of it, your boss is a source of considerable frustration to you.' As so often was the case, he knew far more of what was going on inside her head than he let on.

'Ronald can be a pain and, of course, you're right: I enjoy my job, but I could change if an opportunity came up. But that's hardly going to be in Rome, is it? Besides, conservation's a fairly small sector and there's not a lot of money in charity work, for obvious reasons. At least I'm reasonably well paid where I am.' She took a mouthful of Chilean red and did her best to change the subject. 'Did I tell you about Mario's house? The pool's amazing.'

Unsurprisingly, her mother failed to take the bait.

'So, what about that man you were telling us about last time you were here? A banker, I think you said he was.'

Jo hadn't thought about Markus for a good few days now and she was almost annoyed to be reminded of him.

'I went out with him a couple of times, but he very definitely wasn't my type. That's all over.' She refrained from going into any detail, hoping her mother would change tack. She did, but in an unwelcome direction.

'Oh, dear, that's a shame. But of course, Angela said the problem with Mario's brother is his attitude to women. You really wouldn't want to get involved with a woman-iser, would you? What was it Angela said? He likes to "play the field".'

Jo gave an inward sigh.

'He's a nice guy, but he's got commitment issues.' This sounded like a safe way of describing him.

'She said he doesn't want to settle down, even though he's in his mid-thirties. Of course, you're going to be thirty yourself very soon.'

'Don't remind me.' Jo took refuge in her wine glass.

'Anyway, Angela said it's such a shame he's the way he is, as the two of you get on so well together.'

'She's right: we do. But he isn't going to change, so let's just drop the subject. It isn't going to happen.'

Her parents must have heard the steel in her tone and the conversation turned to her upcoming birthday. As it would be during the week, she agreed, reluctantly, to come back a week on Sunday for lunch with her mum and dad and a bunch of people she hadn't seen for years, whose average age was probably approaching seventy. Still, it kept her mum happy and it wasn't as if she had anything better to do that weekend.

That evening, as she waited for the train back to London, she phoned Angie. After hearing about her sister's success in a show jumping competition the previous day and congratulating her, she turned the subject to Corrado.

'Angie, do me a favour and try to steer mum away from Corrado next time you're speaking on the phone. Dad's already trying to marry me off to him.'

'I'm sorry, Jo. I suppose it's just because now that I'm getting married, they want you to settle down too.'

'I *am* settled – apart from my pain in the arse of a boss. Anyway, we both know any settling down isn't going to be done with Corrado.' She hesitated. 'Have you seen him recently? How's he doing?'

'He hasn't been about much. I imagine he's been working hard to get everything done before the holidays. The laboratory shuts down for two weeks around the middle of the month. Most everything over here closes down in August. It's so bloody hot!'

'Well, if it helps, it's bloody hot here as well, now that it's finally stopped raining.' She wondered what Corrado was going to do for his holidays. A visit to London, maybe? In spite of herself, she felt a frisson of excitement.

It was misplaced.

'I imagine he'll go off somewhere on his yacht. That's what he did last year.'

An alluring image of Corrado in his swimming shorts on the deck of a luxurious boat, floating on an azure sea, came to Jo's mind, closely followed by the less alluring image of a beautiful Italian girl in a sexy bikini lounging on the deck beside him. She suppressed a snort.

'Well, say hi from me next time you see him.'

'He said the same thing to Mario the other day. Mario says he thinks he's missing you.'

'Well I miss him too, but we both know that's not going anywhere.'

'People can change, Jo.'

'That's what everybody's been telling me.' She spotted the yellow front of her train approaching. 'Anyway, got to go. Here's my train. See you.'

'I'll call you on Thursday to wish you a happy birthday.'

That evening as she checked her emails, she spotted one from Ricky in California. It was very friendly, and highly complimentary of the ideas she had outlined for dealing with plastic waste recovered from the oceans. He promised to look into the feasibility of doing something along the lines she had laid out, but then her eyes were suddenly riveted to his final paragraph.

> I've only just got back to LA and I've been meaning to contact you. On my way home from Europe, I had a four-day stopover in New York and I was invited for lunch with Professor Dietrich. We talked about the Rome conference and it's pretty clear she was very impressed by you. I delicately dropped a few hints about a lot of your paper on plastic waste coming from you, rather than Captain Jack Sparrow, and she appeared to be even more impressed. It may come to nothing, but you never know – you might even get a job offer out of her. She's coming to LA next week and I'll see her again. If you're interested, why don't you send me your résumé and I'll pass it onto her. Couldn't hurt…

Jo was genuinely gobsmacked. Professor Dietrich worked for the United Nations. Jo knew she headed a specialist department dealing with climate change and the idea of being asked to join a team like that was amazing. She was still dreaming when her phone rang. It was Victoria.

'Hi, Jo. We've been visiting George's sister in Dulwich and seeing as that's sort of just down the road, we thought we'd drop in to check on how you are. Are you in the middle of anything?'

Jo assured her she would be delighted to see them and told them to come round. Fifteen minutes later they appeared. Victoria subjected Jo to careful scrutiny.

'Hi, Jo. I'm glad to see you looking cheerful.'

Jo waved them in.

'I'm fine. I've just come back from a day with mum and dad and look what I found on my computer.' She read them the last paragraph of Ricky's email and explained what a big deal it would be to work for the professor.

Victoria, ever observant, was the first to point out what this would mean.

'Where does this Professor Dietrich work?'

'New York.'

'So presumably any job would be in New York as well.'

Jo's brain hadn't zeroed in on that yet. Of course, Victoria was right. She stared blankly at the two of them for a moment.

'Yes, of course. I suppose it would have to be New York.'

'So, do you fancy working in the US? New York's supposed to be a really great city.'

Jo turned it over in her head. She had heard the same about New York. It really did have considerable appeal.

Victoria was still looking at the downside of any possible job offer. 'Of course, I daresay your mum wouldn't be too happy, having just lost one daughter to Italy, if she were to lose the other to even further afield.'

'But it's dead easy and not too expensive to get to New York.' George was encouraging, as always. 'Your parents could go over to see you.' He glanced at Victoria and grinned. 'And so could we.'

'I must admit it appeals a lot. There's just one thing, though…' Unbidden, her Italian elephant had just lumbered into the room.

Victoria wasn't her best friend for nothing. 'What's the problem? Are you thinking about being distanced from a certain hunky Italian by any chance?'

Jo bought herself a bit of time. 'Do you guys want tea?'

She filled the kettle and watched it come to the boil, her mind now firmly on Corrado. Yes, it would take her further away from him, but so what? He was just a future relative after all, nothing more. She filled the teapot and turned round.

'You're right, I *was* thinking of him, and Angie and Mario. But, like you say, they could always come over to New York to visit me. Besides, we're only talking about the vague possibility of a job at this stage. There's a long way to go yet.'

At this moment her annoying subconscious served her up a tantalising image of Corrado lying naked beside her on a big bed in a stylish apartment looking out over Central Park. She was gently running her fingers down his muscular chest to his ribbed stomach, while he…

She almost ran across to the fridge, tore the door open and made a grab for the milk bottle, burying herself in the icy interior to cool her flushed cheeks. As she was still hidden by the door, pretending to look for the chocolate biscuits, she heard Victoria's voice.

'Your friend Ricky has a point, though. It wouldn't do any harm to send him your résumé. "Résumé"? Have you ever asked yourself why the Americans use a French word and we use a Latin abbreviation? Surely we should have a perfectly satisfactory English word for it?'

As her friend let her academic curiosity get the better of her, Jo took a deep breath and ran the cold milk bottle across her cheeks. Refreshed, she emerged from the fridge with the chocolate hobnobs in her other hand, thankfully now minus the bedroom image in her head.

'You sometimes hear 'bio', but that's hardly a completely satisfactory English word. Anyway, yes, I reckon I will send him my whatever-it's-called.'

'And if Professor Whatshername offers you a job, you think you might take it?'

Jo filled the teapot and brought it over to the table, along with the biscuits, the mugs and the milk.

'There's a long way to go before that happens. She might never offer me anything. Ricky only said it was merely a possibility, after all. And then my decision would depend upon what they'd want me to do, and how much they'd be paying me. And I'd need a work permit and all that sort of thing. Green cards are notoriously difficult to obtain.'

'Jo, have you ever considered a career in politics? You've just taken a whole minute to say nothing.'

Jo grinned at her. 'I suppose what I'm trying to say is maybe.' She paused for a few seconds, weighing it up in her head. 'But, on balance, I think I'd be tending more towards a yes than a no. Certainly it would be a great career move and it would get me away from my current boss.'

They all sat down and she distributed the mugs of tea. They chatted for a bit and it soon became clear that Victoria and George were very much a couple now. They looked and sounded very happy together and Jo was delighted for them. Victoria soon brought up another subject.

'It's your birthday this coming Thursday, isn't it, Jo? What are we doing to celebrate?'

'I'm not sure turning thirty deserves celebration. Commiserations, more likely.'

'Thirty's the new twenty-five, Jo. Remember that. Besides, you don't look thirty.'

'I feel thirty. And it'll be all downhill from there on.' She kept her tone light, but it was a substantial milestone after all. 'Mum's bullied me into having lunch with them and a bunch of the neighbours next Sunday, but I suppose I should go out for drinks or something on the day itself. There are half a dozen people at work to invite, plus a few old friends living in London. How are you two fixed on Thursday?'

'George is going to Scotland, but Thursday's good for me.'

Chapter 14

Thursday turned out to be far more enjoyable than Jo had expected. By the time she was leaving for work, the postman had delivered half a dozen birthday cards and when she got to the office, there were more on her desk, along with a load of chocolates from the other girls on her floor and emails from more friends and family. But the most interesting surprise by far was the parcel that arrived just after midday.

Carol from the reception desk delivered it personally.

'Here you go, birthday girl. It's got an 'Urgent' sticker on it so I thought I'd bring it straight up.'

Jo took it from her and was immediately struck by the fact it had come all the way from Italy. While Carol leant against the desk and pretended to admire the view out of the window, Jo opened the parcel and pulled out a further smaller package wrapped in tissue paper and sealed in a plastic bag. On the outside of the bag was the single word, 'Gucci', and she stopped in her tracks, gazing in awe at the world-famous name. She set the bag down very carefully in front of her on the desk and pulled the sheets of tissue paper delicately apart. When she saw what was in there, she caught her breath.

It was a bikini. It was a very light cream colour with a delicate pattern of butterflies of many different colours and species. It was simply delightful and any woman would have been happy to own it, but for somebody with a love of butterflies, it was truly superb. Along with it, there was a white envelope containing a card. Her fingers were shaky with emotion as she slit it open and found a short message from the sender.

A very happy birthday to the most wonderful lepi-
dopterist I know. You are always in my thoughts.
    Corrado (and Daisy)

P.S.: Angie told me what size to buy but if,
for any reason it doesn't fit, there should be
a Gucci shop in London who will swap it.

As she sat there, staring in awe at the present, the words 'You are always in my thoughts' echoed through her head and she felt her eyes begin to sting. The fact that he had remembered her mentioning the Gucci bikinis showed he had been thinking of her maybe as much as she had been thinking of him.

'Wow, Jo, that's what I call a present.'

Jo had forgotten about Carol. She surreptitiously wiped her eyes and looked up. Carol had now been joined by two of the other girls from her floor and they were all ogling the bikini.

'Aren't you going to go and put it on, Jo? Wear it all day? I'd never take it off.' Denise from accounts had always had a cheeky sense of humour.

'Not here, ladies. What would Ronald say?'

'Ronald isn't here. Go on, try it on.'

Jo shook her head and wrapped the bikini up again, slipping it back into its own bag for added protection. She was holding something very precious after all. Seeing the disappointment on the faces around her, she opened the biggest of the boxes of chocolates and passed them round and the crowd grew. It wasn't long before she was faced with the question she had been dreading.

'So, who's it from, then?'

'It's not your oh-so-handsome model man, is it?'

Jo shook her head. 'No, it's not from Christian. You might be surprised to know that in the four years we were together, he never once gave me clothes. That was *his* thing. Anyway, that's all over.'

'So, who's this one? Is he another model?'

Jo grinned and shook her head again. 'No, he's a chemist. And he's just a good friend.'

'Some friend!'

'Can we become friends of his as well, Jo?'

'You lucky thing.'

Jo made sure all the chocolates got eaten and mused about just how lucky she was. It was an absolutely wonderful present, both because it was beautiful in itself, but also because of the thought and effort he had obviously put into finding it. In fact, irrespective of its obvious cost, it appealed to her immensely for that very reason. It was also, her subconscious was quick to point out, a very intimate present and, for once, she didn't disagree. Slipping the bikini into one of her desk drawers, she took the lift down to the ground floor and went out into the remarkably warm sunshine.

She took out her phone and called Victoria, who answered almost immediately.

'Hi, Jo. I was just going to call you. Happy birthday, sweetie.'

Jo gave her the news about the bikini and could hear the excitement in Victoria's voice as she replied.

'Amazing, you lucky, lucky girl. You definitely can pick them. If only George was a millionaire... So, have you phoned him up to say thank you?'

'Erm, no. I wanted to see what you thought I should do.'

There was a pause as Victoria deliberated the best course of action.

'The way I see it, there are various ways of responding to something like this. First, you could go into your bedroom, put the bikini on, take a photo of yourself and send it to him. Even better, you could video yourself putting it on and taking it off again and send that to him. If you're not up for the exhibitionist option, my suggestion would be to go home this evening, pour yourself a glass of Prosecco, put the bikini on, lie on your bed and then call him. He wouldn't see you, but I think you might get a real kick out of that. Any good?'

'Vic, I'm not trying to seduce the poor man. We've been through this all before.' Although the sheer naughtiness of the third option did have considerable appeal. 'What I need to know is, do I call him, text him or email him?'

'Call him. Something like this needs verbal contact.'

'Right. And just say thank you?'

'Unless you're going to pledge undying love to him, I reckon "thank you" will have to do.'

'Right, a phone call and "thank you" it is. Thanks for the advice, Vic.'

'See you in the pub later on. Wait a minute. I know, why don't you turn up at the pub wearing it and I'll take a photo of you and send it to him?'

'Not going to happen.'

'I know, sweetie. See you later.'

Jo dashed home after work to change before going to the pub to meet the others. The first thing she did was to run into the bedroom, try the bikini on and check herself in the full-length mirror on the wardrobe door. It looked fabulous and it fitted perfectly. It certainly wasn't any bigger than the one she had borrowed from Angie, but it looked really classy, not obscene. For a moment she glanced at the phone lying on her bed before shaking her head, firmly resisting any temptation to take a photo, and heading for the shower. When she was dressed once more, she sat down at the kitchen table and sent Corrado a brief text. She knew he was a busy man and she didn't want to disturb him with a personal call.

> Hi Corrado. Is it convenient for me to call you now? Jo.

To her surprise, less than thirty seconds later, the phone started ringing. It was him.

'Corrado, hi. Thanks for calling back.'

'Hi, Jo, and happy birthday.'

'Thanks. I wanted to call you, to say thank you. The bikini's amazing. I don't know what to say.'

'And it fits all right? You can change it, you know…'

'It fits perfectly, and it looks wonderful. And with butterflies, I'm really touched.'

'So you like it?'

'I love it, Corrado. If you don't mind me using that word.'

He didn't react to her jibe. 'I'm glad. I've never been great at presents, but the idea came to me the other night while Daisy and I were watching a documentary about endangered species. It made me think of you.'

'I can't thank you enough, and do thank Daisy for her input. But you really shouldn't have. I know how much these things cost.'

'I very definitely should have. I'm just happy you like it.'

'Absolutely, it's wonderful. So, how's my four-legged friend?'

—

Jo got to the pub half an hour late after spending almost an hour on the phone to Corrado. The minutes had just slipped by and she had got real pleasure from the sound of his voice. When she finally hung up, her head was buzzing with thoughts of him and she was still dazed when she reached the pub and met up with the others. She managed to tell Victoria what she had done and she saw a happy expression on her friend's face.

'Verbal communication, you can't beat it. So, when are you going to see him again?'

'The wedding's fixed for April so I'll definitely see him then, if not before.'

'That's nine months away, Jo. Surely you can sort something out before then.'

'He did mention something about maybe having to come over to the UK for business. You never know; he might come here.'

'Well, it would be a very auspicious sign of his interest if he did.' Victoria grinned at her and lowered her voice. They were surrounded by Jo's co-workers, after all. 'It would be ironic if he came to London only to find you'd moved to New York.'

Jo had a good time that evening although she turned down most of the drinks she was offered and got home at just after eleven. Before going to bed, she checked her emails and, to her delight, she found one from Corrado. It just contained the words 'Happy Birthday. Thinking of you', and a delightful photo of Daisy sprawled out on the floor of his terrace with her trademark canine grin on her big hairy face.

Jo glanced across the room at the bikini lying on top of its tissue paper on the dresser and for a moment she contemplated sending him a photo of her own, but just as quickly decided against it. Instead, she just settled for:

Wish I was there. I'll always be dreaming of
Rome and thinking of you (and Daisy). x Jo.

As she pressed 'Send', she told herself the little 'x' was nothing more than a convention, and meant nothing.

She could almost hear her subconscious snort with derision.

Chapter 15

The following day Jo had a visitor at work. Carol phoned up from the front desk to let her know.

'Hi, Jo. I've got a Mr George Wilson down here, asking if he can see you.'

George Wilson? The name didn't mean anything to Jo and she was just about to query what he wanted, when she heard Carol's voice again.

'He says to tell you he's friends with you and Victoria.'

The penny dropped.

'Of course. Send him right up. I'll meet him at the lift.'

George appeared with a smile on his face, looking very business-like in a suit, collar and tie.

'Hi, George. Sorry it took me a moment. I don't think I've ever heard your surname before.' What, she wondered, was he doing here on his own?

'Hi, Jo. Happy birthday for yesterday. Sorry I couldn't make it last night, but I had to go to Edinburgh for a meeting. Thanks for sparing me a few minutes. I'll try not to take too long, it's a work thing.'

Greatly intrigued, Jo led him into her office and saw him close the door behind him before coming over to sit down opposite her. No sooner had he done so than he reached into his jacket pocket and produced a photo. He slid it across the desk towards her.

'Jo, please can you tell me if you recognise this man?'

Jo picked up the black and white photo and studied it. It looked as if it had been taken from a first or even second floor window, and the subject was a man standing by a dark-coloured car. And she recognised him immediately.

'Yes, I do.'

An expression of satisfaction appeared on George's face.

'And what did he tell you he was called?'

Jo couldn't help being struck by his choice of words.

'Markus. His name's Markus.' She searched her memory for a few moments before his surname came to her. 'Finchley, Markus Finchley.' She looked up at George. 'Why? Isn't that his real name?'

'Funnily enough, it is.' He smiled at her. 'You must have made quite an impression for him to give you his real name.' She saw him reach into his pocket once more and produce a laminated card. He laid it on the desk in front of her. 'Before we go any further, I'd better make this official.'

Jo looked down and checked out his ID card. The photo was of a slightly younger, very serious-looking George and it identified him as an agent of Her Majesty's Treasury. She looked up again in some considerable surprise.

'So you really are James Bond.'

He retrieved the card and grinned. 'No, Jo, still double-oh six and a quarter. Anyway, if I can be serious for a moment, I need your agreement to something before we proceed. What I have to tell you is highly confidential information and I have to ask you not to share it with anyone, and that includes your parents, relatives and friends.' He caught her eye. 'Not even Victoria. Can I have your word on this?'

'Of course. My lips are sealed. But what's this all about, George? What's Markus done?'

She saw him settle back in his chair and pull out a little black notebook.

'You remember my sudden arrival in Rome the other week, and my equally sudden departure? Well, I was on the heels of this man, Markus Finchley. He goes by a number of aliases and he's a tricky man to follow. I spent four days with the police in Rome searching for him, without success, and I only got word of his return to the UK on the Friday. He uses different airlines each time, sometimes private aircraft, different airports and different identities. He can easily slip abroad for two days and we're none the wiser.'

'But I met him at the French Embassy. Surely, they wouldn't have let him in if he was dodgy.'

George smiled grimly. 'Oh, he's dodgy all right, but he's also very, very clever. As Markus Finchley in the UK, he's clean as a whistle. He pays his taxes – well, some taxes. He donates to charity – that's no doubt why he was at the embassy. He's a member of his local Rotary Club, and he and his wife are respected pillars of society in Henley-Upon-Thames.'

'Did you say "his wife"?' Jo was aghast.

George nodded and glanced down at his notebook.

'Frances Ann Finchley, née Monroe. Age thirty-seven. They've been married for twelve years. I'm not sure how happily.'

Jo did her best to digest that bit of news. What a slimy toad.

'So why are you after him? You mentioned paying taxes? Is that what this is about?'

'Partly, but there's much more to it than that. The thing is, he's deeply involved with organised crime.' Jo looked up, totally stunned. 'Not at the sharp end. He keeps his hands scrupulously clean. No, he's the money man. We have reason to believe that he's been responsible for laundering hundreds of millions of pounds' worth of dirty money here in the UK, in Europe, and elsewhere in a variety of tax havens overseas.'

Jo was fascinated. A sudden thought came to her. 'When he took me out for dinner, I remember him telling me he'd just come back from the Caribbean. I suppose that's why. But what was he doing in Rome?'

'Have you ever heard of the *'Ndrangheta*?'

'No, never. What's that?'

'It may surprise you to know that currently it's the biggest criminal organisation in Europe. It makes the Sicilian *Cosa Nostra* look like a bunch of Boy Scouts in comparison. They're based in Calabria. You know Italy's shaped like a boot, well, Calabria's the toe of the boot. They're responsible for a vast percentage of all the illegal drugs that come into Europe, principally through the Calabrian port of Gioia Tauro, the biggest container port in Italy. It's estimated that eighty percent of the cocaine arriving in Europe from Colombia comes in through Gioia Tauro, and through the hands of the *'Ndrangheta*.'

'Wow. And Markus is involved with that?'

'Up to his grubby little armpits.'

'How do you know this?'

'Over the past five years there's been a lot more inter-national cooperation between law enforcement agencies, particularly as the American FBI have got more involved, and a number of significant arrests have been made. Some of those arrested were prepared to talk.'

'So why were you following him to Rome?'

'Every month or so, he meets up with his shadowy masters to report back and to receive his instructions. Together with the Italian police, we're trying to use him to lead us to them. I call them shadowy and they really are. It's very much a family business and the top people are all related one way or another. They all come from tiny little villages where nobody dares say a word against them or about them, and they seem to be able to move around Italy like ghosts. Ideally, we'd like to catch them all together *in flagrante*. The problem is, like I say, he's a slippery customer.'

'So how can I help? And how did you know about me and him anyway?'

'I only found out two days ago from Victoria. We were chatting and she mentioned this weirdo who had frightened you in his car and then pitched up uninvited at your conference in Rome. It was when she said his name was Markus that I suddenly began to wonder if it might be the same guy. The real irony is that while I was hunting for him in Rome, you were in contact with him all along. If only I'd known. As for what you can do, that all depends. Have you got any contact details, email or a phone number for him?'

'All I've got's his mobile.'

Jo pulled out her phone and dictated the number to him.

George noted the number. 'And have you any plans to see him again? Vic told me you pretended to be with an American guy so as to get rid of him. Presumably that means you and Finchley are history.'

Jo nodded. 'He definitely got the message he wasn't wanted. I'm sorry.'

'Not at all. His mobile number might be useful to us and, of course, if for any reason you hear from him again, I'd be really interested to know, especially if he's going back to Rome.' He handed her a card. 'My contact details are on here.'

'Of course, George. If I hear anything at all, I promise I'll be in touch, but I think it's very unlikely.' He stood up and she followed suit. 'So, is this why you've been coming to the Italian class?'

'Let's just say that it helps, particularly for speaking to my Italian counterparts. Mind you, the dialect the 'Ndrangheta villains speak is virtually incomprehensible, even to a native Italian. Still, the Italian classes led me to Victoria, so that can't be bad.'

After George had left, Jo sat and wondered for a while. So, Markus was involved in organised crime. Now she was even more glad she had got rid of him. Her subconscious helpfully produced an image of her perched on a barstool in a speakeasy, dressed as a gangster's Moll, surrounded by sinister men carrying violin cases, just to reinforce what she had so narrowly avoided.

–

Early August continued to be stiflingly hot in London and Jo often found herself reminded of her days in equally hot Rome. Of course, Rome had had its compensations, not least a certain hunky Roman man and his canine companion. Since her phone conversation with him on her birthday, she had called him a couple more times just for a chat, and he had phoned her. Certainly, as friends, they appeared to be getting on like a house on fire. As for anything more romantic, a thousand miles between them meant she didn't need to overwork her self-control too much. Then, one night, as she lay curled up on her bed with the phone to her ear, he put the cat well and truly among the pigeons.

'Jo, what are you doing for a holiday this year? Have you got any plans?'

'Not a thing. I've been so terribly busy, I haven't had a chance to fix anything up. In fact, I reckon I've got almost a month of unused holiday entitlement to take. My boss is supposedly returning to work on Monday, and I was thinking about going off somewhere after he's back.'

'It's just… I was wondering…' He sounded unusually hesitant. 'The lab closes down – all but a skeleton staff – for the second half of August, and I've been thinking about going off on the boat for a couple of weeks. Depending on the weather, I thought I might head out to some of the smaller islands like Giglio and Montecristo. I was wondering, if you had nothing better to do, if you maybe felt like coming with me.'

Jo took a deep breath and let the air whistle out again slowly. The idea of a couple of weeks floating around the sunny Mediterranean in a luxury yacht with Corrado was enticing and enchanting, but she felt equally certain that her self-control wouldn't stay the course. And if she gave in to her animal instincts and then things between them subsequently ended in bitter recrimination, as had apparently happened with all the previous women in his life, it wouldn't be the yacht that would be on the rocks, but potentially her whole relationship with her sister, Mario, and his family as well. Her mind racing, she took refuge in procrastination.

'Wow, Corrado, that sounds amazing. The only thing is, I can't commit to anything until I see what Ronald says. Can you give me a few days to let you know?'

'Of course. Everything closes down before *Ferragosto*, that's August the fifteenth, so you've got ten days to make up your mind. Just let me know before then if you can make it.' He was silent for a moment and when he started speaking again, there was unexpected warmth in his voice. 'I'd be really happy if you could come.'

As soon as the call finished, Jo rang Victoria in a state of considerable agitation.

'Vic, thank God, you're there.'

'Hi, Jo, what's up?'

'Vic, I need your advice. Badly.'

'What's the matter? Has something bad happened?' Victoria sounded worried.

'No, definitely not something bad. Potentially something fabulous, but it could also be catastrophic, and I don't know what to do.'

'Tell Auntie Vic all about it.'

So she did, ending up with the crux of the problem. 'The thing is, Vic, I really, really, like him a lot. Under other circumstances, I wouldn't hesitate, but there's so much more to it than just me. He's made it quite clear that he's got no interest in relationships, just sex. I'm a grown-up of thirty and I'd be prepared to take my chances with him, even though I know full well he's got previous. Everybody, including Corrado himself, has warned me off, but when all's said and done, I'm getting to a stage when I know I'd be prepared to jump into his bed and worry about it afterwards. But this isn't just about me. If it all goes pear-shaped between us – and if history's anything to go by, it would do – the ramifications for my relations with his family, and his with mine, starting with Angie, are unthinkable. She's already told him she'll murder him if he breaks my heart.'

'She'd have to beat me to it. I'd be there like a flash with a big bat.'

'So, what do I do, Vic? Up till now, I've been able to put all that on the back burner because of the distance between us. But two weeks on a yacht with him, both of us half-naked…'

'I can see your problem.' There was a pause, before Victoria delivered her verdict. 'It seems to me the most important person in this, apart from you of course, is your sister. You and Angie are very close. You can tell her anything. Give her a call and talk the whole thing through with her. See what she says and let her make the decision for you.'

'Isn't that terribly unfair on her?'

'In a way, yes, but can you think of a better solution?'

After Victoria had rung off, Jo checked the time. It was gone eleven and that meant after midnight in Rome, so she put off speaking to her sister until the following day. She wasn't looking forward to it.

–

Jo waited until lunchtime the next day to call her sister. In the meantime, she phoned Ronald at home to double-check he was coming back to work on Monday and to see how he felt about her taking a few weeks off. He grumbled a bit, but couldn't come up with any valid reason to keep her at work so she knew that, if she decided to go for it, she would be able to get away. The problem was whether or not to say yes to Corrado.

Finally, at just before one o'clock, she phoned Angie, feeling pretty sure they would have finished lunch by what was two o'clock, Roman time.

'Hi, Angie, can you talk?'

'Yes, by all means. Mario's gone up to the restaurant and, at the risk of making you jealous, I'm in the hammock under the pergola and I've just been watching a beautiful red and black butterfly flitting about. A Red Admiral, isn't it?'

'Black wings, reddy-orange bands and white spots? Yes, that sounds like a Red Admiral all right. I don't suppose you've seen one of my elusive Purple Emperors, have you?' Then, remembering the reason for the call, she cut to the chase. 'Anyway, Angie, look, it's about Corrado. I need to talk to you.'

What Angie said next came as a surprise.

'It's about him and the yacht, isn't it?'

'He told you?'

'He's just spent about an hour over lunch bending my ear. He and Daisy only left twenty minutes ago. I was going to give you a call later on to tell you all about it.'

'And what did he say?'

'He did his best to get Mario and me to come with him, and you, for a cruise round the islands. Now, don't get me wrong. His yacht's amazing and he's a very competent sailor. At any other time of the year we'd be up for it like a shot. The problem Mario and I have is that we've got stuff happening here at the Country Club virtually every day this month and it's going to be physically impossible for us to get away.'

'So, he asked you as well...' Jo was surprised, but impressed. It was reassuring that he had thought of getting somebody else along to make sure neither of them did anything impetuous.

'Jo, listen, I wish we could come, but we just can't. He said he's asked you. What're you going to do?'

'That's what I want you to tell me, Angie.'

'Me? You're thirty now, Jo. You're all grown up and you've got to make your own decisions.'

'I know, but it isn't that simple.'

She went on to lay out all the objections that had been running through her head ever since Corrado had made his offer. Angie didn't interrupt, apart from an occasional grunt from time to time. Jo finally ground to a halt with the words, 'The thing is, there's so much riding on this. It's not just a matter of whether or not he breaks my heart. If it was just that, I'd take the chance. But it's you guys, the family...'

She had to wait a few seconds before her sister replied.

'Jo, listen to yourself. I've never heard you like this about a man before. All that bullshit you were spouting about love not being a thing and you not being interested in men is out of the window now, isn't it? You've totally fallen for him, haven't you?'

'It's not *all* bullshit... but, if I'm honest, Angie, the truth of the matter is that I've never felt like this about any man before. Not even Christian at the beginning. I can honestly say that if it wasn't for the complication of our two families, I wouldn't hesitate. Yes, I've been warned by everybody, including Corrado himself, so I know it'll almost certainly end in tears, but I'd be prepared to take the chance.'

'Just like so many other girls have done before you to their cost. You know that, don't you?'

'I know.' Jo felt she was close to banging her head against her desk, but she took a deep breath and pulled herself together. 'The idea of going off with him on the boat is an absolute dream, but I'm only human and I'm under no illusions as to how it'll end when we find ourselves alone together.'

There was another pause before Angie surprised her again.

'I think you should go.'

'You do? But why?'

'For your sanity, apart from anything else. If you don't, you'll regret it for the rest of your life.'

'But what happens if – when – it all falls apart?'

'We'll cope. Believe me, it wouldn't be the end of the world. Everybody here knows what he's like – and that includes his parents. Nobody would blame you. What I can tell you is this: I've never seen him the way he was at lunchtime today, so it's not just you. Maybe he really is changing. And it might interest you to know that Mario says Corrado hasn't been out with anybody for ages, since early July, which coincidentally just happens to be the first time the two of you met.'

'Wow!' That really was a surprise.

'Wow, indeed. You should have heard him today. He just couldn't stop talking about you. He really wants you to come sailing with him and I honestly believed him when he told me – half a dozen times – that he promises not to lay a finger on you.'

'It's me laying my fingers on him I'm more worried about.'

'When do you have to give him an answer?'

'The end of next week, at the very latest.'

'Well, my advice would be to take your time, think it through, talk to Victoria as well. She's sensible. See what she says. If, after you've thought long and hard about it, you still feel like going, then Mario and I will understand and we'll wish you well. Both of you.'

No sooner had Jo put the phone down than it started ringing. She felt her heart leap as she saw who the caller was.

'Corrado, hi. Good to hear from you.'

'Hi, Jo, listen, I was wondering. Are you busy this weekend?'

'Sort of. I'm free on Saturday, but mum's organising a delayed birthday lunch for me on Sunday and I've promised to go, even though it's going to be pretty grim.'

'Ah… right.' There was a pause while he rethought his plans. 'The thing is, I thought I'd see if you felt like flying over for the weekend. That way I could take you riding and out for a few meals and we could just talk. But, above all, I could show you my yacht so you know what it's like.'

'That would have been wonderful.' Jo's mind was racing as she tried to think up ways of wriggling out of the lunch with her parents and the neighbours.

'But you say you're free on Saturday?'

'Yes, absolutely.'

'Right, then maybe I could come over to see you for the day and bring you photos of the boat. I'd just like to see you. Leave it with me and I'll see what I can sort out. I'll call you back this evening.'

Jo spent the afternoon hoping this might be the time he actually came to London to see her. What was it Victoria had said about him maybe coming over? She had said it would be 'auspicious'. Jo felt sure Vic was right and she couldn't hide a growing sense of excitement at the possibility of seeing him again in just two days' time.

She had just got home at six when her phone rang. It was Corrado, but the first thing he said came as a great disappointment.

'Hi, Jo. I've been looking into flights. The bad news is that Italy are playing a friendly against England at Wembley on Saturday and all morning flights from Rome and even Naples to London are sold out. Even Friday night's sold out.'

'Oh…' Jo felt deflated, but help was at hand.

'But the good news is that there are loads of empty seats from London to Rome on Saturday morning and home again in the evening. Would you feel like coming over to see me? I'm sorry it'll be a bit of a sweat for you, but it would be so good to meet up, even just for a few hours and, of course, you'd see the boat.'

Jo didn't hesitate. 'Of course, I'd love to. I'll go ahead and book my flights.'

'That's fantastic.' He sounded really pleased. 'Look, I took a chance, hoping you'd say yes, and I've booked you on the BA flight from Gatwick to *Fiumicino* leaving at eight thirty on Saturday morning, and home again on the last flight which leaves at eight twenty in the evening. You get back to Gatwick at just before ten, so you should be in bed by midnight. Is that okay? It'll be a bit tiring, I'm afraid.'

'That sounds wonderful, but I can pay my own way.'

'I know you can, Jo, but it's my fault for leaving it till the last minute, so let me do it this time.'

'That's not fair. You shouldn't…'

'Well, we can argue about it over lunch on Saturday, all right?'

'All right, but I'm paying for lunch. No ifs, no buts.'

She heard him laugh. 'It's a deal. And, Jo, I'm really looking forward to seeing you again.'

'Me, too.'

Chapter 16

Jo arrived in Rome at noon on Saturday in a state of barely controlled panic. She had got up in the middle of the night so as to have time to get ready and had chosen and discarded three sets of clothing before settling upon a light summer dress and the new underwear she had bought in Rome. All the way over on the plane she had been questioning why her choice of underwear should have been significant, seeing as there was no way he was going to see any of it. Was he?

Corrado was waiting for her in the Arrivals hall and he looked almost as anxious as she felt. He waved to her and, as she approached, he held out his hand to greet her. She shook hands with him almost shyly, not sure whether she was disappointed or relieved not to have been on the receiving end of a hug and a kiss, and followed him out into the baking sun. To her surprise, the Range Rover was parked almost directly opposite the doors, barely fifty yards from the terminal. She looked across at him and smiled.

'Is your little Roman policewoman on duty today or did you just get lucky?'

He grinned at her. 'No, it's all above board. I just paid at the machine. But, yes, I was very lucky to find a space right here. Almost as lucky as I am to see you again.'

As they approached the car, Jo heard a familiar bark and saw a very excited Labrador spinning round on her axis inside the boot, obviously overjoyed to see her best buddy once more. As Corrado opened the tailgate, the dog leapt out, but Jo was ready for her this time and avoided being knocked backwards into the road.

'*Ciao*, Daisy. How's my friend?'

Jo made a fuss of the dog who was emitting plaintive little whines of happiness as she tried to lick Jo's face, and then looked up at Corrado.

'I think she remembers me.'

He grinned again. 'I've said it before and I'll say it again, it must be love.'

Jo didn't reply.

Once they were in the car, Corrado turned towards Jo and took a long slow look at her. She felt the colour flood to her face as his eyes roamed over her body before returning to her face.

'You look wonderful, absolutely wonderful.'

'Well, you don't look too shabby yourself.'

And he didn't. He was wearing a pale-yellow polo shirt and sand-coloured shorts and not a lot else. He looked as gorgeous as the first time she had seen him and her doubts about going sailing with him felt all the more justified. As she had told her sister, he might be able to keep his hands off her, but could she say the same about herself? She decided not to repeat the kiss she had given him when he had picked her up at Rome station a few weeks earlier, and to do her best to keep him at arms' length.

'I thought we could go and have lunch somewhere away from the coast. It's the middle of August, and a

Saturday as well, so the seaside round here's going to be packed. Suit you if we get away from the crowds?'

'Absolutely, but remember our deal. Lunch is on me.'

'I still wish you'd let me do it, but it's your call. If that's what you want, then so be it. I know a great little restaurant where the food's amazing and I promise it won't break the bank.'

As they drove out of the airport and along a series of ever quieter roads through the dead flat countryside, the atmosphere inside the car was also quiet. Partly this was as she didn't want to disturb him while he was driving, but it was also because neither of them appeared to know what to say. Then, thankfully, she spotted a mass of Roman ruins, interspersed with huge umbrella pines, over to the left of them. She queried what they were and he was quick to reply, no doubt pleased to have something to talk about.

'That's Ostia Antica. It used to be the main port of Rome.'

'But it's nowhere near the sea.'

'Not now. The Tiber silted up and sea levels have dropped since those days, so now it's high and dry. If we had more time today, we could go and visit the ruins. It's amazingly well preserved. You can see the Forum, villas, paved streets, hypocausts, you name it. It's very, very impressive.' He glanced across at her. 'Next time.'

'Definitely next time.' She wondered when that would be. Maybe in a week's time if she decided to throw caution to the wind and accept his offer of a holiday on the yacht. Yet again, she turned the conundrum over in her head.

The restaurant was little more than an old stone farm-house. As they parked in the shade of a massive old tree and let Daisy out of the boot, half a dozen chickens ran off in alarm, clucking nervously. Daisy eyed them with interest, but Corrado was quick to make her aware of her responsibilities.

'No chasing the chickens, Daisy. Got that? *Lascia stare le galline!*'

Jo was impressed to see Daisy turn towards him and trot obediently at his side as they walked over to the shady terrace. About half of the tables were full and Jo couldn't see a single tourist among them. A jovial gentleman appeared through a doorway to greet them, wiping his hands on his white apron.

'*Signori, buongiorno.*' He led them over to a table in the shade of a wooden pergola tacked onto the side of the building and covered in vines. It was pleasantly cool under here after the scorching heat of the midday sun.

The menu was verbal, but with a little help from the owner, Jo ordered seafood antipasti, followed by *spaghetti alle vongole*, and then roast lamb, Roman style with sage, rosemary and garlic. It was far more than she would have ordered for herself, but she wanted to make sure Corrado got a good meal. He made no comment until the owner had left them to it.

'That's a lot of food you've ordered, Jo. Are you trying to fatten me up so that I can't fit into my suit for the wedding?'

Jo smiled as she heard him parody the words she had used to him the last time she had been in Rome.

They chatted about everything from cycling to butterflies, global warming to blood tests, but neither of them even once brought up the subject of sailing. The meal was delightful and Jo was surprised to find she was able to eat all of the antipasti, most of the spaghetti with clams, and about half of the succulent roast lamb. She even had room for a lemon sorbet afterwards. As he was driving, Corrado didn't drink much wine, and she firmly limited herself to just a glass and a half, even though the rosé was excellent. She knew she had to keep her wits about her, or, more specifically, she had to be sure her self-control didn't waver. She didn't need to be back at the airport for another five hours and a lot can happen in five hours.

As they sat back with potent little cups of espresso coffee at the end of the meal, Corrado finally brought up the S-word.

'If we had more time I could have taken you sailing this afternoon, but I thought you might like to come down to the marina with me anyway, so I can show you *Ippona*.'

'That's the name of your yacht?'

'Yes, Ippona was the Roman goddess of horses. I imagine you spell it with an H in English, but over here as you know, we aren't into H's. Given my love of horses, it seemed like an appropriate choice.'

'So, your yacht is the horse of the seas?'

'My yacht is the goddess herself. She's very beautiful.' He shot her a quick glance. 'Almost as beautiful as you, Jo.'

'I've said it before and I'll say it again; there's no need for flattery, Corrado.'

He grinned. 'All right then, she's every bit as beautiful as you. Happy?'

Jo grinned back. 'Well, now I really need to see her. Just give me one moment while I settle up with the owner and then let's head for the sea.'

When they got to the marina, Jo found herself surrounded by hundreds of boats, ranging from little rubber dinghies to massive two- or three-deck billionaires' playthings.

'Which one's yours, Corrado? I vaguely remember the photos you showed me. It's got a mast, hasn't it?'

'Correct. And she's a catamaran. You know what that is? Twin hulls. She's over there.'

'Sorry, I should have said "she". I forgot that you sailors treat your boats like women.'

'I probably treat *Ippona* better than I've treated a lot of women.' He looked across at her. 'Sorry, Jo. Shouldn't be talking about my shady past.'

Past? That sounded encouraging, but she didn't dwell upon it.

'What about Daisy? How does she like sailing?'

'I bought *Ippona* about six months before I got Daisy, so she's been on and off the boat all her life. She loves it. And, of course, we're surrounded by water and you know Labradors.' They arrived at the yacht. 'Welcome aboard *Ippona*, Jo. One goddess welcomes another.'

Jo was wearing flat shoes, but she slipped them off anyway, just like he did, before following the dog across the gangway and onto the boat. She stopped and looked around. It was stunning. She had been expecting a cramped cockpit and wooden hatchways leading down into the bowels of the boat. Instead, she found that the open cockpit area was the size of a room, protected from the elements by a rigid white awning, and with seating round a table for a load of people. Above it to one side was the wheel and a dizzying collection of instruments and controls.

Sliding glass doors led to the interior. As Corrado unlocked the doors, she followed him inside and found herself in a massive openplan lounge with panoramic 360-degree views out through the windows, a large dining area with a big table and a horseshoe-shaped bench around it, and a lounge area with twin sofas. The kitchen was ultramodern and the whole impression was light and airy. It was quite unlike any boat she had ever been on before.

'While I'm giving you the tour, let me show you the cabins. There are two in the port hull (that's on the left-hand side) while the whole of the other hull is the master suite. All three have their own private heads and showers.' Seeing her expression, he translated. 'I've done a few sailing courses in the UK and I've learnt the jargon. "Heads" means a toilet. Basically, each of the bedrooms has an ensuite.'

'Wow!' This, too, was not what she had been expecting.

'If you decide to come with me next weekend, you'll have the master suite. Daisy and I will be very happy in one of the other cabins. Here, take a look.'

Jo followed him down a steep staircase into a long, fairly slim space with full headroom and slit windows at shoulder height. The way it had been fitted out was not dissimilar from the room she had had in her hotel by the conference centre. It was comfortable, luxurious and impeccably clean. At one end was a big double bed with, touchingly, Daisy's wicker basket on the floor in front of it. At the other end was a door leading to a beautifully-fitted shower and toilet. The overall impression was of quality and unexpected space.

'What do you think?' He sounded uncertain.

'It's amazing.' She turned back towards him after checking out the bathroom. 'Quite amazing. Now, can I see the other two cabins, please?'

They climbed back into the saloon and crossed to a similar staircase on the other side. She followed him down into the other hull and found two smaller, but equally luxurious, cabins. After she had checked them out, she and Corrado went back up into the saloon again and out through glass doors at the front, leading to a flat sunbathing area where the dog was still rolling about happily. Corrado sat down on a moulded seat and pointed to another one across on the far side.

'Take a seat, Jo. Now, tell me honestly, what do you think of her?'

She sat down, noticing that there were now at least three metres between them. He certainly wasn't crowding her.

'Like I said, this is the most amazing yacht, but there's one thing we need to get settled right now and, if you don't agree then I'm not coming.'

He was beginning to look uneasy now, so she hastened to put him out of his misery.

'If I come with you, if you still want me, then I refuse to kick you and your dog out of the master suite. I'll be very happy in either of the smaller cabins and I won't under any circumstances sleep in your cabin.' As she spoke, she made a prodigious effort to submerge the image her subconscious insisted upon producing of the two of them rolling around naked together in that big double bed. She looked across at him and smiled. 'These terms are non-negotiable. Take them or leave them.'

He grinned at her. 'You drive a hard bargain. I had it all planned. I thought Daisy could sleep in the saloon and keep guard over the two of us. I want you to have nothing but the best.'

'And I'm very grateful, Corrado, but there's no need. You stay in your cabin. I'll be fine. So, do we have a deal?'

He stood up and came across to shake her hand. There was room alongside her for him to sit down, but he remained standing for a few moments before returning to his original position after shaking her hand.

'It's a deal. Now all you've got to do is to make up your mind whether you're coming or not.'

They sat and chatted over a cup of tea for at least an hour with the dog sprawled out on the wooden floor at their feet, occasionally running in her sleep as she chased some imaginary foe. The two sofas were set at right angles to each other and Jo sat on one while Corrado took up station a safe distance away on the other one. It was quite clear that he was either definitely not interested in her or doing his best to demonstrate that he was capable of coexisting with her on this wonderful boat without touching her. As for Jo herself, she was less sure how long she would be able to hold out.

A bit later on, they went out to the sundeck for a brief lie-down in the sun and Jo rather regretted not bringing the new bikini when she saw him peel off his shirt. Still, she told herself, as she lay down on the soft cushions he had brought out, it was maybe for the best if she kept her dress on. He lay down right over at the far side of the deck and Daisy stationed herself in the shade by the door to the saloon, midway between the two of them. Jo closed her eyes and – probably as a result of the early start and the wine at lunchtime – dozed off.

She woke to the feel of a warm touch against her bare leg. There was now a very welcome gentle breeze blowing and her skirt had ridden up a bit. The feel of skin on the naked flesh of her thigh was exhilarating and arousing. She was wide awake in a flash and she lay there, eyes tightly closed, wondering what would happen next.

What happened next was that she felt a tongue start licking her knee. At the same time, she felt a tickle on her thigh as a remarkably hairy chin landed on her bare skin. The licking turned into slobbering and realisation dawned. She opened her eyes to find a pair of big brown eyes looking up at her. Seeing her awake, Daisy roused herself, abandoned her position by Jo's waist and crept up the cushion on her elbows until she was right by Jo's neck. She then stretched out a big black paw and rested it on Jo's shoulder. Jo found herself with mixed emotions. Being the centre of attention of the affectionate dog aroused a lovely comfortable sensation of belonging. However, much as she loved Daisy, she couldn't stifle a feeling of disappointment. She reached out and scratched the dog's ears.

'Hi, Daisy. Did you have a little nap too?'

'Not so little, Jo. You've been asleep for almost an hour.'

Jo pulled herself up onto her elbows and looked towards him, flicking her skirt back down across her legs as she did so. Corrado, now once more wearing his shirt, was sitting on the seat on the opposite side of the sundeck looking at her with a smile on his face.

'Believe it or not, it's half past five. In less than an hour we'll have to set off for the airport again or you might miss your flight. And if I don't get you back to England, your mum won't be too pleased with me.'

'Oh, Corrado, I'm so sorry. What a waste. We could have spent that time talking.'

'Don't even think about it. I could see you were tired. You looked very peaceful when you were asleep.'

Jo got up and took a seat opposite him. She knew the time had come to make a decision. She also knew it was the moment for some straight talking.

'Corrado, about your very kind offer, I've been doing a lot of thinking.' She saw him sit upright. 'I like you an awful lot and I get the impression – hopefully I'm right – that you like me too. Tell me straight, do you think we're going to be able to live alongside each other on your lovely boat for two whole weeks without getting involved? You've been very honest up till now, telling me you aren't interested in a lengthy relationship. I want to be equally honest with you and tell you I'm not up for a transitory physical affair, however appealing it might be. I'm thirty now and I know I need more than just that. Besides, there's the whole question of Mario and Angie to complicate matters. Do you think we can manage to co-exist as just friends?'

He nodded slowly. 'I've been doing a lot of thinking myself, and I believe we can. I know perfectly well what sort of girl you are and I really wish I could tell you I was looking for the same type of relationship you want, but I can't. It wouldn't be right for me to tell you I believe in something when I don't. But, as a friend, I know we can have a fabulous holiday together.' He raised his eyes towards hers and smiled. 'I'll just have to keep thinking of you as a male friend.'

Jo smiled back at him, her decision taken.

'Then, in that case, captain, consider me your first mate. I'll be delighted to come with you.'

She saw a happy expression spread over his face as he leant across the table towards her and held out his hand.

'That's terrific news. I'm really looking forward to it.'

'Me, too.'

'Now that I know you're coming, I'll sail her up to Porto Ercole one day this week and we can start from there. The whole area round there is really unspoilt; just cliffs and rocks, little bays with hidden beaches, and the clearest, bluest sea you've ever seen.'

This sounded fabulous, but Jo added a word of caution. 'I've only ever sailed a bit in dinghies, so I don't really qualify as a real first, second, or even tenth mate. You'll have to teach me everything. I hope I don't annoy you too much. I wouldn't want to have to walk the plank.'

'Don't worry. *Ippona*'s a biggish yacht, but she's rigged so she can be sailed single-handed if need be. The sails unfurl electrically, the anchor winch is electric, and there are all sorts of electronic gizmos so that I can sail her on my own if necessary. Don't worry, we'll be fine.'

'Well, I'm really, really looking forward to it. I can't wait for next week, captain.'

'Me, too, mate.'

Chapter 17

Jo didn't wake up until almost nine o'clock on Sunday morning. Her plane had been late leaving Rome the previous night and she hadn't got to bed until past midnight, but she had slept like a log. Now, in the warm glow of the August sunshine flooding in through the curtains, she reflected on the past twenty-four hours. It had been a wonderful day in Rome and she knew she liked Corrado more and more. Now that the decision had been made, she gritted her teeth and prayed that they would both manage to make it a great holiday and nothing more.

She showered and dressed and put the kettle on. As she waited for the water to come to the boil, she checked her emails and one suddenly drew all her attention. It was addressed to Doctor Joanne Green and it was from Professor Waltraud Dietrich at the United Nations. Its contents were electrifying. She read it carefully, three times. After an introductory paragraph repeating her compliments at Jo's performance in Rome and mentioning that she had spoken to Ricky about her, the second paragraph almost took Jo's breath away.

I was very interested to read your résumé, particularly the subject of your doctoral studies and thesis. Conservation and climate change are very high on the agenda of the UN at present and can only continue to increase in importance as the years go by. It has fallen to me to assemble a team of international experts charged with a task that is vital not only to our different countries, but to the very survival of the planet. I would very much like it if you felt prepared to join us. I am attaching a PDF with details of our mission statement, conditions of employment, salary and so on for your information. Please take your time and consider it carefully. I am returning to my home country of Austria for a holiday in a few days' time and will be stopping off in London on my way back to the States in early September. If this proposal interests you, or if you require any more information, I would be delighted to meet up with you again at that time.

The email finished with a further plea for Jo to give serious consideration to this offer as Professor Dietrich felt sure she would be a major asset to the team. By the time Jo had finished reading it through, she was literally speechless. She checked out the PDF with all the small print and was even more flabbergasted. The starting salary on offer worked out to almost exactly twice what she was currently earning and came accompanied by a comprehensive package of pension, medical insurance and a generous relocation allowance. She read it wide-eyed, overwhelmed by the magnitude of what was on offer.

Her mind still on the email, she made the tea and sat down to drink it while she mulled over the implications of the job offer. From a career point of view, it was ballistic. This would elevate her to the ranks of the very few internationally-known scientists working in this field and she couldn't resist a little smile at the thought of how Ronald would receive the news when she informed him she had decided to accept. And there was little doubt in her mind that she had to accept. Apart from what this would mean for her career and her finances, it would give her the chance to make a direct contribution to the future of the planet, and no scientist could ask for more.

There was no question that this would mean a major upheaval in her life. Moving all the way to New York would separate her from her parents, her sister, Victoria, and all her other friends, both here and in Italy, amongst whom, of course, was Corrado. This development only served to further strengthen her resolve to ensure that during their holiday together they kept each other at arm's length. Falling in love with him – and she knew this was still all too possible – would inevitably end in tragedy, either professionally or emotionally. Or both.

She was still turning this over in her head as she travelled on the train to Oxford. She barely noticed the suburban sprawl around London flashing past and then the gradual appearance of fields and woods. By the time she walked out through the barriers to hug her mother, she wasn't feeling any more settled in her mind. The ramifications of Professor Dietrich's email had certainly shaken her up. Her mother noticed immediately that something was bothering Jo and as they sat down side by side in the car, she made no attempt to start the engine. Instead, she reached across and took Jo's hand.

'What is it, Joanne? Is something wrong?'

Jo did her best to shake herself out of her introspection. She glanced over at her mother and smiled.

'No, mum, nothing's wrong. It's just that I've been offered an amazing new job.'

She saw her mother beam. 'How wonderful! Tell me all about it.'

So Jo told her. As she did, she watched the result of her words on her mother's face. Her expression went from amazed, to delighted, to stunned as the realisation dawned that her daughter was likely to finish up three thousand miles away. As Jo reached the end of her tale, she waited for her mother to react. The reaction took a minute or two to arrive and when it did, it came as quite a surprise.

'You've got to take it.'

'You think so?'

'Of course. It's a wonderful opportunity for you. You must be so excited.'

'But what about you and dad?'

'Sweetheart, we'll manage.' Her mother squeezed Jo's hand tightly. 'Now that your father's mobile again, we'll have to come across to see you in New York. We've never been to America and everybody says it's an exciting country.' Jo could see that her mum was putting on a brave face and she loved her for it. She leant across and gave her a big hug.

'And, mum, I'll come back to see you two as often as I can. It said in the email that the job would involve some travelling, so I'm sure that would include regular visits to Europe.'

As she spoke, she wondered if these visits might include Rome.

Lunch with the neighbours turned out to be quite enjoyable after all. Needless to say, Jo had to recount her exploits in Rome to the assembled group, but she scrupulously avoided any but the most fleeting mention of Corrado. It was only later that afternoon, after everybody had left, that she broke the news to her parents that she'd be leaving next weekend to spend two weeks floating on the Mediterranean alone with him. Her mother was predictably concerned, and her father envious, and maybe a bit concerned as well but, in his case, it was for the nautical part of the holiday rather than the romantic one.

'That sounds wonderful, Joanne. He is an experienced sailor, now, isn't he?'

After her conversation with Corrado the previous day, Jo was able to reassure them.

'He's had the boat for five years and he's done sailing courses in the UK as well as Italy and he's got his Yacht-master certificate – whatever that is.'

Her father knew what this was and looked approving. Her mother, however, was far more concerned about her daughter going off with a man with a reputation as a womaniser.

'Are you sure this is a good idea, Joanne? Aren't you worried he might... you know...?'

'I'm not worried, mum, honestly.'

Jo told her mum that Corrado's behaviour yesterday had been exemplary and she genuinely had no fears of being assaulted by him out in the open sea. She avoided mentioning that she was more worried about how she herself might behave towards him. There was no disguising the fact that she still found him very, very attractive and the fact that he was prepared to repress his natural instincts for the sake of their friendship made him, if anything, even more attractive. Still, her mother didn't need to know this, so she repeated her belief that she and Corrado would be able to co-exist just as friends. Her mother nodded, but couldn't help adding a caveat.

'You'll be going to some very romantic places, I'm sure, Joanne. Just try not to do anything you might regret. And more to the point, remember Angela and Mario. You wouldn't want to mess things up for them, would you?'

'No, mum, I'll be careful, I promise.' For a moment she let her guard slip. 'Besides, what would be the point of getting involved with him when I know I'm going to be flying off to America in a month or two?' And that was the crunch. Now it was even more essential that she avoided falling for him lock, stock, and barrel, or she could find herself three thousand miles away and completely heartbroken. As it was, she knew she was going to miss him an awful lot.

'So, you're definitely taking the United Nations job?'

Jo took a deep breath.

'Yes, I think I am. I'll write to Professor Dietrich this evening and tell her I'm very, very interested.'

–

Jo spent most of the week getting ready for her sailing trip. She spoke to Corrado on the phone most nights and, on his recommendation, went out and bought herself a waterproof anorak, deck shoes and a baseball cap which happened to have the logo of the Royal National Lifeboat Institute on it, hoping this wasn't tempting fate. She also invested in two new pairs of shorts, another bikini – although this was a whole lot cheaper than her Gucci one – and a trip to the beauty salon. She bought sun cream and new sunglasses and even painted her toenails for just about the first time in her life. After all, she told herself, as she was going to be barefoot for most of the time, she might as well add a bit of colour.

On Thursday night she went to the pub with Victoria and George after Italian class and told them all about her day trip to Rome and her decision to go sailing with Corrado in two days' time. Then she told them about the job offer. George, as ever, was very supportive, while Victoria immediately saw through to the heart of the matter.

'This means *arrivederci* as far as we're concerned, and as far as everybody else is concerned here in the UK and, of course, over in Rome.'

Jo caught her eye. 'Yup, that's right, but the operative word is *arrivederci*, "see you again", not farewell forever. And that's the same for you guys and for everybody in Italy.'

'Everybody in Italy? You sure?' Victoria smiled at her. 'Of course, in one way, this simplifies things for you.'

'It does?'

'Here you are, about to set off on a two-week trip around the islands of the Mediterranean just wearing a few strips of clothing, alongside a ridiculously desirable man – sorry George, obviously nothing like as desirable as you – who won't be wearing much more. At least, now you know that if your self-control lets you down and you do end up in his bed, any awkwardness will only last for a few weeks before the Atlantic Ocean intervenes to screen him from you.'

Jo smiled back at her. 'That's a good point, as far as it goes. The thing is, Vic, what worries me is that I really, really like this guy. I'm terrified it won't take much for me to fall head over heels in love with him – even if he doesn't believe it's a thing.'

'And would that stop you going to New York?'

Jo shook her head, although with how much conviction, she wasn't prepared to calculate. 'No, I've got to take the UN job. That's a must.'

'And when do you need to give them a definite yes or no?'

'I've said I'm very interested and I've got an appointment with Professor Dietrich in London three days after I get back from Italy. I suppose that'll be it.'

'Well, at least you'll know by then, won't you?'

Chapter 18

Jo packed all her things into a bulky holdall and lugged it out to Luton airport on Saturday morning feeling excited, but also apprehensive, about what awaited her over the next two weeks. She checked in her bag, went through security, and headed straight to a cafe for a cup of tea and a croissant. She bought a paper, but she barely flicked through it, lost in her thoughts. It was only as she followed the crowd along to the departure lounge that her head suddenly cleared as she got a very unwelcome surprise.

Standing in the queue, only about twenty places ahead of her, was a familiar figure. As his head turned slightly sideways, she confirmed her initial impression. It was, without a shadow of a doubt, Markus. He didn't appear to have spotted her yet, so she shrank down behind the bulky couple in front of her and debated what to do. George had asked her to get in touch if she had any contact with Markus and had given her his card. She fumbled in her bag until she found it and then backed out of the queue and up the stairs out of sight. Slipping off to a quiet corner, away from anybody else, she phoned the number on the card and waited. After only two rings, it was answered by a woman's voice.

'Yes, hello.'

'I'm trying to contact George…' She had to consult the card to remember his surname. 'George Wilson. He gave me this number. It's very urgent.'

'Hold the line please.'

A few seconds later, she recognised his voice. It sounded a bit tinny, as if he was speaking on a mobile.

'George Wilson.'

'George, it's Jo. I'm at Luton airport and I've just seen Markus. He's going to be on the same flight as me to Rome.'

'That's terrific, Jo. Thank you so much. What's the flight number?' She passed it on to him and waited. 'Right, Jo, listen. We got word a couple of days ago that a meeting between him and his bosses was imminent and we've been staking out Heathrow and Gatwick airports. I'm afraid we've got limited resources, so there's no way I or any of my colleagues can get to Luton now in time to catch your flight. I'll pass this information onto my opposite numbers in Rome and they'll be waiting at the other end to follow him.'

'Fine. Is there anything you want me to do? I imagine it's very likely he'll spot me as I get on or off the plane.'

'I wonder… Tell me something, Jo, when your tall American friend scared him off in Rome that time, did you tell Markus he was your boyfriend?'

Jo had to stop and think. 'No, I don't think I did. I just said Ricky'd been in America.'

'So could he maybe have just been a close friend or your cousin, say?'

'Yes, I suppose so. Why? Do you want me to pretend I'm still interested in Markus?'

'Jo, I don't want you to do anything that could be dangerous. *He* isn't a threat, but his Italian connections most certainly are. If he makes contact with you, just be pleasant and, if necessary, tell him the Yank was your cousin so as to keep him sweet, but do not, under any circumstances, go off with him. All right?'

'Of course. Corrado's waiting for me the other end anyway.'

'Fine. Do me one last favour, would you? Send a text to this number once you've come through passport control, please. All right? Just send my name, George Wilson. That'll be enough.'

'Fine. Will do.'

'And, Jo, I wasn't joking. Stay well away from him and his connections once you get to Rome. They are very bad people.'

Jo turned off the phone and headed down to the departure lounge. Fortunately, Markus was now standing a long way in front of her in the Speedy Boarding line which was already moving towards the doors. She handed over her boarding pass and hid herself among the crowd of ordinary passengers until the time came for them to follow the others outside onto the tarmac. Her seat was near the back of the aircraft and she was able to use the rear door and get to her place without catching sight of Markus who was, presumably, much nearer the front.

It was a very smooth flight in near cloudless skies and Jo was able to relax, confident that Markus hadn't spotted her and wouldn't do so. All went well until they landed and trooped off the plane through the forward exit. However, as she emerged up the walkway from the aircraft into the terminal building, she almost bumped into him, standing to one side, digging something out of his bag. He looked up and did a double take. She did her best to look similarly surprised.

'Markus, hello. Were you on the London flight as well?'

'Jo, how lovely to see you. Yes, I've just come over for the weekend. So, we were on the same aircraft!' He hesitated. 'Have you come to see your American friend?'

Jo shook her head.

'You mean Ricky? Tall Ricky, my cousin? He's back in the States now. He was just passing through. We've always been very close.'

She read relief and renewed interest in his eyes. As she turned away to follow the crowd to passport control, she felt a touch on her arm as he started walking alongside her.

'This is wonderful. I've been dying to see you to apologise if I maybe gave you the wrong idea back in London.'

The wrong idea? Jo kept a friendly smile on her face, but it was an effort.

'Water under the bridge, Markus. No harm done.'

'I wonder if you feel like meeting up while we're here in Rome.' She saw him concentrate hard for a few seconds before continuing, 'I'm afraid I have to go straight into a meeting when I get out of the airport, but I should be free by tonight. How about dinner?'

'That sounds lovely. I'll just have to check with my sister first. I'm staying with them, and my brother-in-law's supposed to be waiting for me outside. Can I call you? I've got your number.'

'Ah, no, not that one. That's no good any more. I lost my phone and I've got a new one now.'

He produced what looked like exactly the same phone and dictated the new number. Jo wondered if he regularly changed SIM cards to throw people like George off his scent. She had just added it to her contacts when his phone started ringing. He glanced down at the caller ID and then back up at her.

'Sorry, Jo. I have to take this. Call me later, all right?'

Jo was delighted to get away and she hurried along to the crowded passport control lines and waited impatiently until she got through to the baggage claim hall. Bags from her flight hadn't yet started coming through so she had time to send a message to George.

> George Wilson. Markus has new phone number. He should be exiting in next five minutes or so. Jo.

She added his new number and hoped it would help.

It took another ten minutes before the luggage belt started moving and she was able to reclaim her bag. She kept looking over her shoulder for Markus but assumed he was travelling with just hand luggage and would be long gone by now. Still, it was a relief and a great pleasure to come out of the sliding doors and find Corrado standing right there, waiting for her. He hurried across to her and it looked very much as though he was going to kiss her before he transformed his outstretched arms into a chaste handshake.

'Hi, Jo, great to see you.' He took a closer look at her. 'All well?'

'Yes, thanks. And it's great to see you too.' And she meant it.

He removed her heavy bag from her grip and slung it over his shoulder.

'The car's just a bit further along. I wasn't quite so lucky this time. A five-minute walk.'

They went out of the air-conditioned interior into the full heat of the August afternoon. Corrado led her along, parallel with the front of the terminal building, until they came to the car park. Then, as they were walking past the rows of parked cars, something unexpected happened. Just ahead of them, a big silver people carrier with dark tinted windows suddenly reversed out of its parking space, almost running into the two of them. They jumped to one side and Jo heard Corrado mutter something under his breath. As the vehicle came to a halt beside them, the rear door suddenly opened and, to Jo's surprise, none other than Markus appeared, clawing desperately at the door handle, evidently trying to escape from somebody inside.

Jo and Corrado stopped and stared as a hairy forearm caught him by the scruff of his neck and yanked him back inside. As he did so, his eyes momentarily caught Jo's and she read abject terror in them. Then, as she and Corrado still stood there gawping, a slimmer arm appeared, holding in a manicured hand what was unmistakably a pistol. It took her a moment to realise that the vicious weapon was pointed straight at her. She found herself rooted to the spot, paralysed by fear.

'*Non avete visto niente.*'

The voice was as full of menace as the barrel of the gun and Jo gasped. Then she felt herself pushed out of the way as Corrado stepped in front of her, deliberately placing himself between the gunman and her body. As he did so, there was the sound of the door slamming, followed by a squeal of tyres as the vehicle accelerated away.

'Bastards.' Corrado turned back towards her and enveloped her in his arms. As she felt the tension release, she suddenly found herself weeping into his chest, clutching hold of him as though she never wanted to let him go.

They stayed like that for what seemed like a long time, but which was probably no more than a few seconds, before she heard his voice.

'Did you hear what the thug with the gun said; "You haven't seen anything." In other words, this never happened. Scum!' Not trusting her voice, she just nodded blankly. He reached into his pocket with his free hand and brought out his phone. 'We need to tell somebody. I've memorised the number plate. That might help the poor devil they dragged back into the car.'

Jo took a step backwards, watching him dial the number of the emergency services. He kept a steadying hand on her arm and she was glad of it.

She cleared her throat and spoke to him, her voice sounding strangely distant. 'I'm sorry to be such a wimp, Corrado; it's just that I've never had a gun pointed at me before.'

He glanced down at her as he waited to be connected to the police and gave her a little smile. 'Neither have I. It's not a very pleasant sensation, is it?'

'Thank you for trying to protect me...' Jo's brain suddenly cleared. 'But the thing is, I know the man who was trying to escape from that car.' As instructed by George, she hadn't told Corrado, or anybody else, anything about Markus and his shady dealings and she saw a look of amazement on Corrado's face. As she spoke, she pulled out her own phone and dialled George's number. She was patched through to him almost immediately and she explained what they had just seen, giving him the vehicle's number plate, while Corrado did the same to the Italian police. George took the message, thanked her and hung up.

A few minutes later, they were back at Corrado's Range Rover, being welcomed by an overjoyed Labrador. Corrado stowed her bag in the boot alongside the dog and they climbed inside. This time, Jo knew there was something she really had to do. She reached across, pulled him towards her, kissed him warmly on the cheek and buried her head against his chest. She felt his arms encircle her shoulders and she felt safe again.

'Thank you again, Corrado. My knight in shining armour.'

He squeezed her tightly to him. 'I'm just glad you're all right.' He released his hold on her and lifted her chin with one finger until he was staring down at her. 'And I'm glad I'm all right, too.' He breathed out with a rush. 'No, definitely not a nice experience. Want to tell me what it's all about?'

So she did. After all, the cat was well and truly out of the bag now. He listened attentively and didn't ask any questions. All he said at the end of her explanation was, 'Let's hope the police get them.'

They set off out of the airport and headed up the coast on the road that Corrado told her was the old Via Aurelia from ancient Roman times, now a modern highway. They were about halfway to Porto Ercole when Jo's phone rang. It was George with an update.

'We've got them. You weren't the only people to witness that little scene. Plain clothes officers rammed the vehicle at the entrance to the motorway and have captured the lot of them. I believe one or two were injured, but nothing life-threatening.'

'And Markus?'

'Markus Finchley, who was travelling on a Belgian passport this time under the name of Jean-Pierre Dupont, is apparently a very frightened man, but unscathed. He's also a very lucky man, and he knows it. By the sound of it, he was destined for a very unpleasant fate. We aren't sure why yet, but my Italian colleagues tell me he's singing like a canary so, hopefully, this might be the breakthrough we needed. Jo, I can't thank you enough. If you hadn't contacted me, we would almost certainly have missed him again and he would have disappeared and, along with him, our current investigation.'

'But why were they going to kill him?'

'No doubt we'll find out in due course. Maybe it was just that the bosses got wind that we were onto him and they wanted to dispose of the evidence. Who knows? Anyway, go off and have a wonderful holiday. You've deserved it.'

Chapter 19

They got to Porto Ercole at around four-thirty and were on the boat in the marina ten minutes later. As she slipped off her shoes and stepped off the pontoon onto the deck, Jo caught her breath, feeling suddenly apprehensive. As if being threatened with a gun wasn't enough, she was now about to embark on a trip into the unknown – not so much unknown geographically, but unknown emotionally. Corrado hadn't said much and she had had time to do a lot of thinking in the car on the way up the coast and the thing that had kept coming back to her, over and over again, was the fact that he had deliberately positioned himself between her and the gunman. At the very least, this was a sign of great courage. At best, it demonstrated a depth of feeling for her that he hadn't expressed so far. But for now, she didn't have much time for reflection.

'Jo, I don't know about you, but I could do with a swim… clear my head.' He sounded a bit weary and she wondered if this was just as a result of the drive or maybe some form of delayed shock after their scary experience at the airport.

She glanced round at the crowded waters of the marina.

'I'd love a swim, but do you mean here?' The water looked clean enough, but there were boats in every direction.

'No, definitely not here. Just a short way off to the west of us there are some lovely little beaches. They're pretty rocky, but the water's clear and clean and there's a bar up on the cliff above one of them. Sound good?'

'That sounds fantastic.' Jo was pleased to see him looking a bit more animated.

'Right, first mate, I'll start the engines and then, when I tell you, I want you to cast off. That means undoing the ropes from the rings on the pontoon.' He took her to the low platform at the stern of the boat and showed her what to do. 'Don't leave the ropes behind and don't leave yourself behind. All right?'

'Aye, aye, captain.' Jo gave him a mock salute.

Barely a quarter of an hour later, they were close to one of the little beaches. As he had said, it consisted of little patches of sand interspersed with large boulders. There were three or four people splashing about in the light blue water by the beach, but otherwise it was empty and the scrub-covered hillside behind looked unspoilt and almost uninhabited. As they came to a halt, an electric winch whined as the anchor dropped and Jo watched it slip down to the sea bed. The water was so wonderfully clear that she was able to see a shoal of little silver fish twist and turn away from the chain as it ran out. Seconds later, they were firmly moored and Corrado turned off the engines. She went back into the saloon and met him there, accompanied by Daisy. The dog pretty clearly knew what was coming next and was jumping around in great excitement.

'Daisy doesn't need to change, but I do.' Corrado gave Jo a little smile. 'And I imagine you aren't planning on going swimming in that lovely dress.'

'Just give me one minute.'

Jo headed down the stairs to her cabin while he turned away and disappeared down the staircase on the opposite side of the saloon. She dug out the butterfly bikini and changed as quickly as she could, but he was already up there waiting for her by the time she was ready. He was looking unexpectedly serious and she felt sure the events at the airport must be weighing heavily on his mind. She saw him stop and stare for two or three seconds, before remembering his manners and dropping his eyes, but not before Jo felt the colour flood to her cheeks.

'I'm pleased to see the bikini fits, Jo.'

'It fits perfectly and it's gorgeous. Thanks again.'

'You're very welcome.' He was just wearing a pair of blue swimming shorts, and he looked perfect to her, and this new, more reflective Corrado was, if anything, even more appealing. He looked up and caught her eye. 'Are you going to dive in, jump in or climb in?'

Jo decided that a plunge into cold water was probably the best thing for her after seeing him in his swimming shorts. She had only been on the boat with him for less than half an hour and she was already perilously close to dumping all her good intentions and leaping on him.

'Let's see if I can remember how to dive. I used to be in the swimming team at school.'

She went out onto the sun deck and across to the low guardrail. Stepping over it, she straightened up, took a deep breath, and dived over the side.

The first impact with the water was cold and wonderfully refreshing and when she surfaced, she checked that her bikini was still in place, wiped the hair out of her eyes, and looked up just in time to see a large black object come flying towards her. Daisy hit the water with about as much grace as a sack of potatoes, sending a tsunami into Jo's face, but the Labrador was definitely smiling as she doggy-paddled over, nose sticking up out of the water and her tail like a rudder behind, snorting and snuffling happily.

'*Ciao*, Daisy. Are you a happy dog?' It was a rhetorical question.

'She's a very happy dog. And that was a classy dive, Jo – yours, not hers.'

Corrado appeared a few feet from her. Presumably he had also dived in, but she hadn't heard him.

'By the way, I've hung the ladder on the stern so you can climb out easily any time you want. But, if you're up for it, shall we swim in to the shore and go up to the cafe? See it, up there?'

Jo followed the direction of his pointing finger. Sure enough, a path led up from the beach to a low construction set into the hillside with a shady terrace in front that almost concealed it from view.

'Sounds good to me. I only ever do breaststroke, so you might have to wait for me.'

'We're in no hurry.'

She was a good swimmer and as she swam in alongside him, she duck-dived down from time to time and opened her eyes underwater. The seabed was a mixture of sand and rocks, with lots of little fish darting about. Looking up, she distinctly saw Corrado floating above her, barely moving, waiting for her to emerge. The seabed shelved steeply up as they approached the land, and before long she found she could stand in the water. There were lots of rocks on the bottom, but most were worn smooth by the waves. She picked her way out of the water after him and together with the dog they climbed the short distance to the cafe. The path was well-worn and sandy and it wasn't uncomfortable on her bare feet. As they got there, she had a sudden thought.

'Corrado, I've just realised. I'm afraid I haven't brought any money.'

'I can see that. There isn't really room in that bikini for anything but you.' Seeing her starting to blush once more, he hurried on. 'Luckily these shorts have got a zip pocket and I've brought some cash in a waterproof wallet.'

'That's a relief. I had visions of having to swim back to the boat.'

'We will have to eventually, but not for a while.' He led her across to an empty table looking out over the beach towards the boat. 'At least we can keep an eye on *Ippona* from here.'

'She looks lovely, just floating there. The water's so clean and clear, it almost looks as though there's nothing holding her up.' In fact, it was so very clear, she could even make out the shadow of the boat on the seabed. She returned her attention to Corrado. 'Thank you so much for inviting me. I just know this is going to be a magical holiday.'

He was still looking unusually serious, but he was quick to reply. 'All the more magical because you're here... mate.'

They spent almost an hour sitting there, enjoying the view and the relative cool under the vine-covered pergola. She gradually managed to get him talking and they spoke about all sorts of things, from Angie and Mario to their respective parents, and Jo felt more and more relaxed with him and got the impression he, too, was relaxing. There was no innuendo, no awkward glances at her fairly skimpy bikini, nothing to make her embarrassed. Gradually, she began to get used to being more than half-naked alongside him. Maybe, she told herself, his serious air was nothing more than his having to get used to being with her like this as well.

As if by some unspoken agreement, neither of them mentioned the events at the airport and there was one other subject she didn't feel ready to air quite yet. For now, she said nothing about her decision to move to the US. She knew full well that even though they were just good friends, very good friends, she was going to miss him an awful lot. Somehow, talking about it would only bring that moment even closer.

'Jo, look, there's one of your little friends.'

Jo had been daydreaming, her eyes staring vacantly out over the Mediterranean. Hastily she returned her attention to Corrado. Her friends? Here? Then she saw what he had seen. Barely a metre from them, there was a lovely moth, its wings divided between vivid yellow and black and white segments. The lower half of its body was bright red and the overall impression was of a blaze of colour. It was sitting on a vine leaf, in the shade of the pergola, wings wide open. It wasn't new to her, but it was a beautiful little animal all the same.

'It's a Tiger Moth. They aren't that rare, but it's unusual to see them in the sunshine.' She racked her brains for a moment. 'I think this one's a Cream-spot Tiger Moth, *epicallia villica*.' She turned towards him proudly. 'See, the brain's still working, even if I am on holiday.'

'Impressive.'

She sat and watched it silently until it fluttered away and out of sight. 'Beautiful…' She subsided into reflective silence for a while, just enjoying the moment, the surroundings and his company. It was a good while later when she heard his voice.

'It's gone six. I thought we could eat at Porto Ercole tonight if that's all right with you. So, if you feel like it, shall we head back to the boat?'

'You're the captain.'

They swam back to the boat at a leisurely pace, accompanied by the Labrador. When they reached the low platform at the stern, Daisy flopped her paws onto the deck and – in a no doubt well-practised manoeuvre – Corrado swam up behind her and gave her a hefty push up, out of the water. As Jo was about to climb the ladder after her, she felt Corrado's hand on her arm.

'Hang on. Stay back unless you want a shower.'

Sure enough, Daisy then set about shaking herself dry as the two of them trod water and waited until it was safe to proceed. Once on the deck, Jo realised she hadn't brought a towel out of her cabin and she was still dripping wet, but Corrado pointed forward.

'I've put the cushions out on the foredeck. I normally lie there in the sun for a few minutes to dry off before going in. Good idea?'

'Definitely.'

Jo followed him round the side of the main cabin to the sundeck and lay down on the sun-warmed cushions. As before, Corrado took up station right over on the other side while this time the dog also sprawled in the sun between them, rolling around and grunting happily to herself as she dried out. Jo lay back and after a few minutes felt her eyes begin to close. She was perilously close to nodding off when Corrado's voice dragged her back to consciousness.

'Jo, something very strange happened today...' His voice tailed off uncertainly. This was so unlike his normal confident self, that she was wide awake in an instant.

'What, Corrado? Is something wrong?'

'No, nothing's wrong. It's just that it's something I can't quite get my head round...' His voice tailed off again.

Jo hesitated, giving him time to collect his thoughts. But then, as she let her eyes roam round the foredeck of the boat, she blinked, stared, blinked again and rose silently to her feet. She glanced across at Corrado and put her finger to her lips, mouthing the word, 'Butterfly.'

She made her way across to the coiled anchor chain and stood in wonder. There, shimmering in the light of the setting sun was none other than *apatura iris*, the elusive Purple Emperor in all its deep bluish-purple glory. She stood stock still, hardly daring to believe her good fortune. Seconds later she felt a gentle touch on her bare shoulder and turned her head slowly back to see Corrado, holding out her handbag.

'Here, I thought you might want your camera. I presume it's in here.' He kept his voice to a whisper. 'It's the Emperor, isn't it? I remember it from when I was a little kid.'

Jo nodded and carefully removed the phone from the bag and took a series of photos of the beautiful butterfly as it gently flexed its wings in the sunshine. Then, in the blink of an eye, it was gone. Jo watched it dance away back towards the shore until it disappeared from view. She turned towards Corrado and sighed.

'How... amazing... was... that? And fancy seeing one here. They normally inhabit the tree tops. And thank you for bringing me my camera.'

She glanced down at the phone and checked that the photos had come out well. Reassured, she stuck it back in her bag and looked up at him again, remembering the moment before the appearance of the Emperor.

'Sorry about that, Corrado, you were just starting to tell me about something that happened today.'

He gave her a look that was almost apprehensive, but then mustered a smile. 'Don't worry. It can wait. Now, I suggest we head back to the marina.' His smile strengthened. 'So, Mr Mate, I'll get the engines started and then would you keep an eye on the anchor chain as it comes up and shout if it snags?'

Jo was kicking herself as he went off. Somehow, she had the impression he had been about to speak about something far more important than just a butterfly – endangered or not.

–

The restaurant was right on the harbour side with tables sheltered underneath an awning looking straight out over a little beach and down the coast towards the south. By the time they got there, the sun had disappeared below the low hills surrounding the harbour and lights had begun to twinkle in the distance. Jo took a seat beside Corrado and felt the dog slump down at their feet. It was a beautiful evening and she felt relaxed once more after the stresses of the day.

They were in southern Tuscany now and so Corrado suggested they start with traditional Tuscan bruschetta made with the local unsalted bread and wonderful thick green extra virgin olive oil. After that they both opted for skewers of grilled prawns and squid along with a mixed salad. They drank cold white wine and sparkling mineral water. It took until Jo was already on her tiramisu before Corrado managed to start putting his thoughts into words.

She listened spellbound.

'Jo, listen, I have to tell you something. I don't know what it means. Maybe you'll be able to help me, but it's something that happened today. Back at the airport, when that thug pointed a pistol at you, I felt compelled, no, not compelled, that sounds as if it was a conscious action. I just *knew* I had to protect you. I couldn't bear the thought of something happening to you. I've never felt anything like this before.'

'You were incredibly brave and I'm immensely touched.' Jo could hardly believe her ears. Where was he going with this?

'Not brave. Like I say, it was just instinct.' He reached over and took her hand in his, his eyes catching hers for a moment before returning to the twinkling lights along the distant coast. 'Jo, if you had asked me a month ago if there might ever be any circumstances when I would risk my life for another human being, I would have laughed in your face. We are animals and our two primary instincts are reproduction and survival. The idea of risking my own survival so somebody else can live makes no sense… made no sense. And yet, today, back at the airport, I did just that.' He turned his head back towards her. 'What does it mean, Jo?'

She looked deep into his eyes in the flickering light of the candle on the table in front of them. He looked puzzled, troubled and vulnerable. She squeezed his hand and told him the only thing she could.

'That's something you're going to have to work out for yourself, Corrado. Think it through and it'll come to you. As for me, all I can say is that I feel sure I know what it means.'

'You do?'

She was still reeling from this admission from him. Could it be that the pragmatic scientist was beginning to accept that his actions could be provoked by more than cold hard science? And if this were to prove to be the case, what did this mean about his feelings towards her and his intentions? What did this mean for his future and for hers?

'I'm pretty sure I do. Take your time. I'm sure you'll work it out.'

As she spoke, her mind was still racing. He might not know it, but there was very little doubt in her mind that sooner or later the penny would drop and he would realise what was happening to him. And then? Suddenly her relaxed state transformed into something far more tense, and she struggled to come up with something to lighten the atmosphere. Luckily, at that moment Daisy intervened, producing her usual whine from under the table. Corrado didn't need to translate this time. Jo knew what it meant.

'It sounds like Daisy wants a walk. Why don't I get the bill? And an espresso for you, maybe?'

Predictably, he refused point blank to let her pay for the meal. She fought hard, but in the end had to give way, but only after extorting a promise from him that she would be allowed to pay for other meals. He agreed, although she had a feeling he would offer further resistance next time.

By the time they got back to the boat, it was past ten o'clock and she was feeling exhausted after everything that had happened. She would dearly have liked to sit and talk, or rather listen to him talk, but her eyes were already closing as they stepped on board. By the look of him, he was equally weary. Once they were back in the saloon with the doors closed in case of mosquitoes – although they hadn't been bothered by any insects over dinner – she went across to him to say goodnight. It took a lot of willpower not to kiss him, but she did hug him, repeating her thanks for his bravery at the airport. The hug didn't last long before he stepped hurriedly back and bade her goodnight.

'Sleep well, Jo. The doors are locked, although I'm sure this is a very secure place. Besides, we've got our guard dog on patrol.'

Daisy's wicker basket had emerged from the master cabin and was now in the saloon, midway between the two staircases. Far from being on patrol, Daisy herself had wasted no time in flopping down in the basket and was looking at the two of them through half-closed eyes. Jo went across and scratched her ears.

'See you in the morning, Daisy.' She gave Corrado one more glance and a gentle smile. 'Goodnight, Corrado, and thanks for everything.'

As she lay in her bed after what had been an amazingly eventful day, the thought going round and round in her head was how on earth she might react if he were to come out with a declaration of real love, not just animal lust. While she had no doubts at all that a healthy shot of animal lust was bubbling away just below the surface in her own body, she knew she wanted more than that. And if he loved her, how did she feel about him? Did she love him? And if she did, was she prepared to love him and leave him? Surely she *had* to take the job at the United Nations. Didn't she?

Chapter 20

In spite of all the thoughts racing around Jo's brain, she slept really well and didn't emerge until past eight o'clock next morning. When she climbed up the stairs into the saloon and a wonderful aroma of coffee, she found Corrado already dressed in shorts and a T-shirt, standing at the state-of-the-art coffee machine. Daisy leapt out of her basket as she saw Jo's head appear and gave her a boisterous welcome as her master looked round.

'*Buongiorno*. Sleep well?'

Jo made a fuss of the dog and then went over to Corrado's side. He was looking as desirable as ever and it took a real effort to restrain herself from kissing him. Instead, she just smiled.

'*Buongiorno, capitano*. Yes, thanks, I slept like a log – apart from when those people came past at two o'clock in the morning. What about you?' She took a good look at him in the clear light of day. He was still looking troubled.

'Fine, thanks.' His voice was unusually flat.

She didn't query this, although she felt sure it wasn't true. She had little doubt that his brain had been working overtime. Still, she was pleased to see him manage to return her smile.

'Coffee? Espresso, cappuccino, or something in-between?'

'A cappuccino, if it's not too much trouble?'

She felt like catching hold of him and giving him a big, supportive hug while he continued to struggle to make sense of his emotions, but she didn't. Instead, she went across to the now wide open glass doors and looked out. It was another cloudless day and even at this hour of the morning the sun was hot on her head. She turned back towards him and saw he had been watching her, before his eyes dropped guiltily to the coffee cups again.

'What's the plan, today, captain?'

'A quick cup of coffee and then Daisy needs to go for a walk.' He glanced down at the dog and smiled, and his face lit up. 'She knows that word so very well in Italian. I wonder how long it'll be before she understands it in English.'

He turned away and she heard the roar of the steam as he heated the milk for her cappuccino. He served it up as professionally as any barista and she was impressed. As they drank their coffee, he continued with plans for the day.

'While we're out, I suggest we buy ourselves some croissants for breakfast – unless you want bacon and eggs – as well as some bread and milk and a few other bits and pieces so we can be self-sufficient for a day or two. If you're happy, I thought we could sail around the coast to a lovely bay I know. It's a good, safe anchorage and it's very beautiful. How does that sound?'

That sounded perfect.

It took them most of the morning to get to his little bay and the voyage was a delight. There was very little wind, but a gentle sea breeze gradually came up and propelled them around the coast of the rocky peninsula.

The catamaran was remarkably stable in the little waves and Jo felt very secure. He explained that the Argentario was to all effects an island, barely connected to the mainland by two strips of sand and a causeway. Apart from a few little villages around the coast, it looked almost uninhabited, and its rocky hillsides were covered in scrub and dense Mediterranean forest. It was still remarkably unspoilt.

The bay itself was almost horseshoe-shaped, with a narrow band of sandy beach in the middle. There were half a dozen other boats either anchored offshore or run up on the beach, but there can't have been more than a couple of dozen people altogether. Considering this was the middle of August, this was remarkable. The colours of the water ran from the lightest blue near the shore to a deep cobalt further out, with occasional dark shadows where rocks lay beneath the surface. It was, as he had predicted, almost completely sheltered from the wind and the water itself was virtually flat calm.

They anchored about a hundred metres or so from the beach and travelled to the shore in the inflatable, the Labrador standing proudly up at the front like a figure-head. As they reached the shallows and Corrado killed the outboard motor, Daisy launched herself into the water with gusto and Jo slipped more sedately over the bow after her, walking the inflatable into the coarse sand beach. The spot where they had landed was sheltered by big boulders and they could have been all alone but for an occasional splash or shout from further along the beach.

The water was lovely and warm and they spent ages in the sea, floating about, diving down from time to time to pick smooth pebbles off the bottom and to follow little shoals of silver fish. It was relaxing, it was fascinating, and Jo couldn't have been happier. Finally, they came out of the water, leaving the dog sprawled in the shallows, and settled down on their towels to dry out.

There wasn't a cloud in the sky and as the sun made short work of drying her off, Jo pulled out a bottle of sun cream and rubbed it over her front, legs and face. However, when the time came to turn over, she knew she needed help.

'Corrado, could I ask a big favour of you? I don't suppose you could spread some sun cream on my back, could you? I'm afraid I just can't reach.' This invitation to him to run his hands over her naked body, she told her subconscious, was simply expediency, nothing more. As usual, her subconscious didn't believe a word of it and was probably right.

He pulled himself onto his knees and came across to help. She rolled onto her front and felt the cool cream land on her shoulders and then his hands begin to smooth it over her skin. His fingers ran up her arms and down her backbone. Unasked, he unclipped the strap of her bra as he did his best to cover the whole area. Beneath him, Jo was getting a lot more out of the exercise than just protection from the sun. The feel of his fingers on her skin sent shivers throughout her whole body, and he even commented that she had goose bumps, asking if she was cold. She shook her head, unwilling to try to speak. As he finished his work, he scrupulously clipped her strap up again and sat back, leaving Jo in a state of barely-controlled rapture.

She lay there for ten, maybe fifteen minutes, feeling the sun hot on her back while trying to cool down on the inside. His touch had been magic and she knew, without a shadow of a doubt, that her self-control didn't stand a chance if he ever laid his hands on her again. Friendship was one thing, but she knew full well her feelings for him ran a whole lot deeper than that. Whatever she had told Victoria and Angie about love being an illusion, she was honest enough to herself to realise that something far more serious than friendship was lurking just below the surface of her emotions and it wouldn't take much to bring it to life.

–

His moment of enlightenment didn't come until later.

They sat down to dinner back on the boat just as the last red glow of the sun disappeared below the horizon behind them and the breeze wafted through the saloon, beginning to lower the temperature by a very welcome few degrees after the full scorching heat of the day.

He made pasta with pesto while she prepared a mixed salad with tuna and egg, and then lit a candle, setting it on the table as the light faded. When he placed her plate of pasta in front of her, she was touched to see that he had chosen *farfalle* – so called because of their resemblance to little butterflies. She commented and saw him smile in the flickering light of the candle.

'The least I could do. And I'm really pleased you managed to see your Emperor butterfly. Really beautiful.'

'Although pretty disgusting when it comes to diet. They're particularly fond of rotting flesh or poo.'

'You wouldn't think it to look at them. How something so beautiful can exist by eating that sort of stuff is amazing.'

'Well, to be quite precise, they don't actually eat at all. They get all their food by drinking, sucking it up via their proboscis. And did you know butterflies can taste with their feet? They have sensors in their feet so they can tell what a flower's going to taste like just by landing on it.'

He looked up from his pasta and she saw him smile. 'I can see why you find them so interesting.'

'They're actually such complex little animals. Most people just see them as beautiful little things when, inside, there's so much more to them.'

'Not that different from you, Jo. I can honestly say that although I was immediately struck by your looks, I very soon worked out that what's inside is even more special.'

'I'm delighted to hear it. Never judge a book by its cover.' She set down her fork and reflected. 'This is where your limbic system argument falls down, surely? There's more to us humans than just outward appearance and physical attraction. Our closest relatives in the animal world, monkeys and apes, like the bonobos for instance, are only interested in sexual gratification and reproduction. Humans require more than that, and that's where what's inside comes into the frame.'

For a moment, their eyes met across the table and she read uncertainty on his face in the candlelight. Then he dropped his eyes to his plate, but made no attempt to start eating again. It was a while before he managed to marshal his thoughts, but Jo just sat and waited.

'I've been doing a lot of thinking about my limbic system recently. And it's all your fault.' He took a sip of red wine and Jo found herself tensing, wondering what was coming next. 'I was a perfectly happy hedonist, living for the moment, until you came along. Do you know something, Jo?' He looked back up at her, his magnetic blue eyes flashing with the reflected candlelight. 'You probably didn't realise, but that kiss you gave me when we were soaking wet after we'd been dancing in the rain, that kiss, fleeting as it was, shook me to my foundations. I had never felt anything like it before.'

By now, Jo had lost all interest in her pasta. She, too, took a mouthful of wine before replying.

'So are you saying that you liked it?'

'Liked it? It was amazing. It was as if I'd suddenly been struck by an electric shock that went straight to my brain.'

'Are we back to the limbic system again?'

'Way more than that. It was as if my whole cerebral cortex had been invaded and taken over. Ever since then – maybe even before, I can't remember – I haven't been able to stop thinking about you.'

Jo liked the sound of what she was hearing although it was all so confusing. Could it really be that the leopard was changing its spots at long last? And, if so, would this be the impulse her overstretched emotions needed to finally accept that she really did love him – and had done so for quite some time? She took advantage of his evident honesty to ask him something that had been exercising her mind for weeks now.

'Tell me something, Corrado. When we were supposed to meet up on my last night in Rome, when I was taking you out for a pizza, why was it you couldn't come? Did something happen?'

He didn't answer immediately. When he did, it was with the same bemused tone he had just used.

'I saw you in Piazza Navona with that man. I now know from Angie that he was your ex, but at the time,

I didn't. The thing is, seeing you with him had another very strange effect on me.' He looked up at her. 'I felt jealous, Jo. Do you know what that feels like?'

Jo decided to try to keep things light – if that was possible. 'I know exactly what that feels like, Corrado. Would you believe I've even felt jealous of a member of the Roman constabulary?'

He managed a little smile. 'I'm sorry. The thing is, though, I don't get jealous. Jealousy isn't scientific. Do bonobos get jealous when one of the females engages in sex with another male? No, of course not.'

'I didn't need to see you having sex with the police constable.' She was still doing her best to keep him smiling.

'Of course not, but you know what I mean. Why should it matter to me that you were with another man? I'm not like that.'

'And that bothered you?'

He nodded. 'It bothered me. In fact, I couldn't stop thinking about it and what it might mean. I got so confused, I knew it would be a mistake to go out for dinner with you, so that's why I texted you. I'm sorry, Jo. If it helps, I had a miserable evening all alone. Ask Daisy. She'll tell you.'

She smiled. 'So you weren't completely alone after all. But why exactly did it bother you? Hadn't we established quite clearly that we're just good friends. You're the captain, I'm the mate. Surely there's no need for jealousy.'

'That was the plan, wasn't it?' He sounded almost disappointed. 'This afternoon on the beach, I finally worked out what's happened to me, why I found myself voluntarily offering up my life for yours at the airport. It's contrary to everything I've ever learned or believed, but, like Sherlock Holmes used to say, when you've eliminated the impossible, whatever remains, however improbable, has to be the truth.' He raised his eyes from the table and looked straight at her. 'Jo, I never thought I'd ever hear myself say this, but I can't see any alternative. It has to be love.'

Now that he had articulated the word she had never believed she would hear on his lips, she felt a sense of release, coupled with a surge of emotion that threatened to overwhelm her. Days, weeks of repressed emotion overflowed inside her and she came very, very close to bursting into tears. As far as she was concerned, she could finally admit to herself, if not to him, what she had known all along. She took a tight grip on her emotions and smiled at him.

'Love – that's your scientific conclusion after evaluating all the data?'

She was pleased to see a little smile forming on his lips. 'I can't see any other explanation. It makes no scientific sense but Sherlock Holmes is Sherlock Holmes, after all.'

'You realise this has got to be one of the least romantic declarations of love in the history of the world?'

'I'm sorry, but you have to remember that I'm a complete beginner at this stuff.' He was still smiling, but she couldn't miss the apprehension on his face. 'As far as I can recall from the movies, I think this should be the moment when you tell me you feel the same way about me... or not...' His voice tailed off uncertainly and her heart went out to him. Doing her best to control her growing excitement, she gave him an encouraging smile.

'As a fellow scientist, before leaping to conclusions, I don't think we should discount the experimental method.'

As she spoke, she stood up and went round the table until she was standing by his side. He started to stand up, but she pushed him gently back down again and then leant towards him, encircling his shoulders with her arms. Very gently she let her lips rest against his as her eyes closed. She stayed like this for a few seconds before she felt him stir and reach up in his turn. He caught hold of her, pulled her slowly onto his lap, and kissed her properly for the very first time. She kissed him back with growing passion.

Their pasta was completely cold and the dog was beginning to get worried when Corrado finally sat back, still holding her in his arms, his eyes closed. Night had fallen and the only light in the saloon came from the guttering candle. She reached up and ran her fingers across his face, letting them rest on his lips, his cheeks and finally on his eyelids. While his eyes were still closed, she gave him his answer.

'My conclusion, captain, after a close hands–on examination of all the evidence, is that it very definitely has to be love.' She leant her face towards him again and kissed him softly on the eyelids before releasing him. Then she sat back and took a deep breath. Everything over the past twenty-four hours had been building up to this moment.

'But there's a problem.' She saw his eyes open. 'A big problem. You see, I've got to go to New York.'

'That's not the end of the world. How long for?'

'To work. Maybe forever.'

'I see.'

The tone of his voice said it all. He looked like a little puppy being left at home all alone. She sat there and softly stroked his face with her fingers as she explained all about Professor Dietrich and her job offer. Corrado made no response until she had finished. At that point, he pulled her closer, kissing her on the lips and then gently all over her face until she was in a state of near ecstasy. Finally, he released her, and then he surprised her.

'Well, there's no question. You can't refuse an offer like that.'

'I can't?' She was amazed. In all the different scenarios she had played out in her head, she had imagined him trying everything from bribery to tears to make her give up the UN job and move to Rome to be with him. 'But that would mean we'd be thousands of miles apart.'

'I know, but I think I know you pretty well by now. You told me once you didn't think you were a very ambitious person and I believe you. But I also know that you're passionate about your work and about the future of the planet. I love you very dearly – be in no doubt about that – but I would never want to be the one to make you give up something so important to you. You might not regret it at first but, sooner or later, you would. Besides, I know you're very good at your job and the planet needs all the help it can get. No, you've got to take it.'

'So where does this leave us?'

There was silence for a few seconds before he spoke and when he did, she could hear him doing his best to put a brave spin on the situation.

'To quote you quoting Alfred Lord Tennyson, "it's probably better to have loved and lost than never to have loved at all."'

'But we haven't loved yet.'

'That, at least, we can easily remedy.'

Chapter 21

Over the next ten days they spent most of their time in the sea, on the beach, or in bed. Wherever they went, they were always together and Jo couldn't remember ever having felt happier.

Apart from the question of New York hanging over them like the sword of Damocles.

As the days went by, she grew closer and closer to Corrado, although the looming spectre of separation threatened to take the edge off what was proving to be the best time of her whole life. The sense of relief she now felt as she could finally admit to herself the feelings that had been building in her body for weeks was overwhelming – and very welcome. As for Corrado, she could see he was clearly trying hard to enjoy the moment, without looking any further ahead than a day or two, but little things gave him away. Jo grew ever more convinced that he loved her dearly and the very bizarreness of the experience for a self-confessed unbeliever like him was almost comical to observe. From time to time she would catch him looking at her like Daisy staring at a string of sausages, and when she smiled at him he would blush as if he had been caught out. In the morning she would wake to find him leaning on one elbow, staring down at her as she slept, an expression of adoration on his face, and she loved him for it.

She now knew without a shadow of a doubt that she loved him very much, reflecting that her own days as an unbeliever were well and truly over. Angie and Victoria had been right all along: just because she had had a bad experience with Christian didn't mean love didn't exist. Now she knew it really did, and it felt wonderful.

After a few more lazy days around the Argentario peninsula, they sailed out to some of the other islands, starting with Giannutri, a tiny island with barely a handful of houses on it, but with one of the most spectacularly beautiful coastlines Jo had ever seen. It took them less than three hours to sail across from the mainland with the aid of a good breeze and Jo had a go at taking the helm while Corrado did some fishing. When they reached the island, they moored in a little creek whose waters were a breathtaking, almost unreal, combination of every possible hue of blue from deepest ultramarine to royal blue, cornflower, and the lightest powder blue where the wavelets washed up on the little beach. The only sounds were the cries of the gulls and the gentle hiss of the waves on the sand.

They swam in the blissfully warm water and dived down, collecting tiny blue and yellow shells from the bottom. In the evening they took a little portable barbecue to the secluded beach and grilled the fish Corrado had caught as they had sailed across. They drank white wine, cold from the fridge, and he wedged the bottle in the wet sand on the shoreline to stay cool as they lazed in each other's arms and watched the sun drop below the horizon. If paradise existed, Jo thought to herself as she lay alongside him in the twilight, it most definitely had to look something like this place.

After a few idyllic days they moved on to the bigger, busier, island of Giglio where they managed to squeeze into a mooring alongside a pontoon in the main harbour at Porto Giglio. They went out for dinner that night in a restaurant overlooking the bay, surrounded by noisy crowds, but were perfectly happy with each other's company and ignored the other diners. On their way back to the boat, he bought her a little necklace made of the tiny blue and yellow shells, just like they had found on the sea bed. Next day they stocked up on supplies and then sailed round the island to a delightful little bay where they moored and lazed for a few more days, barely seeing anybody else for hours on end.

From there they headed back across to the Argentario once more and stopped in Porto Santo Stefano where he had an appointment with his accountant. This was a sizeable port, packed with tourists, cars and noisy scooters, and it came as a shock to the system after days of blissful peace and quiet. While he was away at his lunch meeting, Jo took Daisy for a good long walk across the headland and at midday sat down in the shade of a gnarled, thorny old tree, its branches blown horizontal over the years. Across the deep blue of the Mediterranean she could see the Tuscan coast curving northwards, its unbroken sandy beaches fringed with pine forests. As the dog slumped down beside her, Jo pulled out her phone and called Victoria.

'Vic, hi, how's things?'

'Great, thanks. I gather from George that you helped him and his team with some big problem the other day. All very mysterious, but he told me he couldn't have done it without you.'

Jo knew that George had asked her to keep the Markus affair secret, so she made no mention of him and just talked about the silver car and the man with the gun. After she had given Victoria a brief run-down of what had happened in the car park, her friend was far more excited by the fact that Corrado had stepped between Jo and the gunman than what had been going on in the car.

'You know what this means, don't you, Jo?'

'It's got to be love?'

'Exactly, but says who? Just you or him too?'

'Says both of us.' Jo went on to describe the events of the past few days and she heard Victoria whistle.

'I told you he'd change, didn't I? And you... with all that nonsense you've been spouting about love not being a thing! See, Auntie Vic knows best.'

'You were right, as usual. Thank you, Auntie Vic.'

'And I seem to remember saying you needed to check him out in the sack before you could be sure. How did that go?'

Jo found herself grinning. 'Totally amazing.'

'So, what happens now, Jo? You've got your interview with Professor Whatshername in a week or two. What're you going to tell her?'

'What can I tell her, Vic? Even Corrado's telling me I have to take the job or forever regret it.'

'So that's what you're going to do?'

'I honestly don't know, Vic. The thing is, I'm absolutely potty about Corrado. The idea of being separated from him seems unthinkable.'

'I suppose he'll be able to come over to the States and see you regularly.'

'We've been talking about that. Yes, of course we can meet up every now and then but, realistically, that might be all right for a few months, maybe even a year, but if I stay in New York for long, sooner or later it's all going to fall apart.'

'So, what're you going to do? It's an awful choice you've got to make.'

'Tell me something I don't know. I'm damned if I do and damned if I don't.'

Jo spent the rest of the day wrestling with the problem of having to choose between the man she loved and the job she loved. She knew she wasn't the first woman in the history of the world to face this particular dilemma, but that didn't make it any easier. Finally, as she settled down to a well-earned ice cream in a cafe overlooking the port, she even called her mother for advice.

'Hi, mum. It's me.'

'Hello, sweetheart, where are you?'

'I'm back on dry land for a few hours. It's a place called Porto Santo Stefano. Check it out on Google. It's beautiful. This whole area's stunning. Today Corrado's got a meeting, so I've been for a walk with the Labrador.'

'And how's it all going?'

'It's unbelievable, mum. I'm having the most amazing time.'

'I'm so pleased. And how are you getting on with Corrado? He's behaving himself, I hope.'

'He's wonderful. There's just one huge problem.' She took a deep breath. 'I know I'm falling in love with him, and in seven days' time I'm leaving him. Another few weeks after that and I'll be off to America...' Her voice tailed off and she waited for her mother to pounce with a hearty 'I told you so'. But she didn't.

'And is he falling in love with you, dear?' Her mother's voice was unexpectedly soft.

'I really think he is. He has.'

'And you don't think he sees you as just another one of his conquests?'

'Definitely not. It's much more than that, I'm sure.'

'Well, I'm very happy for you, Joanne. So, does this mean you won't be taking the United Nations job?'

'No, mum, I have to take it. Even Corrado's telling me I have to take it.'

'He sounds like a very sensible boy.'

'He's sensible, sensitive, I can't tell you, mum… he's perfect.' In spite of herself, Jo felt tears welling up in the corners of her eyes. Daisy must have noticed something in her voice as the next thing Jo felt was a heavy Labrador paw landing on her lap. She looked down into the big brown eyes and summoned a smile. 'And as if leaving him isn't bad enough, it'll mean leaving his lovely dog as well.'

'You know what they say, Joanne – love me, love my dog.'

'That's what he said, and I do. Both of them.'

'So, are you sure you're going to America?'

'What do *you* think I should do, mum?' This was a first. Jo couldn't remember ever asking her mother for advice about men before.

'That's not up to me to say, dear. You're the one who's got to decide.' There was a short pause. 'But all I would say is there are thousands of jobs in the world, but very, very few perfect men. If you really think this is the right one for you, then maybe you should choose him over the job. I did, you know.'

'You did?'

'When I met your father I was just finishing my degree, but you already know that, don't you? My plan was to go on to do a history PhD and become a university lecturer. Instead, I married your father and the result was you, followed by Angela, and I'm not complaining. You've both turned out so very well. And of course, I got the job teaching at St Margaret's. It wasn't Oxford University, but it was a good job all the same.'

'So you think I should choose him?'

'I'm just telling you what *I* did, Joanne. It's up to you now.'

–

Jo had arranged to meet Corrado at three o'clock at the boat. As she and the dog walked back downhill through the crowded little side streets, she was barely concentrating on where she was going, her mind fully occupied with the conundrum of what to do. She was only vaguely aware of her surroundings until she emerged once more onto the quayside and it was then that she gradually came to a decision. The idea of leaving Corrado was just too brutal for words. Her mum was right, good men were so very hard to find. She couldn't abandon him.

There had to be something she could do here in Italy. She would sit down tonight and scour the internet for something in her field. Rome was home to a number of international and European organisations, after all, from the FAO, the United Nations' Food and Agriculture Organisation, to the WFP, the World Food Programme, and a host of environmental charities. Surely there had to be a vacancy in one of these that would allow her to use her skills to help the world and stay by Corrado's side.

Corrado arrived back a quarter of an hour late, very apologetic. He told her the lunch meeting had lasted longer than expected and he had only just got away. From the expression on his face, it had been a fairly stressful few hours, so she made him a cup of tea and then sat down with her arms around him and the dog at their feet. She thought about telling him she had made up her mind to say no to Professor Dietrich, but then decided to wait at least until she had had the chance to see what jobs were available online.

Tired of the crowds, they stocked up with food and headed back out to sea again, anchoring for the night in another spectacular, and unpopulated, little bay a few miles to the west of Porto Santo Stefano. As they sailed round the rocky coastline to get there, they were joined by a pod of dolphins who swam with them for almost half an hour. Jo couldn't have been happier, although she noticed Corrado still looking a bit glum. After they had anchored, she went to the fridge and poured out a couple of glasses of Prosecco to help cheer him up. She joined him and Daisy outside on the sundeck and settled down beside the two of them.

'So, how did the meeting go? Everything all right? You've been a bit quiet.'

He switched his gaze from the cliffs back to her. The deep blue eyes were smiling, but there was something else, maybe regret, in there. She wondered if this was because of his meeting or if he, too, had been thinking about their imminent separation.

'Sorry if I've been a bit distant. No, everything's all right. We were just going through the figures and I was hoping we might have a bit of leeway to expand, but the advice is to wait.' He shrugged. 'It's a pity.'

'Never mind.' She reached over and caught hold of his arm. 'Angie told me your business has expanded amazingly fast. I suppose it's inevitable the curve will have to level out a bit.'

He summoned a smile. 'You're right, of course. It's just that I was hoping...' He swallowed his wine and set the glass down. 'Anyway, I had a good lunch, so that's something, and Paolo, the head of accounts, is a good friend. Let's forget about business for now. I can think of far more interesting things we could do.'

As he rolled towards her, Jo laid her half-empty glass carefully to one side and pulled herself up on top of him, straddling him and resting on her elbows. As she looked down into his eyes from very close range, she decided there were various ways of cheering him up. The first was verbally. The next would probably involve going down to their cabin, even if this was a very remote place.

'I spoke to my mum today, Corrado. You know what she said? She said there are thousands of jobs in the world, but very few good men.'

'She sounds like a very sensible lady.'

'And you're a good man.'

'You're sure about that? My track record isn't so great.'

'You're a good man. So good, in fact, that I made my mind up an hour ago that I'm going to ditch the UN job and look for something here in Italy, hopefully Rome.' She reached down and kissed him. 'It's quite simple really. I can't imagine life without you.'

He hugged her so tightly she almost couldn't breathe for a moment. When he released her, his eyes were sparkling and his voice was heavy with emotion.

'I can't imagine life without you either. But think long and hard about what you're giving up. This is your life's work we're talking about.'

'But it's also you I'm talking about. There has to be something suitable here in Rome. I'm going to spend the next few days on the internet checking out what's available. We'll see. Now...' She kissed him again and then whispered in his ear what she was proposing as a more practical way of cheering him up. He reached up and crushed her to him.

'I love you, Jo, I really do.'

Chapter 22

The bad news was that over their final week together, in spite of all her best efforts, it soon became clear that there were very few job opportunities for environmental scientists in and around Rome. As their carefree days on the yacht gradually counted down and the end of their holiday approached, Jo trawled the internet from top to bottom, but was no nearer to find a suitable position. She discussed it with Corrado every night and he wasn't surprised.

'Ever since the financial crisis of 2008, Italy's been in dire straits. Unemployment's soared and young people are leaving the country in droves to look for work elsewhere. To be honest, that's what the accountant told me the other day. My company's doing okay, but we have to be prudent. I wanted to expand but he persuaded me not to. He's a good guy and an old friend. He knows what he's talking about.'

'Yes, but the Italian government and the big international organisations must be taking people on, surely?'

'Of course, but for every job that's advertised, there are hundreds of applicants, and don't forget we're in Italy.' He tapped the side of his nose with one finger and sighed.

'What does that mean?'

'It means that the jobs don't always go to the best candidates, if you know what I mean. People know people. Strings get pulled. Favours get called in. It stinks, but it still goes on.' He turned those hypnotic eyes of his upon her, now very serious. 'Think really hard before giving up the chance to work for the UN. It's a great opportunity for you.'

'But it would take me away from you.'

'Not necessarily forever. Maybe just for a year or so until you move on to something even better back here. And, besides, I can come and visit you in New York in the meantime.'

'But it's you I want, Corrado. I've thought it through and there's no doubt in my mind. The idea of being separated from you is unbearable.'

He smiled and kissed her, but his eyes showed how worried for her he was.

They spent their penultimate night, once more, back in the little bay on the south side of the Argentario where he had had his epiphany. It was a bittersweet evening. Once again, they barbecued on the beach, once again, they swam, sunbathed and played with the dog. But both of them knew that tomorrow would be their final night together, at least for now.

Jo was becoming increasingly concerned. Next week she had her appointment with Professor Dietrich and although she had decided not to take the UN job, however enticing it appeared to be, she would have been far happier if she had at least been able to compile a short list of possible jobs in Italy. Once back in London she could then apply for them and fly across to Rome for interviews if requested. The trouble was that there was virtually nothing. The closest she found was a position as receptionist at a small charity in the suburbs of Rome, but it was far from what she had been doing and was capable of.

She and Corrado talked it through over and over again, but she found herself on the horns of a dilemma: take the job and lose the man – the man she had waited her whole life to find, of that she was certain – or take the man and give up on her career.

Their final night together was spent at the marina in Porto Ercole. They ate in the same little restaurant overlooking the harbour and chose the same bruschetta followed by prawns and squid. Afterwards, they took Daisy for a long walk along the shore before returning to the yacht in solemn mood. Their lovemaking that night was even sweeter and more all-consuming that at any time and she fell asleep drained in body and mind, salty tears drying on her cheeks.

The next morning, they barely spoke as they break-fasted and Jo packed her bags once more. Corrado was coming back up to Porto Ercole the following weekend to collect the yacht, so they both said farewell to what had been their very comfortable home for the past two weeks. In Jo's case, it was with very real tears in her eyes. She clung to Corrado's arm as they made their way along the pontoon and back to where the car was still parked, now covered in sand and dust.

However, it wasn't until they reached *Fiumicino* airport that she started crying properly. This was still because of Corrado, but for all the wrong reasons. He found a parking space right opposite the terminal building once again, but made no attempt to get out. After switching off the engine, he turned towards her, his suntanned face unusually serious and drawn.

'Jo, we've got to talk.'

She smiled at him, but it was an unexpectedly nervous smile. She had never seen him like this before. His fingers were drumming nervously on the steering wheel and he seemed incapable of looking straight at her. A sense of foreboding descended upon her.

'Jo, I really don't know how to say this. There's no easy way, so all I can do is to tell you straight.' His eyes met hers momentarily before dropping once more. 'Jo, the whole love thing, I'm afraid I fooled myself... and you.'

Jo sat bolt upright, barely daring to breathe.

'What do you mean?'

'You knew before we set off on this holiday what sort of man you were getting yourself involved with, didn't you? Everybody told you. I told you. You knew.' He paused for a moment and she saw the muscles of his jaw clench and unclench nervously. 'I honestly didn't set out to deceive you, I promise. I really believed things were different this time. I genuinely thought this might be it... love.'

He stopped again and Jo saw him take a couple of deep breaths. As for her, she felt as if somebody had kicked her in the stomach. A cold chill enveloped her as he continued.

'We've had a great time, Jo. I've had a great time. And sex with you was the best I've ever had.' As Jo did her best to digest this remark, he went on again and her heart shattered in her chest. 'But it was just sex. I realise that now. There's no point trying to kid myself, or you. I'm afraid I'm still the same old hedonist. I haven't changed, however much I would like you to think I have. I want what I want, and I can't give you what you want and deserve. Jo, take the UN job. Go to America and forget about me. I'm not worth it.'

'So it's all over…?' Her voice sounded croaky, like an old lady. She cleared her throat and tried again. 'But after everything that's happened…'

'I know, Jo, and I've tried. Believe me. But it's no good. We want different things, we want to lead different lives. I'm not the man for you and even if you don't realise that now, you will, trust me. Forget me and go and live your life in America.'

Of course she argued, pleaded even, but he remained stubbornly convinced that what she had interpreted as love blossoming between the two of them was nothing more than lust. She tried to remind him of all the good times they had had together, but all that achieved was to bring tears to the corners of her eyes. In the end, rather than break down and sob like a little baby in front of him, she scrambled out of the car, hugged the visibly troubled dog and grabbed her heavy bag. Shaking off Corrado's attempts to carry it in for her, she lugged it into the terminal by herself, leaving him standing by the car. And she didn't turn back even once.

The time she spent waiting at the airport was a blur. She sat in the toilet for half an hour doing her best to stop crying, but with little success. When the tears finally stopped, it must have been because she was dehydrated. Certainly, she didn't feel any better. She heard her flight being called and followed the signs to the departure lounge where she queued up with all the other passengers, most of them happy and cheerful, while all she felt deep inside was a void.

In the space of two or three minutes, he had kicked away her foundations and she felt herself close to crumbling. Even after Christian's sudden departure she hadn't felt as bad as this. Over the past two weeks she knew she had developed deep and lasting feelings for Corrado and she had been totally convinced that he felt the same way about her. She knew she loved him with all her heart and yet, in a few short sentences, he had consigned all that to the waste bin and had trampled all over her.

The aircraft was only half full and she was fortunate to find herself with three seats to herself. This was probably just as well for any passengers who would have been unfortunate enough to find themselves seated next to somebody sobbing into her handkerchief for most of the way back to Luton. Upon arrival, she manhandled her luggage through the terminal and onto the train to the centre of London. From there she felt too drained to struggle down into the Underground, so she took a very expensive taxi ride home.

By the time she got back, she was barely coherent and it was very lucky that Justin and Kevin arrived back at almost the same moment. They met downstairs in the lobby and her appearance must have given her away. Justin immediately relieved her of the heavy bag while Kevin took her by the arm and marched her upstairs to their flat. He sat her down on the sofa and settled down beside her. When Justin appeared with a pot of tea and three cups, he sat down on the other side of her and added his support. Their kindness was so touching and sweet, it tipped her over the edge once more and she cried her eyes out yet again.

A mug of hot tea and one of Justin's brownies finally succeeded in staunching the tears and slowly and painfully, she told them all about it. Both men were visibly shocked. When she finally lurched towards the end of her tale, Kevin voiced his opinion.

'The man's an utter, *utter* bastard. How could he? And you genuinely didn't realise it was all a sham until the very last day?'

'Until the very last few minutes of the very last day. I thought everything was going so well. Yes, he was a bit strained towards the end, but then so was I, knowing that this wonderful holiday – and it really was a wonderful holiday – was about to come to an end. It came as a bolt from the blue.'

The boys insisted that she should stay there with them and they ordered in a curry. They opened a bottle of wine, but Jo shook her head. The way she was feeling, alcohol was the last thing she needed.

They bullied her into eating, and by the end of the meal, she was feeling a little bit better. Kevin then asked her the sixty-four-thousand-dollar question.

'So, what about the job in America? Are you going to take it?'

Jo sat back and reflected. Only a few hours earlier she had been rehearsing in her head what she would say to Professor Dietrich in three days' time to break the news that she wouldn't be accepting the UN job offer after all. Now, suddenly, it had all changed. With Corrado revealed as little better than a deceiver – or, at best, a self-deceiver – there was nothing to keep her on this side of the Atlantic. Her last words to the boys before leaving two weeks earlier had been her decision to take the UN job as an important and exciting step forward in her career. Now there was no reason not to. She nodded to herself.

'Of course I'm going to take it.'

'We'll miss you, princess.'

'And I'll miss the two of you so very much.'

'Make sure you get a big place so we can come and visit.'

'Absolutely.'

–

The following day she had arranged to go out to Oxford to see her parents. She didn't sleep very much overnight, but as a result of all the thinking she did as she lay there staring up at the ceiling in the small hours, doing her best not to break down and cry all over again, she had taken a few decisions by the time she dragged herself out of bed and into the shower.

Angie and Mario would be getting married next April and she knew Corrado would be there, as would she. There would be absolutely no way to avoid seeing him. She could no more miss her sister's wedding than Corrado could miss his brother's. Angie had probably been joking when she had threatened to feed him to the pigs if he broke her big sister's heart, but Jo saw no reason to tempt fate. In consequence, she decided to play down the feelings she had been developing on the boat, and she would tell everybody – her parents included – that it had been a lovely holiday and they were good friends, but she had decided to do the sensible thing and accept the UN job as a level-headed, grown-up career move. After all, she told herself, she had set off on the cruise two weeks earlier with that stated intention.

She didn't feel up to speaking to Angie about this as it was all too fresh and raw. Instead, she sent her a short email just saying she had had a lovely holiday and was now back home safe and well, and about to accept the new job. After a considerable amount of internal debate, she then sent a short email to Corrado.

> I have arrived back safely.
> I have decided to follow your advice and accept the job in America. So as not to cause any friction in the family as a result of your behaviour, I intend to tell everybody we had a good holiday and that's all. I see no need to make things any more awkward than they already are.
> Hopefully you and I won't need to meet up again until the wedding and as little as possible after that.
> Jo

As she pressed Send, her overriding sensation was one of bitter disappointment. The more she thought about it, Tennyson, however great a poet he might have been, didn't know a damn thing about love.

Chapter 23

Jo flew across to New York on the fifth of October. As she sat in the aircraft on the runway at Heathrow, listening to the jet engines revving up, she didn't cry, but her mood was far from cheerful. Her farewell party two nights earlier had been bittersweet and even the sight of Ronald visibly upset to be losing her hadn't managed to cheer her up. September had been an awful month, or at least it would have been terrible if she hadn't had so much to do, getting her affairs in order before flying off to her new life three thousand miles away.

Her meeting with Professor Dietrich had been brief and Jo had been glad of that. Only three days after returning from Rome, she had still been feeling very fragile. Fortunately, she had managed to paste a smile on her face and drum up a semblance of enthusiasm for the new job, and she hoped Professor Dietrich had been convinced. Part of the generous relocation package had involved being able to send a certain amount of her personal possessions across to the States by courier, and the selection of what she required and the relegation of everything else to her parents' attic had also helped to take her mind off Corrado and what might have been or, in her case, what *had* been until it had been firmly crushed by him.

There had only been one communication from him, a reply to her email.

> Dear Jo
>
> I totally agree. As far as anybody needs to know, we had a lovely holiday together and that's that.
>
> I'm sorry.
> Corrado

She had cried when she read it and even now, a month later, the thought of it still could still bring tears to her eyes. After all they had enjoyed together, after all the love, how he could spare her just twenty-four measly little words? And, since then, there had been no contact of any kind between them.

She had steadfastly stuck to her story of having had a wonderful holiday, but that nothing had developed between her and Corrado. In consequence she told everybody it had been an easy and sensible decision to accept the offer of the UN job, even though it meant a major upheaval for her. The only people who knew the truth of what had happened were Kevin and Justin and, of course, Victoria.

Victoria, predictably, hadn't taken it well.

'What a miserable, scheming little sod! When you phoned me from that island or wherever it was, you sounded so happy, so blissfully happy. I remember telling George I thought you'd finally found what you'd been looking for.'

'And I really thought I had done, Vic.'

'And then he just calmly waits until you're sitting outside the airport to drop the bombshell that he doesn't

love you after all and that all he'd been after was sex.'
Victoria snorted. 'You'd better tell Angie it's probably not
a good idea to invite me to the wedding next year. If I
see Corrado, I won't be responsible for my actions, and
I'd hate to spoil the wedding for them by smacking the
bridegroom's brother.'

Jo had smiled at that. 'I can't do that, Vic. As far as
anybody else is concerned, we had a great holiday and
we're just good friends. I can't risk screwing things up for
Angie and the family by telling the truth. She'd go ballistic
with him and I've got a fair idea that Mario would blow his
top as well. It could split the family. No, at the wedding,
you and I will be on our best behaviour. A gracious smile,
a few words – not the ones you'd really like to use with
him – and that's that. Hopefully, once the wedding's out
of the way, neither of us will have to see much of him ever
again.'

There had, however, been a lot of regret in her tone.

Fortunately, October turned out to be even busier than
September and Jo found she was able to settle into her new
life in America without too much time for introspection.
Her new office was in a very modern building on the
outskirts of New York and she soon got to know and
like the other people in her department. She was the
youngest member of the team and, as such, she found that
they all seemed to want to take her under their wings.
Fortunately, with a couple of exceptions, this wasn't just
because they wanted to get her into bed. As far as that
was concerned, she had absolutely no interest in any man.
She was invited out for burgers, pizzas, bagels and a host
of ethnic dishes from couscous to tacos. Consequently, it
came as a great relief to find that one of the many perks

of the job was that she had access to a stunningly well-equipped fitness centre with a gym and a pool where she managed to work off all the calories she was consuming. They also had a punch bag there and she found it excellent for those occasions when her mind drifted back to her handsome Roman chemist.

In the middle of November, the weather took a turn for the worse, the temperatures plummeted, and she had to go out and buy a whole new wardrobe. Coming from a warm English summer, as well as two weeks in the heat of the Mediterranean, she had seriously misjudged how cold it could get in New York and she soon added thick tights, fur-lined boots and a wonderfully warm, full length, down-filled coat to her armoury. The apartment provided for her was large and comfortable, and surprisingly not too expensive. She soon got used to American life and American language, buying milk in quarts, taking the subway, and making sure she didn't stray off the sidewalk.

One memorable evening, she was invited to dinner at Professor Dietrich's house. There were just the two of them, along with three very affectionate cats who had an unfortunate, and unpunished, habit of jumping onto the dining table mid-meal. Clearly these were Waltraud Dietrich's surrogate children, and very spoilt ones at that. Waltraud was a good cook and it was a delightful evening. Jo found her very easy to talk to and it was probably this, as much as anything else, that caused her to start talking about Corrado. She ended up recounting the whole sad story, mercifully without doing more than sniff a bit and blow her nose. It turned out Waltraud had already had an inkling that something like that must have happened.

'I felt sure when we met up in London that something bad had happened. You looked very worn, very unhappy... fairly depressed, to be honest. I'm pleased to see you looking and sounding much brighter now, but at the time I was concerned for you. So, have you spoken to him since then?'

Jo shook her head. 'No, no contact. Officially we're just good friends – we have to be because of the family complications – but unofficially all links have been severed.'

Waltraud listened impassively, her eyes tolerantly watching the fluffiest of the cats playing with a bread roll it had stolen from the table. 'So, if he hadn't broken your heart, would you still have come here?'

Jo removed a cat hair from the rim of her glass and took a sip before replying.

'To be totally honest, Waltraud, no. I had made up my mind to thank you, but to turn the offer down. I can see now that I was completely besotted with him. I hadn't found an alternative job in Italy and yet I was all set to throw away this incredible opportunity you'd offered me, all for the sake of love... or what I thought was love.' She caught the professor's eye. 'I'm sorry if that makes you sound like second best. I don't mean it like that. I just wasn't thinking logically.'

'Love can do that.'

Somehow, these four words really surprised Jo. She knew that the elderly lady was unmarried and had assumed her to be as firm in her belief that love was unscientific and unwanted as Corrado himself. Instead, she had used the word without disapproval and with more than a note of nostalgia. Jo listened, fascinated, as Waltraud then revealed secrets from her own past.

'I had to make that choice myself a long time ago, Jo. I was about your age and working at the university of Graz in Austria. I was going out with a man at the time, Klaus, and I liked him a lot. In fact, I thought I loved him. Then, out of the blue, I was offered a job over here in the United States. Those post-war years in Austria were very tough and everybody said I should take it. When I told Klaus, do you know what he did?'

Jo shook her head, touched to hear the great lady talking so openly about such a personal moment in her life.

'He asked me to marry him.' Waltraud took another mouthful of wine and gently persuaded the smaller of the two black cats to get off the table. 'I thought about it. I thought long and hard about it and, in the end, I turned him down. I took the job and we split up forever.'

'But then everything has worked out so well for you here, hasn't it? Surely you have no regrets.'

The old lady looked across the table at Jo and shook her head ruefully.

'Every day of my life, Jo. Every day of my life.' Jo was staggered, but she didn't have time to comment before Waltraud continued. 'He's a very successful scientist in his own right. Or rather, he was. He's now retired, I believe. He married a girl I knew from school and they had three big strong sons. He's had a very happy life.'

'But surely you've been happy too?'

'Yes, I've been happy. I've accomplished a lot in my life and I have a lot to be thankful for. But I'll always regret leaving Klaus.' After a few moments of reflective silence, she looked up again. 'At least your Corrado made the decision easy for you, didn't he?'

These words were still running through Jo's head in the taxi on the way home. In a way, Corrado *had* made the decision for her. What was it he had said about feeling sure she would regret it if she turned the UN job down? Looking back on it now, after a little bit of time for reflection, she realised he had probably been right. Certainly, she was enjoying the job here more and more as the days went by. Here, at least, she had the opportunity to apply everything she had worked so hard to attain and maybe make a real difference. She wouldn't allow herself to go so far as to describe her work as vital to the survival of the planet, but she knew she was doing important work all the same. In a funny way, maybe Corrado had done her a favour after all, even though it certainly hadn't felt like it at the time.

That night when she got home, she sent him an email. It wasn't long, but it said everything she wanted to say.

Dear Corrado

I will always remember those idyllic days we spent together on your lovely yacht. I will always remember you and, of course, Daisy. And I will remember you both with affection.

You were right. I should have known what I was getting myself into. You, yourself, were the first to warn me. I do not regret what happened between us although I will always regret the way it ended. In fact, I will remember the time we spent together as some of the very best days of my life. Thank you.

I love my new job and I'm glad I took it.

I am writing this to let you know that I don't hate you. I thought I did for a while, but I don't.

I wish you a happy and successful life,

Jo

She pressed Send and sat there at the laptop for a few minutes until a single teardrop landed on the keys and she closed it gently, knowing she had done the right thing.

Chapter 24

Twenty-four hours later, she got a reply from him. It wasn't long, but the tone was far less terse than his previous email.

> Dear Jo
>
> I was delighted, and relieved, to hear from you. I have been thinking about you a lot ever since I last saw you. Once again please try to accept my apologies for how it ended.
>
> I am really pleased to hear that you are enjoying your new job. I know you have a lot to offer and I'm sure the planet needs you.
>
> I do hope we can remain good friends.
>
> Corrado (and Daisy)

She read it and re-read it a number of times. As she did, a host of memories were awakened yet again, but this time she didn't cry.

She came close, but she didn't.

At lunchtime next day she phoned her sister. They had only communicated by email once or twice since the summer and this was the first time they had spoken since her holiday with Corrado. Jo had been putting off talking to her, terrified she would end up in tears on the end of the line and spill the beans. Now, after her exchange of emails with Corrado, she finally felt strong enough to try.

'Hi, Angie. Can you talk?'

'Jo, hi. Yes, of course. What time is it with you?'

'Just gone one o'clock. I'm having my lunch.'

They chatted about the Country Club, the weather and the horses before Angie brought up the subject of her brother-in-law.

'It sounds as if you and Corrado had a lovely holiday. He told us all about your visits to the islands. He was very impressed with your swimming, although knowing him as we do, that may just have been the bikini you were wearing.'

'It was a wonderful holiday. Unforgettable. Have you seen him recently?'

'Not for a few weeks now. Mario sees more of him than I do as they've been talking about the new spa we're creating. He's fine, though Mario said he seemed a bit quieter than usual. He thinks Corrado's having a bit of a break from all his women. Maybe you made more of an impression on him than you thought.'

Jo skated round the possible implications of this. 'And his lovely dog? I'm totally in love with Daisy, you know.'

'She's as sweet as ever. Have you spoken to Corrado recently?'

'Only a couple of emails.'

'Has he told you he's going to America?'

'He's doing what?'

'California, I think Mario said. Some business thing, just for a few days.'

'And when's that happening?'

'I'm not sure. Why don't you ask him? Pretty soon, I think. Anyway, Jo, changing the subject, I was going to sit down and send you an email this week to talk about Christmas. Now that dad's back on his feet again, I've managed to persuade them to come over here for a few days at Christmas. Is there any chance you can come over and join us? I know you've only just arrived in America really, but it would be lovely to get the family together.'

And the family would, of course, include her future brother-in-law.

Jo prevaricated. 'That sounds lovely, Angie. I'll speak to my supervisor and see what she thinks. Americans aren't big on holiday entitlement, but I know I should get a few days off. I'll see what I can do.'

When she put the phone down, she sat for a while, mulling over what her sister had told her about Christmas and about Corrado's impending visit to the USA. Of course, California was four or five hours' flight away so it wasn't likely he would be coming to New York but, what if he did? In spite of everything that had happened, she found herself wondering whether they might meet up. If he suggested it, what would she say? On the one hand there was what Victoria had described as the open sore that would just get more and more inflamed by his appearance. On the other was the realisation that, in spite of everything, she couldn't hide the fact that there was a part of her brain that would love to see him again, even if a more logical, sensible part deeply disapproved. As he would have put it, the limbic system wants what the limbic system wants...

That evening she send him another email and got an almost immediate reply, even though it was past midnight in Italy. She mentioned that she had been talking to her sister and asked, casually, about his projected visit to California. The reply was disappointing, or satisfying, depending upon which part of her brain was doing the thinking.

> Dear Jo
>
> Yes, that was the plan, but things have changed. The man I need to see is coming across to Europe in a few weeks' time and we're meeting in Geneva. You maybe know him – Professor Richard Paris from UCLA. I believe he was at the Save the Planet conference in Rome with you.
>
> Has Angie told you about Christmas? I know she's planning to get your parents over. Will you be coming too? If so, do you want me to go away somewhere? I don't want to make things awkward for you, although I know I would love to see you again.
>
> Your call.
>
> Corrado

Jo spent an hour wondering how to reply. In spite of what she had told Angie, she felt pretty sure she should be able to get at least a week off at Christmas and the idea of the family getting together was appealing. It was considerate of him to offer to disappear, but Christmas was a time for families, not for being alone, even with a loveable black dog as company for him. After two cups of tea and a slice of toast, she finally made up her mind.

Dear Corrado

I hope to be able to come over to Rome for Christmas. Thanks for offering to go away, but I wouldn't want to separate you from your family at such a time. No, if I manage to come, I'm sure I'll be able to cope with seeing you again.

As for Richard (Ricky) Paris, I know him quite well. He's a very nice guy. What are you seeing him about (or is it a trade secret?)?

Jo

She didn't hear back from him until the next day. After all, it must have been very late by the time he'd received her email. His reply was interesting.

Dear Jo

Thanks for being so understanding. I do hope you can come and I promise to be on my very best behaviour. As for Professor Paris, we are talking about plastics and how to dispose of them. He's a world expert on that sort of thing. I'll say hi to him from you.

If you do come at Christmas, I can guarantee you a very warm welcome from your four-legged friend. She's lying at my feet at the moment and I'm sure she's dreaming of you. I do.

Corrado

I do. Jo read these two words over and over again, wondering what they meant. In the end, her logical self won out over her limbic system and she decided it must be a sexual thing, just him remembering some of the wonderful nights they had spent together – and they had been wonderful. If she were totally honest with herself, she, too, had had such dreams, but she knew they were best ignored, so she didn't respond. After all, he had made it quite clear there wasn't going to be anything else between them.

As the days ticked by, Jo made up her mind to accept the invitation to the family get-together in Rome, even though this would bring her into contact with Corrado once more. She mentioned the possibility of going to Rome for Christmas to Waltraud and was pleased to hear she had no objections. Then, one day in late November, just as Jo was checking flights and groaning at the way the prices for the Christmas period had all shot up, Waltraud dropped into her office with some very good news.

'You know you were talking about going to see your family in Rome at Christmas? Well, I wonder if you felt like killing two birds with one stone. A friend of mine at the European Commission has just been in touch to see if we could send one of our experts to a climate change summit that's taking place in Milan on the twenty-second, just three days before Christmas for crying out loud! God knows why they've waited until the last minute to contact us. Under normal circumstances, I'd tell them we can't, but it occurred to me that it might suit you. That way, you could go on from there to Rome and then fly back here after the holidays.' She gave Jo a smile. 'And the EU will pay for your flights and your expenses.'

This sounded amazing, but daunting. 'What would I be expected to do?'

'I'll forward the briefing papers I've been sent. By the sound of it, they just want you to sit on a panel of experts to answer any questions thrown at you by the EU heads of state.'

Jo gulped. 'Heads of state?'

Waltraud nodded. 'And before you say it, you'll be fine. Trust me, I wouldn't suggest you for this if I didn't think you were up to it. And the fact that you speak Italian's going to be very much in your favour as well. Besides, I can sort you out with a whole heap of statistics you can use to bamboozle them if you run into trouble.' She grinned. 'Honestly, you'll do fine. Besides, you've already proved your credentials with the Italian media so you know that'll go well if you're approached.'

Jo took a few deep breaths and said yes, but as the days counted down to her departure, she found herself feeling more and more nervous. And, of course, she had two things to worry about now: the summit and Corrado. She wasn't sure which of the two was scarier.

She flew across to Milan on the nineteenth of December. It turned out to be a remarkably comfortable flight in Business Class and she even managed to sleep for a few hours. She was met upon arrival by a uniformed driver in a black Mercedes, who delivered her to her hotel in the city centre. She then had a few hours to herself to visit the stunning cathedral and to do a bit of shopping. Everywhere she looked, there were Christmas decorations, and there was a decidedly festive air about the place. That evening she attended the opening drinks party and was delighted to see a very familiar head looming above the crowd.

'Jo, hi. It's great to see you again.' Ricky appeared at her side and gave her a warm hug.

'Ricky! I didn't know you'd be here.' Jo kissed him on the cheeks.

'I gather we're on the "experts" panel together tomorrow.'

'Well, in that case, I'm counting on you for support. I'm terrified.'

'No need. You'll do just great. And, hey, I've discovered we have a mutual friend. I met Corrado in Switzerland a few days back and your name came up.' He gave her a big smile. 'I may be talking out of turn here, but I definitely got the impression he thinks a lot of you, Jo.' The smile broadened. 'And I mean *a lot*.'

Jo felt herself blushing, but did her best to carry on as if nothing had happened.

'He's going to be my brother-in-law. We get on well. I gather you and he were talking business.'

Ricky looked almost embarrassed for a moment.

'We sure were, but I can't tell you anything about it for now. But yes, exciting times.'

Jo was intrigued and decided to ask Corrado what it was all about. At least, she thought to herself, it would give them something to talk about when they finally met up.

The summit meeting two days later went remarkably well, and Jo was delighted to discover that she didn't have to do any TV interviews. By the time all the heads of state and ministers for the environment of the different European countries had arrived, the meeting itself barely lasted three hours and concluded with a late lunch, after which Jo had the surreal experience of finding herself in the ladies' toilet at the same time as the British Prime Minister. Somehow it had never occurred to her that Prime Ministers needed to go to the toilet.

By mid-afternoon it was all over and she bade farewell to Ricky once again, wishing him and his family a very happy Christmas. Another black saloon delivered her to Milano Centrale station, where she took her seat in the sleek high-speed train that shot her down to Rome in barely three hours. As she emerged from the train at Roma Termini, she found Angie waiting at the end of the platform to greet her. Jo didn't know whether she was relieved or disappointed it wasn't Corrado. The two sisters hugged warmly and walked out to the Kiss-and-Ride car park where Mario was waiting with the car. Jo hugged him and found herself smiling broadly. It was really good to see them both again.

It was just after eight o'clock by the time they arrived out at the Country Club. Her mum and dad were staying in Mario's parents' villa across on the other side of the estate, while Jo was staying with Angie and Mario. She dumped her suitcase, freshened up, and then they went over to the hotel to meet the others for dinner in a private dining room. As they walked into the room, there was a sudden movement and the next moment a very happy Daisy came charging towards her. Jo dropped down on one knee and hugged the rapturous dog, equally delighted to meet up again. And, of course, she thought to herself as she finally returned to her feet, where there was Daisy, her master would also be.

'Joanne, sweetheart, you must be exhausted.' Her mother came across and enveloped her in her arms. 'How are you?'

Jo hugged her warmly. 'I'm fine thanks, mum. Far less jet-lagged than I'd been expecting.'

She released her mum and hurried over to hug her dad and then Mario's mother and father. Finally, she looked round and saw Corrado.

In spite of everything that had happened, in spite of the pain and grief of these past few months, there was no disguising the flash of joy that shot through her at the sight of him. Even her stubborn subconscious couldn't do anything about this. He was looking as gorgeous as she remembered, no longer dressed in shorts and a T-shirt, but in a very smart grey suit. She was still wearing the rather nice formal blue dress she had bought at Macy's a week earlier and was glad she hadn't changed into anything more casual. It was only as she approached Corrado that she realised it was the exact same colour as his eyes. She didn't have time to dwell upon the ramifications of what had made her choose this colour as he stepped towards her and reached out his hand formally. Remembering her decision to keep up the charade that they were still very good friends, she ignored his hand and caught hold of his shoulders and kissed him on the cheeks, much to the delight of her limbic system and the annoyance of her subconscious.

'*Ciao*, Corrado.' She was pleased to hear her voice sounding level.

He smiled back at her. '*Ciao*, Jo. It's really good to see you again.' He sounded as if he meant it.

They didn't have any time to talk as his father, obviously keen to play the perfect host, invited them to all sit down at table. Either by accident or design, Jo found she was sandwiched between her mother and Mario, with

Corrado along the table from them so, throughout the meal, they had little opportunity to talk.

It was an excellent dinner and the two families soon bonded. Jo was impressed to hear her mum resurrecting her rusty Italian to speak to Mario's mum, while Mario's father produced some pretty comprehensible English. The two fathers appeared to be hitting it off and Jo was delighted. Angie looked absolutely radiant and Jo even wondered for a minute if she might be pregnant, but as she was drinking wine, Jo assumed it was just the pleasure of seeing her parents and her future in-laws getting on so well together. From time to time, Jo felt Corrado's eyes on her, but for the most part, she avoided eye contact with him.

Finally, as the pudding plates were replaced by coffee cups and liqueur glasses, Mario announced that he would be taking his future in-laws on a whistle-stop tour of the Eternal City the next day and Jo was welcome to join them. She declined the invitation as she was starting to feel very tired now after all the travelling and the stress of the summit. She decided she would have a long lie-in and then spend the day with her sister, catching up and helping to make preparations for the Christmas party planned for that evening at Mario's house. This, apparently, would be for a load of their friends, some of whom Jo had met briefly at the pool party that summer. That seemed a very long time ago.

The dinner party broke up at around ten-thirty and Jo said good night to everybody, including Corrado and the dog, and went home with Mario and Angie. As she stripped off her dress and went into the bathroom, she breathed a big sigh of relief that things between her and Corrado hadn't been too strained. Of course, she still had five more days to go before she flew back to the States.

Chapter 25

Angie and Mario's Christmas party started at eight and Jo had been busy all afternoon helping to move furniture, prepare canapés, hang Christmas decorations and set out glasses and plates. Mario had been out most of the day with their parents and there was no sign of Corrado. Jo toyed with the idea of opening up to her sister about exactly what had happened on their sailing holiday, in particular how it had ended, but she decided to keep this to herself. Everything appeared to be going very well and she had no intention of making waves.

It turned out to be quite a big party and Mario had even rented a mobile disco. Fortunately, it was a dry night, and although it certainly wasn't anything like as cold as New York outside, it wasn't a balmy summer evening by any means. Even so, as the party heated up, so did the house and soon the French windows into the terrace were all open, with people standing, sitting and dancing outside as well.

Jo had slept remarkably well the previous night and was feeling relatively relaxed – apart from the lurking fear of sooner or later finding herself alone with Corrado. He put in an appearance with Daisy at seven-thirty, but they were all so busy making the final preparations that Jo and he barely exchanged greetings. This was actually quite a relief to her. She didn't really know how she would react as and when she finally found herself alone with him, but she had to admit that she was surprised how little anger she now felt towards him. Whether this was just the passage of time or the success of her first few months in America was hard to assess. Nevertheless, she was happy to put off talking to him for as long as possible.

Angie had warned her in advance that they were planning a party and Jo had come prepared with two dresses – one lightweight and one thicker in case it was cold. She chose the lighter one and had no regrets as the temperature in the house rose and she found herself being dragged onto the dance floor by a string of cheery Romans. At the end of one particularly energetic dance, she thanked her dancing partner and slipped out onto the terrace for a breather.

She was happy to take a little break, sitting on the edge of a huge terracotta plant pot containing an olive tree, as she relaxed in the night air. It was cold, but not too cold. Her moment of relaxation was soon interrupted by the arrival of a slightly older man. He was carrying a glass of wine and, from the colour of his cheeks, it wasn't the first one he had drunk. He gave her a smile and held out his hand.

'Good evening. My name's Paolo. I saw you all alone and I thought I'd come and talk to you, to see if you're all right.'

She stood up and shook his hand. 'Good evening, Paolo. That's very kind of you. My name's Jo. I'm Angie's sister and I'm pleased to say I'm fine. I was just getting a breath of air.'

Paolo took a step back and looked at her with renewed interest. To her surprise, he then proceeded to walk all the way round her in a circle, his eyes glued to her, studying her in great detail. Seeing the expression on her face, he was quick to explain.

'Do excuse me. I just had to take a good look at the famous Jo, the heartbreaker.'

Jo gave him a quizzical look. 'I think you may have me confused with somebody else, Paolo.'

He took a big mouthful of wine and Jo rather wished she'd got a glass of her own. This had the makings of an awkward conversation.

'You're Jo, who went sailing with Corrado this August, right?'

Jo nodded, wondering how he came to know this. She soon found out.

'I'm sorry, I should explain: I'm Corrado's Finance Director and I've known him for years. We're very close.'

'I see. So, you were the man Corrado had lunch with at Porto Santo Stefano.'

'That's right.' He drained his glass and looked round for a top-up, without success. 'He talked a lot about you. It was easy to tell he was head over heels in love with you and then you just went off and left him. Broke his heart.'

Jo was stunned. 'I didn't do anything of the sort. I had the offer of a job in New York and I took it, that's all.' She very nearly went on to tell him that it had been Corrado who had told her to take the job and that if anybody's heart had been broken, it had been hers, but she decided it was no business of Paolo's.

'Well, whatever happened, the result is that you broke his heart.' He shook his head sadly and Jo felt her temper rise.

'How can you say that? It wasn't like that at all.' She could hear her voice getting shrill and she made a conscious effort to cool things down. 'It really wasn't. But what makes you say he's heartbroken? He looks all right to me.'

By this time, she got the impression Paolo was beginning to regret embarking upon this subject.

'It's a sham, an illusion. I've spent a lot of time with him over the past few months and I've seen him at his lowest. We've been talking a lot about you and every time it gets to him.'

'You've been talking about me?'

This time she couldn't miss the guilty expression on his face. 'I'm sorry, I'm speaking out of turn. Please forget what I've said. It was nothing.'

He suddenly looked so ashamed, she felt sorry for him.

'It's forgotten, Paolo. Don't give it another thought. I still think you're wrong, but forget it.'

He managed a little smile before he turned away. 'I'm very sorry, Jo. I shouldn't have said all those things. It's none of my business. But I can see why he's so infatuated with you. You're the most beautiful woman I've seen all night… all day.'

Jo patted him on the arm and smiled back at him. 'Thank you, Paolo.'

As he scuttled off guiltily, she found herself turning over in her head what he had just said. Why on earth, she asked herself, had he used the present tense when he had told her Corrado was infatuated? Surely that was long gone, if it had ever existed?

Just then, she saw Angie appear with a bottle of Prosecco and two glasses.

'Hi. Jo. I've got to sit down. My feet in these shoes are killing me. Remind me never to wear heels ever again and certainly never to dance in them.' She led Jo to a nearby table and the two of them sat down. Angie slipped off her shoes with a sigh of relief, filled the two glasses and looked across at Jo.

'So, sis, how's it going?'

'I'm fine, Angie, but I've just been having a strange conversation with a man called Paolo, Corrado's Finance Director.'

'I just saw him. I think he's had a few too many glasses of wine. He's a nice guy and a close friend of Corrado's, but he's always had a bit of a drink problem. Why, what did he say?'

Jo took a deep breath. 'He said Corrado's heartbroken, and it's my fault.'

Angie took a sip of wine before answering. 'You'd better see what Corrado says about that, but I'll tell you this: he hasn't been himself since you left.'

'...but, heartbroken? He's not that kind of man, surely?'

'He never used to be, but Mario and I have been quite worried about him lately.'

'You mean he's really been upset?'

'Upset, preoccupied, quieter, different. Something must have happened on that boat. But all he says is that it was a marvellous holiday, nothing more.'

Jo was secretly pleased to hear that he had respected her decision not to burden the other members of the family with their problems, but she was still very intrigued. For a moment she almost came right out and told her sister exactly what had happened, but she was saved by the bell. Just as she was thinking about starting, Mario arrived, followed by Daisy. He looked bothered. The dog looked affectionate.

'Angie, we're running out of Prosecco. I thought I'd got enough in the fridge, but everybody seems to be drinking it. Corrado and I are just dashing across to the restaurant for some more. There are hot canapés in the oven. Can you keep an eye on them while I'm away?'

Angie jumped to her feet and Jo followed her. As they headed back into the house, she saw Corrado with his car keys in his hand. Just then, Angie had an idea.

'Jo, would you mind going with Corrado to help? That way Mario and I can stay here and make sure everything's okay.'

Jo was quick to agree and Mario looked relieved. 'Thanks, Jo. That's very kind. Tell Corrado to ask for Loretta. I'll give her a call now.'

Jo and Daisy headed across to Corrado and she explained the change of plan. He nodded and led them out to the little Fiat. They jumped in with the dog and he set off up the drive towards the restaurant. As he did so, she shot a glance across at her.

'You're looking wonderful, Jo.'

'Thanks.' She didn't know what else to say.

They had almost reached the restaurant before he spoke again, this time hesitantly. 'Jo, it's so great to see you again. Could we talk?'

'Isn't that what we're doing?'

'I mean sit down and talk properly.' He drove round to the rear of the restaurant and pulled up by the kitchen doors. 'Please…'

Jo didn't reply, her brain churning. She had imagined this would happen sooner or later and she didn't know how to react. On the one hand she was fascinated to hear more about this alleged heartache he had been suffering, while on the other she had no intention of accepting him back into her life – or her bed – after he had confirmed just what sort of man he was.

The kitchen doors opened and it was the work of a few moments to squeeze four cases of cold Prosecco into the boot of the car alongside the excited dog. A minute later they were on the move again and Corrado was heading down the drive towards his brother's house. They completed the trip in silence. As they reached Mario's house once more, she made her decision.

'Yes, we can talk, Corrado, but we both know where we stand now. You made yourself perfectly clear about that. So, by all means let's talk, but we both know it's over between us. You want what you want and I want something different.'

They carted the wine into the house and restocked the fridge. Once they had finished, he caught her eye.

'If you're free, Daisy could do with a little walk. Do you fancy coming with us?'

She nodded. 'I'm always happy to go for a walk with Daisy.'

They walked out of the back door and along the drive, away from the river in case Daisy should decide to go for a swim. The havoc a soaking wet Labrador could cause to a host of people in party frocks and smart clothes was definitely to be avoided. As they walked, and the dog disappeared from time to time into the shadows either side of the drive before reappearing like a green-eyed ghost, Jo felt the nervous tension between them grow. The atmosphere was so tense, she had to keep reminding herself to breathe. Finally, Corrado began to speak. Jo listened attentively and with increasing amazement.

'Jo, I want you to know something. Telling you to take the job in New York was the most difficult thing I've ever had to do in my life.' His voice was low and strained.

'Being told I was being discarded by the man I thought loved me wasn't exactly a bed of roses for me either, you know.' Her voice was little better.

'I know, Jo, and I'm really, really sorry. But what else could I say? It would have been crazy for you to turn down a job at the UN for an uncertain future over here.' He slowed his step and she saw his shape turn towards her in the darkness. 'If I had told you how I really felt, would you have left? Would you? I've done some pretty shabby things to women over the years – all right, in my defence, I didn't set out to treat anybody badly – but I knew – I know – I would never, ever want to do anything that would harm you.'

'And breaking my heart and reducing me to tears doesn't count as harm as far as you're concerned?' In spite of her bitter words, Jo couldn't help wondering where he was going with this.

'I know.' His voice was low. 'It must have been awful for you. It was awful for me too, you know. But it was the only way. I told you then and I'm telling you again now: you had to take that job. If you hadn't, if you'd ended up as a receptionist behind a counter in some little office in Rome, sooner or later you would have regretted it. And I knew I couldn't be responsible for doing that to you.'

'So you're telling me you deliberately broke my heart so as to save me from some future, unspecified, heartache?'

'So as to prevent you from getting to a stage in a month, a year, five years, when the regret you felt would change into resentment towards me as the cause of it. Without me, you were free to make the right decision. I had to remove myself from the equation and make you go.'

Jo stopped and tried to make sense of what he was saying. 'Well, it worked. I took the UN job and I have no regrets.' No sooner had she spoken than she realised this was a lie too far. 'No, of course I have regrets. Not about the job. I love the job. It's what I've spent the last ten years of my life working towards. But I can't even begin to explain the regret I felt, and I still feel, that the man I loved, the man I thought loved me, could just stab me in the back so callously.'

'I still love you, Jo.' His voice was so low, she could barely hear what he was saying. 'I never stopped loving you, in spite of what I said.'

Jo was totally baffled now. As she struggled to make some kind of sense of what he was telling her, she felt the warm comforting presence of the Labrador at her side and she reached down to ruffle her ears. As she did so, Corrado carried on.

'If I could have done it any other way, I would have, Jo, I promise. I tried all sorts. You know that working lunch I had with my accountant in Porto Santo Stefano?'

'Paolo? I met him earlier on this evening. He accused me of breaking your heart.'

She heard Corrado give an exasperated sigh. 'He had no business telling you that.' There was a pause as he controlled his frustration. 'Anyway, it's like this: I knew you had to take the American job and I knew there was no way a long-distance relationship could ever work for more than a few months. I had a simple choice: follow you to the US or break up with you.'

'Follow me to the US? You considered doing that?'

'More than considered. That's what the meeting with Paolo was all about. I've been thinking about expanding overseas for some time now and where better than the richest consumer market in the world? I called that meeting so as to see if there was any way we could bring our plans forward and set up in the US sooner. Unfortunately, as you know, the reply I got from him wasn't what I wanted to hear. Paolo's an old friend and he's far too fond of his wine, but he's a brilliant accountant. He told me, and then he demonstrated to me with spreadsheets, that it would have been too much of a risk, unless we could find an American partner, and at that time we didn't know anybody suitable. He told me to wait for a few years, and so I was left with no alternative. I was sure you wouldn't have taken the UN job unless I did something radical. So, Jo, I took it upon myself to break your heart and, in so doing, I totally shattered my own as well.'

Jo could feel her head spinning. 'Is there somewhere around here we can sit down?' Suddenly, her legs felt quite weak.

She felt Corrado take her arm and lead her a little way down the drive to a wooden bench, set underneath an old-style lamppost. They sat down on it together with the dog at their feet. As they did so, she shivered and realised she was cold. He must have felt it too, as he shrugged off his jacket and stretched it around her shoulders. She murmured her thanks and sat there for a good minute, turning over and over in her head everything he had said before attempting to speak again. When she did, her voice was barely more than an emotional croak.

'You expect me to believe that everything you said to me in the car at the airport was a lie?' It seemed barely credible. 'You deliberately told me you didn't love me so I would take the job in New York?'

'Yes.'

His voice didn't sound much stronger than hers. At their feet, she heard the dog give a puzzled whine. Jo knew how she felt.

'Well, if that's true and, as you can see, I really am glad I took the job, why tell me all this now? It's too late. There are three thousand miles of ocean between us.'

'Not necessarily.' His voice was still low, but there was a stronger, more assured note to it now.

'What do you mean?' Her eyes were stinging with emotion and she had to clear her throat before she got all the words out.

'You know that meeting I had with your tall Californian friend, Doctor Paris, Ricky Paris? Well, the upshot of it is that we came to an agreement. I just got the contract through to sign two days ago. He represents a big American environmental group – you probably know that already – and together, we're setting up a company in the US specialising in the disposal of plastic waste. By the way, he told me some of the ideas we're going to be working on originated from you.' She felt him take a deep breath.

'And the new plant is going to be situated just outside New York.'

Jo twisted round until she could look up at his face.

'You and Ricky are setting up a factory in New York?'

She saw his head nod and his eyes drop towards hers, the deep blue now green in the orange glow of the street light. 'That's right. And I'm planning on moving to New York to supervise it personally.'

'You're moving...?' So many things were falling into place in her head, she could almost hear the cogs turning. Could it be that her subconscious and her limbic system were singing from the same hymn sheet at long last?

'That's right, Jo. I told you once that I couldn't imagine life without you. These last three months have hammered that home to me.' There was another pause. 'Could I just get something out of my pocket, please?'

She felt him reach into the pocket of the jacket hanging round her shoulders and then, to her total astonishment, she saw him drop down onto one knee in front of her. She sat there speechless, now heedless of the cold, as she saw him holding a little square box. From it he extracted a ring that sparkled in the light. Beside him the dog looked as astounded as Jo felt.

'Joanne Margaret Green, will you marry me?'

Jo suddenly felt an overwhelming urge to burst into tears, but she fought hard to stay rational.

'You abandon me, you break my heart and now you want to marry me?'

She saw him nod uncertainly and her heart almost burst. Her willpower gave way and she felt tears stream down her cheeks as she buried her face in her hands and sobbed. A second later, two things happened almost simultaneously. She felt Corrado lean forward and stretch his arms around her shoulders while a warm, hairy body did its best to climb onto her lap, snuffling at her face, emitting little whining sounds. This, as much as anything, returned her to reality. She raised her face from her hands, wiped the tears from her cheeks and looked up, straight into two sets of eyes barely a couple inches from hers. Addressing herself to the blue ones, she took a deep breath and found her tears suddenly transformed into the broadest smile she had ever smiled.

'The answer's yes. Corrado. Yes, I will, with all my heart.'

She leant her lips towards him and, as she did so, a big hairy canine head threatened to get there first as Daisy – no doubt caught up in the moment – pushed her long nose between them. Jo gave the dog a cuddle and then gently pushed her to one side and reached for Corrado, seeing his eyes sparkle and a smile spread across his face. As her lips approached his, she heard his voice, soft and warm and loving. 'You know what they say; love me, love my dog.'

'I do.'

Epilogue

It was a magical setting, and everywhere she looked there was romance in the warm evening air.

Especially at their table.

They were sitting under the same parasol on the west side of Piazza Navona in the heart of Rome. She was, once more, sipping Prosecco while he had again opted for a cold beer. The sun had dropped low on the horizon by now and the ground was already in the shade, although the residual heat from the scorching July sun still radiated up from the cobbles. All around them were crowds of happy people, mostly tourists, laughing and chatting. Along with the tourists were also lots of Romans, like the man sitting alongside her. She reached over and caught hold of his hand.

'Going to miss all this?'

He glanced across at her and gave her hand a gentle squeeze.

'I love my city, but New York's a good substitute.'

'And we'll be coming back pretty often, won't we?'

'Of course. Besides, as long as I'm with you, I really don't care where I live.'

'And you'll keep the house?'

'Of course. We'll need somewhere to stay when we come back to visit.' He caught her eye. 'Besides, who knows what the future will bring?'

'Does Daisy know she's going for a long flight next month?' Jo glanced down at the dog, snoozing at their feet.

Corrado shook his head and smiled. 'She doesn't even know she's got a passport, but she'll be fine. As long as she's with you and me, she'll be happy.'

'And you're not too freaked out about next Saturday?'

He shook his head again. 'Why should I be freaked out? Marrying you is everything I could possibly ask for.'

'At least you've seen the place and you know what's in store for us.' Angie and Mario's wedding in the spring had gone very smoothly, and all the friends and family from Italy had been blown away by the picturesque little stone church in the equally picturesque little English village.

'And then there's going to be the honeymoon.' Corrado reached across and draped his arm around her neck. 'Three weeks on *Ippona* with my two favourite girls. I'm a very lucky man.' He pulled her towards him and kissed her tenderly on the lips. She rubbed her cheek against his and looked up into those amazing blue eyes as she rested one hand on his bare knee beneath the table.

'You know something, Corrado?' She grinned at him. 'A whole bunch of neurochemicals have just hit my limbic system. There's definitely a bio-chemical reaction happening.'

He kissed her again, harder this time, before replying.

'And I love you, too, Jo.'

Acknowledgements

With many thanks to Michael Bhaskar, Kit Nevile and the whole team at my wonderful publishers, Canelo, for their help and encouragement. Special thanks to editor Federica Leonardis for her knowledge of Rome as well as of English grammar, Robin Fox at ButterfliesinItaly.com for setting me right on Lepidoptera, and to Stephen Leger who knows all about luxury yachts.